Praise for Leta Serafim

WHEN THE DEVIL'S IDLE

(Starred Review) "This classic fair-play whodunit, the excellent sequel to 2014's *The Devil Takes Half* (Serafim's first Greek Island mystery), takes Yiannis Patronas, the endearing chief police officer on the island of Chios, to Patmos, where someone has bashed in the skull of Walter Bechtel, a 90-year-old German, in the garden of his foster son Gunther's holiday residence—and carved a swastika on the victim's forehead. When Patronas asks Gunther about his foster father's past, Gunther becomes defensive and claims that his papa was 'just an ordinary man' and did not commit any atrocities during WWII. Serafim does an especially good job of integrating Greece's current financial struggles into the story line, and Patronas's colleagues, especially an eccentric priest with a taste for seafood, lighten what otherwise could have been a very grim tale without minimizing the underlying horror of the background to the crime."
—Publishers Weekly

4 Stars: "The pairing of cynical Patronas and optimistic Michalis injects some humor in an otherwise moderately paced procedural. Serafim expertly creates the beauty of Greece. However, the real draws of this book are the fully developed, complex characters, and the facts on Greek culture and history. Book two in the Greek Islands Mystery series is sure to satisfy."
—RT Magazine

"*When The Devil's Idle* is loaded with twists and turns and red herrings that will leave you guessing all the while you are flipping pages to find out what happens next. Ms. Serafim has provided us with a marvelous whodunit and I am already looking forward to the next book in the series."
—Vic's Media Room

THE DEVIL TAKES HALF

(Starred Review–Featured as a Best Summer Debut) "Serafim's dense prose is perfect for lovers of literary and scholarly mysteries. Her plotting

is methodical and traditional, with subtle nods to Sherlock Holmes, Greek mythology, and historical events."
—Library Journal

"[An] impressive debut…. Serafim has a good eye for people and places, and sheds light on the centuries of violent passion that have created an oppressive atmosphere hanging over the sunny Greek landscape."
—Publishers Weekly

"The Greeks have a word for it, and in this fast-paced, delightful mystery, that word is murder…. The real buried treasure is pure pleasure in Serafim's debut novel."
—Mary Daheim, *New York Times* and *USA Today* bestselling author of the Alpine and Bed & Breakfast mystery series

"Whether it's police procedural genre convention, the exotic island landscape, or the passionate Greek character, Serafim knows the lay of the land, and she confidently guides the reader. Armchair adventurers will get a solid grounding in Greece's violent and tumultuous past. The quirky pairing of Patronas and Michalis has the makings of an unorthodox investigative team and the beginnings of a beautiful friendship. This immersive escapist mystery should put Serafim on the map."
—Kirkus Indie Reviews

"The Greek setting gives this book not only an exotic locale but also characters that have a different way of looking at life and often, motives that wouldn't exist if this happened in… Cleveland. Take a literary visit to Greece. You won't regret it!"
—Jodi Webb

To Look on Death No More

To Look on Death No More

Leta Serafim

coffeetownpress

Seattle, WA

Coffeetown Press
PO Box 70515
Seattle, WA 98127

For more information go to: www.coffeetownpress.com
www.letaserafim.com

All rights reserved. No part of this book may be reproduced or transmitted in any form or by any means, electronic or mechanical, including photocopying, recording, or any information storage and retrieval system, without permission in writing from the publisher.

This is a work of fiction. Names, characters, places, brands, media, and incidents are either the product of the author's imagination or are used fictitiously.

Cover design by Sabrina Sun

To Look on Death No More
Copyright © 2016 by Leta Serafim

ISBN: 978-1-60381-192-7 (Trade Paper)
ISBN: 978-1-60381-193-4 (eBook)

Library of Congress Control Number: 2015949760

Printed in the United States of America

For my husband, Philip, and my father, John E. Naugle

This book could not have been written without the insight and support of both of them, especially my late father, whose experiences as a prisoner of war in Germany during World War II color every chapter and form the heart of the book. He, like my main character, Brendan O'Malley, was an Irishman and a reluctant warrior, fond of laughter and a good story, and he worked unceasingly all his life—both professionally as associate administrator of NASA and personally—to serve justice and further peace and understanding among men.

My husband, Philip, also had a tremendous impact on the writing of this book, educating me about the war in Greece and the suffering of the civilian population during the Nazi Occupation. His description of the heroism of the Greeks stirred my imagination and eventually led me to Kalavryta and the telling of this story.

I am profoundly grateful to both of them.

Also by the author:

The Devil Takes Half
When the Devil's Idle

1

GRIPPING THE STRAPS of his parachute, Brendan O'Malley watched the landscape unfold at his feet. Below him he could see the long blue flame of the plane's port engine, a nimbus of burning fuel, a blur in the air around it. He took a deep breath, remembering the German paratroopers who'd landed in Crete—the terrible price they'd paid, thousands of them shot to death. Silently he prayed that would not be his fate. Unlike them, he'd be jumping at night. He hoped the darkness would cover him.

The rising moon had been an unwelcome surprise. Not taking it into account was a gross miscalculation on the part of the British major who had dispatched him here. The Americans on the plane said parachuting into Greece now was unwise—that he'd be dead before he hit the ground. "The moon's like a searchlight," they said, wanting to abort the mission and return to Cairo, but O'Malley had been determined to go ahead.

In the end, O'Malley had prevailed. The pilot gave in to his shouting and bluster, fearful of the gun O'Malley was waving around to make his point. But by then he'd lost valuable time, overshooting his rendezvous point by more than three miles.

God Almighty, what a fool he'd been.

"Off you go," the American shouted a moment later, glad to see the back of him, still chafed at him for pulling the gun.

O'Malley's chute caught the wind and he drifted, moving farther and farther away from his target. The earth rose up to meet him, the mountains of Greece slowly emerging and taking shape below. The wind picked up and swung him around, slamming him full force against a jagged strip of rock.

O'Malley screamed as the rock tore into his side, and then again when he tasted blood.

* * *

Unbuckling the chute, O'Malley staggered to his knees, but fell back, blood trickling down his chin. He wondered how long he'd been out. Six, seven hours at least. He wiped the blood from his mouth with the back of his hand. In a moment, it was wetting his lips again. His chest was on fire, every breath an agony. Had he punctured a lung? No matter. He'd have to move out and soon.

He heard someone chamber a round and ducked, clutching his bleeding gut. Germans must have heard the plane and tracked him here. Silhouetted against the moon, he'd have made a fine target, his parachute like a Victorian cut-out, scissored out of black paper. It was a wonder they hadn't shot him out of the sky.

But it was only a girl. She was so striking, standing there with the rising sun at her back. He'd have thought her an angel come to bear him to heaven, save for the gun in her hand. He'd seen angels with swords. *Aye*, the image was common enough, especially in Ireland. But angels with guns, never.

Unusually tall for a Greek, she was dressed all in rags, a blood-stained man's jacket thrown over her shoulders for warmth. Her eyes were enormous, gray-green with flecks of gold. Her braided hair was hidden by a tattered scarf. Keeping well back, she coldly took his measure, holding the gun high like a sniper. *Probably working for the Germans*, O'Malley thought. *Took the jacket off a murdered hostage.* He guessed she was around seventeen, old enough to have chosen sides.

A child was with her, a bespectacled boy of six or seven. He kept well back, watching O'Malley with a strained expression on his face. He was caked with filth, his curly black hair matted and stiff with it. His glasses were too big for him and were tied to his head with a length of grubby string, the lenses so thick they distorted his eyes. Judging by the cheap frames, the army-issue look of them, they'd been scavenged, too.

The boy gave a nervous laugh and pretended to shoot him, making a series of loud hiccupping noises like a machine gun.

Not the full shilling, O'Malley thought, studying him. Standing there in his old man's glasses, hopping up and down and jibber-jabbering. The way he cocked his head as if he couldn't hear, laughed at nothing …. *Aye*, something was wrong with him.

His posture was formal, one knee down, right arm extended. Seen a firing squad, the kid had. No wonder he was so skittish.

The boy danced closer. "*Alepou!*" He reached out and touched O'Malley's hair. "*Alepou!*"

The girl started going through O'Malley's things with a practiced hand, digging out his tobacco and pocketing it along with his emergency food rations, a little smile on her face. The smile faded when she saw his surgical tools, the scalpels and glass syringes in the leather case.

She gave him an appraising glance. "Medic?"

O'Malley nodded.

He doubted the Greeks would welcome an Irish doctor into their midst, but with a war on, sooner or later they'd have need of his services. The surgical tools would be his entry ticket, might even save his life down the road.

He squinted at the rifle she was holding. A battered Bren, it was his, no doubt about it. She must have taken it off him while he lay there unconscious. He slid his hand down the side of his pants and surreptitiously checked his holster. It was empty. So, she had his revolver, too. At least she hadn't taken his compass, sewn as it was into the fly of his pants. No, a Greek girl, she wouldn't have touched it, even if she'd known it was there.

"*Siko.*" She motioned for him to get up.

Gathering up the parachute, O'Malley reluctantly got to his feet, nearly passing out from the pain. They were near the summit of the mountain, well hidden in a thin scrub of pine.

The girl pointed to a path beyond the trees. They started toward it, O'Malley in the lead, she and the little boy behind. As before, she kept well back, keeping the rifle on him, her glossy black braids swinging from side to side.

O'Malley didn't know how far he could walk. He ached all over and the taste of blood was heavy in his mouth. He was beginning to panic. Day would soon be upon them, and with it would come German patrols. *Goddamn those bastards in Cairo!* Sent him here to die, they had.

Nudging him with the gun, the girl urged him to hurry. "*Ela, Angle.*" Come on, Englishman.

"Irish," he gasped.

She shrugged, indifferent to the distinction.

Ahead lay an abandoned village. An old cemetery occupied the hill above it; they ran toward it, ducking behind the tombstones as they made their way forward. Most of the graves were shallow crypts, faced with white marble. The girl paused in front of one and fiddled with the stone siding. It gave way easily, the marble squealing as she pushed it aside. Below was a dank, evil-smelling space.

She waved O'Malley and the boy inside and then climbed in after them. Taking care to leave an opening for air, she repositioned the marble over their heads, effectively sealing them in.

Done this before, O'Malley thought, *she and the boy both.*

"*Alepou!*" the boy cried again.

"What's that mean?" O'Malley asked the girl. "Why does he call me that?"

She surprised him. "Your hair, the red," she said in perfect English. "It means fox."

They spent the rest of the day in the crypt. At one point O'Malley heard voices shouting in German, the scrape of boots overhead. Terrified, the little boy began to rock back and forth, "*Germanoi!*" he whimpered, pointing to the top of the crypt. "*Germanoi!*"

He grew more and more agitated and wet himself, a stream of urine trickling down his legs and making a puddle on the dirt floor. Afraid he'd give them away, O'Malley put a hand out to steady him. The kid was trembling all over, terror roiling him like a seizure.

The footsteps gradually faded and silence returned to the crypt. The little boy curled up on the ground and tried to sleep, batting weakly at the flies settling on his legs. The stench of urine was strong in the crypt.

The girl didn't move, just sat with the rifle across her lap and stared at O'Malley.

She was a fine bit of stuff, he thought, staring back at her. Something out of a storybook, the face on her. *But fierce, my God*; she was fierce. Singe a man's balls right off, she would. Turn them to ashes.

He wondered who the crypt belonged to, if her relatives were buried there. She hadn't stumbled upon it by accident. That was for sure. Judging by the boy, they'd had a bad time of it.

As soon as the sun went down, the three of them moved from the cemetery. A full moon was rising, and the raised tombs were spectral in the half-light, the marble headstones alive in the growing darkness.

Not a good time to be traipsing through a war zone, O'Malley told himself, watching the light play across the landscape, *not a good time at all.*

But the girl knew what she was doing; and they soon found themselves walking along the edge of the rockbound gorge. The moon illuminated the limestone cliffs, the savage slabs of rocks on either side. Countryside here was too rough for Germans. Too rough for anything, save goats. He'd been dropped in to Greece to make contact with Greek partisans and build a landing strip— an impossibility, he saw now, given the terrain. He could see his rendezvous point, the village of Kalavryta, at the southern end of the gorge. The town looked small from where he was, the whitewashed houses like a handful of dice in the moonlight.

Ahead lay nothing, just the stony backside of yet another mountain. They were totally exposed and had been for some time, the trees having given way to loose rock that clattered underfoot, as brittle and porous as old bones. His chest ached, and the straps of his pack were tearing deep into the skin around his shoulders.

Again, O'Malley thought what a fool he'd been. How he'd argued against the plan from the beginning. Landing in mountains, constructing airstrips. The British commander in Cairo had sent him off anyway with a pickax and a copy of *Oliver Twist*, 'to pass the time.' O'Malley knew he was in trouble when he saw the book. He'd traded it for a spiral notebook, thinking he'd keep a journal. A record of his adventures.

"Be hard pressed to find words for this," he muttered, looking back at the girl and her brother. Set upon and rousted by children, marched off at the point of a gun, *his* gun. *Ah, sweet Jesus*, how the men in his unit would mock him if they knew.

He wondered again who she was working for. She hadn't turned him over to the Germans in the cemetery, nor had he seen any evidence of guerrilla activity in the area she'd marched him through. Odd, all of it.

The cave was about halfway up the mountain, well camouflaged behind loose pine boughs, less than ten feet square. O'Malley judged it to be man-made, a natural opening widened by hand at some point in time. A blanket was folded up in one corner, and there were jugs of water—evidence of a camp fire.

Partisans? he wondered. *Or just these two?*

"You stay here," the girl said.

O'Malley watched her leave with mixed feelings. He'd once found a dead fox in a trap. Even though its leg was crushed, the animal had somehow managed to drag itself and the vise that held it more than a hundred yards before it died. He was that fox now, broken and unable to get away. He'd never get down off the mountain without their help, not in the condition he was in. He'd been well named by the boy.

"When are you coming back?" he yelled.

The girl glanced over her shoulder. "Tomorrow, *Angle*."

English. There it was again.

"I'm Irish, damn you," he yelled. "Irish from the roots of my bloody red hair to the bottoms of my bloody big feet. Irish, well and true. Irish, in point of fact. Irish, for the love of God. Irish, you hear? Irish!"

2

Exhausted, O'Malley collapsed on the floor of the cave and slept. When he awoke, he felt better; the searing pain had abated and blood was no longer seeping from the cut on his side. He crawled outside and took a look around, seeking to orient himself. The view took his breath away—a vision of mountains unfolding one after another as far as the eye could see. He imagined he could trace the curve of the earth, the outlines of the seven continents and all the briny seas. Hitler had a place like this in the Alps, he remembered. Berchtesgaden, it was called. *No wonder he likes it there, the evil bastard. Up so high, a man's no longer a man. He's the kin of eagles.*

Although he'd been in Greece off and on since 1941, this area was new to him. The men in his unit—Australians mostly, he'd been the only Irishman—had run for their lives in April of that year, fleeing Athens the same day the Germans marched in. They'd ended up on a beach in Pylos far to the south of here. The Germans had been relentless, strafing them from the air the whole way. It hadn't been Dunkirk, but close.

In ancient times, the Spartans had massacred most of the inhabitants of Pylos, one of the Australians had told him, and sold the rest into slavery. And so it was again in 1941, only at German hands this time—slavery and death.

He'd been shot not long after in a field that smelled of sheep. A farmer had found him and tended to his wound, dressing it with iodine and strips of worn sheeting. Too weak to travel, O'Malley hadn't made it to the British ships waiting to evacuate his unit off the coast and had ended up hiding out in Greece for well over a year. He'd learned the language as a result and come to appreciate the men who lived and fought there—these modern-day descendants of the Spartans, whose ancestors had been the first guerrillas and who were guerrillas still.

A fisherman had ferried him across the southern Mediterranean Sea in the spring of 1942, and from there he'd made it on his own to Egypt. A British major in Cairo had arranged for him to return this time in the autumn of 1943, citing his previous experience in the area. His stated mission: to make contact with Greek partisans and construct an airstrip. O'Malley scanned the mountains again. A futile mission if ever there was one.

"You'll do better in Greece as an Irishman," the British officer had told him this last round. He should have asked why that was. Why the Greek partisans weren't welcoming British soldiers anymore.

The Americans in the plane had been only too glad to tell him. Greek leftists were killing British field officers, they said, had killed the last man in before him, executed him as a spy. "Churchill's against them and they know it. Going to be a lot more blood spilled in these mountains before this thing is over. Civil war."

But by then it was too late. O'Malley was standing there at the door of the plane with his chute strapped on, the wind tearing at his clothes.

Before the war, he'd never been farther than Dublin and then only once, the time he'd taken the train from Cork to sit for his degree examination and become a licensed doctor. A right yokel, he'd been that day, riding the train from Cork in his Sunday clothes.

Soldiering would fix that, he'd thought at the time, a British uniform his ticket to the outside world. And fix him, it had. Aye, fix him it bloody well had.

He unzipped his pants and urinated off the mountain, wishing that the British major was there now, wishing he could piss in his eye. He shouted at the sky, cursing him, all the bleeding idiots in Cairo. "May vultures feast on your living flesh and your filthy, wormy entrails fall out! May your wives all be whores! May their cunts grow teeth!"

Feeling better, he removed the two pieces of his compass from his fly and buttoned himself up. He fitted the compass together and fiddled with it. He'd head toward Sparta and link up with the guerrillas there. Travel at night and hide during the day. Complete his mission and get the bloody hell away.

He searched for a cigarette before remembering the girl had taken them. He wondered what else she'd taken and emptied his pack out on the ground. His tools were still there—the shovel and pickax—as were the medical instruments, but his cigarettes and every scrap of food was gone.

He knew the path the girl had taken was somewhere below and searched for it, working his way down over the rocks one foot at a time. He'd gone about twenty feet when the rock he was standing on suddenly gave way, sending him flying in an avalanche of stones and gravel.

"No! No!"

Screaming and clutching at air, he plummeted straight down. He reached out and grabbed at the cliff with his hands, trying to break his fall, tore off his fingernails and skinned both his palms.

"Oh, God, no!"

He landed hard on a ledge of rock. Pebbles continued to rain down, gritty dust settling in his eyes and hair. O'Malley spat on the palms of his hands and rubbed them on his pants, nearly weeping from the pain. A near one, that.

Slowly he fought his way back to the point where he'd started, leveraging himself up the vertical face of the cliff, taking a step and pulling himself up with his hands, burying his bleeding fingers in the loose gravel. The cuts on his palms stung and he had to stop and rub them against his shirt. By the time he reached the cave, he was soaked with sweat. He crawled inside and lay there, panting. He was well and truly fucked. A captive not just of the girl and her comrades, but of this inhospitable land, these malevolent mountains.

* * *

O'MALLEY STARED AT the ceiling of the cave. After what he'd dubbed, 'the fall from grace,' he loathed the place, the rocks, the stagnant air inside the hole.

He'd foraged for food but found nothing. No matter. He'd eat spiders, dirt if he had to. 'Starvin' is part of being Irish,' his father always said. 'Part of the heritage like the singing and the faith.'

O'Malley smiled at the memory. His father had been like that, turning adversity into laughter, a bit of wit, always. An Irish patriot, he'd been furious when O'Malley enlisted. "Are you daft?" he'd shouted. "Have ye no sense at all?"

"Pa, there's a war on."

"Aye, an English war. 'Tis them you should be fighting, not the Germans."

" 'Tis the Germans, Pa, the Germans this time. Enslaving the world, they are. Don't you read the papers?"

It was September 1940 and London was burning. O'Malley knew then he'd have to fight. They all would.

"Taking orders from an Englishman, you'll be," his pa had declared. "Send you to your death, they will. Sooner slit your throat as look at you."

"I'd fight in the Irish army if there was one. If de Valera hadn't decided to sit it out."

"Rightly so, he did."

And so it had gone until the day O'Malley left—his mother pleading with the two of them to keep their voices down.

His father drove him to the station, stood there awkwardly while his mother cried, uncomfortable with the leave taking, still angry at him for going. "Remember, Brendan," he said, softening a little and patting his arm, " 'tis better to be a coward for a minute than dead the rest of your life."

"Aye, stands to reason," O'Malley replied, making a joke of it.

He touched the stained rocks above him and closed his eyes. He'd been at war for three years now, fought in Crete and across the deserts of North Africa, been wounded twice and fought on.

At first the show horse nature of the British operation in Cairo had appealed to him—sending agents like himself behind enemy lines to blow up bridges and the like—but no longer. The major he'd served under had been full of himself and waged war, not out in the field with his wits and a gun, but in a clean hotel room, by sticking pins on maps, as a game almost. He and those like him had gotten men he knew killed with their foolishness. Good men he'd relied on and trusted. Lying there in the cave, he silently vowed he'd not be one of them

* * *

NIGHT WAS FALLING when the two turned up again. The girl was outfitted like a guerrilla this time with O'Malley's revolver and army-issue dagger stuck in her belt, his rifle and a bandolier of shiny, brass cartridges slung over her shoulder. O'Malley wondered what had become of his grenades, if she had them secreted somewhere on her person. He most fervently hoped she had them and not the boy.

She frowned when she saw his wounded hands and shook her head at his foolishness.

"I told you stay," she hissed.

Holding up a roll of bandages, she gestured for him to take his shirt off. He turned away as he undid the buttons, embarrassed at his whiteness, the seeping fissures where the straps of his pack had cut into his shoulders. Working quickly, she rubbed him down with a dampened rag that smelled of rosemary and bound him up. She knew what she was doing, her hands sure. She probed his side and worked her fingers over the gash the rock had left, seeking to piece the torn flesh together. He pretended to be a xylophone, making different sounds as she moved her hands over his ribs, thinking to amuse the boy and take the drama out of the bloody mess he'd become. Laughing, the boy immediately joined in the game, drumming his gut with his fingers and making sing song noises, a crude kind of music.

As soon as she was done, she stepped away. O'Malley missed her touch, the warmth of her hands on him. It had been a long time since a girl had touched him, held him even briefly.

She never smiled, he noticed, kept her face averted and never met his eye. Was it shyness, or had she been wounded as women sometimes were during a war? Painfully thin, she reminded him of the feral cats he'd seen in Athens—the way she darted about as if a pack of dogs were after her, a pack of dogs only she could see.

She signaled for him to hold out his hands, poured water on them and gently wiped them, then bandaged them up as well. Again, O'Malley was struck by her skill.

After she finished, she handed him a packet of food wrapped up in newspaper. It wasn't much—a chunk of stale bread and a single, damaged tomato—but he fell on it, licking and sucking the crumbs off the paper until it dissolved.

Although his hands pained him bitterly, he reached out and touched her sleeve, tried to thank her in Greek. She wouldn't have patched him up if she intended to betray him. Bandaged or not, he'd fetch the same price from the Germans. Come to the same end.

The girl jerked away. "*Mi*," she said loudly. Don't.

"*Ela*," she called to the boy. Come.

"Stay," said O'Malley.

"*Grigora*." Fast.

"Stay."

She shook her head and was gone.

* * *

As soon as it was light, O'Malley ventured down the path. There'd be hell to pay if the Germans caught those two. In the hands of the SS, death would be a blessing.

He'd watched the girl leave the previous night and made a note of how she'd edged down from the cave, inching along the jutting shelf of limestone that traversed the cliff as if on a tightrope. The wind was brisk and it stirred the brush along the trail, the aromatic clumps of oregano and thyme clinging to the rocks. He could see treetops in the distance, the beginnings of a pine forest, and walked toward it, intending to take shelter there.

He'd left most of his gear in the cave, thinking that if the Germans captured him, it would go better for him, make the charade of his being a Greek farmer more plausible. A vain hope, he knew. Noting his fair skin and freckles—he was 'well speckled,' as they said at home—they'd assume he was English and shoot him for sure.

Ah, Jesus, the sad irony of it.

He was almost to the bottom of the slope when he spied the goat caught in a crevice. A large ewe, it hadn't been milked in a long time, and it bawled when it saw him, the sound echoing eerily off the cliffs. The animal made

O'Malley nervous, and he looked around, worried about who it belonged to, if there were partisans operating in the area.

The goat waggled its head and brayed again, its lifeless eyes upon him. It was a homely creature with little devil horns. Still, O'Malley felt sorry for it, imprisoned as it was, and wanted to do something to help. Milk it, he figured. He'd milked cows in his time. Stood to reason he could milk a goat. After he finished, he'd try and free it. But when he reached for a teat, the goat lowered its head and butted him with its horns, catching him in his wounded side.

"Aw, ye bleeding ingrate, ye skin full of shit!"

The milk, when it finally came, was thin and bluish. Filling a tin cup, O'Malley poured the foul-smelling liquid into his canteen. Truth be told, he was in no hurry to build an airstrip for the British. Might as well stick around and nursemaid the goat until the girl arrived, milk the beast again as the need arose. From the look of them, those two were starving. A spot of milk would do them no harm.

He shook his head. A strange kind of soldiering this was turning out to be. Goats and children and naught but milk to drink.

The goat's leg was well and truly stuck—the fur bloody where it'd rubbed it.

O'Malley flashed again on the dead fox, the way it had dragged itself off to die. He'd seen a soldier do the same in Athens—an Australian lying wounded in the street, his gut torn open by mortar fire. Clawing at the pavement, he'd tried to get away. O'Malley would never forget the look on the man's face when he realized it was too late, that the German tanks had begun to move. The sadness in his eyes.

He couldn't bear the thought of another thing dying.

Getting out his pickax, he began tapping at the rock above the goat's leg, thinking he'd dig it out. This quickly proved impossible. The infernal beast sought to gore him every time he came near and about deafened him with its cries.

"Mother o' God, will ye not be still?"

As before, his two captors appeared at twilight, the little boy singing as he followed his sister up the path. Hearing the guttural sounds the child was making, O'Malley guessed he must be imitating the Germans in his village. Aye, it was "*Deutschland über alles*" the kid was singing. The strident melody was unmistakable, Nazi to its very core.

O'Malley handed him the canteen. "Help yourself, lad. It'll do you good."

Tipping the canteen back, the boy gulped down the milk. "*Danke*," he said when he finished, wiping his mouth with his hand.

"Thinks I'm German, so he does, the little bugger." Laughing to himself, O'Malley didn't bother correcting him. There were those in Ireland who'd have approved—considered it better in fact—his own father among them. The greater insult to be judged English.

He led the girl over to the goat, gestured to the pickax and made a hopeless gesture. The animal cried out when they approached, raised its head feebly and bobbed it up and down.

The girl's face brightened and she knelt down beside it. Cooing softly, she stroked its fur and rubbed its ears, appeared to call it by name. O'Malley was about to warn her of its horns when she grabbed the animal's leg, twisted it and in one smooth motion, pulled it loose it from the crack. The goat shook itself once and ambled off as if nothing had happened.

She gave O'Malley a triumphant look. "Is no hard," she said in English.

She quickly secured the goat, tying two of its legs together with a rope so it could graze, but not run, then marched O'Malley back to the cave at gunpoint. It was a strange procession, the three of them edging up the cliff with a goat in tow, the girl poking him in the back with his revolver, reminding him every step of the way, who was in charge.

When they reached the cave, she looked him up and down, searching for a way to tether him, too, eventually settling on his boots. "Give them to me."

"The hell I will!" O'Malley could almost hear the Australians in his unit, the fun they'd be having right about now. "I'll warm your ear, I will. Smack you senseless, you try and take my boots. Anyway, they'll not suit you. They're far too big. Troughs."

"Now." She raised the revolver.

"Oh, bloody hell." Sputtering with rage, O'Malley undid the laces, pulled the boots off and handed them to her. He was willing to die in combat. *Aye*, that was to be expected. It came with the soldiering. It was another thing entirely to be shot to death by a girl over footwear. Be embarrassing, a death like that. Shameful.

Tying the laces together, she slung the boots over her shoulder. ""You will stay here. You will not leave." Her accent was stilted and formal. Learned English from a book, she had. Lessons in school.

"You hear, *Angle*? If you leave, I will kill you."

* * *

NOT MUCH POINT in mountain climbing in one's bare feet, O'Malley soon discovered. He'd tried to get down the path in his socks, but the rocks had been like razors underfoot, and he'd fallen into a mess of brambles—thorny brambles that stuck to him. He'd plucked them out as best he could, but couldn't reach all of them. A mass of pain he was.

"Not enough she's got my guns. No, the sly bitch, she had to take my boots as well."

She was carrying a dented kerosene lantern when she reappeared the next night, swinging it back and forth in her hand. She'd brought him food, too—a haunch of rabbit in a clay pot.

Sitting there in his bare feet, the thorns he'd missed still paining him, O'Malley did not feel particularly grateful. He thought about clobbering her with the pickax the British had outfitted him with, splitting her from—how did the poem go—"her gurgle to her snatch," but decided against it.

It would be a Nazi-like thing to do, braining a girl with a pickax. That's why they're in the trouble they're in, everyone in the world against them, cause they go mucking about like that.

Also, there was the boy. Coming apart at the seams, he was. Any more bloodshed and he'd be done.

O'Malley had taken off his socks, hoping to shame her into giving him back the boots, and made a great show of wiggling his toes. They were a little bluish, he thought, the color of uncooked chicken. He sat there sullenly, thinking over his options. Without his boots, he hadn't many. None, when you got right down to it. It had been a stroke of genius on the girl's part, taking them. Might as well have cut his legs off.

The boy pulled O'Malley's parachute out of his drop pack and slipped it on, the silk trailing after him in a long, billowy cloud. Extending his arms, he imitated a plane, running around in circles and buzzing loudly, the parachute drifting in folds around him. A few minutes later, he jumped, fell to the ground, and lay there, then got up and pretended to fly again.

Kid knows my story, O'Malley realized with start. Had probably watched him drift down and slam into the side of the mountain. Perhaps his first encounter with the two of them had been a form of rescue.

But then why'd they strip him of his gear and take his boots away? Insist on holding him captive in a cave? It didn't make sense.

"Is it the Germans you're waiting on?" he asked her. "Going to peddle me to the SS? Use me like a poker chip to better your lot?"

The girl didn't seem to hear. Keeping her head down, she dug her finger into the butt of the rifle, scratching at the wood with a nail.

"You can't keep me here forever, you know," O'Malley said. "I'm a British officer, Sergeant Brendan O'Malley. Churchill himself set up my group in July of 1940, told us 'to set Europe ablaze.' I'm on an important mission. I'm supposed to build airstrips here, arrange supply drops for your people."

He had her attention now.

"You said you were Irish. 'Irish, in point of fact. Irish, as God made me.' Irish this and Irish that. So loud you were." She spoke quickly, rattling off the words as if English were her native tongue.

O'Malley nodded. "I am that, truly. Born and bred in Ireland."

"So why are you working for the British? Burning things for Churchill?" Her voice was full of contempt.

A good question, given how things had gone. She'd feel right at home with his pa. He wondered where she'd learned to speak English, what her story was.

He wasn't sure he was up to explaining how he, an Irishman and a Catholic, had come to serve in Churchill's clandestine army. How he'd felt like he was doing God's work the day he enlisted, but didn't feel that way so much anymore. It wouldn't matter anyway if her people were leftists, supporters of the Communist guerrillas in ELAS. British or Irish. It'd be all the same to them.

"Ireland was neutral and I wanted to fight."

"Neutral?"

"Means sitting it out, not participating in a war."

"In Greece, you must fight. There is no choice, no 'neutral.' War, always war in Greece. 'Summer, autumn, war.' " Looking over at him, she raised her eyebrows, smirked a little. "Ancient words, from Sparta."

Top this, her expression said. *Go ahead. I dare you.*

O'Malley didn't like being patronized, never had. He got up and limped over to where she was sitting and shook his fist in her face. "Damn you and your bloody Spartans. Give me back my boots, you hear?"

Looking up at him, the girl shook her head, enjoying the wrangling, the power she had over him.

"How do you expect me to survive without boots? What the hell do you plan to do with me?"

"I don't know, *Angle*," She smirked some more. "Maybe I hold you for ransom. Sell you back to Churchill."

3

O'Malley had resigned himself to staying in the cave. Without boots, he couldn't climb down from the mountain, nor brave the stony ground underfoot. His wound wasn't healing properly and he needed to preserve his strength. He'd doctored it as best as he could in the squalid confines of the cave, gritting his teeth and lancing the wound with a scalpel, praying it would drain properly and he wouldn't die of infection. He remained confused as to what the girl wanted with him.

Like the witch in "Hansel and Gretel," day after day, she gave him food. Only she wasn't fattening him up, no, just the opposite. Last night's dinner had been *horta*—grass—as it had been every night for more than a week. Grass and more grass, sometimes with a little splash of olive oil on it, more often, not. A two-legged beast of burden, he was fast becoming. A wonder he didn't grow hooves.

His clothes were unholy, so coated with dirt they were like cardboard; and he could smell the stink rising off him. He ran his hand over his face; his beard was growing apace, his hair, too, stiffening up just as his clothes had, rising out from his head like the mane of a lion. Soon he'd be as wild-looking as his ancestor, Cúchulainn, when he stole the brown bull of Cooley. *Aye,* a great battler he'd been, Cúchulainn. Not like him, Brendan O'Malley, brought low by a girl.

She was wearing a different dress this time and had washed and braided her hair, tied it back with a ribbon. The braid was as thick as a man's wrist, the natural curliness of that wild mane of hers barely subdued. *Must be an amazing sight when she sets that hair free*, O'Malley thought. *Rippling all down her back, it would be like the hair of a mermaid, an angry mermaid in a storm-lashed sea.*

She had been going back and forth between the two languages for some time now, not sure which was better when she spoke to him. The British had had similar trouble, asking him to speak up and stop mumbling when he gave a report. 'Enunciate, if you'd be so kind,' his commanding officer was always saying, openly contemptuous of his Irish accent. O'Malley figured that his Greek must be well nigh incomprehensible.

Sometimes a certain quality crept into her voice when she told him things, like now with the word *horta*. He'd known girls like her in Ireland, ones who paraded their knowledge around and used it to show off. They usually weren't pretty, those girls. Being smart was all they had. This one, on the other hand, was lovely. Helen of bloody Troy.

Although they hadn't talked again about what she intended for him, he'd come to believe she meant him no harm. Sometimes she dozed in the cave, the rifle across her knees. She always awoke with a start at the slightest noise. Spooked, she was. She and her brother both. Like horses pulled from a burning barn.

During the retreat through Athens, a girl of the same age had led O'Malley into a pastry shop, loaded him up with bottles of brandy and kissed him full on the mouth. She'd urged him to kill all the Germans he could, to die if he had to in that killing, and kissed him again and again.

All the Greeks had been crazy that day. A man had wrapped himself up in the Greek flag and jumped to his death off the Acropolis. Another had rigged up a blockade to stop the German tanks, a blockade made of orange crates and dining room furniture. Children had handed beers and cigarettes to the Australian POWS the Germans had captured and were marching away. All heroic, but more than a little mad, given the penalty the Nazis imposed on such deeds.

Perhaps she's just another one.

O'Malley watched her in the light of the lantern.

Like the others, just one more war-crazed casualty. Perhaps that's all this is.

Tonight's bread had a strange texture to it. O'Malley broke off a piece and ate it, wondering what the baker had used for flour. Nothing he was familiar with, neither wheat nor rye.

"*Bobota*," the girl volunteered. "Chick peas."

Famine fare. Like the Irish when the potatoes failed, making soup out of nettles, out of stones.

He handed the bread back to her. "Here, you eat it."

"No, no. Is for you."

"Look at you. You're bloody well starving, you and the boy both. It's no use pretending. I see how it is. You got no business feeding me the way you been doing, not when you got naught in the larder yourselves."

He grabbed her by the arms, shook her a little. "I'm a soldier. I can fend for myself. It's too risky what you're doing. You got to let me go."

"Germans catch you, they will kill many people," she whispered. "They call it *Sühne-Maßnahmen*—'atonement actions.' They burn people alive."

O'Malley nodded. He was familiar with 'atonement actions,' had come upon the gruesome results of one in Crete and helped the survivors bury the bodies. As an explanation, it would suffice.

"Is that why you took my boots?"

She nodded. "Is better you stay. Better for you, better for all the people."

"Are you with the partisans, the *antartes*?"

"No." She seemed surprised by the question.

"What about your folks?"

"We are nothing." Her voice broke. "Only poor village people. Hungry."

"You're not going to give me up? Get me shot as a British spy?"

She shook her head.

"I am saving you, *Angle*," she said sadly.

* * *

SHE STAYED WITH O'Malley for a long time that night, sitting beside him, cross-legged on the floor of the cave. She told him she'd learned English from her aunt, who'd lived in the United States. "All the time English, English. 'I am, you are, we are. I have, you have.' Over and over. She wanted to go back to America, wanted us to be ready."

"What happened? Why didn't you go?"

"My father. He didn't want to leave, be a stranger in America."

Better to have braved it, O'Malley believed with all his heart. Better to have braved the new world than to be perishing in the old, eating grass to stay alive, eating grass like cattle.

He told the girl how his parents had argued about America, his father wanting to join his brother, who lived in something called a 'triple decker' in Boston, and his mother's tears. " 'Heat and hot water all hours of the day and night,' my pa said. 'Must be a wondrous place, America.' "

Then 1929 had come and photos of the breadlines had appeared in *The Southern Star*, the weekly newspaper of Cork, the shantytowns Americans were living in. "Pa quit his talking about Boston that year. ' 'Tis better to starve among one's own,' he told us,, 'if starving ye be.' "

The girl nodded. "My family, we were the same. My aunt crazy for America, my father only for Greece."

"What about your ma?"

"My mother died with Stefanos."

Her situation still puzzled him. Perhaps she'd lied about being a partisan, a member of ELAS, the Greek communist forces. There were women fighting all over Greece. One of the most effective intelligence groups in the resistance was run by a woman, Lela Karagianni. Another, code-named 'Thiela,' was a legend in Roumeli. Still, he doubted the girl would drag her brother into it, him being the way he was, half-blind and so clumsy he could barely stand upright. In Ireland they called such kids, 'specky four eyes.' *He'd have a hard go, a boy like that, on the playgrounds of Ireland.*

"Where's your father now?"

"Moving our goats away from Kalavryta."

O'Malley laughed. "So it was *your* goat."

"Yes. He took the bells off so no one would hear and it got away. We were looking for it the night we found you."

She picked at the crumbs with a finger. "Is bad now, Kalavryta. Everyone hungry, like Hodja's donkey."

"Hodja?"

"Foolish Turk. Greeks say stories about him."

"Tell me one." O'Malley wanted to keep her talking, didn't want her to leave.

"I say best. Hodja very poor and he decides to teach his donkey how to live without food. To help donkey get used, everyday he gives it less and less to eat. Donkey doesn't complain so he keeps going. 'What happen?' people ask Hodja after time. 'I don't know,' Hodja say. 'Donkey, he was just getting good at it when he died.'"

Her face was somber. "Germans, they are Hodja now, take food away, and Greeks, they die, same as donkey."

The little boy was roaring around in the parachute again. He'd found O'Malley's goggles, too, and was wearing them on top of his glasses. He bent down so his sister could see, but she waved him away.

"He has many problems, my brother," she said. "He can't see good. Is no good for school. Looks like boy, but is a baby still."

"Is that why you always bring him with you?"

"Yes. In village, Stefanos is like a ball they kick."

* * *

O'MALLEY DREAMED OF them that night, dreamed he was swimming with the two of them in the sea. It was a hot day and the sky was bleached nearly white by the sun. The wind came up in his dream and stirred the water, making it grow dark and raising huge waves, which carried them away. He swam after them, but the current was too strong and it held him back until it was too late; they were gone. He awoke with a sense of foreboding.

He needed to leave and be quick about it, be gone from the mountain before winter set in. He pulled the blanket around him. The ground was rimed with frost, the air so cold, he could see his breath.

She'd given him back his dagger the night before. It wouldn't be much use against the Germans, but it was a start.

Venturing a short distance down the trail in his socks, he found an old olive tree and cut off a branch. He skinned off the bark and made a spear, thinking he'd build a trap, catch a rabbit and surprise them with it. He paused, looking down at the spike he was holding. What if it didn't catch the rabbit proper and the poor creature lingered, nailed to the stake there like Jesus on the cross? The thought made him sick and he threw the branch away. He'd carve a toy for the boy instead.

He'd completed two pieces by the time they got there, a horse and little pig, part of a set of barnyard animals he intended to make. They were crude things, clumsy and lifeless, four legs and misshapen heads; but the boy was thrilled when he saw them and dragged them back and forth across the floor of the cave, neighing and snorting in turn.

Over the next few days, O'Malley carved other animals for him. People, too. A chimney sweep with a ladder he blackened with soot from the fire, and a farmer leading a cow. He was also at work on a corral—pieces of wood looped together by scraps of fabric torn off his clothes. At first, he sang to himself while he worked:

> They passed around the whiskey and they passed around the ale
> And if the glasses weren't big enough they used a wooden pail.
> Everyone was feelin' good, no one was feelin' dry.
> All around the glory and the glory it was high.
> Someone asked Clancy, "Would he sing a song?"
> Clancy said he would, but his voice was gone.
> Up jumped Maloney and he gave a recitation
> All about the kind of wood that grew in every nation.
> That was the signal and they all began to fight and the women hollered, "Murder!" and they said it wasn't right.
> All kinds of wood went flyin' through the air.
> Brady hit O'Grady with the round of a chair.
> Murphy took Sullivan and threw him on the bed
> Stabbed him with a clothespin and left him there for dead.

But the sound of his voice bouncing off the walls of the cave depressed him, and he stopped. By his calculation, it was Sunday, September 30th, and he'd been in Greece two weeks.

His mother had probably gone to mass that day. She'd been a great one for prayers, his ma. Always after him about it when he was young, she'd given him a rosary the day he shipped out. Blessed by the pope, it'd been—one of her life's great treasures. He'd left it behind, taking care to hide it so she wouldn't see. He was off to war. What need had he for rosaries, women's things?

He was sorry now he'd done that. Sorry he'd been young and so bloody full of himself.

"Ah, ma, where are you now? You with your piety and your hope, your cupboard full of saints." St. Jude had been a favorite of hers. St. Jude, the patron saint of desperate cases.

"Remember me to St. Jude, Ma, Oh God, Ma, remember me to St. Jude."

With a sigh, he picked up the knife and attacked the wood again. He wondered if he'd ever see his mother again.

Somewhere off to the west, he heard an owl and frantic rustling in the rocks below. He hoped whatever it was had been quick enough and not been swept away by the beating wings.

He shook his head. "Friend, you are brother to dragons now and the companion of owls."

* * *

THE LITTLE BOY occasionally acted out stories about the carvings. They didn't amount to much, his little vignettes, hunger being the prominent feature—the pig eating the cow's share and the like, barnyard wars between those that had food and those that didn't. Sometimes O'Malley would join in, entertaining him with nonsense rhymes he remembered from childhood.

The girl would listen in the shadows. "Irish, foolish people," she'd say. "Silly with words."

Laughing, O'Malley would chant,

> Lord, confound this surly sister
> Blight her with blotch and blister
> Cramp her larynx, lung and liver
> In her guts, a galling give her.

until the girl covered her ears with her hands and begged him to stop.

He told himself beguiling her was part of his plan; he'd lull her into complacency. As if anyone could lull this girl into anything—complacency least of all. He knew he was strong enough now to overpower her and get his rifle back, yet he held off. He welcomed their time together and on occasion would sing to her, 'The Rose of Tralee' and other romantic ballads. The songs brought Ireland closer and made her seem a part of it.

One night the little boy began to sing, too. "Tralee, tralee."

"Stefanos, right?" O'Malley made it a question.

The boy smiled, nodded. *"Nai, eimai o* Stefanos." Yes, I am Stefanos.

"I'm Brendan, and you're Stefanos. And she's …." He gestured to where the girl was sitting.

"Danae. *Einai i* Danae." She is Danae.

Danae.

* * *

O'MALLEY CONTINUED TO plead with the girl to give him his boots back. "You got to understand. I'm a soldier. 'Tis tough work, soldiering. Takes a lot out of a man. Got to be properly dressed if you're to do it right, especially when battling Germans. Can't be taking on the Wehrmacht in bare feet, no ma'am. Be undignified, that. Be a thing of laughter."

A proper son of Ireland, he was a shy man, poor when it came to talking women into doing things. Oh, he'd had a few in Athens, urged on by the Australians in his unit. But they'd been sows, those women, greasy and fat, with the smell of men on their skin, cigarette smoke in their hair. Scrubbers. He'd had to wait in line for them, pay his money and take his turn. Nothing like this one, this savage beauty before him.

He looked over at her, studying her face in the yellow glow of the lantern. He was warming to her. *Aye*, no doubt about it. Could feel his cheeks grow hot just looking at her. So beautiful she was. Solemn. Like a Madonna in an Italian painting.

He didn't understand it. She wasn't even a proper girl, one you could put your arm on, soft and smelling of flowers. No, she was a dirty twig of a thing, mulish. Like one of the elements on the periodic table. Zinc, iron. Basic-like. Everything reduced to its essence. In her case, eyes. *Aye*, it was the eyes with her.

"You're a fool, O'Malley," he muttered. "A different kind of fool than you were in Cairo, but a fool just the same."

Still, he felt something when he heard her voice, her footsteps outside the cave. A quickening, a sense of being more alive.

He shook his head. And him a soldier.

4

THE KID HAD had a bath since O'Malley had last seen him and been barbered within an inch of his life. "*Geneia*," the boy said, bowing his head so O'Malley could feel.

"*Geneia*" Whiskers.

O'Malley dutifully ran his hand over the child's scalp, praying it wasn't nits that had generated the shaving, another form of vermin. "Aye, little friend, the barber's been at you good, given you a proper going over."

Standing there in his glasses, his little head clipped so closely it gleamed, he looked so forlorn that O'Malley took pity on him, hoisted him up on his shoulders and began to spin around with him.

The child squealed with delight. "*Peta!*" Fly!

O'Malley continued to swing him around, but his weight tore open the cuts on his shoulders; and he began to bleed again.

The girl gasped when she saw the stream of yellowish liquid soaking O'Malley's shirt. "No good, no good this."

Worried, she brought him charcoal and a box of matches the next night, a bowlful of stringy mutton. She wiped his wounds with a cloth soaked in brandy and bandaged him up as best she could. O'Malley sucked on the cloth after she'd finished, praying there was enough left in it to deaden the pain.

He began to run a fever, his wounded shoulders streaked with all manner of colors.

" 'Tis nothing," he told her. "A spot of bother."

But she wasn't fooled. "Ach, *Angle*."

Angle.

O'Malley turned away. He no longer had the strength to correct her.

* * *

HE LIT SOME of the charcoal and buried himself in the blankets. Although it smoked up the cave, the fire took the edge off the cold and he was able to sleep. He was no longer afraid of starving to death or being killed by Germans. It was being carried off by gangrene he feared now. His own rotting, suppurating flesh.

He wished he'd ask her to bring some paper and a pencil. He wanted to get his specifics down. Who he was and where he was from, how to get word to his mother and father, should he perish. Perhaps if he told the girl, she'd remember.

"I'm Brendan O'Malley," he said hoarsely when she reappeared. "Brendan O'Malley from County Cork."

"I know. I know who you are."

"Irish."

"Yes, yes. 'Irish in point of fact.'" She had tears in her eyes.

O'Malley threw the blankets back and tried to stand, but found his knees had gone all rubbery. Sinking back down on the blankets, he watched while Danae loaded his pack, carefully stowing the carved animals he'd made inside. He liked the way she moved, the deftness of her fingers and her prideful stance. He longed to touch her, to run his fingers along her collarbone and her neck—that long neck like an Egyptian queen's. She was in a red dress, a proper girl's dress this time, with a little buttons down the front and touch of lace. If he never saw another woman, if he died on his way down the mountain, the vision of her this night would suffice.

"Come now." She was all business. "We go to Kalavryta."

She helped him on with his boots and laced them up for him, then draped the blanket around him. Gasping for breath, he fought not to vomit in front of her.

Putting her arms around him, she helped him down the path, the boy running along behind. O'Malley longed to explain himself to her. To have her understand what the last three weeks had meant to him. His lonely youth as an only child on an isolated farm with naught but a dog to play with. How he'd longed for company his whole life, brothers and sisters. Only to find them now in this place with the two of them, to find them now as he was dying.

Half-delirious, he rambled on about Ireland as they walked. The breath of the horses on a winter's morning and the great wash of green in the spring. The sheep, all burly, on the hillsides, their coats like patches of dirty snow.

He kept losing track of his thoughts. " 'Tis the fever," he muttered to himself. "Rendered me useless, it has. Like whiskey, it's gone and loosened my tongue while melting my poor brains.

"Where are you taking me?" he kept asking, growing more and more confused, uncertain now as to where he was, what language he was speaking. "Where are you taking me?" he asked again.

Later he remembered grabbing her hand, and kissing it again and again.

* * *

O'Malley didn't know how long it took them to get down from the mountain, but the sky was full of light by the time they reached Kalavryta. Every now and then the girl would stop and let him rest, his shoulders throbbing with pain. He longed for a word of comfort from her—evidence that if he died of his injuries, he'd be missed, grieved over even—but she said nothing,

He tried not to cry out, lest he scare her or the boy, but it took more effort than he was capable of, and he moaned and gibbered like a fool. He called for his ma like a child afraid of the dark. But mostly it was Danae. Dark-eyed Danae he wanted, Danae he cried for.

Worried, the little boy grabbed him and tried to prop him up. "*Siko! Siko!*"

O'Malley sought to reassure him, but found he couldn't get his mouth around the words. "And me an Irishman." He wondered if this was death come to take him, this silencing a part of dying.

His shoulders were sticky with blood, and he kept slipping in and out of consciousness. He could see the town clearly now. One more stony rise and they would be there.

The girl climbed up on a rock and watched the sleeping village with a strange expression on her face, intent, like a dog waiting for the crackle of gunfire, its quarry to fall from the sky. The rifle was lying on the ground within easy reach, but O'Malley let it be. No point now.

A thick fog was rising from the river, and it wafted across the lowlands, the fields and orchards surrounding the town. The mist gave the village a dreamlike appearance, clouds of it washing over the cobbled streets and gray stone houses and making them gleam like pewter. Soon only the bell tower of the church was visible. O'Malley rejoiced when he saw the fog; it would give them cover.

The girl didn't cross the fields as he'd expected, but headed north toward the gorge. She took her time, staying well hidden in the trees as she led them forward. A few minutes later, they reached a railroad bridge high above a boulder-strewn glade. A light rain was falling, and overhead the metal trestles were glossy with damp. Secreting themselves beneath the pilings of the bridge, they stayed there until nightfall, the water coursing at their feet.

O'Malley was grateful for the cold, the way it eased his suffering and seemed to lessen the fever. Seeing him shivering, the little boy pulled off his sweater and laid it across O'Malley's shoulders. The child had quieted down since leaving the cave and kept looking around, obviously frightened.

The girl roused them a little while later. Walking single-file, they moved from stone to stone across the river, taking care to leave no prints in the mud. It continued to rain, red clay washing down from the banks like rivulets of blood.

Seeing it, O'Malley was reminded of the River Styx and the ferryman who transported the dead across it for a fee. Stories of Hades he'd learned in school. It was somewhere here, he remembered, that ancient hell, somewhere here in this part of Greece.

The girl nodded when he asked her about it. "Before Jesus came, people said hell had three doors and this place was one."

Hidden in shadows, it was as dark as night in the gorge, the roaring of the river the only sound. He could hear the wind howling outside, but nothing stirred at the bottom of the gorge where he was. The air was utterly still. *Aye*, it was easy to imagine hell here.

He guessed she'd come this way because it was easier for him; the ground was level and there were no cliffs to climb. They left the gorge, passed through a strand of rain-washed olive trees, and rested there for a few minutes, the gray-green leaves fluttering above them like clouds of mica.

He looked around. The fog was starting to burn off. They'd have to hurry.

* * *

THE GIRL PUSHED open the door of the shed. "Fast," she whispered.

O'Malley stumbled inside and collapsed on the floor. The place was filthy—moldy feathers and chicken shit encrusting the wooden walls and cobwebbed windows. Although the chickens were long gone, the ammonia-like scent of them lingered in the air and made O'Malley's eyes sting. Germans must have passed through and taken them, God knows what else. Hopefully, that had satisfied them and they'd let him be, let him die in peace.

Trying to help, Stefanos fussed about, tucking the sweater around him and feeling his forehead. "*Eisai kala?*" he kept asking. Are you all right?

O'Malley pushed him away. "Stop your rabbiting about. Get along with you."

Danae returned a few minutes later with a middle-aged woman.

The woman recoiled when she saw O'Malley and took a step back. "What's wrong with him? Typhus?"

"No," the girl said. "His wounds got infected."

Taking care to keep her distance, the older woman walked around, inspecting O'Malley.

He watched her with a sinking heart. *As if I'm a leper, a bleeding leper, lying at her feet.*

"How do you intend to feed him?" the woman asked in an aggrieved tone.

Hands on her hips, she stood there in her apron, stout and implacable, rooted to the earth like a tree. *An old farm horse*, O'Malley judged, taking her in, the massive legs and heavy haunches. *The kind bred to pull wagons.*

"He can have my share," the girl said.

"No, no. You've got to get him out of here. It's too dangerous."

"He's sick."

"I don't care. Let him be sick somewhere else."

* * *

THE WOMAN LET the door slam when she left the coop. The boy had taken care to stay out of her way, backing himself into the corner and staying there. He'd seemed diminished by her presence.

"My father's sister," Danae said after she left. "My *theia*, Aunt Toula, from America."

"She's in charge here? The one who looks after you?"

"Yes. She came to live with us after her husband died."

"Seems a right dragon."

Using his last ounce of strength, O'Malley propped himself on his elbows. "I heard what you said about the food, that you'd give me your share."

"I will. Stefanos, too."

Closing his eyes, he lay back down. "Be wasted on me. I'm a goner, Danae. Might as well stuff your faces."

* * *

O'MALLEY CLOSED HIS eyes. He could feel his shoulders burning, the heat coming off them. He wanted to be home. He didn't want to die in Greece among strangers.

Later that night Danae reappeared with her father and another man. The latter brought a lantern with him and a leather bag with a flat bottom full of medical instruments.

The doctor peeled off what was left of O'Malley's bandages and washed out his wounds with alcohol, then signaled the other man, who gave O'Malley a little bottle and nodded for him to drink it. "*Ouzo*," he said. Alcohol. It burned on the way down with a familiar whiskey-like fire that took the edge off the pain. After he finished, the man gave him another. "Drink," he said in English.

The two men then stood by for a few minutes, watching O'Malley and whispering in Greek. O'Malley fought to stay awake, unsure what they planned to do with him. He was deeply frightened. Afraid the gangrene was too far gone and they'd have to cut off his arms.

The doctor gave him a wet sponge, motioned for him to bite down on it, then tied a gag around his mouth. He removed the cover of the lantern and set it down on the floor, close to O'Malley's right shoulder. The kerosene hissed as it burned, smoke rising in threads from the burning oil. O'Malley watched the exposed flame for a moment, fighting not to be sick.

"God Almighty," he screamed. "Here it comes."

When the doctor nodded, the girl's father knelt down and gently straddled him, his weight pinning O'Malley to the floor. He grabbed O'Malley's arms and held them down while the girl did the same to his ankles. The doctor got a scalpel out of the bag and passed it back and forth over the flame, then dug it deep into the wound on O'Malley's right shoulder.

O'Malley bellowed and cried. He could smell his flesh burning, feel the heat of the hot scalpel cutting into him. The girl and her father fought to hold him down, wrestling to keep him still. The doctor continued to work, first on one shoulder, then the other, passing the scalpel back and forth in the fire, then pressing it into O'Malley's infected flesh, searing away the gangrene and cauterizing the wounds.

O'Malley bellowed and sobbed, his mouth all stopped up with rags.

5

When he awoke, he was lying on a cot, his shoulders swaddled with crisp white sheeting. He lifted first his right arm, then his left, tears starting in his eyes. Wiggled his fingers.

He bowed his head and thanked God, thanked Him again and again. He'd do right when he got back to Ireland, buy something for the church, candlesticks or a statue, put coins in the poor box. From this day forward, he'd be the son his mother always wanted. A holy Joe.

He kissed each of his hands in turn, what he could reach of his upper arms. The pain was terrible, like he'd been skinned alive, but he didn't care. He'd been spared. He'd not have to spend the rest of his life with hooks, frightening children, no hope of a wife.

O'Malley glanced around, wondering where he was. The room had a low ceiling and no windows. The walls were crumbling in places; and the air smelled of mildew and damp earth. The room had no door, naught but a length of burlap strung up on a rope. What light there was came from beneath it.

A cellar, it looked like.

He dozed off and on, waking and dropping off again. The doctor returned at some point and changed his bandages. He seemed well pleased with his work and told O'Malley in Greek all had gone well. He'd been lucky. The pain was diabolical. O'Malley couldn't turn without setting it off again, great waves of it, so intense it made him sick to his stomach. "Lucky?" Yes, he supposed he was.

A jug of water had been left for him. It tasted sweet, as if it had sugar in it or perhaps honey, and he gulped it down, only to vomit it up a few minutes later. After that, he sipped more slowly, taking his time, fighting to keep it down. The jug continued to be refilled, though he never saw who did it. Someone also emptied the chamber pot beneath the cot. Later food began to appear. Meat, which surprised him, on a battered metal dish. Like the cot he was lying on, the dish looked to be army-issue.

It was strange how the jug refilled itself, food came and went. When he soiled his sheets, he'd wake up to find they'd been changed. His clothes, too. Almost as if sorcery was involved. He seemed to remember a fairy tale where the same thing had happened, but he couldn't recall the ending, whether it had gone well or badly for the people involved.

Lying there on the cot, unable to tell if it were night or day, O'Malley lost track of time, how many days it had been since his surgery. *Three*, he guessed, *maybe four*. The first forty-eight hours had been a blur, every move he made pure agony, the torn flesh in his shoulders paining him to the point of paralysis. He'd longed for oblivion—alcohol, opium, anything that would take him there—and begged the doctor for it. "We've nothing," the doctor told him. "I'm sorry. You'll just have to bear it."

O'Malley remembered the sounds he'd made, so loud they'd woken him, pulled him back to consciousness. "What's that?" he remembered asking, only to realize it was him—he was the one screaming like a pig on its way to the slaughterhouse.

The doctor continued to slip in, so quietly O'Malley would look up and be surprised to see him there. He'd smile at O'Malley, inspect the wound, and leave.

O'Malley saw no one else. Stretched out there in the shadows, he sometimes felt as if he'd been buried alive.

He got up from the cot and walked around the room, holding on to the wall for support, then pushed aside the burlap and looked out. A shallow passageway led off to the right, as narrow as a mine shaft. It had an earthen floor and didn't lead anywhere, only to a wall about ten feet away. O'Malley paused for a moment and listened. Hearing nothing, he ventured on. At first he'd thought the wall was whitewashed stone like the rest of the cellar, but soon discovered it was wood, carefully disguised with paint. It rested in a groove in the floor and proved easy to move. Pausing now and then to catch his breath, O'Malley slid it away. He could hear the wind blowing outside and feel the cold. Like a horse set free in a pasture, he would have galloped off if he'd been able to, neighed even.

Bracing himself, he took a step and then another. He was outside now, standing in a depression on the side of a house. He recognized the shed in the distance and the ruined garden he'd passed through with Danae.

He leaned his head back, letting the sunlight wash over him. He was in the same clothes he'd worn in the cave, but they'd been washed and ironed. He touched his face, his hair, sniffed at himself. Someone had cleaned him up as well. His arms were painted up and down with mercurochrome or iodine, something streaky and orange. He sank down on the ground and sat there, watching the clouds pass overhead, their shadows moving rapidly across the fields, and gazed at the distant mountains. He found himself crying at the sight of them.

"Not right this. Not manly." But still he cried, sniffling and wiping his nose on his sleeve.

Knackered, he was. Broken down entirely.

It was growing dark when O'Malley returned to the room, taking care to put the wall back in place, leave it as he'd found it. The space was a priest's hole, he'd decided, albeit a modest one. Probably dated from the time of the Turks. There'd been such places all over Ireland, where people would gather in secret and take communion, celebrate the rituals of their outlawed faith, where priests could hide from their English persecutors.

He wondered what the Greeks had used theirs for. Probably something similar, the Ottomans being what they were the Germans of their day.

* * *

DANAE SLIPPED INTO the cellar that night. After O'Malley's walk, his shoulders had begun to burn and he'd been unable to fall asleep. He turned and looked at her. She was dressed in a white shift with a crocheted shawl over her shoulders, cloth slippers on her feet. She stood there for a moment, watching him, trembling a little from the cold.

"Evening, Danae," he whispered.

"Evening, *Angle*."

"Good to see you."

"Good to see you, too."

"Why'd you come so late?"

"My aunt doesn't want me here. Doesn't want Stefanos and me anywhere near you."

"Why? 'Twas only gangrene plagued me. Nothing contagious."

"She thinks you'll bring us trouble."

O'Malley thought it over, nodded sadly. *Aye*, he very well might.

"I just wanted to see how you are." She sounded embarrassed. Given her aunt's antipathy, she must be the one who'd refilled the jug while he slept, caring for him all these days. A guardian angel of sorts. A guardian angel with neither feathers nor wings.

He motioned her over. "Come sit with me for moment. I'm perishing of loneliness."

She stayed where she was, even drew back a little. "You were very sick. The doctor said you might die."

"Gangrene's a nasty business. Saw a lot of it in North Africa. Shrapnel wounds."

He could barely see her in the darkness, the whiteness of her dress and shawl the only indication of her presence. He wondered if her hair was loose, undone for the night.

"Doctor said another week and he'll take the bandages off."

"Then what? I go back to the cave?"

Wrapping the shawl more tightly around her, she continued to stare at him. "I don't know," she said. "They're talking about taking you to the *antartes*, sending you back to war."

* * *

AFTER DANAE LEFT, O'Malley lay awake, wondering what he should do. Part of him wanted to call it a day, find his way to the coast and be shipped back to Egypt. Another part of him wanted to see it through. To stay in Kalavryta and feast his eyes on Danae, play the fool with her little brother. He'd arrange for the British to drop food in for them. Be a hero of sorts, Father Christmas.

Might not be worth the risk, however. If the Germans found him, they'd shoot him for sure. Be a shame after all the patching up the doctor had done—the stitches and the surgery, the days he'd spent lying here, recovering—to land in German hands, get done to death now. His ghost to roam these infernal hills, damned to speak Greek for all eternity, damned never to be understood.

Not to mention the destruction it would bring on Danae and her family. The trouble he'd bring in such a case would be biblical. They might not salt the land, rain frogs and plagues down upon people, but the Germans were more than equal to the rest of it.

"Be best if you don't get captured."

He thought again of Danae in her slip. The sound of her voice in the darkness.

Aye, be altogether better if he stayed alive.

6

It grew too cold to stay in the priest's hole, and they moved O'Malley upstairs a few nights later. The aunt held a lantern, supervising Danae and her father as they helped him across the yard. O'Malley looked up at the night sky, impressed by the brightness of the stars and the strange positioning of the constellations, so turned around and different from what he remembered in Ireland.

He pointed to a familiar cluster. "What do you call that one there?" he asked Danae.

"*Megali arktos*. Big bear. Same as in Latin. *Ursa Major*."

"It's 'the Crann' or 'King David's chariot' in Ireland. Its little mate, that one there, is 'fire tail.'"

He would have liked to linger outside, soaking up the darkness with her, but the aunt didn't want them talking; neither did the father, who stood off to one side, watching them with a frown on his face. As if a bill had come due, a high one he hadn't anticipated.

He called the aunt to lend a hand. The fact that he'd summoned her, not Danae, was not lost on O'Malley. He wondered if the man knew—if his lovesickness was that obvious.

Like the room in the cellar, the house had a cloth door. It consisted of three, maybe four rooms. It was bitterly cold inside, smoking metal braziers the only source of warmth. What furniture there was had obviously been handmade, pine tricked up with varnish to look like mahogany; an old calendar tacked up on a wall for decoration. Rugs were scattered throughout—some hand-loamed, others simple goatskins.

Outside, a wooden privy served as bathroom. Inside the privy there was no place to sit, which didn't surprise O'Malley, having seen it before all over Greece—nothing but a porcelain platter on the ground with a hole at the center. The father showed him how to position his feet on either side, squat down to do his business, then wash everything down with a bucket. At 6'2", O'Malley had always found it a perilous contraption, requiring great balance and concentration.

"Shit on my shoes, I will, I'm not careful."

When it came time to sleep, the man gathered the goatskins, piled them up, and shook a sheet over them. Handing O'Malley a blanket, he said, "Germans sometimes pass here. If you hear them, you put rugs back and hide. Come, I show you."

He led O'Malley to a closet in the kitchen. A trap door was secreted in the floor, a short ladder leading down into the priest's hole. "I can't show you now with your arms so bad, but if Germans come …."

Arms or no arms, the man's expression said. *Run for your life.*

Fastidious and self-contained, the man seemed restless as he stood there, filled with energy he didn't know what to do with. O'Malley's father had damped that down with drink. He wondered what Danae's father used.

"You smoke?" the man asked.

When O'Malley said he did, Danae's father handed him a cigarette and lit it for him, then did the same for himself, treating the tobacco as a precious thing. Leaning his head back, he blew a smoke ring and laughed to himself. He had a gold incisor, O'Malley saw. Glinting slightly, it gave him a jaunty air that didn't match the rest of him, his dour and stolid manner. He didn't try to make conversation, just stood there smoking with his eyes closed, grunting with pleasure.

He had the same ox-like weightiness as his sister, Toula—the same unyielding flesh and heavy limbs. They worked better on him, O'Malley thought, made him seem powerful and serious, a person others would listen to.

Talking apace and joking around, O'Malley worked to befriend him. "I grew up on a farm in Ireland," he said. "Raised sheep same as you. In Dublin, they call people like me 'bog trotters,' 'culchies.' Don't think much of us." He went on talking for some time, long after their cigarettes were finished, speaking of his parents and the life they'd lived, how he'd gone to medical school at his father's behest and become a doctor, planned to start a practice in Cork when the war was over. He made sure to include his father's antipathy to the English and how his people had suffered at their hands.

Let it be said. Let him hear me say I have no allegiance to Churchill.

The man turned and gave him a searching look. "Go to sleep," he said.

It wasn't until O'Malley bedded down for the night that he realized he'd seen no food in the house, nothing whatsoever to eat. The aunt must have hidden it before they moved him upstairs. Been afraid he'd devour it and her both.

* * *

THE TEA WAS weak and tasted like medicine. O'Malley swirled the liquid around in his cup. Greener than what he was used to, it had grassy bits floating in it. He assumed that like the bread made of chick peas, it was something forced on the Greeks by the war.

He thanked the aunt politely, taking care to use the third person when he spoke to her in Greek. She was someone who cared how others addressed her, whether they showed her proper respect.

Danae drank her tea in silence. She seemed relieved to see O'Malley on his feet again and patted his hand when her aunt's back was turned.

"What day is it?" he asked.

"October tenth."

So he'd lost less than two weeks to the gangrene. Not much, considering.

She'd undone her braid and shook her head a little, smiling as though sharing a great secret, aware of the effect she had on him.

After they finished eating, Stefanos pulled a ball out from under the bed and kicked it toward him. O'Malley kicked it back and they played together until the aunt put an end to their game.

"Break glasses, is bad for Stefanos," she said in English. "Hurt shoulders again, bad for you. You need to get better, go back to army."

Although she spoke in a solicitous way, gesturing to O'Malley's bandaged shoulders with a concerned look on her face, he understood: the old heifer wanted him gone. She picked up her broom and pointedly began sweeping around him, tidying up as if he wasn't there.

"I didn't ask to be brought here. It was your lot who took me in."

The woman didn't answer. Setting the broom aside, she removed the covers of the bed and shook them out, straightened the edges of the sheet.

"I'm sorry for any trouble I've caused."

She turned and faced him. "Do you know what will happen if they catch you? How dangerous it is for us? Barely enough to eat and now you come. My brother says we must shelter you. We're Greek, he said. It's demanded of us. When I told him 'no,' he said I spent too long in America, only care for myself, that America ruined me." Her voice was choked with rage.

Pushing him aside, she picked up the broom and began to sweep again, her eyes on the dirt at her feet.

* * *

"What are you doing?" Danae asked O'Malley.

"Sitting out in the yard with Stefanos. Had a bit of set-to with your aunt this morning. Thought it best if I stayed out of her way."

He hauled himself to his feet, and the three of them walked around to the back of the house, taking care to stay close to the trees in case anyone was watching. There was the remnants of a vegetable garden and Danae stayed there, saying she wanted to search for food and motioning for them to go on. Giving a cry of victory, she discovered a couple of tomatoes and held them up for O'Malley and the boy to see, an eggplant and a desiccated pepper.

The day was overcast, clouds overtaking the sun like shifting gray mountains. O'Malley found an abandoned nest on a tree limb and gave it to Stefanos, who in turn shared a dead beetle. The bug's body was iridescent, a jewel almost, and it seemed to glow in O'Malley hand.

The boy wanted to show him the rabbits his father kept. He led O'Malley toward a river at the far end of the field. The banks were heavily overgrown, and the area was shadowy and damp. The river was sluggish, brown with silt, and there were sandbars everywhere, breaking through the surface of the water like islands. A few had trees growing on them, adding to the darkness.

The hutch was well hidden, buried deep in a thicket of pines by the river. An ingenious structure, it was more than four feet long and made of weathered wood the same color as the surrounding brush. A length of chicken wire provided ventilation for the animals, but kept them contained.

Stefanos told him his father had moved the hutch there to keep the rabbits away from the Germans and camouflaged it with pine boughs. There were a goodly number of the animals, their noses twitching as they caught their scent.

"*Ela* Foufou," the boy said, feeding a handful of grass to one of the rabbits, a young one with a floppy ear. "*Ela*, Bobo *kai Kiki*."

They lingered by the hutch for a few more minutes, O'Malley keeping a watchful eye out. He noticed an old woman hanging up clothes on the far side of the river and retreated back into the trees, pulling the boy with him. Although he knew he was too far away to be identified, it scared him to be so exposed.

"Time to go back, Specky," he told the boy.

The wind picked up as they left the glade, stirring the dead leaves underfoot and bending the pine trees almost double.

Feeling its power, O'Malley wished he had a kite, a length of string to play out. No telling how high a kite would go on a day like this. Maybe he could make one when they got back to the house. He looked up at the darkening sky.

Aye, he'd have just enough time before the rain came.

* * *

Using old newspapers and scraps of wood he found in the cellar, he constructed a kite on the kitchen floor, tying the framework together with twine and laying old newspapers over it. Clumsily made, it was a crude thing, but with any luck it would do the trick.

"*Aetos, aetos!*" Stefanos shouted. Kite, kite.

When O'Malley finished, Danae gave him a length of yellow cloth for a tail. "Old dress," she said with a shrug. "Too small now."

Once they were outside, the boy ran back and forth, string in hand, struggling to get the kite airborne. The wind took it a few seconds later, but its weight was poorly distributed and it careened wildly, spinning around like a plane shot out of the sky.

O'Malley stepped forward and helped the boy steady it, demonstrating how to work the string up and down with his hand. Shuddering, the kite began to rise, its cloth tail switching back and forth.

Calling to it in Greek, Stefanos coaxed it not to fall. "*Min peseis, aneva ston aera kai milise me ta poulia.*" Take to the air and speak to the birds.

O'Malley left him to it. He was tired now and his shoulders hurt.

Danae chased after her brother, running back and forth and yelling instructions. Caught by the wind, her skirt billowed up. She batted it down with her hands, her cheeks red with cold.

The string broke a moment later and the kite slowly tumbled down, breaking into pieces as it fell. Frantic, Stefanos tried to get it back up again, but it kept coming and crashed into a tree.

"*Spasmenos.*" All broken.

"No matter, sport," O'Malley told him. "I'll make you another."

He tugged the tail free and stowed it in his pocket. A souvenir, he thought, a memento of this day, this hour before the rains came.

* * *

The storm broke a few minutes later, sheets of rain engulfing them as they ran toward the house. O'Malley grabbed Stefanos and swung him over the puddles, the sea of red mud that was suddenly everywhere. Lightning splintered the sky above their heads, exploding across the low lying clouds like mortar fire.

Open-mouthed, Stefanos stopped to watch, counting off the seconds. A moment later, a clap of thunder shook the ground beneath them.

"Come on, come on!" O'Malley cried, grabbing the boy and running toward the house.

Danae's aunt was standing in the doorway. "*Ela, paidi mou,*" she called to Stefanos. Come, my child.

As soon as Stefanos got inside, she pulled off his wet clothes off and wrapped him in a blanket. "Why did your sister let you get so wet, my boy? Why didn't she take better care of you?"

Danae ran into the house a moment later, soaked to the skin. Without a word, the aunt got up and retrieved the mop, handed it to her, and went back to fussing over her brother.

Funny that, O'Malley thought, studying the two of them. In Ireland, it was girls who were favored, not like here, where it was always the boys. Maybe it was the cost of marrying a girl off in Greece, the dowry required. Or maybe the custom went back to ancient times, the need for men to fight that everlasting war Danae spoke of. Not that Stefanos would ever make much of a warrior, fight with anything besides his shoelaces, the cowlick on his head.

The boy squealed as his aunt dried him off. O'Malley looked over at Danae. The expression on her face was hard to read.

She's used to it. Bloody Cinderella.

The aunt lit the brazier in the front room and settled the boy in front of it, bringing a blanket from the back room to tuck around him. Pulling a chair close to the brazier, she called to O'Malley to come and join her, ignored her niece completely.

Speaking English, she boasted to him about her life in America, how she and her husband had lived in a big apartment in Chicago with an elevator that took them up and down. They'd had a car, too, a Buick. "It was good for me in America. Food, so much food. A woman to clean. Beautiful clothes."

A real Lady Muck, she spoke as if he alone would understand. As if their experiences were the same because they both spoke English.

How little she knew. O'Malley supposed that's where her dress had come from, the silly high heeled shoes she was wearing. Fine for getting in Buicks, not so good for going hungry in Greece.

He didn't think the show she was putting on was for his benefit. No, it had something to do with Danae.

"Then my husband died and I had to sell everything and come back here." She said 'here' as if it were a pigsty, someplace dirty. "All my life, bad luck." She reached over and grabbed Stefanos, pulled him close to her. "All my life. Eh, *paidi mou*?"

O'Malley wished she'd leave the kid alone. He didn't like the way she was playing with him, petting him like he was a puppy.

Danae walked over to the window and pulled the curtain aside. "Where did my father say he was going?"

"To Kalavryta. He said he had work to do."

O'Malley looked at her sharply. There was something in the way she said it, something she wasn't saying.

"Again?" the girl asked in a pained voice.

"Yes." Something passed between them, some hidden message.

"Panagia mou," Danae whispered. "How many this time?"

The woman shrugged. "Who knows?"

It rained the rest of the day. The aunt retreated to the bedroom with Stefanos to take a nap, leaving Danae and O'Malley alone in the parlor.

Opening up an old wooden trunk, Danae got out some family trinkets and showed them to him. A photograph of her parents on their wedding day, a copper dish from Rhodes. "My mother's wedding dress," she said, smoothing down the front with her hand. It was a poor thing with ruffles made of cheap lace and high neck, yellow now with age.

Dana pulled it out of the trunk and held it up to herself, then getting to her feet, began to waltz around the room, spinning as if in the arms of an invisible partner. The white fabric set off her skin and dark hair, her ever-watchful eyes. O'Malley had never been to a ballet, had only read about them, but he thought a ballerina might look the way Danae did just then, all thinness and grace and draped in white cloth.

"You'll be wearing that?" he asked. "Same as your ma, the day you wed?"

"I'm just playing. I will never marry."

O'Malley stepped closer, intending to dance with her, but she quickly spun away.

"You're beautiful, Danae," he said, reaching for her hand. He succeeded in grabbing her and they danced for a moment, the dress between them.

"In Ireland, men would be buzzing around you like bees. By the hundreds, they'd be, swarming wherever you went."

"Not in Greece. I have no dowry, nothing to bring to the wedding."

"What about this place?"

"It belongs to Aunt Toula."

"Hardly fair, that."

"Much in life isn't, *Angle*," she said in a tired voice, done with her dancing. "You're a grown man. Haven't you noticed?"

Folding up the dress, she carefully put it back in the trunk. Her one great treasure. "My mother was my age when she got married. She only saw my father twice before the wedding. He was from another village."

O'Malley wondered how her mother had felt on her wedding night, bedding down with a stranger. "Were they happy together?"

"They were poor." Wealth was a condition for happiness, apparently. For love.

O'Malley remembered his father's words when he'd asked him about women, a husband's duty in marriage. "To care about her and the children, that's what it is," his pa had said. "Make sure they're warm enough and have food in the larder, that the fence stays mended so the sheep don't stray. Never let the drink take you and get your work done. Be the one the rest look to, her most of all.

" 'Tis simple, son. Just the daily job, done right."

* * *

THE AUNT FED them something called *trahana* for lunch, a watery broth with odd bits of dough floating in it. Although it left a sour aftertaste, O'Malley held it in his mouth, fighting not to swallow it right away, to make it last. He looked around the kitchen, curious as to where Danae's tomatoes had gotten to, what the aunt had done with them.

Stefanos was banging on his bowl with a spoon. "*Peino, Peino!*" I'm hungry.

"Once the war's over and there's enough to eat, I'm going to eat breakfast three times a day," O'Malley said in Greek, wanting to engage the boy in the conversation.

Stefanos got a dreamy look on his face. "*Paidakia*," he said, thumping his spoon again. Lamb chops.

"*Loukoumades*," said Danae, joining in the game.

"What the devil are *loukoumades*?" O'Malley asked.

She thought for a moment. "Donuts, *loukoumades* are donuts."

Tightlipped, her aunt gathered up the dishes. "You should be glad for what you've been given," she said, aiming her remarks at O'Malley. "Vinegar for nothing is as sweet as honey."

There was nothing at all for dinner.

Later O'Malley asked Danae why they didn't kill one of the rabbits.

"My father won't let us. He says they are our—how you say—protection, in case things get worse."

Worse than this, they'd be eating their shoes, same as Chaplin did in the movie. Twirling the laces on his fork as if they were spaghetti.

* * *

THE RAIN CONTINUED on through the night. O'Malley stacked up the *flokatis* and lay down on top of them. After eating the *trahana*, Danae and the other two had disappeared. Probably sleeping in the back room. No point in trying to do anything in this weather.

O'Malley didn't know how long he'd been asleep when he heard the first sound. A dull thud, it rattled the dishes in the cupboard and made the floor shake. His heart pounding, he lay there in the dark, trying to figure out where it had come from. *Ach, you're dreaming*, he told himself finally, rolling over and going back to sleep again.

He'd just dozed off when the sound came again. This time there was no mistaking it or the voices that followed. Mixed up in it, O'Malley thought he heard a motor start somewhere close by. He crept to the window and peered out, wiping the moisture off the glass with his sleeve. Nothing.

The brazier had gone out and the stone floor was as cold as ice.

Worried, he shook the *flokatis* out and spread them on the floor as Danae's father had instructed, then opened the trap door in the kitchen and climbed down the ladder as fast as he could, two steps at a time. He sensed rather than saw the people, the mass of them crowded into the small space at the bottom. He could see their eyes shining in the weak light, their faces glimmering faintly as they looked up at him. There was a woman with a baby, an older man with a bandaged head, and five or six others. O'Malley smelled the dampness on their wool coats, the wet dirt they'd carried in with them. They didn't move. Just stood there and watched him like a herd of deer. Foolish the same way deer were. As if their stillness would make them invisible, protect them from bullets.

O'Malley could sense their fear. Clinging to them, it was, like the rain on their clothes.

Danae's father came forward, pushing his way through the throng. "Go back to bed," he said. "This doesn't concern you."

"Who are they?"

"People the Nazis are after." He spoke rapidly in Greek to the group. It broke the spell and everyone started talking at once. "They don't want you here," he told O'Malley a few seconds later. "They're afraid you'll betray them."

"Tell them who I am. Why I'm here."

"They don't care. All they care is you're a stranger."

Stung, O'Malley climbed back up the ladder. The noise must have been the false wall, sliding back and forth, the people talking as they took their places in the cellar beneath him. Danae's father had waited until it rained to move them into the house. Thought the bad weather would protect them from Germans.

Pure foolishness, that. Like lobbing rocks at tanks.

* * *

THE NEXT MORNING O'Malley questioned Danae about the people. They were in the ruined garden, sent there by the aunt in search of food. The rain had stopped and mist was rising from the damp earth, wisps of it drifting up between the trees.

"Where'd the people come from?"

"I don't know. At the beginning, they were Jews. Children from Salonika. A man from Vrestena was helping them escape. Spiliakos, his name was. He'd go to the Jewish part of town, take them and lead them out of the city."

"How'd he get them past the Germans?"

"By acting drunk. 'Oh, papa,' the children would scold, pretending to hold him up. 'Not again. Mama's going to be so mad at you.' He rescued dozens that way. The Germans never caught on, never realized that every time they saw him, he was with a different group of kids."

She recited this as if it were nothing, this saving of children. As if it was a routine matter.

"What happened to them?"

"I don't know. All I know is they got away."

Brushing the hair out of her eyes, she went back to searching for food. "The people who come now aren't Jews. I don't know who they are or where they come from. All I know is that they have to get away."

"Who's helping him? Your aunt involved?"

"No. She hates what he's doing. She wanted to charge them money for staying here, for the food. The rotten tomatoes we feed them."

"Are the partisans a part of this?"

She glanced at him, suspicious now. "Why do you care?"

"I'd like to be a part of it. It'd be better than building an airstrip, helping the British colonize this place after the Germans leave."

"You won't be here."

"How do you know?"

"I heard my father talking. They're taking you away next week."

Stefanos was kicking his raggedy ball across the field. Made of cloth, it was so heavy with mud, it barely moved. "*Ela*," he yelled to O'Malley. "*Ela, Angle*."

O'Malley held up a hand, signaling for him to wait his turn.

"He'll miss you." Danae nodded to her brother.

"What about you? Will you miss me?" O'Malley kept his voice light.

"I don't know." Keeping her head down, she returned to her digging. "Maybe."

* * *

WHEN O'MALLEY CREPT down the ladder that night, the people were gone. He was impressed by the smoothness of the operation. He hadn't seen them go, hadn't heard a sound. As a clandestine mission, it had been flawless, a bloody magic act.

The father had to be part of a network, probably similar to the one that had rescued him in 1941, the farmers who had passed him from one place to another before finally spiriting him across the Libyan Sea to Egypt. He imagined he'd travel the same route as the people here when he left Kalavryta.

He looked around the empty room again. The air still smelled of rain, their wet wool clothes.

"God speed," he said aloud.

7

O'MALLEY WOKE TO the sound of men shouting in German. He bolted for the cellar and stayed there huddled down in the dark, his heart in his throat. Judging by the sound, it was a large patrol, twenty men at least. He inched over to the false wall, thinking he'd throw it down and run if they came for him. For once, he welcomed the gloom in the cellar, the impenetrable dark.

He pulled the wall open a notch and watched them go by. They were marching in a tight formation, a seemingly endless line. His initial estimate had been wrong. There must be fifty men out there.

"Partisans blew up a bridge south of here," Danae's father told him. "The Germans are searching for them." He handed him a lantern, cautioning him only to use it when the sun was up. At night, the light would attract the Germans and reveal his hiding place.

Over the next few days, German patrols continued to pass back and forth in front of the house. Always in a hurry. Always with their helmets on and their weapons on display.

O'Malley stayed in the cellar. The cot was still there as was the jug of water, the one that had filled and refilled itself after his surgery. If they threw a loaf of bread down to him occasionally, he could probably last out the war.

The father had given him a chamber pot, too, saying his sister would collect it twice a day and empty it for him. The aunt never spoke to O'Malley as she went about this task and made a great show of her distaste, holding the chamber pot as far away as she could.

O'Malley chuckled to himself. *Lady Muck and her bucket of piss.*

Dressed to the nines, she'd swept out the cellar the previous day, questioning

O'Malley as she went about the chore. How big was the farm he grew up on? Did his father own a car, his mother a proper washing machine? She spoke sentimentally of her time in America, how well off she'd been, describing the fur coat her husband had given her one Christmas.

O'Malley thought at first the questions were her way of taking his measure. People did the same in Ireland. As a stranger, you expected it. But when the questions continued, he decided it must be something more. A way of distancing herself from where she had ended up, of letting him know she hadn't always lived here in this slum of a house, that she'd been somebody once.

The Greeks who'd cared for him in Pylos had questioned him, too. Mainly to see if he could be of use to them, if he had anything they wanted. He'd doctored a few relatives, even looked in on a sick cow. He assumed it was the same with this woman. For all her time abroad and her fancy airs, Danae's aunt was at heart the same as those others.

He answered her as truthfully as he could, though it made him uneasy. Danae stayed in the background, listening. Making faces behind her aunt's back, sashaying around and mocking her when she wasn't looking.

As the days passed, the aunt grew friendlier and friendlier. Even going so far as to make jokes about not being seen in public with O'Malley. "A handsome man like you," she said, nudging him with her elbow. "People in the village would talk."

As if this were peacetime, their only worry the gossip of neighbors.

For the most part, Greek women kept their eyes averted in the company of men, never stared at them the way she was doing. Perhaps this was a style she'd picked up in America, the red lipstick she insisted on wearing and the brazen manner, a bit of foolishness she'd brought home with her.

She was a woman who would say anything, his ma would have said. Mass in church if she were allowed.

Later, Danae told him her aunt was the same with everybody and that it had gotten her in trouble. "The other women don't trust her. They think she's a harlot."

"Why'd she come back? From what she said, she had a good life in America."

"Her husband died and she was alone."

"But why here? You said she had money."

"My father asked her to come after my mother died. She always wanted children. Taking care of Stefanos when he was a baby was like having one of her own."

One, he noted, *not two*. "You don't like her very much."

Her expression was bleak. "She only loves Stefanos. She's never been a mother to me."

* * *

DANAE'S FATHER TOOK the boy with him to Kalavryta two days later to search for food. They'd been gone about four hours when the child came bursting into the house. "*O Germanos pethane! Pethane, pethane!*"

O'Malley felt a chill. Although his Greek was poor, he understood what the child was saying. Died. The German died.

The father's voice was grim. "Someone shot a German soldier in front of the bakery. I was in the shop next door, but Stefanos was right there when it happened. He saw the rifle in the doorway and heard the shot."

"Anyone see him?"

"The woman who owns the bakery. 'The rifle? It was no one I knew,' she said. 'I don't want you to think my family had anything to do with it.' She offered Stefanos a loaf of bread, wanted to buy his silence. But I wouldn't let him take it. 'You insult me, you insult my son,' I told her. 'He knows what's at stake. He will never speak of what he saw today.' "

He said all this quietly, only the slight tremor in his voice betraying his fear for his son.

Together he and O'Malley secured the wall of the cellar, then the front door, replacing the burlap with a ratty length of wood. They nailed the shutters closed and ordered the women and boy to stay out of sight.

If it hadn't been so pathetic, O'Malley would have laughed out-loud.

As if any of this would protect them. If the Germans wanted in, they'd come in. More rocks at tanks, this was. Toy guns and cardboard shields. They needed to take action, to spirit Stefanos away from Kalavryta and be quick about it.

"Germans won't rest till they find the killer," he told the boy's father. "Stefano is a witness. You need to get him out of here. They'll be going from house to house soon. You don't have much time."

Danae's father seemed to make up his mind. "Tomorrow, then."

The plan was simple. They'd travel as a family group, all five of them, with their belongings and a herd of sheep, act like they were refugees, intent on resettling elsewhere. If the Germans stopped them, they'd probably lose the sheep, but the animals were necessary, would disguise their true purpose.

"We'll leave you and Stefanos in the cave," Danae's father said. "I'll get word to the *antartes* and let them know you're there and they'll come for you."

* * *

"WHY DIDN'T YOUR father let Stefanos have the bread?" O'Malley asked Danae when she brought him his supper that night. "What harm would have come of it? He's a sickly child. He needs to eat."

"If people saw, they'd think Stefanos was a part of it." Her tone was unemotional. They were at war. Everyone had to make sacrifices.

"But he's a child."

"Makes no difference."

They were alone in the cellar. Above him, O'Malley could hear Stefanos crying, unsettled by the events of the day, and his aunt soothing him, trying to settle him down. Danae's father had gone into town and wouldn't be back until morning.

"He's a hard man, your pa. Hard."

He'd grown up believing hardness was a good thing in a man, especially in wartime. Now he wasn't sure. To deny a starving child a loaf of bread. It seemed wrong to him. Cruel even. Like the Spartans leaving the broken babies out to die.

"Never mind my father," Danae said.

She seemed in no hurry to leave and lingered there, grinning at him, her eyes full of mischief.

Reaching for her hand, he pulled her toward him. "In olden times, a lady would give a soldier her colors to wear when he headed into battle. I'm a soldier. What will you give me?"

Watching her all the while, he raised her hand to his lips and kissed it, letting his mouth linger on her skin. He untied the ribbon that held her hair back and buried his face in it, then undid the buttons of her blouse one by one. Gently, he caressed her, drawing her closer and kissing her neck, her mouth.

"*Oxi,*" she said, laughing and struggling a little. "*Oxi, Angle.*" No.

" 'Tis wrong calling an Irishman, '*Angle.*' 'Tis an insult."

He wouldn't let go of her even when she pulled away. He kissed the palms of her hands, each of her fingers in turn. "Danae," he said hoarsely. "Danae."

"*Angle,*" she said, mocking him. "*Angle.*"

He ran his hands all over her, kissed that long length of neck and buried his face in her hair. He could feel her trembling beneath him, her eyes shining in the darkness as she watched him expectantly. They fell to the floor and rolled over and over, laughing softly. She soon lost her shift, her naked breasts exposed, the whole of her.

"Danae?!" her aunt called. "What are you doing? Get back up here!"

O'Malley stood there for a long time after Danae left. He felt as if he'd been branded, a fresh scar searing his flesh where he'd touched her with his hand and felt the beating of her heart. He looked up at the darkness. Imagined her sleeping above him. He touched his lips with a finger, remembering the taste of her skin, the briny flavor of her. Wanted her more than he'd wanted anything in his life.

He began to sing softly, 'The Rose of Tralee,' the saddest ballad he knew. A song of love, longing:

> The cool shades of evening their mantle were spreading
> And Mary all smiling was listening to me
> The moon through the valley her pale rays was shedding
> When I won the heart of the Rose of Tralee.
> Though lovely and fair as the rose of the summer
> Yet, 'twas not her beauty alone that won me
> Oh no! 'Twas the truth in her eye ever beaming
> That made me love Mary, the Rose of Tralee.

"I'll have you yet," he said to the shadows. "You hear, Danae? Have you and have you and have you."

* * *

It was still dark when the father shook O'Malley awake. "It's time."

After settling O'Malley down on a stool in the kitchen, the aunt set about dyeing his red hair, combing out each strand and dabbing it with a brush. She then painted his beard and eyebrows in turn, his eyelashes and the hair on his arms, chest and legs.

Homemade, the dye stung his skin. "Burning me, you are," O'Malley cried. "Killing me with your woman's poison."

Danae's aunt handed him a mirror without a word, glad to be rid of him. She'd have made him drink the foul brew if she'd had any say, buried him afterward out in the field.

He turned his head from side to side, inspecting himself. The business with the dye hadn't made him look Greek, only filthy to the point of unhealthiness. The liquid had trickled down and stained the skin of his face, made it look moldy. The glass in the mirror was cracked, cleaving his image right down the middle. The two halves didn't match up, which was about how he felt.

"It's the business," he said, trying to make the best of it. "My own mother wouldn't know me."

The aunt had been against the plan from the start, saying a cave was not a fit place for a child. "He's the one who'll cause us trouble," she'd said at one point, nodding in O'Malley's direction. "Him and only him."

O'Malley wondered if she'd heard them in the cellar last night, if she knew what had gone on between him and Danae. It didn't matter. Too late now—too late for everything.

Stefanos showed O'Malley his suitcase. Made of lacquered cardboard, it was a small thing, not much bigger than a metal lunchbox. He'd wanted to bring the broken kite, too. "*Fere ton aeto.*" But there hadn't been enough time to get it down from the tree. He seemed eager to be underway, happy even.

In the kitchen, O'Malley and Danae quickly divided up whatever food the aunt had seen fit to give them and stored it in their packs. The girl surrendered his grenades and watched as he secured them to his belt, then retrieved his rifle and revolver from the cupboard.

The last gift was a heavy cape made of goatskin bestowed on O'Malley by Dane's father.

"Shepherds wear them," he said. "Put it on."

The cape had a peaked hood and reached almost to the floor. A good disguise, it was big enough to hide his weapons under, his pale Irish self. As for the rest, his face and hair, well, he'd deal with them later.

Standing there in the kitchen in the cape, he felt a little like the girl in the story, the one in the red riding hood who set off to visit her granny and almost got eaten by the wolf.

A man named Wolff was now second in command of the SS, a coincidence not lost on O'Malley.

8

Danae quickly retraced the route she had followed when she brought O'Malley from the cave, walking beneath the girders of the railroad bridge. As a soldier, he would have preferred high ground, but deferred to her. She would know better where the Germans had positioned themselves, possible sites for an ambush. The river was running high, and garbage clung to the wet grass along its banks—rusting tin cans and potato sacks, a headless doll. He saw a dead cat spinning in the shallows, its teeth exposed in a rictus of death.

Spume was rising and beads of water clung to O'Malley's cloak. The other three were well back, herding the sheep along the muddy banks of the river.

"Dye's washed off," he told her, looking down at his hands. "All your aunt's handiwork. They catch me now, they'll know I'm not Greek."

"No matter."

"How will you explain my coloring?" He stroked his cheek, larking about, overjoyed to have her near him. "The fairness of my complexion?"

"I'll say you're an albino."

"One of those white rabbits? The kind with the red eyes?"

"Yes, a rabbit."

In case he missed the point, she put her hands on her head and wiggled them. "Big rabbit."

It was quiet under the bridge. There was no sign of the German patrols Danae's father had spoken of, but that didn't mean anything. They could be anywhere.

A donkey was pastured in a nearby field, watching them with its slanted eyes. It ambled off peacefully a moment later and disappeared into the brush.

O'Malley hung back when they reached the bare rocks above the town, worried about the empty stretch of earth that lay ahead. Once they started across it, they'd have no cover for more than two hundred yards. It wasn't a long distance, but it would be enough. If anyone was watching, they'd spot them. They'd be totally exposed.

Danae's father was evidently thinking the same thing. "Should we run?" he asked.

"Might be better to walk. Act like we belong here."

"Only if we go as a group. Otherwise, they'll think we're partisans, heading back to camp."

They ended up tackling the mountain from a different angle, scaling immense walls of rock, heart-stopping in their bleakness. The aunt quit a few minutes later, saying she'd sprained her ankle and could go no farther. They were in a stretch of meadow, thick with grass, and the sheep quickly spread out to graze.

O'Malley guessed they were about a half mile from the cave. He searched for signs of military activity, the glint of metal in the trees or telltale trail of dust, but saw nothing. Aunt should be all right. Given the steepness of the slope and the weight of their weapons, the big howitzers and Sig 33s, no Germans would venture here.

* * *

O'Malley helped Stefanos and Danae up the last few yards to the cave. In the end, the father had stayed back with his sister, who didn't want to be left alone, and the three of them had gone on ahead. The cave was as he remembered it—a hole whittled out of rock, as empty as the tomb in the scriptures the day the angel rolled back the stone. Exhausted from the journey, Stefanos collapsed on the ground and quickly fell asleep. O'Malley sat down next to him and motioned for Danae to join him.

He wasn't inclined to romance, not today, not suited up as he was in war paint and dye, the kid sleeping underfoot. Sopping wet, his cloak reeked of its goatish origins. Perhaps Pan could get away with it, have his way with the girls as a goat, but O'Malley doubted he could. Besides he didn't feel much like Pan. No, standing there in his animal hide, soaked to the skin and foul-smelling, if he felt like anyone, it was John the Baptist.

Also, there were the grenades. He'd been warned off sex as a boy, told fornication would lead straight to hell. Given the grenades, it very well might. *Best not to chance the arms.*

Besides, Danae was no scrubber. She was a good girl and deserved something better than a quick tumble.

Inching over, he bent down and kissed her gently on the lips. She grabbed his hand and pressed it against her face. It was covered in dye and left an impression on her cheek, a tattoo of sorts.

He moved to wipe it off, but she shook her head. "No, no."

Getting to his feet, he gathered her up in his arms, holding her as close as he dared given the grenades, and danced her around the cave. He sang as he danced, bending her low the way he'd seen men do in the movies, fancy folk in tuxedos and slicked back hair.

He kissed her a second time. A sad kiss, this last. A kiss of farewell. "I'll be back for you. I'll not be letting you go."

She touched his cheek again with her hand. Standing there in her shawl, she looked like she'd stepped out of a Renaissance painting.

"*O Theos mazi sou*," she whispered. Go with God.

* * *

"A MAN WITH boots does not have to worry where to put his feet," they said in Ireland. *Aye*, boots were the thing. Unlacing his boots, O'Malley pulled them off, stretched out next to Stefanos, and tried to sleep. He kept thinking he heard Danae coming back up the path. But there was nothing.

Her father had cautioned him not to make a fire, saying the smell of wood smoke would draw the Germans, but it was so cold, his bones ached. Venturing down the path, he gathered up an armful of twigs, brought them into the cave and lit them. He relaxed a little as the air warmed, wished like a caveman he had a big bloody rib to gnaw on.

He didn't know how they'd done it, those first humans. Chasing woolly beasts four times their size, sleeping in caves like this one. Given the choice, he'd go with the church's teaching. Adam, he'd be, living it up in the Garden of Eden. At least it'd be warm there, fruit for the taking. Eve beside him, stark naked and willing, at least until she fell in with the snake, bollixed up everything. Yes, indeed, he'd take the Bible version of the thing if it were up to him. The start of it all.

He'd reviewed his supplies and taken stock. If he was careful, he and Stefanos had enough food to last out the week. After that, he didn't know what they'd do. Hopefully, the partisans would come by then. Otherwise, he'd have to do like the cavemen and hunt for their supper.

He longed for a human voice, any sound save this, the mournful drone of the wind.

9

O'MALLEY WAS CURLED up close to the dying ashes of the fire when he heard footsteps outside the cave. Grabbing his rifle, he hid himself in the shadows. "*Ela, Angle,*" a man called.

Fearing a trap, he kept silent.

The man called again. "*Ela,* O'Malley."

"In here," he answered in Greek.

"Show yourself."

Revolver in hand, he cautioned Stefanos to keep quiet and left the cave. Three men were standing there in the darkness waiting for him. Two were wearing civilian clothes, the third, a military jacket with epaulettes. Unshaven and grubby, they were close to O'Malley in age and held their guns with easy familiarity. Veterans, same as him.

"*Fere to paidi kai akolouthise,*" one of the men said. Bring the child and follow.

When O'Malley didn't respond, he repeated the order in heavily accented English. "Hurry. It will be light soon."

Climbing steadily, the four of them crossed over the wind-swept summit of the mountain and headed down into the trees on the other side. Ahead, O'Malley saw horses pastured in a meadow, a second group of men resting in the grass nearby. Unlike the clean-shaven youths who'd rousted them from the cave, these men were heavily bearded and far older. One was dressed in a uniform from another age, white leggings and a black *foustanella*, the skirt barely reaching his knees. Bristling with weapons, the men had bandoliers crisscrossed over their chests and curved daggers stuck in their belts.

Brigands, O'Malley thought, one of the outlaw bands he'd heard were operating in the region, men who took advantage of the war to loot and pillage. They watched him come toward them with undisguised hostility, as ferocious a group as O'Malley had ever seen.

One of the men seemed to be expecting him, and he got up and lumbered over to where O'Malley was waiting. Unlike the others, he wore a greasy khaki uniform. "Why are you here?" he asked O'Malley in English.

"British Command in Cairo sent me. We're supposed to build an airstrip together, so they can fly in supplies." He nodded to the landscape. "Seems they forgot about the mountains." O'Malley let a little contempt show in his voice, his low opinion of the officers who had ordered him here.

"Guns?" the same man asked.

O'Malley studied the rifle the man was carrying. A Carcanos carbine, it was Italian and dated from the beginning of the war. The weapons the other men were cradling were far older. Single bolt rifles from the turn of the century, most of them. They probably had been passed down from father to son. *Aye*, the men needed guns, all right.

"I can try and get you weapons," he said, seeking to win them over. "Maybe a howitzer."

"Man said you were Irish."

He was careful, O'Malley noted. Didn't use names when he referred to someone.

"Aye. I'm Irish, all right. Born and raised in Cork."

"And yet you serve the British."

O'Malley had anticipated this and rehearsed his answer. "I was a foolhardy lad of twenty-four when I enlisted, determined to save the world from the Nazi menace. Been struggling to stay alive ever since."

"Where'd you fight?" He lit a cigarette, watched him through the smoke.

"I served in Athens. Got wounded in the retreat, stranded to the south of here. Farmers shuffled me about, got me to Egypt. Been with the British Command in Cairo ever since, fought in Crete, North Africa. They're the ones sent me here, arranged with the Americans for the drop." O'Malley's smile was grim. "Been warring forever, so I have."

"Where in Crete?"

"Chania, Souda. I kept moving. Had to."

The man seemed to relax. "You ride?"

"A little. I'll not win a steeplechase, but I can hold my own on a horse."

The horse proved to be a mule, an arthritic slow-moving animal with a mind of its own.

O'Malley hoisted himself up in the saddle and pulled Stefanos up after him. Putting his feet in the stirrups, he gave the beast a kick. It took two steps, laid its ears back and stopped dead in its tracks. Smirking, the Greeks stood around and watched as he tried to propel it forward.

Stefanos kept yelling to go faster, which added to the humiliation. "*Pame! Pame!*"

O'Malley slapped the mule on the rump with his reins, but it stayed where it was, posed with its head up as if listening to something, some far off mulish song only it could hear. A true tinker's mule, it was, full of naught but piss and wind.

The Greek who'd questioned him was on a proper horse, a magnificent bay, and he galloped around O'Malley, yelling instructions while the others catcalled and laughed. Still the mule refused to move. Finally, the man reached over and grabbed the reins and led it away like a pack animal. More derisive laughter followed. O'Malley wondered if he'd been set up. If the mule had been an initiation of sorts, a ritual humiliation.

* * *

THE MULE WAS so bony, O'Malley could feel its ribs moving beneath him and hear its labored breath. Judging by the moss on the trees, they were heading north, into the desolate mountains O'Malley had wanted no part of.

Ahead lay the same shadowy gorge he and Danae had passed through. Vouraikos, she said it was called. In ancient times, there'd been a waterfall deep within the gorge, a magnificent waterfall that reached all the way to Hades. He'd made a joke of it, telling her if it was all the same to her, he'd rather not go that way, and yet here he was, riding toward it like Don Quixote with his own little Sancho Panza—Stefanos—asleep in his arms. Be hard pressed to say who was the bigger fool.

The ravine was pleasant at first, the banks of the river thick with poplar trees, their yellowing leaves rippling in the wind, but then it narrowed, walls of rock rising on either side and blocking out the sun. Heavy with sediment, the river too became a thing of shadows, the water collecting in deep pools, a faint mist clouding the air above them.

He saw a group of stone buildings in the distance. Chiseled out of limestone, they ran up the side of the gorge.

"Mega Spileon," the Greek told him, pointing to the distant walls. "*Paleo monasteri.*"

O'Malley quickly translated the words. Old monastery.

His mule was flecked with sweat, and he worried it would give out on him and die, but it kept ambling along at its own pace, stopping now and then to eat grass. It seemed to know its way.

The Greek urged his horse forward, heading for a small chapel in the distance. It was less than a quarter of a mile from the monastery, so close O'Malley wondered if it was part of the same complex. The walls of the canyon were less steep here and heavily forested. The Greek skirted around the church and galloped up into the trees. Hidden in a thicket of pines was a path.

They rode up the path single file, climbing steadily toward a massive band of limestone at the top of the cliff. Far below, O'Malley could see the river winding through the gorge, coiling and uncoiling like a serpent. He spied a man with a rifle watching them. They must be getting close.

They rode a few hundred feet farther, crossing up over the limestone crown and down the other side. Beyond it lay a slight depression in the earth. Arching slightly, the limestone formed a ledge above it, a kind of natural roof. The camp was secreted there.

Dismounting, the Greek led his horse to the far side of the hollow, then helped O'Malley and Stefanos down from the mule.

The mule gave O'Malley a baleful look, then lowered its head and began to scrounge around in the dirt, pulling up tufts of grass and chewing them. A thousand years old, the thing must be, O'Malley thought as he watched it work its mouth, its hideous yellow teeth. Charlemagne might have ridden it. It didn't bode well for the Greeks if this was their cavalry.

Shielded by the rocks, the camp was impressively sited, difficult to spot from the air, and given the mountains behind it, nearly impossible to bomb. *Aye*, they'd be safe here, he and Stefanos. A frontal assault would be suicide.

A group of thirty-five to forty men were standing around, waiting for them. "Leonidas!" they cried, welcoming the man who'd brought him here "*Kalos orisate.*"

Stefanos relaxed when he heard the Greek. "*Patrides*," he told O'Malley. Countrymen.

The man called Leonidas quickly introduced O'Malley to the rest. As before, he only used first names: Fotis, Lakis, Haralambos. No rank was given, nothing that could identify them to the enemy. The assembled men were dressed in a mix of military and civilian clothes from a variety of sources—including Italian and German, judging by the cut of the jackets. The same held true of their weaponry, which ranged from German Mauser C96s and American Thompsons to antiquated World War I stock and flintlock muskets dating from the last century.

Curious, O'Malley asked if they were ELAS—Communists.

"What's it to you?" Leonidas asked.

The men studied him with guarded expressions, uncomfortable in his presence.

"Going to kill me, are you?"

"Might," one said.

A battered radio pack was set up on a table, various wires and tools laid out around it. O'Malley recognized it as a Paraset transceiver, the kind the

British supplied their field agents with. "Where'd you get that?"

"Got passed along," Leonidas said. "Same as you." They were watching him closely now. "You know how to use it?" asked Leonidas.

"Never had cause to use one in the field. Always had a radio operator traveling with me who worked the thing."

Leonidas pushed the radio toward him. "Try," he said.

Like the mule, another challenge.

Opening the pack of the radio, O'Malley inspected the three tubes. All appeared to be in order. He put on the headset and jiggled the toggle switch. Given the mountains, he doubted he'd be able to reach Cairo, but perhaps he could contact another British agent operating in the region. Before he'd left, he'd been given the code name Barabbas by the British major. The Greeks were taking a risk. If the Wehrmacht was listening, it wouldn't matter what name he used. They'd know he wasn't German.

He got into it immediately with the British Liaison Officer on the other end, the man asking him where he'd been all this time, why it had taken him so long to make contact. "A spotty performance, Barabbas. Entirely second rate."

Fighting not to lose his temper, O'Malley described what had befallen him, the gangrene in his shoulders. He left out his capture by Danae, his being led away by children.

He spoke quickly, not wanting to give the Germans time to track his signal.

One of the Greeks understood English and quickly translated for the rest. The men looked at O'Malley with sympathy. It was an old fight they were listening to, the enlisted man versus the officer, a poor man versus his betters. A fight they understood well.

"*Oi Angloi*," Leonidas spat. The English.

The officer continued to berate O'Malley, reiterating his orders and suggesting 'he'd do well to follow them,' condescending to him with every word.

O'Malley finally exploded. "Listen, you feckless son-of-a-bitch, don't you be telling me what to do! If you know what's good for you, you'll go back and tell those bastards you serve under, those bloody bastards in Cairo, that I've made contact, you hear? That Brendan O'Malley, code name Barabbas, has made contact."

Before signing off, he asked the officer's name; threatened to cut his balls off if he saw him in Cairo.

The Greeks nodded approvingly, even offered to help him castrate the officer should the opportunity arise, making scissors with their hands and using a host of Greek expressions, all of them vulgar.

"*Tha ton evnouchisoume!*" We'll make him a eunuch.

* * *

UNLIKE OTHER UNITS O'Malley had served in, this one was casually organized without a discernible hierarchy or chain of command. He estimated around forty-five soldiers were housed in the camp, though it was hard to tell. The men came and went as they pleased, disappearing back to their villages for days at a time. They did follow a routine of sorts, keeping their weapons clean and organizing guard duty, feeding themselves and the horses twice a day, but they did so with no sense of urgency, casually even. There was no military discipline, no daily inspections or latrine duty, there being no latrine. No obedience was asked for or given.

They slept under the stars, urinated off the rocks, and defecated in the tall grass on the far side of the camp. Having gone exploring, O'Malley had found this out by accident his second day there. He'd done his best to clean his boots afterward, washed them like a man possessed. Not that it mattered. By and large, hygiene was nonexistent in the camp. No one shaved or bathed that he could see. If the Germans came calling, the stench alone would kill them. Worse than mustard gas, it was.

They didn't know what to make of O'Malley and enjoyed teasing him. Leonidas even went so far as to lift up a lock of his hair one morning at breakfast. "You should shoot your hair dresser, my friend, your *kommotiria*. Execute him as a saboteur."

O'Malley patted his head self-consciously. " 'Twas a woman did it. Dyed my hair so I'd look Greek. Did me up proper, so she did."

The men took to calling him 'Samson' after that. 'Samson' as in 'Samson and Delilah,' a man like O'Malley who'd been ruined by a woman with scissors.

A makeshift kitchen occupied the center of the camp; and supplies were stored in two locked chests there. The area was overseen by the cook, Roumelis, a wall-eyed giant with a belly that hung low over his pants. He resented O'Malley and always chafed him when he ladled up his dinner.

O'Malley nicknamed him Cyclops and did his best to stay out of his way. Food was plentiful. The stew the cook prepared was a luxury after his days starving in the cave. He had no idea where the meat and vegetables came from, whether they had been donated to the cause or the men had stolen them—looted the farms for provisions just as the Germans did.

A filthy young boy named Giorgos helped the cook and ran messages back and forth. He was a little older than Stefanos, eleven or twelve, and had a cheerful, open way about him, smiling as he peeled the potatoes or washed the pots, laughing and telling jokes. They usually involved shit and the smells attendant with it, be they his or someone else's. He liked to play cards for money and cheated unashamedly, stuffing aces down his shirt and pulling them out, cackling with glee as he raked up the coins the others had anted up. He smoked cigarettes—which he stole, running off with whole handfuls of them—and drank wine he siphoned off from a jug. Sometimes he stole food, too, grabbing a chicken leg or a sausage from the pan and eating it while the cook shouted at him.

Once or twice, he shared his food with Stefanos, bullying him a little and making him beg for it first. He enjoyed showing off and bragged to the boy of his exploits, claiming he'd fired mortars at the Germans. Killed more than anybody.

O'Malley doubted that, but let him be.

After the precision of the British unit in Cairo, the saluting and 'yes, sirs,' the whole partisan operation seemed a little, well, loose to him. More like a summer camp than a military installation.

Most of the men were local, less driven by ideology than by the desire to free their country, to protect their crops and keep their livestock out of German hands. When O'Malley questioned them, they laughed and said they were *kleftes*, bandits like the ones who'd battled the Ottomans in the nineteenth century, living in the *limeria* or lairs of their ancestors. They denied political affiliations, claimed to be neither ELAS Communists nor right-wing members of EDES.

Leonidas was the only constant. Although the others came and went on a regular basis, he never left the camp. A dark bear of a man, he was stoop-shouldered and walked with a heavy, shuffling gait, favoring one leg over the other. His black hair was shaggy, his untrimmed beard as thick as fur. He reeked of cigarettes, and the front of his uniform was gray with ashes.

Judging by the way the other men deferred to him, he was the officer in charge, though he rarely gave orders or pushed himself forward. If something needed to be done, he'd nod at one of the men and it was taken care of. No fuss or saluting. No, 'yes, sir' or 'no, sir' with him. He rarely spoke, and when he did, he chose his words carefully, took his time and made sure everyone understood.

"I've no home to return to," he told O'Malley one night. "The Germans took everything. Burned us out."

Having drawn guard duty, they were sitting high up in the rocks, watching over the camp.

"Shepherding the wind," the Greek called it.

"I watched the houses burn from the mountain," he said. "The Germans had been looking for us, settled on the village instead. Thought that if they destroyed it, they'd deprive us of food and we'd have to surrender."

He showed little emotion as he described the death of his parents, the people he'd grown up with. Sitting there on the ground, he might well have been made of stone.

"What'd you do?"

"What could I do?" His voice was quiet, whatever pain there'd been long since leeched away. "I fought."

"Aye. Freedom or death, all that."

They both laughed.

Leonidas always kept him close during maneuvers and bedded down next to him at night. O'Malley had come to believe the Greek did this to protect him, to keep him from getting murdered because of his British masters, the language that he spoke. Without Leonidas, he'd be lost in the camp, he was sure of it.

"Who were those men the first day?" he asked. "The ones all festooned with knives."

"Another group of *antartes*. Different from us."

'Right wing' was left unsaid. In Ireland, they called folks like that 'blue shirts.' O'Malley wondered what they were called here.

"What were you doing with them?"

"Nothing that concerns you," Leonidas said in English.

Leonidas knew some English, O'Malley had discovered, though he refused to speak it with him, preferring always to speak Greek. This time had been an exception. A warning.

O'Malley went on as if he hadn't heard, "Seems a whole lot of people pulling in different directions. What's going to happen here after the Germans leave?"

"That group you saw the first day, the men here. We're going to kill each other."

* * *

He looked out at the darkness, thought of Danae and the boy. It was a clear night, the stars like a swath of gauze across the sky. It was so quiet he could hear the river coursing through the gorge, the wind in the pines. *Throisma*, the Greeks called it. They had a name for most everything, the Greeks, their speech staccato and precise.

A fog was drifting in and it slowly enfolded the rocks, the soldiers asleep on the ground. Made the camp look as if it were inhabited by ghosts.

O'Malley thought again of Danae, her words about the region, its proximity to hell.

He wanted to ask after her, but he wasn't sure of her last name. All those weeks and he hadn't thought to ask. She'd just been Danae. Not enough, not hardly enough.

He'd noticed the area close to the ledge was warmer than the rest of the camp. The limestone provided rudimentary shelter, a windbreak as it were. He often stayed there with Stefanos, huddled down in his cloak with his arms wrapped around the boy. Occasionally, one of the Greek partisans would join him, a light-hearted fellow named Lakis. He had lived in New York for a time and had befriended O'Malley. Neither was completely fluent in the other's tongue and it was a challenge sometimes communicating with Lakis, the two of them relying on hand gestures to make themselves understood. Almost like a game of charades.

"I met someone in Kalavryta who lived in the States," O'Malley told him late one night. "Maybe you know her. Toula? She lives with her brother and his two children."

"Sure. Toula Papadakis." Lakis drew a woman's figure with his hands, laughed in a crude way.

"That her married name?"

"No. The name she was born with. I never knew her husband."

Danae Papadakis. O'Malley breathed a sigh of relief. Worse came to worst, he could find her if he had to. Ask where she and her family might have gone.

"Toula took to America," Lakis said. "I didn't. Cold people, Americans. Money's all they care about."

"You're saying they're capitalists?"

"Yes, yes. That's what I'm saying. Capitalists."

Slapping his knee, Lakis laughed and laughed.

As leftists, most of the men were like Lakis, not too far gone, their focus mainly on ridding Greece of the Germans. Oh, there were one or two fanatics. A dour, bespectacled school teacher named Haralambos was the worst. A thin, praying mantis of a man, he had a mouthful of crooked teeth and constantly lectured the others. Basic Marxist cant. 'Capitalists drink the blood of the working class,' and the like.

Him, O'Malley dubbed 'Spittle.'

"Be careful of Haralambos," Leonidas warned O'Malley one night. "He thinks you're a spy."

"Who does he think I'm spying for? The Germans?"

"No. Churchill."

"Hell, I'm just a hapless bastard deceived by the British, caught up in a web of their lies and deceit. A fool, I might well be. But a spy, never."

"I told him that, but he doesn't believe me."

A handsome young man named Alexi often accompanied Haralambos on his rounds, striking poses in his ELAS uniform and seeking to call attention to himself.

Leonidas had little use for him either. "Alexis licks where he used to spit. Before the war, he was *fascistas*, now he's ELAS."

"In Ireland, we call men like that 'slinkeens.' Folks you can't turn your back on."

"Here we say, 'His word isn't worth the fart of a donkey.' "

"A grave insult, that."

The Greek nodded. It was one of the few time O'Malley had ever seen him smile.

"Watch out for him, too," Leonidas said, growing serious. "He thinks hurting people makes him a man."

* * *

UNCOMFORTABLE IN THE camp, Stefanos dogged O'Malley's every move. They ate together, cleaned guns together, even unbuttoned their pants and pissed off the cliff together. O'Malley made a bed for the kid on the ground close to where he slept and spread the *flokati* over him when he saw him shivering at night. Seeking warmer clothes, he'd opened the child's suitcase, but found nothing useful, only the carved animals and his terrible ball. Ripped in places, the latter was falling apart, sodden with mud. O'Malley smiled. Aunt Toula had had no hand in this. Stefanos must have packed for himself.

To pass the time, they played soccer with the ball. O'Malley's pa still called soccer 'football' and followed it religiously, recalling with pride the time the Cork team, the Fordsons, won the cup in 1926. O'Malley played it well. So well, that he'd once dreamed of a place on the national team. Still did sometimes when he'd had a pint or two.

"*Balla?*" the boy would ask.

"Aye, Specky, *balla*."

When the muddy ball gave out, O'Malley made a second one out of his parachute, hacking up the silk and wadding it up, tying it together to form a rough sphere. It never amounted to much, the games they played. Stefanos would inevitably miss when he went for a goal, knock himself off balance and fall down. He never cried, even when he hurt himself. No, with him it was only laughter—crazed, hysterical laughter. His joy to be playing the game was so profound, it was like madness.

Family members appeared at the camp on a regular basis, a seemingly endless stream of them. An old woman in black turned up one day, leading a donkey laden with blankets, jars of honey secreted in the folds of the cloth. The men called her *yiayia*, grandma, and kissed her on her withered cheeks, made as if to carry her off. Smiling a toothless smile, the old woman joked with them good naturedly for a time before she left, leading her donkey back down the footpath to the village. O'Malley wondered how old she was, how far she'd traveled to get there.

Most of the people came at night, led as he'd been by men in the camp. A young Jewish couple from Athens arrived late one evening, identifiable by their city clothes, the story they told. The Grand Rabbi of Athens had fled the city, they said, after the Nazis demanded he give up the names and addresses of the Jews there. He'd urged other Jews to flee as well.

"The Germans have sent two officers to Athens now to organize the deportations. They're the same SS men who were in charge in Salonika. They said the Jews there were being resettled, but no one has ever heard from them again. The SS just put them on a train and they disappeared."

They said that the Greek archbishop, Damaskinos, was personally signing thousands of false baptismal certificates in a desperate effort to save the Jews. He'd filed a formal protest with the German authorities against the deportations, but they didn't think it would do any good and were determined to flee Greece.

The couple kept to themselves, speaking to each other in a language O'Malley didn't understand.

"What do you suppose happened to the people they spoke of?" O'Malley asked the *antartes* after the couple slept. "The ones the Germans put on the train in Salonika."

"They're dead," Haralambos said flatly. "They were supposed to go to work camps, yet they deported everyone—persons over ninety, amputees, children and pregnant women, people who would be of no use to them. The driver of one of the trains is a cousin of mine. He said the Germans stopped the train at one point and threw out the bodies of the children who'd died along the way. The people inside the train didn't have food or water and beat against the wooden sides, screaming and crying. The Germans gave him a handful of watches to keep quiet about it."

Leonidas had been listening to the discussion. "*Kolasmenoi*," he said in a low voice. "Means 'condemned to hell.' The Germans aren't resettling them, no matter what they say. They're killing them."

O'Malley never saw the Jews leave, had no idea how the system worked, how word was passed or where they went. He searched for Danae's father whenever a new group arrived, but didn't see him, not then.

A short while later, a young Jewish boy from Lefkada was brought into the camp, having recently escaped from a German transport. "We were all standing together on the quay in Patras," he said, "hundreds and hundreds of us. A friend of mine from school saw me and told me to wait there while he brought me some food. While I was waiting, the Germans cordoned off the area where my family was and I lost track of them. I didn't know what happened to them, where they were, and I started to search. But a stranger took me away, saying it wasn't safe. Germans were moving people away, killing them."

The boy started to cry. O'Malley wanted to comfort him but didn't know how. Neither did the rest of the men, judging by the bleak expressions on their faces. Lies wouldn't help, not in the long run, not with a thing like this. Besides, he couldn't do it, couldn't stand there and tell the kid everything was going to be all right when it wasn't. They were gone, his folks. Gone to whatever heaven Jews believed in. There'd be no reunion with them in the future. No joyful scene after the war. They were dead, or soon would be. Dead, and with them, the boy's dreams, his vision of a benevolent universe and his place in it. Just thinking about it made O'Malley's eyes well up. The boy looked to be the same age as Danae, and already the best part of his life was over. He just didn't know it yet.

He, too, was gone by morning.

Sometimes the visitors contributed food or clothing to the camp. O'Malley couldn't establish whether the parcels they brought were given in payment—demanded by the soldiers for the service they rendered—or if they'd been freely given. Leonidas took offense when he asked about it. Said neither he nor any of the others would take payment for rescuing a person, no matter who they were or what their religion was. It was their duty to save people from the Nazis; it was a matter of *filotimo*, honor, and required of them as men.

"An ELAS unit fought to save the Jews in a village in northern Greece and smuggled their leader in Athens, Rabbi Barzilai, out of the city. They're Greeks, same as us."

Local Greek villagers also arrived at the camp with sacks of potatoes, olives, and walnuts. Most were related to the partisans, their generosity less patriotic than familial. Occasionally, one of the men would share his bounty with O'Malley and Stefanos and give them fistfuls of nuts or a boiled egg. O'Malley wished he had cigarettes to share in return or chocolate, a way he could repay them in kind.

Most nights the soldiers made a fire, always in the same place in the deepest part of the trench, laboring to make sure that smoke wasn't visible from above. They purchased sheep and goats occasionally from farmers, paying with gold sovereigns. Leonidas kept the money in a leather pouch and was tightlipped about where it had come from, doling it out coin by coin to the team making a run for food. O'Malley had gone on one of these forays, standing by while the men negotiated with the farmer then helping them drive the purchased animal back to the camp for Roumelis to slaughter. He'd hated that part—the choked bleating of the animal when the cook grabbed its throat, the pool of blood darkening the ground afterward.

A theater troupe appeared one night, setting up a portable stage they'd carried up to the camp on their backs. Not much bigger than a puppet theater, it was made of hinged wooden planks that folded up and had a curtain, a strip of velvet hanging across it. There were five actors in the troupe—three men and two women—and they performed clumsy skits with socialist themes, using the same vocabulary Haralambos used when he got wound up. They also sang songs and told jokes, again with a political theme. The price of admission was cheap: something to eat. An egg or a rusk dipped in oil. Young and enthusiastic, the actors were deeply committed to ELAS, and said they'd been all over Greece.

One of the men played a hand-held drum, thumping the rim as well as the skin exactly the way Irish minstrels did the bodhran. The dull sound of the thing made O'Malley homesick.

He recognized two of their songs. '*Synefiasmeni Kyriaki*,' was about the war. Cloudy Sunday, cloudy like my heart. '*Saltadoros*,' was another. I jump. The lyrics described people who stole food and cans of fuel off the backs of German trucks.

When the actors finished their show, O'Malley stood up and took his turn, entertaining the soldiers with songs from Ireland, patriotic songs from the Troubles, shouting out the bitter words, seeking to make the anguish come alive for the men assembled there. The killing sadness.

"In my country, we call music like that 'high lonesome.' "

The actors brought word of a massacre near Corinth. Fifty-six people, some of them women, had been sent to the St. George Monastery by the Nazis and executed there, their throats cut.

After the actors departed, O'Malley wrapped his cape around him and settled down for the night. Stefanos was fast asleep, but Leonidas was still awake, sitting with his back against the ledge, smoking a cigarette.

"Do you think they'll try something like that here?" O'Malley didn't refer to St. George's. There was no need. They both knew what he was talking about.

"Probably."

So he'd had the same reaction. The thing was heating up. O'Malley had been warned that the average British agent only lasted six months in the field. So far he'd been in Greece for two months, which meant he had four to go. March, 1944. He wasn't sure he'd make it until then, not if the Germans were slitting throats. Not at all sure he'd get out alive.

"We'll go on reconnaissance tomorrow," Leonidas said. "Find a site for your airstrips."

"You know a place?"

"Yes. It's to the east of here."

* * *

The sun was rising when the two of them set off, the slopes of Mount Helmos awash with pink light. Reining in his horse, O'Malley sat and watched the dawn, enjoying the play of light across the bare slopes. Clouds were rolling in and they momentarily overran the sky, but then the sun broke through again and revealed itself

"Aw, sweet Jesus. Just look at it."

Like watching the world being born, it was. Being God on the first day of creation.

A beam of sunlight played across the darkened land like a searchlight, then the clouds shifted and it was gone. The battle continued for a few more minutes, darkness alternating with light. Seemed to sandblast everything, the sun in Greece, expose the world with fresh clarity.

As always, the beauty of the landscape took his breath away. No wonder the ancients chose this place and their descendants were fighting so hard to keep it. The light alone was worth dying for.

He was on a spirited horse Leonidas had given him. Not knowing the mare's name, he'd dubbed her Elektra, it being close to 'electric,' which she surely was, throbbing with energy, the sparks just flying off her. Her coat was black, save for a patch of white on her forelock. When she galloped, it was with every fiber of her being, her legs extended like a race horse. Even now, O'Malley could feel her fighting to run. Like Man o' War at the starting gate, Elektra was a thing possessed.

He and Leonidas talked a little as they cantered through the trees, the Greek asking him about Ireland, what it was like growing up there.

"Monotonous. Nuns in school and Mass every Sunday. Even as a lad, I was at it, taking communion, confessing my poor sins to the priest."

"Your family was Catholic?"

"Aye. Defined us, so it did, the faith."

Leonidas gave a wry grin. "Before the war, I wanted to be a priest."

O'Malley stared at him. He couldn't imagine Leonidas as a priest, couldn't see him bowing his head to anyone.

"What happened?"

"I became a soldier instead. Now I believe only in myself." He thumped his chest. "Who I am. What I'm capable of."

"An atheist then?"

"Yes."

The casualness with which he said this shocked O'Malley. "Lonely business, that."

"My mother wanted me to be a priest. When I was little, she used to say I had a 'bishop's hands.' " Reining in his horse, Leonidas sat motionless for a moment. "She was very devout. Fasted forty days before Christmas, forty days before Easter. Knew the words to every prayer they chant in church. The Germans burned her alive."

O'Malley looked up at the sky, watched the clouds for a time. "Grievous thing what happened to your folks. You having to watch. Grievous."

"There's a Greek saying: 'Where many die, there is no fear of death.' " Leonidas gave a bark of laughter.

He shifted in his saddle, the leather creaking under his weight. "You said you were a doctor."

They were speaking English. *A measure of trust*, O'Malley told himself. The beginnings of a friendship.

"That's right," he answered carefully. "I'd just hung up my shingle when the war broke out. Pa was beside himself when I enlisted. 'Never thought I'd live to see the day,' he said. 'A son of mine in the English army, doffing his cap when they play 'God Save the bleeding King.' "

"How'd you end up here?"

"Volunteered for it, fool that I was. I served as a medic for a time, but couldn't stand it. Men dying all around and me being unable to save them. I remember seeing a man get killed by a bomb. Sad pigeon-toed kid, name of Devon. Got caught, he did, blown completely apart. Sometimes when I can't sleep, I hear him screaming still. Him and all the dead men I served with. A chorus, it is, ringing in my head."

Leonidas raised his face and something passed between them. *He knows*, O'Malley thought, seeing the bleakness in the Greek's eyes. *Leonidas knows. He hears them screaming, too.*

He followed him up the hill. Felt good, pounding across the countryside on the back of a horse. Made him feel like a boy again, when speed was the ticket, when it seemed to be the only thing that mattered.

Ahead lay a vast alpine meadow. Surrounded by mountains on three sides, it was open to the north.

O'Malley slid off his horse and handed the reins to Leonidas. "Wait here."

He paced it out, measuring the length and breadth of the meadow, the incline of the land. He did a rough calculation when he finished. With some help, he should be able to construct an airstrip 1200 yards or longer here. The land was relatively flat, free of large rocks and standing puddles of water. It was protected to a degree from the blistering wind. A plane could approach from the north, fly in and land. *Aye*, it would do.

The ground was covered with brown grass and patches of dead wildflowers.

O'Malley bent down, took up a fistful of earth, and crumbled it between his fingers. Gritty and light. If he got to work before winter set in and the ground froze, he'd have an easy time of it.

Maybe he'd make it to March after all.

10

O'MALLEY STRAPPED A shovel to the back of the saddle and headed off at first light, eager to start to work on the airstrip. He'd asked for volunteers the previous night, and two men had stepped forward, Lakis and a farmer from Kalavryta named Fotis. They'd promised to come later and help him level off the field.

He'd been relieved when Haralambos had declined to help. He'd come to hate the sound of the man's voice, the incessant whine about capitalists like the buzzing of an insect in his ear. The teacher was gaining in stature; the other men stopped what they were doing to listen to him now when he spoke. He encouraged them to come forward and discuss the sins of their neighbors, give him the names of those who'd aided the Nazis. Preparing for future show trials, O'Malley guessed, a day of reckoning after the Germans left.

As a 'pawn of Churchill,' one of Haralambos' favorite phrases, O'Malley had no doubt he'd be one of the first to get shot. The officer in Cairo had told him there were still independent right-wing groups operating in this part of Greece and that he might want to seek them out, have better luck with them, though he doubted it. There'd been skirmishes the previous year between the two groups, ELAS units forcing the others to join them. When the right-wing soldiers refused, ELAS forces attacked and murdered them. It wasn't a good time to be in Greece. He could get killed either way he jumped.

Stefanos had wanted to come with him, but he told the boy to go back to sleep. "Naught for you to do, child. I'll be back before you know it."

Watching over the child had worn him down, and he welcomed the solitude. The fighting in the region had increased. He'd heard mortar fire the previous night and the hushed talk of the men, speaking of a village named

Kallithea where the Germans had killed close to thirty. Heating up, it was.

Snow dusted the upper reaches of the mountain. Not much, but still it surprised him. It was only November. What would befall him come January? He had no gloves, no coat to speak of, save for the awful *flokati*.

Seeing how cold it was, the Greeks had offered to steal a German overcoat for him and laughingly measured his shoulders. "A meter," they said. "Have to be a big German." But O'Malley waved them off, saying he was fine, unsure that they were playing. *Aye*, it felt good to be away from them.

A moment later, something spooked the mare and she took off at a gallop. The dampness in the air made her coat glisten, her mane go all bushy. Bending low, he rode her like a jockey for a few minutes before gradually bringing her to a halt.

"You're something, horse, you are."

A cloud of mist swept over them as they entered the meadow. Rising from the ground, it quickly covered the airfield, drifting in like smoke borne by the wind. Reining in Elektra, O'Malley watched it engulf the land—the limestone ridge where the camp was, the mountains on all sides—and he reached out a hand to touch it. The mist continued to swirl around, wafting around the feet of the horses. Perhaps it was the earth itself sending it forth, trying to cleanse itself of the blood, the unspeakable events of the war.

He sympathized with the earth and its desire to be clean again. To be free of the stench of cordite.

Looking around, he tried to picture the airfield. When he had it fixed in his mind, he dismounted, pulled his shovel loose from the saddle, and began scraping out a crude rectangle in the dirt—an outline for Lakis and Fotis to follow. He was glad that Lakis was coming, welcoming the man's cheerfulness, his lopsided grin. Fotis he didn't know well. Quiet, he was younger than most of the men in the camp and kept to himself, never speaking more than was necessary. He'd been wounded at some point—a jagged scar marred his face— and walked with a slight limp. O'Malley took care as he worked, figuring out the angle the plane would come in on, remembering the formula he'd been taught in Cairo. The land was stonier than he'd anticipated, full of rocks deeply embedded in the earth.

He worked for a couple of hours, digging up stones with his shovel and casting them away, flattening the earth and smoothing it out. When the goatskin cape got in his way, he threw it off, thinking the effort would soon warm him. He looked back over the five or six yards he'd completed. Like farming in Ireland, this was—a struggle with little to show for it.

When he finished what he'd intended, he leaned against his shovel and wiped his brow. Two weeks it would take him if he kept on like this. Less if he had help.

The hawk was circling high above him, screeching in protest at his presence. He watched it, wondering where its nest was, if it had a mate or like him was all alone up here. The sun was high in the sky, the mist of the morning long since gone.

* * *

WHEN HE RODE into the camp, O'Malley saw the men standing around Leonidas. At first, O'Malley thought they were listening to the radio, but then he saw the blond-haired man at the center. A young German soldier with his hands tied behind his back.

"We met a German patrol leaving Kalavryta," his friend explained. "They attacked us and we fought back, threw grenades at them, everything we had. We found this one after the smoke cleared. Must have lost contact with his unit."

The soldier was young, no more than nineteen or twenty years old, wearing a standard-issue Wehrmacht uniform and thick boots. He hadn't been long at it, judging by condition of his tunic, the luster of his buttons. The emblem on his hat—a spiky flower—indicated he was a mountaineer from General von Le Suire's unit, the 117th Jäger division.

Leonidas saw O'Malley eyeing the boots. "Take them," he said.

"What are you going to do with him?"

Leonidas made a gun with his hand, fired off an imaginary shot.

"You can't be doing that, Leonidas. He's a prisoner of war."

The Greek's eyes were bloodshot, his voice charged with anger. "You remember Giorgos? The boy who helped out in the kitchen? Germans caught him today. Burnt him with cigarettes and cut off the soles of his feet. He crawled away on his hands and knees, screaming. Haralambos found him, brought him back to camp on a mule."

The German was crying openly now, tears coursing down his face. He'd been beaten, probably dragged a fair distance. He raised his head and addressed O'Malley directly in English, begging him not to let the others kill him. "Please," he said over and over again. "Please."

Another voice for my collection, O'Malley thought. He turned away, unable to listen.

The soldier's black leather harness and belt looked new, the brass hooks and D rings unscratched. For some reason, the newness, the untested quality of the German's gear, upset O'Malley. Poor bugger. Captured on his first patrol.

"Hold him for ransom, Leonidas. Don't shoot him. Von Le Suire will retaliate if you kill him, torch more villages."

"They will never find his body."

Leonidas led the young soldier away a few minutes later, the German still babbling and calling out in English, whimpering for O'Malley to save him. They were heading toward the deep ravine at the south of the camp, the place where the *antartes* dumped their garbage.

"Wait," O'Malley yelled, running after them. He reached around the German's neck, yanked out the man's metal identity tag and broke off the bottom half.

The soldier began to scream then, switching to German in his final moments. "*Bitte nicht, bitte nicht!*" Falling to his knees, he crossed himself and began to pray. "*Gegrüßet seist Du, Maria, voll der Gnade.*"

Leonidas quickly stripped the German of his gear, his boots. Carrying Giorgos in his arms, Haralambos joined him a few minutes later.

O'Malley couldn't believe what he was seeing. "Don't be doing this, Haralambos. 'Tis an ugly thing, murder. Nothing to show a child."

Giorgos' bandaged feet were wet with blood; and he, too, was crying, writhing in pain. Leonidas waved his gun at the German, asked Giorgos what he wanted him to do with him.

"Kill him," the boy shouted.

Taking a deep breath, Leonidas placed his gun up against the skull of the German and pulled the trigger. The sound was deafening and reverberated off the rocks. The soldier's head exploded and he fell to the ground.

Leonidas doused the body with kerosene and set it on fire, then threw the flaming corpse off the mountain. He spat on it as he kicked it off into space. "Finished," he said, wiping his hands on his pants.

O'Malley fingered the German's tag in his hand. The man's name had been Gunther. As always, the Germans were nothing if not efficient. The top half of the tag was designed to stay with the body, the bottom half to be broken off and collected so that others might learn of his fate.

Leonidas dumped the German's hobnail boots down in front of O'Malley. "They're yours now. Put them on."

* * *

DEEPLY SHAKEN, O'MALLEY followed Leonidas back to the camp. "You shouldn't have done it. Killed him like that. You're no better than they are."

Leonidas grabbed O'Malley by the front of his shirt and shoved him hard. "Stay out of it," he warned, adding "Englishman," in case O'Malley didn't get the message.

"Or what? You'll shoot me, too?"

Making a noise deep in his throat, Leonidas lunged at O'Malley and threw him to the ground, hit him hard in the mouth. "Shut up!" he screamed.

"You bastard!" Wiping his bloody mouth, O'Malley got to his feet. He took a step toward Leonidas and swung, burying his fist in his gut.

Clutching his stomach, the Greek staggered back. He turned his head away and vomited a little, sweat beading his forehead, then came at O'Malley again, flailing away at him with his fists.

After that, they went at it like prize fighters, clawing and biting, wrestling and pounding each other, falling down and getting up again. They went banging and tumbling through the camp, smashing into a pile of wooden boxes and sending ammunition and supplies flying. They upended a jug of wine and the basin full of water the men used for washing.

The other men stepped back to give them room. "*Skotose ton*," one of them shouted to Leonidas. Kill him.

Dancing back and forth, O'Malley worked to stay out of the larger man's way. He could feel his ribs throbbing. "The Greeks are in a frenzy now. I go down, they'll kick me to death."

Leonidas might have the advantage of weight, but O'Malley was faster. He darted in and out, landing a punch and backing away. He continued to duck and weave, only drawing close when he saw an opening, where he could smash his fist into Leonidas' kidneys or groin. Desperate, he fought dirty, digging his nails into the Greek's eye and grinding his knee into his balls. Yelling, the Greek tried to pin him down, his black eyes full of rage, spittle and sweat flying off him. Moving in, O'Malley grabbed his beard and yanked out a fistful, made a swipe at his ear.

He'd miscalculated the distance between them, and Leonidas grabbed him. Pushing him up against the rocks, he pummeled him with his fists—left, right, left, right—starting on his face and working his way down. O'Malley felt blood wet his scalp, start to trickle down both sides of his face. One of his eyebrows split, then his cheek.

Lakis finally intervened. "Stop," he cried, pulling Leonidas back. "Stop!"

But O'Malley wasn't ready to be rescued. Wiping the blood out of his eyes, he took a wild swing at Leonidas. "Kill me, too, will you?"

His knuckles were raw, both his eyes swollen shut. The blow didn't connect and he lost his balance. Still he kept swinging, raising his fist feebly in the air. "You're a dead man, you are. I'll clobber you good, I will."

He'd torn his shirt in the fracas, exposing the scar tissue on his shoulders, the livid welts where the doctor had dug out his decaying flesh. A murmur went up in the crowd when they saw the wounds.

Leonidas retreated, stood there heaving, panting like an animal.

Spent, O'Malley sank back down. "They say the British always win the most important battle, the last one. Same thing's true of the Irish. I'll beat you yet, Leonidas. I will. Given half the chance, I'll beat you senseless."

He translated this into Greek and the others laughed, nodded. They'd liked the passion O'Malley had brought to the fight, his willingness to brawl in spite of his wounds, his crippled shoulders.

Dampening a cloth, Lakis tried to staunch the bleeding, gently wiping O'Malley's face and dabbing at his scalp. Roumelis stepped forward with a flask of ouzo, nodded for O'Malley to take a swallow. One by one the men in the camp did the same, bringing him cigarettes and patting him on the back, sharing their vials of homemade fruit brandy, crusts of bread, and hard-boiled eggs. Even Haralambos paid homage, handing him a grimy pamphlet printed in English.

Strange. In Ireland no one would give you anything if you lost a fight. Let alone reward you with liquor and hard-boiled eggs. There'd be harsh words said in Ireland at the very least a bit of mockery, a questioning of one's muscle and blighted manhood. But gifts, never.

After dinner, Leonidas came and sat with him. "You all right?"

The fight seemed to have cleared the air between them, pushed back the event in the ravine.

O'Malley nodded, though it cost him; a wave of dizziness passed over him.

Leonidas gestured to his shoulders. "What happened? The men in the camp have been asking."

"Gangrene."

"And the hole?" He touched his sternum.

"A bullet in Souda. Been warring for a long time, I have. Been at it since the beginning."

Leonidas gave him a cigarette and lit it for him. "How many men have you killed?"

"Lost track." O'Malley didn't want to think about it. Didn't want to remember.

A long moment of silence followed. "It ever bother you?" Leonidas asked softly.

"I'm not a machine. 'Course it does."

Might as well tell him. Let him think me a coward. "Worst was in Crete. Time they shot the paratroopers out of sky. Didn't have a chance, those men. They were dead the minute they jumped out of the plane. Five thousand we killed. I went through the gear of one. I'll never forget it. Him, lying in the dirt with a hole in his face, all tangled up in his chute." He fought to keep his voice steady. "No more than eighteen, he was, with hair the color of wheat. I found a photo of him and a girl, both of them smiling. It was well worn, the photo, creased where he'd folded it. They were holding schoolbooks. Schoolbooks."

O'Malley's face tightened. "I wanted to throw away my gun. Quit the war and run away. Then the mortars started up again and the Germans killed a man I knew not far from where I was standing. And I was back at it, blasting away at them with my gun. That's war, that is. I shoved the body of the yellow-haired kid away so I could aim better, so I could shoot more of them."

He flicked the cigarette into the air. It made an arc, a trail of red sparks in the darkness. He felt the weight of the war pressing down on him, the sadness that came over him whenever he thought about the things he'd done, the dead on both sides.

Aye, he knew what Leonidas was about tonight. "It does no good, brooding about it. You're a soldier, same as me. Killing the enemy is what we do." He'd not have killed the man, Gunther, but then he barely knew Grigoris, felt no kinship with him.

Leonidas made a clumsy gesture with his hands. "I … I …."

"Leave off, I say."

The camp was quiet, the men lying on the ground all around them. Suddenly, one of them screamed in his sleep. Lakis, it was. It was eerie, hearing him go off like that.

"Aw, Jesus, Lakis." O'Malley nudged him with his foot. "Shut up, will ya?"

Leonidas leaned back against the rock, wincing a little. "You're a good fighter."

O'Malley grinned, welcoming the change of subject. "Irish. Known for it, we are. Brawling is our national sport. Never tire of it. And once we start, we never stop, never. Just keep coming at you. Coming and coming. As long as there's breath left in our bodies."

"Breath? What does it mean, 'breath?' "

"It means as long as we live. Staying alive, Leonidas. That's the key, that is."

* * *

THE NEXT MORNING O'Malley inspected himself in the mirror above the communal wash basin.

"Mother o' God. I look like I fell out a tree and hit every branch coming down."

He turned his head from side to side, taking inventory. His eyebrow, cheek, and lip were all split; and one of his eyes was swollen completely shut. He'd lost the fight with Leonidas, no doubt about it. Napoleon at bloody Waterloo.

Not wanting to make trouble, he donned the German's boots and laced them up. No good would come of it, he was sure. Ghost might rise up and take possession of him, drag him off to some beer garden in Bavaria, some sauerkraut-infested hell.

Before they'd turned in for the night, Leonidas had asked him for the German's tag. "I'll write the letter. I'll tell his people he died in battle and we buried him here, that there's a cross on the mountainside, marking the place where he fell."

He'd help Leonidas put up the cross, O'Malley decided, paint 'Gunther' and the date across it. Penance was a good thing, or so the nuns had told him.

His relationship with the men in the camp improved after the fight. Apparently getting half done to death by one of their own had done the trick, finally made him one of them. A few had approached him during the morning mess and introduced themselves, saying they wanted to help build the landing strip.

They began to prepare the ground as soon as they got there, O'Malley overseeing the work and making sure they stayed inside the rectangle he'd etched in the dirt. Way things were going—Germans cutting people's throats—he might need the British to pull him out, the *antartes*, too, come to that. Be prudent to be prepared.

A morose lot, for the most part, the *antartes* labored in silence. Although they dug steadily, the ground was hard and they'd only completed half of the airfield by the end of the day. Working steadily, it took them another day and a half to finish.

* * *

Leaning on his shovel, O'Malley surveyed the completed field. The surface was smooth, the soil well packed, even. Day or night, a plane would be able land there. He went from man to man, shaking their hands and thanking them for their help.

"*Bravo!*" he declared, patting Lakis on the back. "Fair play to you!"

When he and the others returned to the camp that night, they found Roumelis roasting a lamb on a spit, the meat sizzling over an open fire. The smell of it kept wafting across the hollow and they quickly grabbed their tin plates and lined up to eat. When O'Malley's turn came, Roumelis cut off a haunch and put it on his dish, then another for Stefanos.

"*Bon appétit,*" he said with a laugh.

O'Malley and the boy stood there, eating with their hands. Stefanos grinned from ear to ear, his face shiny with grease.

O'Malley grinned back at him. "Aw, Jesus. This is heaven, Stefanos, this is."

He was in a great mood, 'riding on the pig's back' as his pa would say. The *antartes* were friendlier than in the past, even Roumelis, the Cyclops. No longer Samson, he was *Irlandos* to them now. Irishman.

Once he completed his mission, he'd be free to go back to Kalavryta. Find Danae and finish what they'd started that night in the cellar.

* * *

Early the next morning, O'Malley radioed the British liaison officer. After identifying himself as 'Barabbas,' he gave him the map references for the airfield. "Finished it, I did. There's a big opening to the north, clear passage through the mountains. Planes should have no trouble getting in here, landing where I told you."

The officer repeated the coordinates back to him and signed off. O'Malley was relieved the man hadn't asked when he planned to return to Cairo. He wasn't eager to leave. "See it through, I will. Soldier on a bit longer."

He asked Leonidas to keep an eye on Stefanos, then saddled Elektra and rode to the clearing to wait for the plane. If possession was nine tenths of the law, then by rights, she was his. He fed her every night, mostly weeds he pulled from the hillside, and groomed her after a fashion. Watering was harder, requiring a trip down to the river with a bucket and a long climb back up. Still, he was glad of it and rode her whenever he could, galloping across the frozen ground and whooping like an Apache.

Around noon, he saw a plane pass overhead. It was flying at a high altitude. Bound for Egypt, maybe. Although he waited the rest of the day and well into the night, he saw no other planes. The air drop he'd been counting on had failed to materialize.

Gathering up some sticks, he built himself a crude lean-to in the rocks above the field and crouched down inside, rubbing his hands together, trying to get warm. Around midnight, it started to snow and the ground slowly iced over, a glass-like sheen that made walking treacherous and landing a plane an act of suicide. He thought it would probably melt when the sun came up and left it, too tired to scrape it away with his shovel. It snowed the rest of the night, huge gusts of white drifting down from the mountains and sweeping across the plain.

A Stuka buzzed the airfield early the next day, the pilot firing bullets across the rectangle in the dirt before seeking a higher altitude.

Well hidden in the rocks, O'Malley watched the plane maneuver with a sinking heart. The Germans had obviously spotted the airfield. If the British didn't come soon, the Luftwaffe would claim possession and land their planes there.

"Later this week," he was told when he radioed the British liaison officer.

Never stirring from the airfield, O'Malley waited three days. But no plane ever came near the clearing.

He continued to see vapor trails high above the mountain, and once or twice heard aircraft in the distance. But the planes could have been German for all he knew. They were too far off to identify, to make out the markings on their fuselage.

"Where the hell is the plane?" he shouted when he radioed the officer again. "Airstrip's in the mountains. It snowed last night. I'll have to plow you out, you don't get a move on."

"British command vetoed the site," the man told him. "Another agent is operating to the north of you. He's afraid your antics will draw the Germans and compromise his supply line."

"Antics?" O'Malley yelled. "We slaved building that thing."

That pool of whore's melt.

Ignoring his outburst, the man instructed O'Malley to abandon the airstrip and construct another farther to the south.

"South's where the Germans are," O'Malley said, furious now. "There's a whole division down there. The one hundred seventh Jägers. Well established, they are. Been there for weeks now."

"To the south," the man repeated. "Those are your orders."

"Are you not hearing me? Where would you have me build the bloody thing? In their mess hall? It's well nigh impossible what you're asking for. Mean my death and the death of the men helping me. I won't do it, you hear? I won't."

He yanked off the headset and slammed it down. *Operation Bloody British Airfield.*

Oh, Jesus, sweet Jesus in heaven, what a fool he'd been.

He felt hard done by. They didn't care what happened to him. No, they'd sent him off to Greece to get slaughtered without so much as a 'by your leave.' Bloody maggots. No wonder field agents only lasted six months.

"You're going to hear from me!" he shouted to the heavens. "I'll join the IRA, I will! Shoot your king. Shoot your bloody king."

11

"I QUIT MY POST," O'Malley told Leonidas when he got back to camp. "As of this moment, I'm no longer a member of His Majesty's Forces. I'm a free agent. Irish by birth and loyal to none."

The Greek raised his eyebrows. "You deserted?"

"Aye. Something like that."

O'Malley recounted the conversation he'd had with the British officer, the order he'd been given to abandon the airfield and build another near Kalavryta. The officer's casual disregard for his safety, the safety of the *antartes*.

"I'll not be speaking to that can of piss anytime soon, that's for sure. Thick as two planks, he was. 'Build an airfield in the south.'" O'Malley snorted. "Get us all killed, that will."

He was glad to be back in the camp, sitting around the fire with the others, his vigil at the airfield finally over. He thought again about the man on the radio: a bigger fool never put his arm through the sleeve of a coat.

They'd never miss him in Cairo. No, they'd just chalk him up as another dead field agent and move on. Wouldn't lose a moment's sleep, worrying about how or why Brendan O'Malley came to be lost. They'd just summon up the next fellow and put him in harm's way.

It was one thing to be in the RAF, defending London, or battling Rommel in the sands of Africa. Another thing entirely, soldiering here. What did the British need airfields for anyway? Germans were in retreat, the war in Greece nearly done. He'd stay on and help Leonidas and the rest. He believed in their cause. Was willing to die for it, come to that.

"A man entering the camp," the sentry shouted.

The *antartes* grabbed their guns and walked out to meet the new arrival. It was Danae's father, carrying blankets and a bag of food for his son.

Eager to hear news of Kalavryta, the men crowded around him.

The German soldier had survived the attack outside the bakery, he reported. Determined to find the person responsible, they'd brought in a local collaborator in a black mask and two Gestapo agents. The owner of the bakery was the first person they questioned. Apparently, the collaborator had seen her son inside at the time of the attack and they were looking for him now, turning the village upside down. All was chaos.

Danae's father was worried they'd want to speak to him, members of his family, question them, too. Growing angrier and angrier, he threw open his palm and made an obscene gesture. "*Nazistes!*"

Raising his hand, Stefanos mimicked him. "*Nazistes!*" The Greeks nudged one another and laughed, calling on the boy to do it again.

"*Nazistes!*" Stefanos obediently cried. "*Nazistes!*".

Another fool's errand, O'Malley thought, watching them. Teaching a child to insult the Germans. Get him killed, that would.

Before Danae's father returned to Kalavryta, O'Malley cornered him and asked after her.

"You said the Germans were speaking to everybody in the village. What if they come for her, too?"

The thought of her being questioned by a Gestapo agent made him sick. He paced back and forth. It was as if his fears had taken on a life of their own, acquired a heartbeat, a pulse.

"I will see to Danae," her father said, turning away from him. "She is my daughter. She is no concern of yours."

* * *

AT FIRST O'MALLEY had enjoyed looking after the boy, but gradually the kid's presence began to grate on him. It was hard minding a child who never shut up and found infinite ways to get into trouble. Wore one out, so it did. Like a radio full of static, with no knob to turn it off.

"Jesus, Mary, and Joseph. Will you not be still?"

Planning a solitary ride through the trees, he'd saddled the horse early that morning, but Stefanos had woken up and followed him.

"*Pame!*" he yelled. Let's go.

"Get back, Specky," O'Malley said. "Not so close. She's a skittish beast. She'll trample you, sure."

Ignoring the warning, the boy continued to flick Elektra's tail with his hand. "*Pame!*"

"A right bloody torment you are, Stefanos. As stubborn as the day is long."

Reluctantly, O'Malley hoisted the boy up into the saddle and the two of them set off.

It had rained during the night, and the branches of the pines were beaded with moisture. Stefanos pointed to a cobweb hanging suspended in space, its filaments glimmering with droplets of water. "*Arachni!*"

They cantered up to the airfield, Elektra shouldering their weight easily. O'Malley could feel her breathing beneath him, the smooth rhythm of her gait as she charged ahead. She started to gallop when they reached the clearing, dirt flying in all directions.

Taking his hat off, O'Malley whipped her flanks with it, driving her faster and faster as he rode around in circles, slowly obliterating the airfield he and the *antartes* had created, erasing the lines in the earth.

The Stuka had strafed it, which meant the Germans now knew it was here. Better to destroy it than let them use it. Land here, they'd be upon the camp in no time.

"Off with you!" he bellowed to the horse. "Come on, come on!"

"*M'aresei!*" Stefanos shouted. "*M'aresei to alogo.*" I like the horse.

O'Malley took his time returning to camp, quizzing the boy about Danae as they ambled through the trees. "Your sister ever talk about me? Ever speak about our time together in the cave?"

Stefanos thought for a moment and shook his head. "*Oxi.*"

"Not a word?"

He pushed his glasses up. "*Tragouda to tragoudi sou.*" She sings your song. Giggling, he imitated his sister, singing a mishmash of English words.

Recognizing the melody, O'Malley gave a bark of laughter and began to shout the lyrics, too, amending the words.

> She was lovely and fair as the rose of the summer,
> Yet 'twas not her beauty alone that won me,
> Oh, no, 'twas the truth in her eyes ever beaming
> That made me love Danae, the Rose of Tralee.
> The cool shades of evening their mantle were spreading,
> And Danae, all smiling was listening to me.

"*Nai, afto. Afto to tragoudi.*" Yes, that's it. That's the song she sings.

O'Malley sang on, wishing Danae could hear him, could answer him in turn. His music, a bridge between them.

He'd ask her to marry him one day. 'Care to hang your laundry alongside mine?' he'd say, the way men did in Ireland.

After supper that night, the boy dragged his suitcase over and got out the animals O'Malley had carved for him. He bedded them down on a dingy cloth and gave them a fistful of grass to eat. A blue bead was mixed in with the carvings.

"*Mati*," the boy said, pointing to it. A talisman against the evil eye.

Stefanos' treasures. O'Malley touched the animals, wishing he'd done a better job, made a proper Noah's Ark for him with giraffes and lions and monkeys, all the animals known to man.

They played with the animals for a time, O'Malley pecking the ground with the chicken, Stefanos braying and heehawing with the donkey. Hearing them, Leonidas got down on the ground and joined in, snuffling and snorting with the pig and pretending to gobble up the boy. "*Fage, gourounaki, fage.*" Eat, little pig, eat.

Another difference from Ireland, O'Malley thought, *where two grown men would be taking a risk if they played with a child like this. Get bloodied, if not killed, if one of them tried it alone.*

The following day, O'Malley organized another soccer game, using the ball he'd made, thinking it'd give Stefanos a leg up in his village if he mastered the game, lessen the child's terrible awkwardness.

Lining up the ball, he demonstrated how to lift it with his foot and bounce it up and down; then he drove the ball forward and kicked it over to Stefanos, who went down after it on his hands and knees.

"Aw, Jesus. What's up with you? I told you, you can only use your feet. You're not a goalie. You can't pick it up with your hands." He passed it to him again, shouting for him to kick it, to try and score.

They were using clay jugs the cook had given them as goal posts. The ball went careening and took out the first jug, smashing it to smithereens.

Stefanos jumped up and down. "*Kai ti ekana!*" Look what I did.

O'Malley snatched the ball away. "Are you mad? 'Tis no cause for laughter, destroying a goal post. Get you banned for life, that will."

He set it down between them. "Here now. Try it again."

This time the boy shot it directly where he was supposed to.

"Fair play to you. Well done."

They continued to play until Roumelis shouted it was time for dinner. The kid was getting good at it, O'Malley thought, developing a keen sense of when to feint and when to brazen it out. Another week and he'd have it down.

Starved for activity, the men in the camp quickly took over the game, assigning O'Malley and Stefanos and nine others to the first team, which they dubbed the 'dungdogs,' and Leonidas, Fotis and others to the second, called the 'Greeks.'

O'Malley objected. " 'Dungdogs' is an insult. You can't call us that."

"How about 'whore's sons'? Is better?"

The game helped break up the tedium, the hours of waiting that seemed to be an intrinsic part of war.

Unhappy with the frivolity, Haralambos insisted the soccer playing be restricted to two hours a day, the rest of the time to be used for education. He volunteered to teach anyone who wanted to learn how to read. O'Malley thought he'd use this opportunity to brainwash the men. But it was Greek grammar he taught them, alpha and omega and all the rest.

Stefanos never asked where his father was or when he'd be back. He accepted his absence without complaint as he did most things—sleeping out in the open, the grammar lessons, the games. Laughing with O'Malley and the others. Laughing as if nothing was wrong.

His front tooth had come loose and he fussed with it, wiggling it back and forth with his finger, saliva wetting his chin.

O'Malley slapped his hand away. "Stop that. It'll come out when it's ready."

And so it did. Sometime after two a.m., about three hours after O'Malley had fallen asleep. Squealing, the boy woke him up and handed him the wet tooth, a gift of sorts. It was a foul thing, none too clean, and slick with blood. O'Malley tried his best to act pleased. "Ah, bless you. Now go to sleep."

But Stefanos refused to settle down. Absurdly pleased with himself, he kept grinning at O'Malley, pointing at the place the tooth had been, holding his lip back with a bloody finger so O'Malley could see the gaping hole in his gums.

"*To donti vyike, to donti vyike,*" he kept saying. Tooth gone, tooth gone.

O'Malley wanted to eat him alive. "For the love of God, will you not hush? 'Tis only a tooth fell from your mouth. Not the Holy Grail."

12

THREE DAYS LATER, a convoy of German soldiers rolled into the gorge. They rode in on three trucks, the sound of their engines echoing against the rockbound cliffs, the gears grinding as the vehicles fought for purchase. Eighty to a hundred men, O'Malley estimated, heading in the direction of the old monastery.

"Someone betrayed us," Haralambos said, watching the soldiers approach through binoculars. "Probably Papadakis. He was the last one here."

The others argued with him. "He'd never give up our location, not with his son here."

They continued to bicker, Haralambos eventually acquiescing. But O'Malley knew the teacher had made a note, added the name 'Papadakis' to the list he kept of people who bore watching—scores to be settled after the war.

He'd have to warn Danae's father and urge him to get out of these mountains before the teacher and his comrades took over.

The Germans had taken them by surprise that morning. The *antartes* had been sitting around the campfire, drinking coffee, when the sentry came running in, yelling a German patrol was in the area.

Grabbing their guns, the Greeks wasted no time. "Take out the first truck," Leonidas shouted. "After that, blow up the other two."

O'Malley held back, worried about Stefanos.

No good, having the boy out in the open with a battle raging. Especially that one, who'd try and shoot back with the branch of a tree. Call the Germans names and jump up and down.

O'Malley looked around for a place to hide him and spied a wooden barrel near the fire. He tipped it upside down and emptied the wine inside out on the ground, then rolled it through the makeshift latrine on the far side of the camp, back and forth through the stinking piles of waste.

"In you go," he told the boy.

"*Mirizei skata!*" It smells like shit.

"Off with ya! Get in there!"

"*Oxi!*"

Swearing, O'Malley grabbed him by the scruff of his neck and threw him in. "Don't you go brickin' about and shitting yourself, Stefanos, you hear? I don't care how scared you are, you stay quiet."

The boy shoved an open hand in his face, giving him the *mountza*, the Greek equivalent of the finger. "*Malaka!*" Jerk.

The little maggot.

Laughing in spite of himself, O'Malley put the lid back on the barrel, taking care to leave a slit open for air. He thumped it three times, two long raps and one short. "That's the signal, Stefanos. Don't come out until you hear me do that."

Kid should be all right. Barrel was well hidden and reeked of shit. Even if the Germans succeeded in overrunning the camp they wouldn't touch it. No, they'd think it was a primitive Greek privy and leave it be. Stefanos would be well out of it, safe once the fighting started.

He grabbed Elektra by the reins and led her into the same thicket of trees. The horse might draw the Germans if they came busting in and lead them to the barrel where the boy was hiding, but he felt like he had to try and protect her. As a precautionary measure, he gathered up piles of loose brush and built a little fort around her, then gave her some feed to keep her quiet.

"Mind yourself, horse," he said.

Taking a last look around, he sprinted to the place where Leonidas was waiting. He was excited in spite of himself, a little tremor running up and down his spine.

* * *

Leonidas tossed a submachine gun to O'Malley.

O'Malley's face fell when he saw it. "Bloody hell." The damned thing was a Sten.

'Stench guns,' the Australians had called the weapon, claiming they were best used as clubs; they always jammed in battle. On Crete, they'd thrown them away, preferring the German MP 38s they took off dead paratroopers.

Leonidas was carefully doling out the ammunition. Like the gun, it, too, didn't amount to much.

"Aim carefully, my friend," he said.

Fotis and Lakis were readying a mortar on the ridge, assembling it and locking the mechanism in place. Others were manning a second mortar at the entrance to the gorge. They were laboring silently, and so far the Germans were unaware of their presence.

The convoy halted suddenly about midway through the ravine. It had been moving at a steady pace when the engine of the lead truck apparently overheated and quit. O'Malley could see steam pouring out of it. The strip of land along the river was too narrow for the other two trucks to maneuver around the stalled vehicle; and they stayed where they were, waiting with their engines idling.

O'Malley watched the convoy through his binoculars. Whoever their commanding officer was, he'd violated every rule of war coming into the gorge. He should have dispatched a smaller group first to make sure it was safe before driving the trucks in. O'Malley doubted General von Le Suire was with these men. Also the soldiers never should have stopped, even when the truck broke down. They should have kept going no matter what, on foot if necessary, doing everything in their power to get to safety, out of the canyon. *Aye*, a veteran like von Le Suire would have known better.

Two of the soldiers were bent over the engine of the stalled truck, trying to fix it, while the rest of the men began fooling around. Calling to his friends, one man was teetering on the rocks, while another beat the bushes with a stick like a gamekeeper, rousting a man shitting there. Like their commanding officer, they were inexperienced and grew ever more boisterous, clowning around and shouting loudly in German. Finally, an older man emerged from the first truck and set about restoring order.

He moved with a kind of debilitating weariness, his skin pasty and damp. He was sweating profusely, his hair soaking wet and plastered to his forehead. At one point, he put his hand on the fender of one of the trucks to steady himself.

"Shit," O'Malley muttered. "Bastard's got malaria."

The sick officer spoke to the other men, evidently ordering them to get back in the trucks. They ignored him and continued to horse around, if anything growing even louder.

So much for German discipline.

"Officer in charge has malaria," O'Malley whispered to Leonidas. "He blundered into the gorge by mistake."

The two of them were lying on a shelf of rock about fifty feet above the riverbed on the eastern side of the gorge. Fotis and Lakis had climbed up the western side and secreted themselves there, while two other groups moved into place on the north and south, effectively sealing the Germans in.

"Into the valley of death rode the six hundred," O'Malley said under his breath. That's what the gorge would be in another minute or so. *A fucking valley of death.*

Poem had made no sense to him in school, made even less to him now. Why celebrate a group of men who'd blundered into a valley like this one, ridden to their awful deaths? All that 'doing and dying' the British loved so much, it didn't amount to much that he could see. He'd been given a manual when he first enlisted, a sort of military textbook that stated the 'courtesy of a salute was to be dispensed with in battle.' He always thought that about summed up what was wrong with the British.

He looked around, wondering how the Greeks would do. Hidden high in the rocks, they were nearly invisible, holding their guns at the ready. Been at it since 1940—three long years—they knew what they were about. *Warriors true.*

Leonidas reached for the rifle. "First this, then the mortar."

O'Malley nodded. Mortars might be effective, but they were loud and you could hear them coming from a long way off, follow their trajectory and get out of the way. A sniper's bullet was different. It gave no warning and was far more terrifying.

Taking careful aim, Leonidas fired at the German in the river. The bullet hit him square in the chest and he pitched forward into the water.

The other soldiers immediately began to scream, pointing to the cliff and trying to gauge where the shot had come from, if it was one man or many. The officer again urged them to take cover.

"*Macht schnell!*" he kept yelling. "*Macht schnell!*" Hurry.

"Now, Leonidas!" O'Malley made a chopping motion. "Hit 'em with the mortar!"

Nodding, Leonidas slid a shell into place in the mortar and took aim at the soldiers, his finger on the trigger.

The shell hit the first truck in a blinding flash and exploded against the door, spewing flames and oily black smoke high in the air. A group of soldiers got caught in the blast and began scrambling away on their hands and knees, beating at their burning clothes with their hands. A second explosion followed when the truck's gas tank went up, showering flaming chunks of metal down on the fleeing men. The metal sizzled when it hit the river.

The driver of the truck staggered out of the cab, his entire body aflame. The other soldiers pulled him down and rolled him back and forth in the sand, babbling hysterically in German. The driver kept screaming. Even from where he was, O'Malley could hear him, hear the other men still trapped inside the burning vehicle.

Gagging, he buried a fist in his mouth, willing the men to stop, praying he'd be spared, not have to listen to them die.

A few seconds later, Leonidas fired off another round. The mortar hit the third truck in line, effectively trapping the Germans in the gorge. The middle truck went up immediately after. O'Malley could hear men shrieking and crying as the fireball engulfed them. A few ran into the river and began wading upstream. The Greeks there opened fire on them and they tumbled headfirst into the shallows, bloody water pooling and eddying around their bodies.

The diesel fuel continued to burn, black smoke gusting around the trucks and slowly filling the ravine, turning the sky dark, day into night.

Anchoring himself against the rocks, O'Malley raised the submachine gun and fired off a round. He couldn't see through the smoke, so he focused instead on the inhuman cries he heard coming from the trucks. Be an act of mercy, killing whoever was making those sounds. Put an end to their suffering.

The German officer in charge just stood there and watched it all come apart. He made no move to call for reinforcements. The poor fool didn't even have a radio. The barrage continued for another fifteen minutes, the air heavy with burning fuel, the cloying stench of burning flesh.

One of the soldiers in the gorge raised his weapon and let loose a volley in O'Malley's direction. Quickly retaliating, O'Malley stood up and letting out a blast from the machine gun. Shrieking, the man dropped back and grabbed at his neck. Seconds later he dropped to his knees, soaked in his own blood, his gray uniform wet with it.

A group of Germans were wrestling a piece of artillery free from the wreckage of one of the trucks—an LG 42 or one of its kin. Seeing it, O'Malley dropped back down behind the rocks. He had come up against the LG 42 in Crete and seen the destruction it caused.

"We got to get it away from them," he shouted to Leonidas. "Take down the mountain, they will, they fire that thing."

The force of the explosion threw him flat, the blast from the LG42 tearing up the ledge he was on and clipping the trees behind. Hoping to get out of range, O'Malley began crawling backward as fast as he could. He'd gone about ten feet when the Germans fired again. Although the ledge absorbed most of the impact, the noise of the blast nearly crippled him. His head hurt and his field of vision was suddenly awash with bright scarlet light. He felt his face with his hands, afraid his eyes were gone, that he'd been blinded.

Another round whistled through the air and exploded nearby. O'Malley could feel the ground vibrating beneath him and feared it would set off a landslide. Blast after blast followed in rapid succession as the Germans adjusted their sights and began focusing on where he and Leonidas were hiding. O'Malley felt like he was being flayed alive, guts and bones and pounding heart out in the open. Chips of rock grazed the flesh of his face, his wounded eyes.

O'Malley banged at the ledge with the butt of his gun, desperately trying to dig a fox hole, knowing all the while it was hopeless. If either he or Leonidas tried to return fire, the Germans would instantly know their position and blow them apart.

The Germans continued to shell the ledge.

Crying out, O'Malley curled up and covered his head with his hands. He was breaking apart, the pounding forcing his ribs loose, his skull from his spine. The sound was deafening, each blast penetrating deep within him.

Seeing they were in trouble, Fotis ran toward the LG42, a stick grenade in his hand. "Cover me!" he shouted.

O'Malley took a deep breath, raised his gun and fired off a round. "A knife in your eye, you bastards!"

Skittering down through the trees, Fotis hurled the grenade at the Germans. It exploded in a blast of fiery dirt, making a crater under them and taking them out. Within seconds, O'Malley was tearing down the cliff toward the LG42, intent on seizing the weapon.

The burning trucks had ignited the pine trees by the river and there were flames everywhere, sparks shooting high in the smoky gloom. The grenade had torn off the arm of one of the Germans and nearly decapitated the other. Blood darkened the sand beneath them and was slowly seeping into the river.

Grabbing the LG 42, O'Malley spun it around and fired at the soldiers in the river. His aim was off and the shell tore a great hole in the sand. He raised the gun higher and fired it again. This time the shot was true, blowing a column of water high in the air. The shrapnel from the blast caught two of the Germans, killing them instantly.

"*Nein*," a man cried, raising his hands in the air. "*Bitte nicht!*"

Keeping his hands up, he stumbled out of the water. "*Bitte nicht!*" he cried again.

Hands in the air, the rest of the Germans quickly followed. The majority came from the river, eight or nine from behind the smoldering trucks. Like coal miners, they were covered with soot, their eyes red and inflamed. Eighty-one of them there were by O'Malley's count, including four who were lying on the ground, badly wounded. The officer he'd seen earlier had survived the attack and now stepped forward. He gave his name, Wilhelm Reiss, and stated the group was part of the 177th Jäger Division.

The Greeks quickly lined the soldiers up at gunpoint and stripped them of their gear, piling their weapons up on the riverbank. They took their packs, everything they could pull off them. The officer watched them in a dispirited way. As before, his men ignored him.

O'Malley logged them in as best he could, interviewing each in turn and asking for his name, rank and serial number. It was a waste of time as he didn't understand German, had neither a pencil nor a paper. Still he went on, asking them if they were married and how many children they had. All this in Greek. He'd never had men surrender to him before and wanted to do it properly, make the capture official. The questions about the Germans' children and the rest, he'd added for the *antartes'* benefit, hoping to make the captured soldiers seem more human and stave off a massacre.

It was one thing to kill in the heat of battle. Part of warring, it had to be done. Another thing entirely to shoot men who had their hands in the air, who were waving a white flag. It didn't much matter to the dead how they died, he knew; still, it was a question of decency, fair play, and a sporting chance. Otherwise, it was all for naught, the soldiering, nothing but pure muck savagery.

They were young, the Germans, hadn't seen much combat. Hitler had to be getting desperate, boys like these finding their way into the mountaineers, the almighty Jägers.

Fotis was kneeling alongside one of the trucks, counting the bodies.

"How many?" O'Malley asked.

Fotis kicked one of the dead Germans, cocked his gun, and shot him again. The bullet made a small black hole in the front of the man's uniform, momentarily raised his body in a puff of air.

"Not enough," he said.

* * *

HOLDING HIS MACHINE gun on the prisoners, O'Malley stayed by the river. Although his eyes stung, he could see fine now. Whatever had happened to him up on the ledge had been minor, scrapes and cuts mostly.

He tried not to look at the Germans, to block out the animal sounds coming from the four wounded men by the water, the sad lot who'd been burned in the fire. He doubted they'd get medical attention in the camp, doubted they'd survive the night.

A corpse was spinning around in the river. The dead man had been badly burned, the side of his face nearly gone. O'Malley waded into the water, removed the man's identification tag from around his neck and pocketed it. Another letter to write some day.

He drew back when Alexis showed up. The Greek had been against him since the day he arrived, calling him a "British whore" and inciting the others against him. He'd only stopped after O'Malley pulled a knife and threatened to disembowel him if he kept it up.

Alexis rarely addressed O'Malley now, and when he did, he patronized him, making fun of his red hair and freckles, calling him, *vloyiokomenos* behind his back. Pox.

For the most part, O'Malley was amused by the Greek's antics. Alexis was noticeably younger than the rest of the men in the camp, barely had a beard. Still, he took care never to provoke him needlessly. From what he'd seen, it was soldiers like Alexis—the ones who had the most to prove—who were the most dangerous in wartime.

Stepping forward, Alexis ordered the captured Germans to turn their pockets inside out, then went through them, unbuttoning their tunics and inspecting them. When he finished with the living, he began to paw through the clothes of the dead.

O'Malley didn't much care for what Alexis was doing, the way he was manhandling the dead soldiers, the blood on his hands.

"What's he doing?" he asked Leonidas in a undertone.

"Searching for Iron Crosses, things he can sell."

"Leave off," O'Malley called loudly to Alexis, making a joke of it. "There's not a medal to be had here. Bloody amateurs, the lot of them."

Leonidas and Haralambos moved off to the side a moment later and began conferring in low voices. When they finished talking, Leonidas retrieved a length of rope and handed it to O'Malley, demonstrating how he wanted him to loop it around the Germans' wrists, first one man, then the next, until they were all tied together in a long line.

After O'Malley finished stringing the Germans together, Leonidas marched them at gunpoint out of the gorge. O'Malley stayed well back. As he'd anticipated, the *antartes* left the dead to fester and the four wounded men lying where they'd fallen.

When they passed Mega Spileon, a handful of monks came out and watched them go by, holding their black hats with their hands against the wind.

Nodding respectfully, the majority of the *antartes* acknowledged the monks, a few even going to far as to cross themselves as they walked by the old monastery. Only Haralambos and Alexis turned away, pointedly ignoring the robed figures.

As if turning away would ever diminish the power of the church or make it disappear, O'Malley thought as he watched them. Good luck to those two if that's what they were about. Church had its problems, but without it, there was nothing. Just pure muck savagery. They would find that out soon enough.

Reluctantly, he followed the *antartes* up the path. Leonidas was in the lead, moving at a furious pace.

Less than two feet wide in places, the path followed a natural break in the rock and wound steeply up the face of the cliff. Portions of it were clogged with gravel, and bound as they were, the prisoners were on their hands and knees, struggling not to fall.

Again, O'Malley held back, watching the long line of men crisscross the cliff. He could see the entire length of the gorge from where he stood, the burned trucks and dead bodies in the river. The trees were already thick with crows, black with them.

The birds reminded him of the legends Danae had told him about this place. How '*styx*' meant 'hate' in ancient Greek and was a portal to hell. No one knew for sure if the gorge was the actual site of the Styx, but O'Malley, for one, was sure that it was. The smoldering trucks convinced him. Hell could only be that. It required nothing more.

When they reached the top of the cliff, Leonidas ordered the Germans to kneel. As before, it was hard for them, and the Greeks were rough on them, hitting and kicking them. The Germans began to murmur, growing more and more agitated as they were forced to the ground.

Alexis drew a finger across his throat. "*Sie sterben*," he shouted with a laugh.

"What's that mean?" O'Malley asked.

"You die." Alexis was pleased with himself, O'Malley saw, the position he found himself in.

"They're POWs. You can't be killing them. Geneva Convention's very clear on that."

"Fuck the Geneva Convention."

Leonidas pulled O'Malley away. "Stay out of it. You don't know him. He'll kill them just to prove he can."

Same as his ancestors had done the crippled babies, O'Malley thought. You wouldn't have heard the babies, but the men—God Almighty, you'd hear them, all right. Sear your heart, that would. The pitiful cries of the men.

O'Malley knew if the situation had been reversed, von Le Suire would gladly have shot the prisoners, yelled 'see you in hell' as they died. But that was von Le Suire and von Le Suire was a Nazi.

"Your lot really going to kill 'em?"

Leonidas didn't answer for few minutes. "I don't know," he said at last, his voice weary. "We haven't decided."

"You kill 'em, Germans will retaliate. They'll destroy Kalavryta."

Once more, Leonidas took his time. "I know."

O'Malley continued to plead the Germans' case, his fear for the village driving him. "Don't do it, Leonidas. They're soldiers same as us. POWs. Surrendered fair and square."

"We can't keep them here. There's nothing to feed them."

"Feed 'em grass." O'Malley was shouting now.

Leonidas signaled for him to keep his voice down. "I don't know if I can save them." There was a pleading note in his voice, a cry almost. "Some of the men want revenge for that massacre near Corinth."

O'Malley looked back at the seventy-seven trussed-up men, felt their fear coursing through him. "Sweet Jesus," he whispered.

* * *

"I'm taking the wounded Germans to Kalavryta," O'Malley told Stefanos the next morning. "I'll stop by your house on the way back. Bring you word of your family."

The boy grabbed O'Malley and wouldn't let him go.

"*Meine edo*," he said in Greek. "*As pethanoun oi Germanoi. As pethanoun oloi*." Stay here. Let the Germans die. Let them all die.

"It'd be best if you stayed in the barrel, Specky, same as before. Don't get out until I get back and rap on the top, give you the all clear. We captured seventy-seven Germans yesterday, and they're sitting outside the camp. You don't want to run afoul of them."

Without another word, the boy scampered back to the barrel, called out from inside that he'd wait there until O'Malley came back. O'Malley was sure the kid would keep his word. Wouldn't stir from that place. No, not with Germans so close by.

Leonidas had given the order to save the wounded Germans, the four men in the gorge, saying the risk to Kalavryta was too great should they die. A group of farmers had been summoned to help with the transport and had brought canvas stretchers with them. The cloth was ripped and bloody, the wooden poles, worn with use. The farmers knew what they were doing and worked quickly, hoisting the poles onto their shoulders and carrying the Germans to Kalavryta, two men shouldering each of the stretchers. They were surprisingly gentle and spoke softly to the wounded men as they walked along, comforting them as best they could.

"*Mi fovasai*," they kept saying. "*Mi fovasai*." Don't be afraid.

The Germans kept drifting in and out of consciousness, the awful pain of their burns reviving them as they knocked against the poles. O'Malley wished he had something to give them, a way to dampen down their suffering. They were about the same age he was. Too young to die.

The Greeks debated whether or not to bury the dead men in the gorge before moving out, but decided there wasn't enough time. They had to get the wounded men to the hospital in Kalavryta before they died. "Later," Leonidas said.

A young doctor met them at the entrance. He'd been trained in Athens, he told O'Malley, and been posted here at the start of the war. Dressed in a white coat and wearing wire-rimmed glasses, he seemed a careful man. Slowly peeling back their clothes, he examined the Germans and studied their wounds, then motioned to bring them inside. There was one ward in the hospital—a chilly room with two long rows of iron beds. It was largely deserted. Two of the beds were occupied by elderly women. The yellowish walls were pitted and stained, and the cement floor was cracked.

The place didn't have much in the way of supplies, O'Malley saw. The cloth bandages laid out on a table looked to have been laundered repeatedly, and most of the pill bottles were empty. He doubted the doctor had anything for pain.

Tipping the stretcher, he helped roll the first German onto a bed. The man screamed, his seeping burns dirtying the white sheet beneath him.

The doctor quickly cut away the wounded man's clothes and threw them to the floor.

O'Malley nodded to the prostrate man. "I'm a trained doctor myself, if you need help."

"You have any experience with burns?"

"Some, in a military hospital in Egypt."

"I'll see how it goes. Maybe I'll send for you."

* * *

SELF-CONSCIOUS ABOUT HIS blood-stained clothes, the stench of battle still clinging to him, O'Malley knocked awkwardly on Danae's door.

"You'll be wanting word of your brother and I came to tell you the lad is fine," he told her when she appeared. "Took to the military like a duck to water, he did. I see to him mostly. Leonidas, too, sometimes. One of the men, a school teacher named Haralambos, is teaching him to read in the afternoon. *Grammata, grammata*, and all that. He's lacking for nothing, Stefanos. Having the time of his life."

Danae smiled but said nothing. As usual, giving him no help.

"Your father about?" O'Malley asked.

"No," Danae said. "He and my aunt went to Kalavryta to buy supplies."

Taking his cap off, O'Malley stood there awkwardly. "We got into a firefight yesterday and I helped bring the wounded to the hospital. Told your brother I'd check on you. That's the reason I'm here."

She had just washed her hair and it hung loose on her shoulders and gave off a lemony scent. He had a trouble concentrating and had to look away.

Eyeing him, Danae shook her hair out a little to dry it, lifting it up and letting it fall. Flirting, she was. He was sure of it.

O'Malley took a deep breath. Might as well get down to it. "The men I was with already went back to the camp. I told them I'd be along presently, that

I had to see my sweetheart." He made a deep bow. "My *filenada*, Danae. The queen of my heart."

"I'm not your *filenada*," she said in that matter-of-fact way of hers. "I'm just a poor girl from Kalavryta."

"To me you are, Danae. To me you are and always will be. I think about you all the time. Can't live without you, seems. When all this is over, I plan to come back here. Hang my clothes on the line next to yours."

O'Malley's aunt had looked at his uncle in a funny way after he took up talking to himself, holding long, involved conversations with historic figures no one else could see—Jesus, for one—conversations that went round and round but never led anywhere, only to a bed in St. Patrick's, the state lunatic asylum in Dublin. 'Pickled his brains, he has,' his aunt had said of him. 'Can't be relied upon.'

It occurred to him that Danae was now looking at him in much the same way. *Thinks I'm gone in the head, she does, same as my poor uncle.*

Perhaps he'd been too hasty. Should have bided his time and led up to the thing.

Blushing furiously, he blundered on, "That's how a man proposes where I come from. We're a shy lot, the Irish, not good at speaking what's in our hearts, what goes on between a man and a woman."

"And so you talk of laundry?"

"Aye. Seems that we do."

Bending down, he gathered up a bit of clover, twisted it and wound it around her finger. "One day I'll give you a gold one, Danae, with jewels encrusted upon it. Diamonds I'll fetch from Africa. Pearls from beneath the sea."

She played along, holding her hand up and pretending to admire the ring. She let him kiss her, too, even went so far as to put her arms around his neck and draw him to her, albeit cautiously. He could feel her heart beating through the cotton of her dress, racing it was. He was gentle with her, kissing her on the forehead and eyelids before finding her mouth again.

Like holding a wild bird in his hands, it was—a lark or a swallow. He didn't want to crush it or cause it to fly away.

* * *

The men in the camp were exuberant that night. They urged the cook, Roumelis, to break out the *raki* to celebrate. "Seventy-seven Germans captured. Von Le Suire's going to shit himself."

"Shit you more likely," O'Malley said under his breath. "Shit you and Kalavryta both."

He walked over to the barrel and rapped on the top with his knuckles. "Specky? You in there?"

The child's voice was muffled. "*Angle?*"

"None other. You can come out now."

Stefanos crawled out on all fours, smelling nearly as rank as the barrel.

"I saw your sister. She sends you greetings."

"Danae?"

"Aye, lad. Danae."

She'd run back into the house not long after he'd kissed her and stood at the window, watching him through the glass. It occurred to him that she hadn't said anything when he'd made his declaration, hadn't indicated she felt the same way. It'll come, the love, he told himself. A fine looking fellow such as himself. 'Course it would.

She'd kept the grass ring on her finger, he noticed. Waved hesitantly as he turned to go. *Aye*, it was on its way already, the love.

The boy told O'Malley that even though he'd been scared, he'd done what he was supposed to and hadn't made a sound, not one. Nor had he ventured forth when he had to go to the toilet. Meaning O'Malley got to do laundry that night while the other men drank, the pants being the boy's only pair. It was tedious work, boiling the water first and then the pants, scrubbing at the stains he'd rather not think about while the boy stood there trembling, wrapped in the *flokati*.

"I couldn't just be your bleeding nursemaid. No, you had to go and add washerwoman to my duties."

He draped the pants over the branch of a tree to dry and got ready for bed. Roumelis had insisted Stefanos sleep next to the fire where it was warmer, had even gone so far as to give the child a blanket to wrap himself up in. Although O'Malley was soaked to the skin from the sloshing of the bucket, no such offer had been extended to him. He'd sleep where he always did, with his back up against a rock at the far end of the camp.

He fed Elektra and saw to it that she had water, a fresh armful of hay. Her warm presence gave him comfort. The feel of her hide under his hands was like touching Ireland again, recalling the boy he'd once been, who'd dreamed of racing in the steeplechase and winning a pot of gold.

With a sigh, he returned to the camp and settled down for the night. He could see his breath in the cold air above him, feel his joints stiffen as he lay there on the ground. He feared he'd be covered with frost come morning, ice in his whiskers and hair. His joy at seeing Danae slowly ebbed away as he lay there. He thought about the German prisoners up on the cliff, bound like chickens on a spit, waiting in the dark to die, the dead soldiers in the gorge, shattered by the grenade. He wished with all his heart he could walk away, be done with all this.

He could still hear the guns, the fierce roar of mortar fire rattling around in his head. He remembered the way the men inside the trucks had screamed—the inhuman sounds they'd made when the fire rose up and took them. He wiped the tears from his face, glad for the darkness, relieved that the others couldn't see him.

"Holy Mother of God, preserve me."

13

One of the Germans had managed to free himself during the night, Fotis said. After which, he'd undone the bounds that held the men on either side of him. They in turn had freed the others.

Alexis and Lakis had been assigned guard duty, ordered to stand three meters back with their machine guns trained on the prisoners. Leonidas had been very clear on that point: three meters back, no more, no less. They hadn't taken the order seriously and been sprawled on the ground, dozing peacefully, when the prisoners overpowered them, coming up on them from behind and bashing in their skulls. They'd killed Lakis outright. Alexis had survived the attack, only to regain consciousness bound hand and foot, a pair of dirty socks stuffed in his mouth.

Dirty socks. O'Malley shook his head. A nice touch, that.

The prisoners had taken the two machine guns and whatever ammunition the two Greeks had on them. Not wanting to alert the camp, they hadn't risked firing on them, had resorted to using rocks instead.

They wouldn't get far, not with the *antartes* baying at their heels. Still, O'Malley didn't blame them for running off. He'd have done the same, torn the shackles off with his teeth if he'd had to. Chanced it, same as them.

Alexis was surrounded by the men from the camp, trying to argue away what had happened. "I was awake when they attacked. There were too many of them. I couldn't do anything."

The Greeks were angry he hadn't made a stand, fought harder to save Lakis. "You fucking asshole," one of them said to Alexis. "You worthless bastard."

He was done here, O'Malley thought. Judged a coward by his fellows, silenced by a pair of socks. It had been Fotis who'd found him when he came to take over guard duty. Alexis had worked the socks lose by then but hadn't screamed or tried to alert the camp in any way. Had just sat there, wringing his hands like a woman and waiting to be rescued while Lakis bled out on the ground in front of him.

* * *

"Get the horses," Leonidas shouted.

O'Malley trailed after them on Elektra, but took care to stay well back. Germans might be preparing an ambush, waiting just around the bend with the machine guns.

"Here," someone shouted, picking up the trail.

The brush was trampled down, a bit of gray fabric caught on a branch.

"Come on," Leonidas yelled.

Not a posse, O'Malley thought as he watched them. *No, something uglier.* He remembered the description of the Spartan women from a book he'd read in school—how they'd given their men a choice when they went into battle. Win or come back on their shields. In other words, 'victory or death.' The Greeks had modified this in 1821 during the war against the Turks to 'freedom or death,' but it was the same thing: either you won or you died. That's what this band was about tonight. Hell bent on retrieving their prize. Those seventy-seven desperate men making a run for safety. The Greeks were going to have them or die.

He wanted no part of it. Turning his horse around, he headed back to camp. All was quiet. Stefanos was fast asleep next to the campfire, his glasses carefully folded up next to him. O'Malley tucked the boy's blanket tight around him and threw a log on the fire, then walked back to his pallet and lay down. The moon was high overhead and it bathed the camp in pale, blue light.

O'Malley heard a sudden spurt of gunfire. Leonidas must have found them. Hoisting himself up on the rocks, he scanned the gorge, searching for movement. A flash of fire illuminated the trees for a second, the shadowy forms of men on horseback. More flashes followed and then the staccato bark of a machine gun. They weren't far off, O'Malley judged. If the prisoners retreated back this way, he and the boy would be pulled into it whether they liked it or not.

But he heard no more shots. Perhaps Leonidas had captured them, he thought. Perhaps that part of it was already over. He drew the goatskin tightly around his shoulders. The night was very cold—'perishing,' as his pa would say. The promise of snow in the air.

* * *

It was close to daybreak when Leonidas and the others returned, marching the prisoners ahead of them at gunpoint. One of the Germans, a blond youth, screamed something when he entered the camp.

"*Skasmos,*" Haralambos shouted. Shut up.

Most of the prisoners looked like they'd been beaten. One man's hand had been broken, the fingers bent at odd angles, his thumb smashed. Leonidas hadn't killed them, O'Malley thought. No, he'd let the men work off their rage a different way.

The Greeks quickly fenced the prisoners in behind barbed wire. "Shoot to kill, should they try and escape again," Leonidas instructed the men.

A cry of protest rose from the Germans. Fotis grabbed the ringleader, pushed him hard against the wire, and ground his face up against it.

O'Malley didn't blame him. Fotis' brother, Andreas, had been grabbed by a Gestapo agent the week before, a man called Radomski who was well known in the region for his sadism.

They were evil that way, the Germans, truly satanic.

The thought stopped him and made him wonder why he'd ever championed their cause or pleaded with the Greeks to spare them. Sure, they were young, but so was he. So what if they were new to the ways of war. That didn't make them innocent. No, that didn't make them innocent.

The majority were sitting on the ground with their backs against the ledge, their expressions insolent, contempt for him and the place they found themselves in unmistakable. O'Malley stared back at them.

"You will be spat on and reviled in every assembly," he said, quoting St. Patrick.

It would come to that one day, he was sure of it. These men and the cause they served remembered only as a thing of evil. Like Herod slaughtering the babies in Jerusalem, the Nazis black deeds never to be forgotten. To be recalled time and time again as long as there were humans left on the planet to tell the story.

"Your kind will disappear like the froth of the river, a river all fishes hate."

He'd chosen the right cause, had fought for it and was fighting still. He'd see that the Greeks obeyed the Geneva Convention and did right by these men, even if they were scum, see that they fought a proper war. The idea amused him. A 'proper' war? As if there'd ever been such a thing.

One of the Germans pointed at him and said something to the others, who nodded and laughed. Taking the piss, he thought. Having at me because I'm Irish and don't look like I belong, because I'm pale and talk funny. A cuckoo hereabouts. A cuckoo in a nest of robins.

Must be that the POWs were going on about. They were big on those sorts of things, the Germans. Differences between folks.

"Dry up, you scangers!"

The passageway where the *antartes* ate and slept was already narrow. The prisoners crowded the space, made getting around nearly impossible. Leonidas had wanted to keep an eye on them and so they would, he thought, morning, noon, and night. There'd be no getting away from them here.

Roumelis produced a watery gruel for them to eat, and the Germans fell on it, nearly drowning themselves in their haste to slurp it down.

With the death of Lakis, the number of Greeks in the camp was now down to thirty-nine, including the boy, Giorgos, whose feet were still healing and couldn't fight, and Stefanos, who'd shit himself if it ever came to that. Which meant the Germans outnumbered them more than two to one. A fact not lost on Stefanos, who retreated to the barrel and wouldn't come out.

"They can't hurt you," O'Malley said, trying to coax him out. "They've no guns and their hands are bound. You'll be all right, Specky. Truly you will. I promise."

"*Oxi*," Stefanos yelled from inside. "*Oxi, oxi, oxi.*"

"Why are you so afraid of them?"

"*Kremasan ton thio mou.*" Sticking his head out of the barrel, he acted out the hanging of his uncle, clawing at his neck with his hands and gasping for breath, doing his best to make his eyes bulge out. It was pretty vivid and O'Malley wished he'd stop. "*Pirovolisan to skilo mou.*" They shot my dog.

According to the boy, the Germans had been conducting a *blocco*—one of the lightning raids they occasionally undertook to subdue the civilian population—and a man in a black mask with cut-out eyes, a *maskoforos*, had entered the house with four of them. The man in the mask had singled out his uncle, who'd been in the kitchen talking to his father, and the Germans took him away. His hands had been all bloody the day they hanged him, Stefanos said. Something bad had happened to his hands. The boy went on to say that though he was sad about his uncle, he was glad it had been him they took and not his father.

"The man in a mask was Greek?"

"*Nai, milouse Ellinika.*" Yes, he was speaking Greek.

"Did you recognize his voice?"

"*Oloi xeroun poios einai.*" Yes, everyone knows who he is.

The dog had growled when they entered the house and one of the Germans shot it. It fell to the floor and died a few minutes later, its fur matted with blood.

"*Itan kalos, o skylos mou. To onoma tou itan* Babikos." He was a good dog. His name was Babikos.

O'Malley let him be. Perhaps it was better if he stayed in the barrel. If the Germans escaped again, they'd report to von Le Suire and he'd bring in the planes and the heavy artillery. The revenge operation, the *Sühne-Maßnahmen*, for the dead men in the gorge would take place here, not in some hapless village.

Still, O'Malley felt bad for the child. Seeking to cheer him up, he sang to him that night after dinner, entertaining him with an old Irish standby.

> When Mrs. Murphy dished the chowder out, she fainted on the spot.
> She found a pair of overalls at the bottom of the pot.
> McGinty, he got roaring mad, his eyes were bulging out,
> He jumped onto the piano and loudly he did shout,
> "Who threw the overalls in Mrs. Murphy's chowder?"
> Nobody spoke, so he shouted all the louder,
> "It's a rotten trick that's true, I can lick the drip that threw
> The overalls in Mrs. Murphy's chowder.

Stefanos laughed when O'Malley translated the words; and he asked him to sing it again. "*Alli for a.*"

"Don't you worry, Specky. You'll soon be back in Kalavryta with your pa. We'll build you a tree house down by the river. Fly us some kites."

"*Kai i* Danae." And Danae.

"Of course. She'll always be with us, Danae will."

Stefanos asked if they could ride the horse again, and together they spun a great tale about how the two of them would ride the horse to Kalavryta and gallop inside the house, chase around and wreak destruction while the boy's aunt fought them back with the broom. The boy liked the idea and fell asleep still speaking of it. About what his aunt would say if they set a place at the table for the horse and fed it dinner, taught it how to eat with a spoon.

"*Tha tou doso olo to fai mou.*" I'll give it my food.

* * *

A DELEGATION FROM KALAVRYTA arrived at the camp two days later. It consisted of a middle-aged priest named Father Chronis and two other men. Village elders, O'Malley judged, noting their air of self-importance. In Ireland, such folk had aligned themselves with the English. Here, apparently, it was with the holy fathers.

O'Malley shook his head. *Ah, Jaysus, will you not listen to yourself? Going on as if being rich were an almighty sin, an act of treason. It's living with all these Bolsheviks, done it to you. Turned you into a red, it has. Ruined you entirely.*

"Antonakis," the older of the two men said, introducing himself. It was a cold sort of greeting, patronizing in its way.

"The bishop has been approached by General von Le Suire, who demands you release the German POWs you are holding. The bishop is afraid if you don't comply, the Germans will attack Kalavryta just as they did Komeno. They killed over three hundred people there, many of whom were women and children." All of this was said in a reasonable voice as if they were discussing a routine matter, the paving of the streets, say.

Leonidas interrupted. "It was Roser who ordered that raid, not von Le Suire."

The man started again. "The bishop is afraid—"

"*Den eixei tharos*," Alexis cried, pushing his way forward. The bishop is not courageous.

The man continued on as if he hadn't heard. "His Eminence requests your cooperation. He is convinced that if you do not surrender the prisoners, von Le Suire will massacre the people of Kalavryta. They will be the ones who suffer, not you."

Perhaps it was the man's condescending tone or the fact that he represented the bishop, but Leonidas and the other men refused to listen.

The next day, the priest returned alone. He described how he'd been mobbed by the residents of Kalavryta when he returned to the village the previous day. "Women were crying. Everyone is afraid."

"The Germans will never attack Kalavryta," Leonidas said. "It's of no strategic importance to them."

"The situation has changed. The resistance has stepped up its attacks. They dynamited two railroad bridges and attacked a convoy of German engineers in Tripoli. Two days later, they blew up eleven trucks. Eleven trucks! And now this: eighty-one German soldiers captured."

He searched the faces of the Greeks. "Sooner or later, they'll retaliate. Kalavryta is known to them as a center of resistance activity. It's where they will go."

He was a commanding figure in his black robe, dignified and polite. He had a heavy beard, touched with gray in places, and deep-set, intelligent eyes. "I urged everyone to leave. I told them, 'the Germans are going to kill you. Kalavryta will be erased from the map.' " Fingering the cross around his neck, he spoke with infinite sadness.

"They've warned us and warned us. Three months ago they ordered everyone to come to the square, and they read a decree from Major Ebersberger, von Le Suire's second-in-command. It was very clear: if the village continued to support the resistance, they would level it. They warned us again last week. Twice, we've been warned. Twice!"

"The prisoners are a negotiating tool," Leonidas said. "They're the only negotiating tool we have."

"I'm asking you to consider the village. I beg you, do as the bishop says. Negotiate with the Germans. Give up the POWs."

Leonidas lit a cigarette and inhaled. "With all due respect, Father, how would we go about negotiating with the Germans? We turn up at their headquarters, they will shoot on sight."

"Rope the POWs together and march them there, then let go of the rope and tell them they are free to go. It can't be that difficult."

* * *

"Von Le Suire refused to meet with us," Leonidas told O'Malley later that week. "His aide, Ebersberger, said he has no desire to negotiate with *kommunistischen Verbrecher*. Communist scum. The general will 'impose his own terms.' All the prisoners are to be returned to him unharmed along with their weapons."

"Their weapons, too." O'Malley whistled. "What's he giving you in return?"

"Nothing."

The priest, Father Chronis, had brought word of von Le Suire's refusal. He was close to tears. "The situation's hopeless," he said. "The Germans are the winners and the Greeks are the losers." Gathering his robes, he started down the path to Kalavryta, saying he needed to warn the villagers. Silhouetted against the cliff, his black cloak billowed in the wind, lofting out like the wings of a great bird.

O'Malley thought it might be a good idea to start cleaning his gun.

The stalemate continued for the next few days, the men in the camp arguing back and forth about what to do—whether to release the Germans as von Le Suire demanded or march them to their own headquarters many miles to the west.

Sick of it all, O'Malley decided to pay Danae a visit.

"Out with you, boyo," he said, rapping on Stefanos' barrel with his knuckles. "We're going to see your sister."

Stefanos emerged a moment later, blinking rapidly and shielding his eyes from the sun. He'd been cooped up for days now, so long, he'd begun to grow pale, his movements slow and crab-like. He was fast becoming a creature of the dark, the boy, a mole.

O'Malley waited until nightfall, then saddled up Elektra and took off with the boy. He could see the lights of Kalavryta to the west and he rode toward them.

"You can't tell your pa we came here tonight, Specky, you hear? You gotta keep it a secret. He'll have my guts for garters he finds out."

They tethered the horse by the river and walked back through the field to the house. Danae was still up and they threw pebbles at the window to get her attention. She motioned for them to be quiet, laying her head on her hands to show her father and aunt were asleep.

She crept out of the house a few minutes later. "What are you doing here?" she asked O'Malley.

He pushed the boy forward. "Lad wanted to see you," he said, self-conscious in front of her, as always.

Stefanos buried his face in her apron. "Danae! Danae! *Mou elipses*!" I missed you.

The three of them ended up on the back of the horse, riding along the banks of the river. Elektra's hooves beat a steady rhythm in the sand. It was close to midnight and the glade was very dark—the only illumination, the moon breaking through the clouds. They forded the river and galloped across it to the other side, water splashing high around them, silver in the moonlight.

O'Malley was in the middle, holding Stefanos with one hand, Danae behind him with her arms around his waist.

"Where'd you get the horse?" she whispered in his ear.

"One of *antartes* gave it to me."

"What's her name?"

"I don't know her given name. I call her Elektra, 'cause she's a wild thing, full of energy. Fastest horse in the camp, she is. Maybe in all of Greece. It's like flying being on her. Flying."

He told Danae to close her eyes and imagine they were leaving the earth behind, that Elektra was bearing them up into the sky, the way Pegasus did in the stories. "Feel the wind there? That's her wings beating the air. The dampness? Those are the clouds we're passing through."

Throwing her head back, Danae laughed and laughed. "I love this!" she cried.

O'Malley returned two more times with Stefanos to see her, always late at night after her father and aunt were in bed. They spent many hours on the back of the horse, thundering across the moonlit fields. Once they stayed out until dawn and watched the sun come up over the mountains, Stefanos falling asleep in O'Malley's arms as the sky slowly filled with light.

* * *

RETURNING TO CAMP was always hard after he and the boy had been with her. Stefanos would cry and say he wanted to stay at the house, that he didn't want to go back to the barrel. O'Malley did his best to quiet him down.

The situation with the POWs remained unresolved, and three days later, Leonidas asked him to accompany him to German headquarters, to try to negotiate together in person. "Might be good if von Le Suire knows the British have an interest."

O'Malley nodded. "You're right. Might count for something, that."

Before the two of them left, O'Malley asked Roumelis to cut his hair. "I can't be sitting down with a man like von Le Suire looking the way I do. No, sir, I am a representative of the British Government and His Royal Highness, King George, the seventh."

After Roumelis had finished barbering him, O'Malley boiled a bucket of water and set about washing himself. It was a desperate kind of bath, standing outside with his feet in the bucket, splashing water up and down the length of him. The water was soon cold and he had neither soap nor a towel. The Germans watched him from inside their barbed wire enclosure and made fun of his pasty nakedness, the size of his shriveling man parts, holding up their index fingers and thumbs with barely an inch between them.

O'Malley splashed water on them. "Away with you, you bloody Krauts."

Undeterred, the Germans went on jeering. They'd gotten to know the men in the camp over time, and a reluctant camaraderie had sprung up between them. One of prisoners, a fresh faced youth named Hans, had studied ancient Greek at the University of Heidelberg and used it to converse with Leonidas, translating in turn for the rest of the POWs. Everyone in the camp found this hilarious, charming. The *antartes* dubbed him Homeros—Homer—and sought him out every chance they got. Most of the POWs were from Alsace and had been pressed into military service against their will and were—or so they claimed—unwilling pawns of the Nazis.

Lions and lambs lying down together, though who was the lion and who was the lamb was hard to say. The *antartes* were far more ferocious than their German counterparts, especially their commanding officer—the man named Reiss—who'd remained as he'd been that day in the gorge, bewildered and sickly, totally unsuited for the position he found himself in. His men ignored him, preferring to laugh and joke with their captors. It wasn't quite as it had been during the First World War, when the German and English soldiers had thrown down their arms and sung 'Silent Night' together on Christmas Eve, but it wasn't the battle of Stalingrad either.

The man who spoke Greek had offered to teach Leonidas and him some rudimentary German, a few words to smooth the way with Ebersberger and von Le Suire. They'd spent the previous evening going over various German expressions. Leonidas had balked at *Sieg Heil* so they'd compromised on "*Guten Morgan, Lt. Oberst. Wie geht es Ihnen?*" Good morning, Lt. Colonel. How are you?

O'Malley remained hopeful about the POWs. The Germans had had time to ponder the situation. Surely they didn't want their men to die. It was in their best interest to negotiate. *Aye*, it would all work out. He was convinced of it.

He wrapped the goatskin around his waist and went in search of a uniform. From what he'd seen in Cairo, officers were a breed apart, preferring to socialize in their own mess, drink with their own kind. Given a choice, they'd only have spoken to one another, never the enlisted men under their command.

He assumed the Germans were the same. He'd need braid on his shoulder if he were to impress von Le Suire. Proper garb.

He spoke to Fotis, who was in charge of such things and told him what he needed.

The Greek was hard at work, building another barbed wire corral for the POWs. It was located near the barrel where Stefanos was hiding, the area the *antartes* used as a latrine. Fotis said he planned to move the Germans there as soon as he finished. Give the Greeks more space.

O'Malley chuckled. *Poor Germans.* Smell was bound to get to them. Be a hardship they'd not soon forget.

Digging around in a wooden crate, Fotis pulled out a khaki uniform and handed it to him. It was too short all around. O'Malley could see his wrists and ankles sticking out a good two inches.

Too tall by half.

He sighed, remembering how his mother had despaired of him, "Second time I've let out these pants," she'd said when he was fourteen. "Will you not stop growing for a week at least?"

She'd be scared if she knew what he was about and urge him not to go. His pa would be another story. He'd be proud of the courage his son was displaying, marching into the German headquarters as bold as brass, pretending to be a British officer. Doing his best to save the German POWs, as great a thing as he had ever done.

Idly, O'Malley wondered what had become of the British soldier whose uniform he had on, if he was still alive. Or like the boots he was wearing, it had belonged to a dead man. The thought depressed him. Suited up from top to bottom in the garb of corpses. Pure folly, this.

Leonidas was beautifully kitted out in a sheepskin hat and black leather tunic, boots that reached the knee. He'd tucked his pants into the boots, Russian-style. *Like a member of the Red Army*, O'Malley thought. *Politburo.*

"Be quoting Marx and Engels to me now, will ya?"

The Greek had also trimmed his beard, given the ends of his moustache a bit of a twirl. The tunic was tight across his chest, his powerful shoulders. It did little to alter his slouching homeliness—the sad, dark look of him.

O'Malley straightened his own uniform. "Not bad, eh? In Ireland, girls see a fine figure of a man such as myself, they'd be lining up, wanting to give him the business."

Leonidas actually laughed. "An ass thinks an ass is a pretty fellow."

"What rank in the British Army should I be giving myself?"

"I don't know." Leonidas' mouth twitched. "Corporal."

O'Malley fingered one of the buttons on his uniform. He was looking forward to playing the fool in front of the Germans, pretending to be a British officer. Braying and carrying on like something out of Kipling. He'd even gone so far as to practice his speech, aiming for exactly the right tone—that astounding mix of aristocrat and imbecile that had characterized his British masters in Cairo.

"Forget all that," Leonidas said when he told him. "Don't talk."

"Away with ya. Won't we do better if von Le Suire thinks I'm a decorated personage, a peer of the realm?"

"He'll never think that, you open that Irish mouth of yours." He lit a cigarette and inhaled. "If you're not careful, von Le Suire will hang you."

"I can't just stand there," O'Malley said, unwilling to give it up. "I'll look stupid."

Leonidas went on smoking. "Stupid, yes, but not dead."

"How about I say I'm Australian, a representative of the British Commonwealth?"

"You keep quiet, that's what you do."

* * *

NOT SURE WHEN he'd return, O'Malley fed Elektra and filled her bucket with water. After he finished, he shouldered his rifle and filled his pockets with ammunition.

Stefanos' voice startled him. "*Pou pas?*" he asked sleepily, crawling out of the barrel.

"I'm heading to German headquarters with Leonidas. Got some business to tend to."

"*Pame mazi.*" Take me with you.

"Can't, child. There are a lot of soldiers where we're going. Worse than here. Place is infested."

O'Malley steered him back to the barrel. "Go on now, off with you. Go back to sleep."

The boy hesitated. "*Panagia mazi sou.*" May the Madonna protect you.

"And you, Specky," O'Malley said, touched in spite of himself. "And you."

* * *

HE AND LEONIDAS left on foot. Worried von Le Suire might detain them, the Greek hadn't wanted to risk losing the horses. He had a canvas ammunition bag slung over his shoulder with a captured Luger inside and a handful of

German bullets—proof positive that he had the POWs and was negotiating in good faith.

They were almost to the path when the cook, Roumelis, came chasing after them. He begged them to add sheep to the deal as the camp was running out of meat.

"Germans will never take us seriously if we do that," O'Malley told him. "A man's a man. A sheep's a sheep. Can't go trading one for the other."

Roumelis argued for a few minutes, then turned on his heel and left. "*I peina kastra polemaei kai kastra paradinei*," he bellowed over his shoulder.

"What's that mean?" O'Malley asked Leonidas.

"Wars are lost to hunger."

"Hell, he's a cook. What does he know?"

14

O'MALLEY TOOK HIS cap off and shoved it in a pocket so he wouldn't lose it to the wind. *Not snow*, he judged, studying the gathering clouds. *Rain*.

They had hiked north along the cliff, following the course of the river. "Beyond the monastery is a railroad bridge," Leonidas said. "We'll cross there. It's better than wading across."

O'Malley nodded. Danae had taken him across the same bridge when she'd brought him to the cave. He scanned the walls of the gorge, searching for signs of movement. They'd be totally exposed once they started down the path, pinned against the cliff with no place to hide.

He regretted he hadn't done a head count of the prisoners. "You get all of them the night they ran away? The guns they stole?"

Leonidas frowned. "One's missing."

Shit. They'd made a dog's dinner of it. O'Malley slowed his pace. German might already be dead, come to that, slaughtered by the *antartes* that night. If not, he'd be up ahead, roaming the territory they'd have to pass through, roaming it with a gun.

Evidently, the same thought had occurred to Leonidas, who slowed down and began to move more cautiously. He took his time when they reached the path, inching down with his back against the rocks, gun in hand. O'Malley followed close behind, flattening himself, too, against the face of the cliff.

"I'll speak to the monks," Leonidas said. "They keep an eye out. They'll know if anyone passed this way."

"Sure. Talk with them. Be prudent."

Leonidas said the monastery was called Mega Spileon and that it dated from the fourth century AD. It had been rebuilt many times, most recently in the 1930s after a powder magazine from the War of Independence exploded and burned the place down.

Ammunition in a church? O'Malley chuckled. Would that the Irish fathers had been so brazen.

A monk in a gray habit greeted them and bade them enter. Fingering his beard, he said the others were in the refectory eating and insisted O'Malley and Leonidas join them. It was a humble meal: lentils and bread, a carafe of homemade wine. Although the wine was rough, O'Malley welcomed it, the momentary peace it brought him, the quieting of the buzzing in his head. He drank and drank, recounting stories from Ireland that Leonidas translated as well as he could for the monks, who looked at one another, shocked by O'Malley's loudness.

Still talking, O'Malley lit a cigarette. "Ah, tobacco, soothes you, so it does. I was but eight the first time I smoked a cigarette and didn't I go and set myself ablaze with the thing? Pants were smoldering, smoke pouring out of my skivvies. Pa heard me yelling and came running. Quick as a wink, I stuffed the cigarette down in the sofa—burning all the while, mind you—so he wouldn't know what I'd been up to. My mother's prized possession, it was, that sofa, held pride of place in the family parlor. Torched it good and proper, I did. In a panic, I picked up a pillow and began batting at the flames, took out the lamp next to it and their wedding picture. My pa was ready to eat me."

"My friend talks like a woman," Leonidas said drily. "He has an electric tongue."

O'Malley pretended to take offense and they clowned around for a moment, the monks laughing timidly.

The two of them visited the church before they left. The smell inside reminded O'Malley of the Catholic sanctuaries of his youth, the tallow and lingering trace of incense. All of it was deeply familiar. Facing the altar, he knelt down and crossed himself, prayed for the success of their mission.

An elderly monk walked out of the church with them, and he and Leonidas lingered on the steps for a minute, talking. He was wearing a stiff, conical hat with a heavy black cloth draped over it, similar to the wimple nuns wore, only with a much higher crown. Worried, the monk kept pointing to the monastery, repeating something over and over.

When they were underway again, Leonidas explained the cloth was a symbolic veil, designed to prevent the monk from seeing the world. "It's called *kalymafki*."

"He seemed pretty stirred up. What was he going on about?"

"What they should do if the Germans come."

"What'd you tell him?"

Leonidas' smile was grim. "I told him to get away as fast as they could."

What a sight that would be. The monks holding on to their hats as they ran, their black cloaks flapping in the breeze. Four and twenty blackbirds baked in a pie. He wondered what the Germans would do—if they'd hesitate at killing holy men, if the monks' vocation would stop them.

* * *

"How we going to keep von Le Suire from killing us the minute he sees us?"

"He goes by the rules. We'll be all right."

"What about your lot? From what I've seen, they're not big on rules. Chasing hither and yon. Like something out of the Dark Ages, you were, the night the Germans got away. Had the bloodlust in your eyes, you did. You should have seen yourselves. Burn 'em alive, they will, I thought, same as they did the heretics during the Inquisition. All your lot needed was kindling and a match. If they kill those POWs while we're negotiating, we're done for."

"They won't kill them. They gave me their word."

Wasn't much, but it would have to do. O'Malley didn't know what the word of a Greek was worth. In Ireland, it meant a great deal, a man judged poorly, shunned even, if he didn't abide by it. He prayed the Greeks were the same.

The two of them walked on in uncomfortable silence, reaching the railroad bridge a few minutes later. Spanning the river, it was smaller than O'Malley remembered. It had started to rain and the river was rising. They'd have to walk on the tracks of the bridge, he saw; there was no place beneath it that was dry enough.

"We'll have to wait," Leonidas said. "It's dangerous to cross the bridge when the trains are running."

Holding their hands over their heads, they sprinted toward the bridge. The slope was already slippery, thick with mud, and they clutched at each other for support. They sat down under the bridge, clinging to the metal pilings with their hands, a few feet above the raging water. The rain continued to drum down.

O'Malley could see the monastery in the distance, the path running like a scar up the cliff behind it. The cliff was streaked with rain, the white limestone shiny and glossy with damp. Aside from the path, there'd be no way to traverse it that he could see. You'd have to climb it same as you did a mountain, banging out toeholds with a hammer.

As always, the land was the Greeks' greatest ally, far better than an army at keeping the enemy at bay. It made him feel better, knowing Stefanos was there; the Germans would never get him, not up there.

"The cliffs are impassable," Leonidas said, following his gaze. "The only way around them is along the river. That day with the trucks is the only time

I've ever seen the Germans attempt it. That man commanding them, he didn't know what he was doing."

"Happens. Officers misjudge the distance and back their tanks over their own men. Read a map wrong and order units under their command straight into enemy fire. British were always carping at us about the proper way to address them, never cared a farthing that I could see about keeping us alive. It's the nature of the thing. Officers stay well back, away from the line of fire, while the poor eejits at the front get destroyed."

At midday, a train went by, pulling two wooden passenger cars. German soldiers were in both of the cars, looking out the open windows, watching the world go by in a bored way.

Seemed a funny kind of troop train, O'Malley thought. Perhaps they were on leave, the soldiers, taking in the sights. The train slowed a few minutes later, jerking as it inched up the steep grade, its metal wheels clicking like a roller coaster's.

"Cogs," Leonidas told him. "That's how it pulls itself up. Greeks call it '*odontotos*,' tooth train. The Italians built it."

The train continued to climb, swaying back and forth as it bore its load up over the mountain. O'Malley could hear its wheels clanging against the metal track long after it had disappeared from view. "Be a good target."

"You a demolitions expert?"

O'Malley nodded. "Blown up a few things in my time."

They talked about setting charges and blowing up the train, both of them knowing it would come to nothing. The train was too small and had no military value. Wouldn't be worth the dynamite it would take to destroy it, the risk to the men.

"The British Army dynamited a bridge on the way to Salonica," O'Malley said. "Kept the Germans from supplying Rommel for close to six weeks. They'd been running forty-eight supply trains a day on that line. It was a great loss to them."

He studied the tracks overhead, remembering the sad little train that had passed over them. *Nothing like that here. Nothing anyone would ever notice.*

"It was a Greek, Napoleon Zervas, not the British, who blew that bridge," Leonidas said quietly. "Zervas and EDES."

Surprised, O'Malley stared at him, open-mouthed. Zervas was a well-known right wing guerrilla, one of the few Greeks his overseers in Cairo had trusted.

"I'm neither ELAS or EDES," Leonidas said by way of explanation. "I am only a patriot."

"Why are you in this outfit, then? Fighting alongside the likes of Alexis and Haralambos?"

"They were the best fighters at the beginning. More disciplined and better organized than the rest. Now ...." He made a hopeless gesture. "Now, they are different."

It continued to pour. A proper Irish storm, it was, O'Malley thought, remembering the way the clouds had boiled up over Cork, rain washing down and turning day into night. Not the people, though. No, the Irish people, they were full of light.

Curious how that was. Here, it was the people who were dark. He'd listened to the men complain about their mothers-in-law and the sourness of their wives. A form of combat, it seemed, marriage here, love rarely entering into it. Unlike his ma and pa, who'd laughed and joked always, turning adversity into a kind of triumph.

He pulled the damp *flokati* away from him, worrying the smell would transfer to his uniform. He sniffed at himself. *Damnation*, it was there. *Eau de bloody goat.*

Wasn't just the smell. Weighted down as it was, he'd have a hard time walking in the thing, let alone impressing the German high command.

"Train's come and gone. Why are we sitting here? Why don't we cross?"

"There's another one due."

"Bloody hell."

The other train passed by a few minutes later. "Now," Leonidas said.

They were about to cross the bridge when the first stone came crashing down. Bouncing off the cliff, it fell into the river with a loud splash. A second stone followed and then a third. They weren't big stones, but they made O'Malley nervous. Squinting against the rain, he looked up at the cliff.

"Cover me," he told Leonidas.

Dropping to the ground, he crawled on his belly through the mud. He paused when he reached the path, wiped his face, and studied the cliff again. *Aye*, someone was there all right, stoning them from on high. Pulling out his gun, O'Malley crouched down and started running toward him.

He stopped dead a moment later. "Christ Almighty. It's Specky."

Oblivious to the rain, the boy was apparently on patrol, standing tall and swinging his arms back and forth. He had his suitcase in one hand, a long stick in the other, which he held like a rifle, imitating the men in the camp. When he saw O'Malley, he threw down the stick and rushed toward him.

"*Se vrika!*" he crowed. I found you.

"Lord, child, what are you doing here?"

Fotis had shifted the Germans in the camp, the boy reported, and parked them in the field next to the barrel. He'd been afraid, hadn't liked the sound of men speaking German, and had gone in search of him.

"You should have stayed in the camp, Stefanos. It's no good, you coming here."

"*Se vrika,*" the boy repeated, softer now, tears in his voice.

Standing there in his dripping clothes, he looked like something that had been dredged up from the sea in a net—a damp, wiggling creature. An otter, maybe. Waterlogged and none too steady.

He took his glasses off and wiped them on his sleeve. "*Den tha pao mazi sou. Tha pao piso ston patera mou.*" I won't go with you. I'll go back to my father.

No point in telling him the danger he'd be in. No point in scaring him further. "*Aye*, home, Specky. That's the ticket."

Home.

Reaching for the suitcase, O'Malley steered him down the path. "Leonidas, we have a visitor."

* * *

O'Malley argued against taking the boy back to the camp. It would only delay them and Stefanos would just run away again. At least this way, they could keep an eye on him. It remained a riddle how the boy had found them in the first place. Seen them from the top of the cliff and rolled the rocks down to alert them of his presence.

Could be he'd underestimated Specky, O'Malley told himself. Maybe he had unknown abilities, was a kind of human bloodhound, able to track people for close to two miles in the pouring rain. Maybe he could see things other people missed through those foggy glasses of his.

The rails of the bridge were slippery, and O'Malley warned the boy to watch his step. He could feel the trestles shifting underfoot, a faint tremor as the wind tore through the girders. The storm was picking up, blinding flashes of lightning erupting from the sky.

"*Keravnos!*" Stefanos yelled, transfixed.

Yanking him by the arm, O'Malley fought his way forward. A suspension bridge was no place to be in a thunderstorm. A bolt of lightning hit the metal, it'd kill them instantly, the charge running through their bodies and electrocuting them. Leonidas was already across, and he called for them to hurry.

They followed the railroad tracks for nearly a mile, rain lashing their faces. Although it was easier than slogging through the mud, O'Malley didn't like being out in the open on the tracks, fearing they were too exposed.

"We going to follow the train all the way to Kalavryta? Seems a risky thing to do. German patrol passes by, they'll spot us."

"There's a tunnel up ahead. Once we pass through it, we'll head down to the river."

Stefanos didn't like the tunnel and began to wail, his high-pitched voice ricocheting off the stone walls until O'Malley thought he'd lose his mind.

"Lord above. Will you not stop your yapping? Hear you in Berlin, they will!"

The child quieted down after they exited the tunnel, intent on rescuing a lizard that had fallen into a pool of rainwater a few feet from the tracks.

Leonidas pulled him back. "*Oxi! Narkes!*" Mines.

That set him off again. "*Narkes!*"

It'd been a bad idea, bringing the boy along, O'Malley now realized. Lad was going to pieces. He had no business trudging alongside Leonidas and him in the pouring rain, following two soldiers into a war zone.

He wondered what the kid would have been like had the war not come, if he would have been a normal boy. He'd been damaged by it, that much was certain. Broken down entirely.

"Let's not go near the burnt trucks. The dead festering there along the shore. Boy's about done in—no need to make it worse."

He'd no need of a view himself, come to that. He'd seen his share of dead in medical school—skeletons dangling on hooks, their vertebrae jingling whenever the wind blew. Worse still had been in Athens, the piles of bones he'd seen in a cemetery there. The custom in Greece was to disinter the dead after five years and place their remains in a metal box, but the war had disrupted the process and there'd been bones everywhere, femurs, tibias, and skulls scattered across the dusty ground.

If he'd had any illusion about what would become of one's earthly remains, those bones had dispelled it. He'd seen firsthand the way flesh changes as it decays and surrenders to the earth. The Bible had it right: ashes to ashes, dust to dust, and so it was with man.

Be altogether better if he and Leonidas went a different way.

They were deep in the gorge now. Engorged with rainwater, the river was spilling over the banks, and the air was saturated with moisture. Shivering, O'Malley burrowed down in the flokati.

Stefanos sat down a few minutes later and refused to move. "*An ixame to alogo den tha perpatousame.*" If we had the horse we wouldn't have to walk.

O'Malley wanted to throttle him. "We don't have a horse."

"*Tha itan kalitera an ixes feri to alogo.*" It would have been better if you'd brought the horse.

"Enough of your cheek. Get up and start walking."

A few minutes later, he sat down again. "*Yiati den eferes to alogo?*" Why didn't you bring the horse?

"Drive me out of my wits, you will. Get up, you hear? Get up before I skin you alive."

Stefanos continued to fuss about the horse, the never-ending journey and how tired he was. Finally, O'Malley hoisted him up on his shoulders, thinking it'd go better. At least then he'd be quiet. He was heavy, but not as heavy as he should have been, given his age. The war had cost him there, too.

Delighted, Stefanos reached for the branches of the trees as O'Malley passed beneath them, tugging them down and releasing them like catapults, showering them with raindrops. He thought this a great game and screamed with laughter. The sky was clearing, weak sunlight filtering down to the floor of the gorge.

"*Tragouda*," Stefanos ordered. Sing.

O'Malley obediently yodeled "Mrs. Murphy's Overhauls" in a high-pitched voice, translating the words into Greek as he went along.

"*Pantalonosoupa*," the boy yelled, clapping his hands together. Pant soup.

To pass the time, they concocted recipes for even odder kinds of soup—soup with stones, soup with bed sheets.

"Socks," Leonidas offered.

"*Sferes*," Stefanos said. Bullets.

"That'll do you nicely, that will. A spicy broth, that'd make."

Giggling, the child sang the Irish song. It was difficult for him to get his mouth around the foreign words, but he kept trying. As always, he was good natured and smiled down at O'Malley, made funny faces.

They were nearing the area where they'd captured the POWs. Heeding O'Malley's advice, Leonidas led them to higher ground, away from the burned-out trucks. The trees near the vehicles were thick with crows. Tens of them cawed raucously in the branches. There were vultures, too, black and ungainly, perched in the highest branches, drawn as the crows had been by the scent of death. Wings extended, one floated down near a corpse in the river and began pecking at it, pulling off strips of flesh and gobbling them down.

Sickened by the sight, O'Malley pulled out his revolver and aimed it at the bird.

Leonidas stayed his hand. "The noise," he warned.

The vulture raised its head, watched them indifferently, then returned to its feeding.

It was the ugliest thing O'Malley had ever seen. Hunchbacked, with shiny, black eyes and a tuft of moldy-looking feathers around its wattled neck, it was like something out of a Bosch painting, sinister and grotesque—of this world and yet not.

"What do you call a bird like that?" he asked Leonidas.

"*Gypas.* Always hungry."

And so the thing was. As close to an embodiment of death as O'Malley had ever seen. He longed to shoot it. Kill it and all its fellows. Belonged to the devil, a beast like that. God had played no hand in its creation.

"Why didn't your lot bury them? Be better than this."

"There wasn't time. We had to get away."

"I've got a shovel. I'll bury them on the way back. Can't leave them like this, Leonidas. Fodder for crows."

They continued to walk, moving away from the trucks and deeper into the gorge. O'Malley's shoulders ached and he longed to rest. "Why don't we stop for the night?" he asked. "Bed down and walk the rest of the way in the morning."

Leonidas nodded. "There's a little island in the middle of the river. We can sleep there."

The clouds were breaking up when they finally halted, a new moon rising over the rim of the canyon. O'Malley heard an owl call from the shadows. Just once, the sound as piercing as a train whistle. Seeing how tired he was, Leonidas volunteered to carry Stefanos across the river. The boy was very sleepy and patted O'Malley's head as they made the transfer.

"Go on ahead," O'Malley said, sinking down on the sand. "I'll be along in a minute. Just let me catch my breath."

He dozed off and woke up with a start. Disoriented, he looked around, wondering where Leonidas and the boy had gotten to.

Taking off his boots, he stepped into the dark water, thinking he'd head for the island. He inched toward it one step at a time, afraid he'd lose his balance and get swept away by the current. The ancient Greeks had been afraid to enter the Styx, Danae had told him, believing its waters could dissolve glass, silver, and gold—all manner of things. Only a horse's hoof could withstand it. Old people were still afraid of it. Her grandmother had called it *Mavroneri* until the day she died, Danae said. The black water.

"Can't tell if my feet are dissolving," O'Malley muttered. All sensation was lost to the cold. "But my balls are sure having a time of it."

He stumbled ashore and called out to the others. "Leonidas! Stefanos! Damn it, where are you?" But all was quiet, the undergrowth deep in shadows. He took off his pants and wrung them out, then put them back on and laced up his boots. His legs ached as sensation returned to them, tingling painfully as if someone was sticking hatpins in them. He looked back at the river. It was indeed a black thing, winding sluggishly around the rocks like a snake. Here and there a flicker of moonlight caught the water, furthering the illusion of movement, of scales.

The reeds around him rustled in the wind, creaking and groaning in a way that was eerily human. Yelling for Leonidas, he pushed his way through the thicket, the sharp edges of the reeds raking his face and cutting into his skin. He tripped a moment later and went sprawling. The ground was frozen and he hit it hard. Cursing, he stayed where he was for a moment, spitting dirt out of his mouth.

Something was moving on the ground next to him. A scorpion crawled out of the reeds a moment later, its barbed tail jiggling slightly as it came toward him.

O'Malley looked around for something to kill it with. It was then he noticed the others. The reeds were alive with them. He must have fallen into a nest. He lay very still, forcing himself not to flinch as the insects crawled around him. The sound of their scrabbling filled him with terror. "Oh God, Leonidas, help!"

The Greek came running. He stopped when he saw the scorpions and took a step back. "Don't move," he cautioned.

He set one of the reeds on fire with a match and waved it at the bugs, stomping them to death as they ran. In a few seconds, he had burned a wide circle around O'Malley. The smoke made the bugs sluggish, their bodies slowly curling up as they died.

O'Malley got to his feet and brushed himself off, unable to shake the feeling he still had bugs crawling on him. "Put the heart crossways in me, so they did."

"You're lucky they didn't sting you."

Leonidas continued to wave the smoldering twig back and forth. "It's an evil creature, the scorpion, can poison even in death."

To illustrate his point, he recited a story he claimed was from Aesop:

"A scorpion and a frog met by a river. The water was high and the scorpion knew he couldn't get across, so he begged the frog to carry him.

" 'Please,' the scorpion said. 'Please.' " Pretending to be the insect, Leonidas spoke in a squeaky voice.

" 'But you'll sting me,' the frog said."

Raising his arm over his head, Leonidas curved it, imitating the tail of a scorpion. " 'I would never do that,' " he said in the same squeaky voice. " 'If I sting you, we will both drown.'

"The frog thought this over and agreed, and the two of them set out across the river. They were almost to the other side when the scorpion reared up and stung the frog.

" 'Why,' the frog croaked as he sank beneath the water. 'Why?'

"The scorpion shrugged. 'It is my nature.' "

Stefanos loved the story and clapped his hands. "*Skorpios! Skorpios!*" Brandishing a stick, he re-enacted the fiery battle against the scorpions, stomping his feet and shouting, "*Psofise! Psofise!*" Die, die.

O'Malley smiled. " 'It is my nature,' that's good, that is. You're a man of many talents, Leonidas. You make a fine scorpion."

"Been fighting the Nazis a long time. Had to learn their ways."

The three of them bedded down for the night on the island. O'Malley shook out the boy's blanket, picked him up, and deposited him down on top of it. "Now don't you move, you hear? You stay on the blanket." He was afraid the boy would kick over his gun in his sleep, accidentally blow a hole in him.

With Specky, one never knew. He always brought trouble with him. It was his great gift.

15

Stefanos got up before O'Malley and Leonidas made them breakfast, laying out leaves and twigs on the ground, a snail that he claimed was an *avgo*. Egg.

He reprimanded it when it crawled off the leaf, its little feelers wiggling, chased after it and brought it back, handling it gently as he set it back down.

Sitting cross-legged, O'Malley pretended to gobble up the leaves. He told Stefanos he didn't like eggs and that Leonidas could have them.

Leonidas picked up the snail and licked its shell. "*Poli nostimo*," he told Stefanos. "*Mporo na exo kai allo?*" Very tasty. May I have another?

The boy shook his head. "*Ftani pia*." That's enough for you.

Although the air was so cold it hurt to breathe, Stefanos took no notice. Lying next to the river, he dipped his hand in the icy water and came running over to O'Malley. "*Café*," he cried, pouring it out at his feet.

He then opened up the suitcase, set the carved animals out, and fed them too, chastising the pig when it took too much. He seemed calmer today, less hysterical.

Must have been those long hours alone yesterday, O'Malley thought, *him chasing after us in the pouring rain, worrying the whole time the Germans were after him, braying at his heels like a pack of Dobermans.*

The water had risen during the night, and O'Malley had to carry him back across the river. The boy kept bouncing around, complaining that he was getting wet.

"Drown me, so you will, you little gobshit, same as the scorpion did in the story. Drown the only one who ever showed you a spot of kindness."

The sun was up, slatted light filtering down and illuminating the floor of the gorge. He could see tendrils of grass at the bottom of the river, coiling and uncoiling like the hair of a drowned woman. So it was the grass that gave the water its black color …. *Not a gateway to hell*, he thought sheepishly, only clumps of seaweed, stirring in the current.

* * *

THEY SKIRTED AROUND Kalavryta and headed west. They climbed a series of low-lying hills and passed through a rockbound valley, eventually emerging on the side of an ancient lakebed.

"German headquarters is on the other side," Leonidas said, "two, maybe three kilometers away."

O'Malley didn't approve of the route. It was too open. They should have come another way. "We'd best be careful. Very soon there'll be no place to hide."

They studied the landscape for a moment, then made their way forward and started across the plain. Leonidas was in front, O'Malley and Stefanos to the rear. They spoke idly as they walked.

O'Malley saw now the plain was much larger than he'd originally thought, not a lakebed. The remnants of some vast, prehistoric sea. Looking out across it, he could almost hear the cry of gulls, smell the cleansing tang of salt in the air. He wondered how old it was, when the water had receded for the last time. It was being farmed now, he saw. Furrows were etched in the red earth as far as the eye could see. Long lines of saplings and brush divided the landholdings, forming windbreaks and separating one man's plot from another. Bare hills rose on three sides, bearded here and there with stunted pines. To the south lay a rocky highland. A large olive orchard covered area in between. O'Malley signaled for Leonidas to head toward it.

Staying well back, the Greek proceeded cautiously. Crouching low to the ground, he entered the orchard first and then nodded for O'Malley and Stefanos to follow. The olive trees were very old, their thick gray trunks as gnarled and lifeless as driftwood. To O'Malley, they seemed in pain, twisted like the body of an Australian POW he'd seen a photo of, caught on an electric fence outside a German prison camp. They seemed to embody the same agony.

A kind of no man's land separated the orchard from the rest of the plain, a slight rise covered with trees. O'Malley welcomed the shelter the trees would provide. *Safer*, he told himself.

They stayed in the forested area as long as they could, the yellowing grass underfoot deadening the sound of their passage. No one spoke. Sooner or later, they'd have to move out into the open and cross the plain. There was no other way to go.

Uneasy, O'Malley kept looking around. He didn't understand it. There were no Germans about. He'd have heard them long before.

He pulled Stefanos behind him and motioned for Leonidas to get down. They waited like that for a few minutes before continuing. Still worried, O'Malley kept an eye out and gestured for Leonidas to stop again. Ahead, he saw a lighted opening, the place where the forest gave way to open ground. Afraid to go forward, they stayed in the trees, whatever had bothered O'Malley now affecting the other two.

Suddenly, a flock of birds took flight and filled the sky. There was a copse of poplar trees on the far side of the plain. Whatever had startled the birds had come from there.

The boy dropped immediately to the ground and set about burying himself in the leaves. Aside from the screeching of the birds, all was quiet.

A crack of gunfire broke the silence, set the birds in motion again. "Is it the birds or us they're after?"

Leonidas already had his revolver out. "Gun's big, nothing a hunter would use."

"Germans, then. They see us?"

"I don't know."

O'Malley looked down at the boy, the leaves he'd mounded around himself for protection. "Any chance we can get away?"

"They're close. I don't think so."

"A white flag then?"

"Can't. Not with the boy."

Aye, he was right. Even if they surrendered, Stefanos would go to pieces in German hands. He wouldn't stand a chance.

A volley of gunfire ended the discussion. The bullets tore up the red earth in front of them.

"Back," O'Malley urged.

Stefanos didn't move. He just lay where he was, buried in his little pile of leaves. O'Malley grabbed him by the ankles and pulled him away, deep into the trees. As soon as he let go, the boy burrowed down into the leaves again. He was trembling all over.

"Come on, Specky! We've got to get out of here!"

The boy was crying softly, trying to muffle the sound with his hand. O'Malley didn't want to grab him a second time, afraid the movement would alert the Germans if it hadn't already. He could see Leonidas crawling through the underbrush on his belly, heading to a stony rise to the left. There were stones piled at the top of it, what looked like the ruins of a house. O'Malley pointed them out to the boy. "There" he whispered. "It's our only chance."

Motioning for Stefanos to follow him, he began inching toward the rise on his hands and knees. He fumbled to get his gun out, to get ready.

"*Perimene me!*" the boy cried. Wait for me.

The Germans fired again, the bullets tearing chunks of bark off the trees.

"*Perimene me!*" Stefanos cried again.

Getting up, he began darting in and out of the trees. He started running toward O'Malley, but then seemed to change his mind. Pausing for a second, he picked up a handful of leaves and threw them over himself.

"Specky, stop, stop! They'll kill you!"

The boy didn't seem to hear. He just stood there rooted to the ground with leaves in his hair.

Getting to his feet, O'Malley raced toward him, thinking he'd throw him to the ground, anything to keep him still. But the boy scampered off before he could reach him. In a burst of speed, he turned and lit out across the lakebed.

"Christ, child, stop your running! Get down!"

Stefanos almost got away. He was moving that fast. But then two soldiers emerged from the copse of trees.

Stefanos hesitated for a moment, then turned and started back toward where Leonidas and O'Malley were hiding.

For a moment, O'Malley thought he was going to make it, but then, sensing movement, one of the soldiers raised his gun and fired. The shot hit Stefanos in the stomach. Clutching his bleeding gut, the boy staggered and fell.

Then like vultures, they descended.

Without saying a word, the two soldiers ran to where Stefanos was lying and rolled him over. They hadn't been expecting a child and looked around nervously when they saw what they had done. Both of them had dead rabbits slung over their shoulders. Hunters.

O'Malley held back, afraid that if he fired at them, he'd hit Stefanos and wound him further. The Germans hastily retreated, backing away and disappearing over the hill.

A child, he hadn't been worth a second bullet.

Disturbed by the noise, the birds wheeled around in circles, shrieking and cawing.

The child lay crumbled up on the ground like a broken toy. While Leonidas kept watch, O'Malley gathered him up in his arms. He tried to stop the bleeding with his hands, pressing his palms hard against him, all the while knowing it was useless. He could feel the life ebbing out of him, see it pooling there on the ground.

The frames of his spectacles were shattered, the glass ground into his eyes. O'Malley wondered if he could even see him. "Specky," he whispered.

The boy turned his head, reached out his hand, feeling feebly along the ground for him.

Remembering how the boy had loved Elektra, O'Malley told him the horse was coming for him now.

"With wings, lad, huge white wings beating the air to carry you home. It'll be the ride of a lifetime. Up through the stars you'll go. Horse will be wild, battling comets and dancing on the rings of Saturn. Higher and higher you'll go. Her mane will be on fire, sparks flying from her hooves. She'll guide you to the heaven, she will, lead you safely through the darkness, the long, endless night." Choking back tears, O'Malley continued, "It'll be grand, lad, you'll see. Grand."

The boy gave a weak smile. He died a moment later.

Grabbing his hand, O'Malley held it up to his face.

Stefanos' mouth was open, a new tooth breaking through the gums. Sobbing, O'Malley clutched the child's shattered body, repeating his name over and over.

"Ah, Specky, Specky. Would it had been me. Lord God, child, would it had been me."

* * *

LEONIDAS CROSSED HIMSELF when O'Malley told him Stefanos was dead. The Germans had vanished, and all was quiet again, save for the clamoring of the birds.

"I'll take him back to Kalavryta. Bury him there."

He picked up the body and raised it onto his shoulders, held Stefanos by his lifeless arms. He stopped about halfway across the plain, thinking he'd felt the child stir, but it had just been the shifting of the body, the dead weight of it.

16

Later, O'Malley didn't remember much about the journey. The body of the boy stiffening on his back, the screeching of the crows overhead. Worse was the cold, the terrible cold that seemed to come from within. The day was overcast, the fields by Kalavryta drained of color. Borne by the wind, dead leaves whirled around, skittering and clawing at the ground by his feet. O'Malley walked heedlessly, not caring what became of him.

He occasionally talked to the boy, telling him the things he'd do when he grew up, where he'd take him and what they'd see. But mostly he wept.

Leonidas accompanied him, saying he'd never find his way back to Kalavryta on his own.

O'Malley had cleaned Stefanos up as much as he could, removing the broken shards of glass from his face and eyes, not wanting the child's family to see what had been done to him. He'd wetted his cap and used it to wash the congealed blood off the boy's clothes and hands. He'd been wounded terribly, O'Malley saw, the bullet catching him at an angle and ripping him apart. The Germans hadn't known how to kill a kid. They'd made a mess of it.

O'Malley made no effort to hide himself or his ghastly burden on the trip to Kalavryta. Although Leonidas cautioned against it, he did it on purpose, hoping to provoke the Germans, wanting a chance to bloody them the way they had the child.

The streets were empty when they reached the town. This surprised O'Malley. Somehow he'd expected shouting and screams to greet them, for the village to give voice to his grief.

"Where is everyone?"

"Sleeping. It's early."

Again, he felt that same sense of surprise. Sleeping? Yet Stefanos was dead.

They crossed through the field where he and the boy had flown the kite. Parts of it still hung from the tree, string tangled in the branches, the rest scattered on the ground below. The newspaper that made up its body was waterlogged and a remnant of the yellow tail was awash with mud. O'Malley had to stop then, couldn't see for his tears.

* * *

DANAE SCREAMED WHEN she saw the body. She'd been hanging up laundry outside and had smiled at first when she saw O'Malley approaching, singing out '*Angle*' and laughing a little.

But now she was on her knees, bent nearly to the ground, keening and weeping over her brother's lifeless form. "Stefanos! No! It can't be! It can't, it can't!"

She yelled for her father to come. Hearing her distress, he rushed out of the house a few seconds later, her aunt close on his heels. They knelt down beside the boy's body and began stroking his face, his arms and legs. They smoothed down his matted hair, brushing their hands against him and pulling back quickly as if the boy's icy flesh stung them.

O'Malley helped the father carry the body into the house and lay it out. The father then left with Danae to alert the priest and prepare the grave.

O'Malley had been expecting recriminations, questions as to how he'd let the boy die, but there'd been none of that. Only grief, this solid wall of grief, sealing them in and shutting him and all he represented out.

Shaking out a tablecloth, the aunt stretched it out over the table in the kitchen and set out plates and glasses, preparing for the mourners she said would come.

"I thought he'd be safe. His father told me, 'You don't have to worry about Stefanos anymore. He's with the *antartes*.' 'Where?' I asked, 'at the top of the gorge? Above Mega Spileon?'" She dabbed at her eyes with a handkerchief.

"Everyone told me he'd be safe there, everyone." Her voice was petulant, as if she were the one who'd been betrayed, the child's death a broken promise.

O'Malley said he needed to get some air and stepped outside. If Toula Papadakis knew the location of the camp, others did, too. He'd have to warn Leonidas. Warn him the Germans probably knew, too, and would be coming for them, that they needed to shut the camp down and be quick about it.

He could hear the aunt weeping inside. He had no desire to comfort her. "Bloody fool."

Danae and her father returned a few hours later. "The man who takes care of the cemetery won't dig the grave," the father said wearily. "We have no money to pay him and he won't do it for free."

"I'll do it," O'Malley volunteered.

Grabbing a shovel, he followed the father to the cemetery. Close to the river, it was a far poorer place than the graveyard he'd hidden in with Danae and the boy that first day.

There were no crypts to speak of, only mounds of earth surrounded by little, gilded fences. Serving as headstones, metal boxes held oil lamps and books of matches, faded photographs of the deceased edged in black. A few had wreaths on them, the flowers gone nearly white from the sun.

Picking up a stick, Danae's father drew a long oblong shape on the ground and told O'Malley that's where he wanted it. At first, O'Malley didn't understand his haste, but then he remembered: the Greeks buried their dead quickly, within twenty-four hours if at all possible. The grave was to face east, the man said, as was the custom.

Damp with rain, the soil was soft and malleable, and O'Malley quickly dug a deep trench. He cried as he worked, wiping his eyes on his sleeve of his jacket.

Danae appeared at some point and stood watching him. Dry-eyed, she didn't speak.

Keeping his head down, O'Malley continued to labor. " 'Twas all my fault, this," he said after a time. "Every bit of it."

In a dull voice, he described the child's death to her. How the Germans had seen them and Stefanos had panicked and ran. "I tried to stop him, but he was going too fast. Trying to get home, he was. Back to Kalavryta."

Climbing out the grave, O'Malley came and stood beside her. "I tried to stop him," he said again. "I'd have gladly traded my life for his. I didn't want this, Danae. I didn't want this."

* * *

SOMEONE—THE AUNT, O'MALLEY guessed—had dressed the boy's body in new clothes and combed his hair. The clothes were far too big, the fabric shiny and cheap. She'd probably purchased them in the *laiki*, the open-air market, that morning. His shoes were the ones O'Malley knew, freshly polished.

He helped the father lift the boy and settle him in the little coffin. How strange Stefanos looked without his glasses, he thought, those grandfatherly goggles he always wore. His coffin was a small pine box, so short they'd had to struggle—bend the boy's knees and tuck his head down—in order to fit him in. It was lined with purple cloth, and the top was flimsy—light as cardboard.

The father propped the boy up on a pillow filled with earth and placed a small wooden icon on his forehead. A group of elderly women arrived shortly after, dressed entirely in black. They filed past the open coffin and kissed the icon, then pulled up chairs and sat down in a circle around it and talked for few minutes, recounting the news of the village. Finally they sat back with their hands on their knees, and one of them began to chant in an angry tone, her voice rising to a crescendo as she complained to God in Greek. After a long moment, the cry was taken up by a second woman. The call and response continued until each of the women had had her turn, singing out in protest at the death of the child, mourning him in a kind of rough poetry.

When they finished, they paused for a moment, then started up again, wiping their eyes as they chanted:

> I had a little bird in a cage and it was tame, O Mother
> I fed it on sugar, gave it balm to drink, O Mother
> It fled its cage and left me, come golden bird
> Where you once drank sweet wine, I now drink vinegar

On and on it went. Some of the verses were directed to the body in the coffin:

> Stefanos, the earth has eaten your childhood.

While others gave voice to their own losses:

> I had my child as the sun.
> My child was light to me and now I walk in darkness.

Their ancestors had probably sounded the same when the news was brought back from Troy, O'Malley thought. Or Jerusalem, as Mary and the myrrh-bearing women prepared Jesus' body for burial. The eternal cry of the mother, the keening of a heartsick mother whose child is lost—somewhere between a dirge and a howl.

O'Malley's people had been stoic, tight-lipped in the presence of death, and the old women's grieving unnerved him. It was like listening to an animal being torn to pieces in front of him. Out of the Old Testament, this was. *Absalom, Absalom.*

In the old days, women used to do similar sorts of things in Ireland when someone died. But it was more prayerful, he remembered, the wailing directed at God, imploring Him to accept the soul of the departed. It wasn't this angry, animal bleating. He could still see his grandmother, the way she'd rocked herself back and forth the night his grandfather died, chanting and mumbling inarticulately. At times she'd imitated the death rattle, only to give a shriek of triumph a moment later. She'd grabbed a handful of ashes from the hearth and scattered them by the open door of the house, as was customary in Ireland, to exorcise evil spirits that barred the soul's flight to Paradise. After she'd finished, she'd stood up and cried with great feeling, "God of glory! Have mercy now and open your gates."

"Amen," his mother and father had intoned. "Amen."

The priest arrived at the house the next morning. He was older than Father Chronis, with a white beard and a clumsy, palsied gait. The old crones had arrived before him and stood up when he came into the room. Holding a lighted candle, he mumbled some prayers over the body and led them outside. One of the women came forward as the coffin left the house and flung a clay pitcher out the door, taking care to break it on the steps as the body passed. *To protect the living*, O'Malley thought, same as his grandmother had done with the ashes, to keep evil spirits and death from returning here. Another woman slipped a coin into the child's lifeless hands.

There was only a small group of people at the church—Danae, her father and aunt, the men who'd served as pallbearers and the old women who'd chanted the laments. The latter trailed after the coffin in a group, holding aloft a platter of boiled wheat and a bottle of wine. All the women wore black dresses, kerchiefs, and stockings. The father had on a black tie and a black armband.

Seeing the armband, O'Malley again was reminded of Cork—the black, diamond-shaped patches people sewed on their sleeves and wore for a year following the death of a loved one. *We're all the same*, he thought. *In death, we are all the same.*

Danae looked over at him and smiled faintly, her eyes glassy with tears.

He and Leonidas had kept well away from the square as they made their way to the church. Leonidas counseled against attending the funeral, saying it was unsafe, but O'Malley insisted. Seeing how few people there were, he was glad that he had.

The villagers had drawn back at the sight of the procession, standing in doorways and crossing themselves as the coffin passed by. It had been very quiet. No one in the church turned around when Leonidas and O'Malley entered. The women especially seemed frightened by their presence.

"They don't want us here," Leonidas whispered. "They worry our presence in the village will draw the Germans."

Swinging the censor, the priest chanted the service. He spoke quickly, as if in a hurry to be done. "Give rest, O God, unto your servant and appoint for him a place in paradise, where the choirs of the saints, O Lord, and the just will shine forth like stars."

After the service, everyone walked behind the coffin up to the graveyard. Again, the priest was hasty, emptying wine over the body in the shape of the cross and chanting, "You shall sprinkle my body with hyssop and I shall be clean. You shall wash me and I shall be whiter than snow …."

The aunt stumbled when she reached the grave. Throwing her scarf back, she tore at her hair, yelling, "*Xriso mou, xriso mou! Agoraki mou!*" My little golden boy.

Danae put her arm around her and nodded to the priest to continue. He quickly resumed the service, swinging the censor, the burning incense a white cloud over the open grave.

"You are dust, and to dust you shall return." He threw a clump of earth down on the coffin. "Let him not be forgotten."

After he finished, the others walked by the grave and did the same. O'Malley had taken the lantern and gone back in search of Stefanos' suitcase the previous night, found it and removed the ball. Lacking flowers, he threw it into the grave.

He whispered, "May the angels embrace you, child."

After the family left, O'Malley retrieved the shovel and filled in the grave. When he finished, he looked down at the mound of fresh earth.

He didn't buy the bunk people comforted themselves with when something like this happened, the crap about earthly suffering and heavenly reward. Perhaps there was some rationale for the death of a child, some divine purpose. Perhaps on the day of reckoning, it would all make sense. He didn't think so. 'Spare me the explanations,' he'd tell God when that day came. 'Spare me the reasons.'

* * *

HE AND LEONIDAS spent the night in the cellar of Danae's house. She brought them food at some point. It was a poor meal—hard rusks and glasses of sweet wine, a plate of boiled wheat, pomegranate seeds and nuts, dressed in sugar.

"*Kolyva*," Leonidas said. "Represents eternal life."

Together, they ate the food and O'Malley took the dishes back up to the kitchen. Hoping to see Danae again, he lingered there, but she was gone. The house was freezing. Had they run out of charcoal or had the father in his sorrow forgotten to light it? O'Malley went into the front room to check. The brazier was empty.

"Jesus, Mary, and Joseph, 'tis only November," he swore under his breath. "How are they going to get through the winter?"

Danae was standing by a window and looking out at the garden. She turned when she heard him, her face streaked with tears. "*Angle*," she said softly.

O'Malley came and stood beside her. The moon was up, lighting the fields around the house and casting the trees into shadow. In the distance, he could see the river glistening in the pale light, beckoning almost, as it had the night the three of them had ridden Elektra.

He whispered the expression the Irish used when confronted with death. "Sorry for your trouble." Words he'd heard all his life. Inadequate as they were, they were all he knew. Poor comfort they seemed now.

She didn't seem to hear.

"I should have insisted he go back to the camp. I never should have let him come with Leonidas and me."

"It was the Germans who killed him. Not you."

O'Malley felt tears start in his eyes. He desperately wanted to be forgiven, absolved for the child's death, but found that he couldn't accept it. "No, it was me. It was me who got him shot."

She put her finger to her lips.

They stayed in the cold room, staring out at the moonlit night for a long time.

Finally, he took her hand and kissed it. She fell against him and started to cry, beating at him with her fists. "Oh, God, I want Stefanos back. Please God, give my brother back to me."

* * *

"I THINK THE Germans know about the camp," O'Malley told Leonidas. Numb with grief, he felt like he was under water, as if he spoke from some far-off place. Still, he went on, relating what Danae's aunt had told him, how everyone in town knew of its location.

"I heard the same thing," Leonidas said. "They say a known collaborator was asking whether we were at Mega Spileon."

He thought for a minute. "I'll talk to my sources again, figure out something." He looked over at O'Malley. "You'll have to wait here. I can't risk taking you with me into the town."

"That's okay. I want to stay here. See if the family needs anything."

"See if *she* needs anything. I saw how you looked at her. The hunger in your eyes."

O'Malley felt himself redden. "What of it?"

"She's a path you can't take, my friend. In case you've forgotten, there's a war on. And after this war ends, there'll be another. Forget her. Forget all of us here. Go back to Ireland. Get on with your life."

"No. I'll fight till the end, same as you."

"Your end and mine are different." Leonidas' expression was hard to read, his voice cold.

"So it's back to that, is it? Me being an outsider?"

"Don't be a fool. I'm talking about Greek against Greek, civil war. You don't want any part of what's going to happen here after the Germans leave."

* * *

Seeing O'Malley in the kitchen the next morning with Danae, her father drew him aside and asked him to leave. "You don't belong here. Leave us and go back to the camp."

O'Malley begged him to reconsider, but the Greek was adamant. "We're done with you and the *antartes*. Take your guns and get out of here."

"Leonidas asked me to wait here for him."

At first O'Malley thought the man's anger came from seeing Danae and him sitting together there at the table, the way he kept looking at her, but then he realized it was something more.

"Not in this house," the man said, "not any longer."

"Where will I go?"

"Wherever the *antartes* take you. It's no concern of mine."

O'Malley retreated to the river. The day was overcast and the wind was cold. Even in his goatskin, he could feel the dampness rising from the earth. To pass the time, he pulled the broken bits of kite down and wound the string around his hand, weeping a little as he did so. He longed to return to that day when he and Stefanos had run the kite out before the rainstorm, to hear the boy laughing beside him. Danae's father had been right to banish him. He had nothing to offer any of them now.

Leonidas returned that afternoon. "People in Kalavryta say the man who was asking after us is not to be trusted." He lit a cigarette and inhaled, his fingers stained with nicotine. "They say if he knows where the camp is, von Le Suire does, too, and that he'll be coming for us. Any day now. It's only a matter of time.

"What are you going to do?"

"You willing to go back to the camp by yourself? Warn the men?"

"You coddin' me? 'Course I'll go." O'Malley looked back toward the house. "Nothing for me here. Her father ran me off."

"I'll meet with von Le Suire in the meantime. Draw the negotiations out as long I can. Give you a chance to get well away. He won't bomb the camp as long as he thinks his POWs are there."

Reaching over, he patted O'Malley's cheek. "Don't worry, Casanova. You can come back to Kalavryta afterwards. See to the girl."

17

O'MALLEY VISITED THE cemetery before he left the next day. Although it was still dark out, Danae was already there, sitting beside the grave. She pushed her hair back when she saw him and rose to her feet.

They stood there awkwardly. It had started to rain again and the ground was muddy, water puddling on the ground around them.

"He had no chance, my brother," Danae said, shaking her head. "No chance—ever."

O'Malley had to look away, remembering the child's final moments, his crippling terror. "Lord God, how I wish this hadn't happened, that I could have saved him."

"And I wish the Germans hadn't come and there'd never been a war." Her voice was shrill. "It makes no difference what we wish."

Sitting back down, Danae touched the grave with her hand. "He was afraid of everything, my brother. He had no business with *antartes*."

Here it comes, O'Malley thought. *Her lambasting me for the boy's death.*

But it wasn't him she was angry with. "I told my father to keep him at the house, that the camp was not for Stefanos. 'He's just a boy,' I said. 'He doesn't belong there.' But he insisted."

"Your father didn't do this, Danae. It was the Germans who killed him."

Danae went on as if she hadn't heard. "Poor Stefanos, all shut up there in the dark. I lit a candle, but the wind took it. I'll buy him a lantern. That will be better. A big one, made of glass. He'll be able to see if he has a lantern. He won't be afraid."

She touched the mound of earth tenderly. "I'll keep it lit always, I promise, Stefanos. I'll never let it go out."

"The *antartes* have lanterns," O'Malley said quietly. "I'll bring you one from the camp."

Looking up at him, she seemed to see him for the first time. "The camp?"

"Aye. The Germans learned its whereabouts and I have to warn the men."

Touching his face with her muddy fingers, she whispered, "*Panagia mazi sou*." May God protect you.

O'Malley choked back a sob. Stefanos had once said those words, blessed him in exactly the same way.

* * *

O'Malley paused as he left the cemetery and stood watching her. *Sweet Jesus*, she was lovely, even now all shrouded in grief.

He opened the gate and called to her. "Walk with me a bit, Danae."

Taking her by the arm, he led her toward the river. It would be light soon and he didn't have much time. At some point she stumbled and he grabbed her to keep her from falling, held her for a moment before letting go. She smelled of winter, he thought, of cold earth and damp. Underfoot, the fallen leaves were stiff and beaded with frost. An abandoned nest clung to the branch of a tree, the twigs that formed it slowly unraveling in the wind.

Danae moved mechanically, putting one foot in front of the other, her eyes dull. Respecting her grief, O'Malley let her be. They sat down and watched the water for a time. It had receded over the last few days, a line of muck marking its passage on the rocks.

"You going to be all right?" he asked.

"What choice do I have?" Her voice was muffled, seemed to come from far away.

"I know this isn't the right time, but something's been preying on my mind, something I need to ask you."

She shrugged. "Ask."

It was wrong doing this now, O'Malley told himself. Pestering her when she was all stove in with grief, but soon he'd be back in the thick of it, might get killed and never have the chance. He wanted to help her before he left, to bind up her wounds as she'd once done his, give her something to hold on to. A bit of light amidst all the darkness.

Not knowing where to begin, he stammered a few words about what she meant to him, his face slowly reddening. Then he remembered a poem he'd had to memorize in school. Yeats, it had been. "The Cloths of Heaven."

Softly, he recited the part he remembered:

> But I, being poor, have only my dreams;

I have spread my dreams under your feet;
Tread softly because you tread on my dreams.

And so he would, spread all he was beneath her and all around her. Enfold her in it now and forever. Not gold and silver maybe, nothing heaven would have any use for, but true nonetheless, his yearning heart.

He wouldn't always be poor. *Aye*, one day he'd be able to take proper care of her, to make sure she had enough to eat, decent frocks to wear. He'd not be standing here as he was today, empty-handed, with nothing but words to offer her.

"I love you, Danae," he said.

She didn't react.

"I love you," he said again in a louder voice.

Not knowing what to do, he picked up a stick and began to dig furiously in the ground. "Will you have me when all this is over? Will you marry me and be my wife?"

"Marry you?" She stared at him.

"Aye. In a church with a priest and whatnot. Doesn't have to be a Catholic priest. I care naught about that. All I care about is what we say to each other." Taking her hand, he repeated more words he remembered from Ireland. "By the power that Christ brought from heaven, mayst thou love me. As the sun follows its course, mayst thou follow me. As light to the eye, as bread to the hungry, as joy to the heart, mayst thy presence be with me, oh one that I love, 'til death comes to part us asunder."

Gathering courage, he rushed on. "I'll do right by you. I'm good with my hands. I'll build you a house, a proper house, with little boxes under the windows where you can plant flowers and heat you can turn on and off with a switch. It'll be grand, I tell you. We'll eat roast beef every day, puddings we'll set on fire—way the English do on Christmas. You'll want for nothing. I swear. Love least of all. I'll sing to you and laugh with you and love you till the day I die. You hear, Danae? I'll love you till the day I die."

She closed her eyes.

"I'll take care of you. Give you every shilling I have."

"I'm Greek, *Angle*. What need have I of shillings?"

There'd been a flicker of something in her eyes, something in her voice as she'd said it. *Hope*, O'Malley thought it was. *Aye*, hope that her life, instead of ending in this place, might be beginning.

"Will you not call me Brendan? Just this once? Will you not say my name?"

"Yes, *Angle*," she said with a hint of spirit. "I'll do that. After we get married, I will call you 'Brendan.'"

And then she laughed.

* * *

O'Malley pondered that laugh all the way back to the camp. Whether it had been a 'yes, I'll marry you' laugh or something else. When he got back, he'd have to ask her again, get it clarified.

He heard no birdsong as he walked, no noise at all, save for the rushing water. Even the crows, heavy in the trees, had fallen silent

Shivering, he picked up the pace. The trees were stippled with rain, their bare branches skeletal against the sky. Although he was very tired, he pushed on, determined to reach the camp before nightfall. Bands of ice were forming along the edge of the river, freezing in lacy whorls and ripples. Tapping his foot against the ice, he watched it splinter and break up. The crackling was louder than he'd expected and he drew back, afraid someone might have heard. The sky remained overcast, the distant mountains dusted with snow.

He studied the canyon walls, searching for movement, but there was none. Save for the burned trucks in the gorge, the war didn't seem to have touched this place. Someone had even seen to the dead, buried them beside the river.

Taking a deep breath, he sprinted across the bridge, made for the path and started to climb, walking as fast as he dared.

The *antartes* were eating supper when he arrived at the camp. Roumelis greeted him warmly, pulled him down close to the fire and handed him a plate of stewed meat. The rest of the men nodded once to O'Malley and went on with their eating. No one mentioned Stefanos.

Tugging off his wet boots, O'Malley relaxed by the fire. The *flokati* was rank, steamed a little as it dried. Between mouthfuls, he told the men the Germans were coming. "We need to shut down the camp and be quick about it."

"'*We?*'" Haralambos' lips were pursed.

"You then. Just as long as it gets down." He hastily relayed what Leonidas had discovered in Kalavryta, that a known traitor was discussing the location of the camp. Leonidas had written a note to this effect and he handed it now to Haralambos. The school teacher read it, crumpled it up and threw it in the fire.

"He's right. We need to leave."

At O'Malley's request, Leonidas had used no names, said nothing about the identity of the collaborator. He'd simply stated the facts: the Germans had discovered the location of the camp and the *antartes* must go and go fast. If they stayed, it would be all-out war, the enemy throwing everything they had at them—planes, tanks, flame throwers—an onslaught no one could survive. He himself would try again to meet with von Le Suire, stall the Germans as long as he could.

* * *

Leonidas' voice was stripped of emotion. "Again, von Le Suire refused to negotiate. Bastard said he will only meet with members of the right wing—EDES—not us, not with 'the communist forces of ELAS.' "

They'd been packing up the camp when Leonidas arrived, hadn't yet finished. His friend was exhausted, O'Malley saw. He had dark circles under his eyes and could barely stand. He must have been walking for hours.

"They exhumed the bodies of four dead Germans in Tripoli," he went on. "I imagine they'll do the same with the dead men in the gorge. The German high command is investigating every death, apparently. Looking to see how the men died, whether it was from wounds received in battle or if they'd been executed."

He dipped his cup in the pail and took a deep swallow of water. "Best keep the prisoners alive," he said, wiping his mouth with the back of his hand. "Give them no cause."

"How can we feed them?" Roumelis protested. "We are running out of food."

The group appeared to be about evenly divided. Half the men were for executing the Germans, the other half against it. Their motives were complicated. One man went so far as to say it'd be a kindness, shooting them, far better than letting them starve to death. Alexis was the most vocal, urging the others to throw them off the cliff.

Surprisingly, Haralambos opposed him. "Remember what the priest said. The Germans will destroy Kalavryta. Remember that."

He'd distanced himself from Alexis, O'Malley noticed. He wondered how it would go in the future between the two men. Who would be Trotsky, who Stalin, the one wielding the ice pick?

O'Malley didn't participate in the debate. As far as he was concerned, Roumelis was right. There wasn't enough food left to keep them all alive. Whether the *antartes* shot the prisoners or not, it was all going to end the same way: the Germans would die.

The next morning a man brought a message to Leonidas from ELAS headquarters. Leonidas refused to reveal its contents with O'Malley. "A new set of orders," was all he said. He seemed deeply troubled.

He and a few other men withdrew shortly after and spoke in low voices. They began to argue heatedly, waving O'Malley away when he approached, saying that what they were discussing was no concern of his. At one point, Alexis pointed to himself and said, "*Tha to kano.*" I'll do it.

The group dispersed a few minutes later. Leonidas announced they would be taking the prisoners with them when they broke camp. If they perished from hunger along the way, well, they'd started the war, hadn't they?

"Let's get started."

Alexis took it upon himself to announce to the prisoners they would soon be set free. In a long speech worthy of a party leader, he told them that General von Le Suire had agreed to the terms of the exchange and that it was scheduled to take place the following day. The prisoners would remain in ELAS custody until that time and should comport themselves accordingly. They would march single file to German headquarters, a journey of some ten kilometers, where they would be handed over.

When he finished, he shook hands with their commanding officer and thanked him in advance for his cooperation.

The POWs cheered when Hans translated Alexis' words into German, laughing and babbling together. "*Frei sind wir den. Freiheit!*" We're free. Freedom!

The *antartes* quickly bound each of the prisoner's wrists together and tied them to a second, longer length of rope. After they finished, they set water out for them to drink, what bread there was left in the camp and a bucket of *trahana*. Bound as they were, the prisoners would have to eat like dogs, O'Malley saw. Fight for every mouthful of food.

Although it was contrary to everything he'd been taught by the Catholic priests at St. Joseph's, he rejoiced at the prospect of the Germans groveling, struggling there on the ground for a miserable bite of *trahana*, rejoiced with all his heart that they would suffer.

Haunted by the death of Stefanos, he'd avoided being around them since returning to the camp. The Greeks, too, for that matter. Spent his time out in the field, caring for the horses. None of the *antartes* had noticed that the boy was missing. The thought made O'Malley even sadder. Like him, Stefanos had been alone up here. No wonder he had run away.

"Ach, Specky."

Only Grigoris had spoken openly of the child's absence. "Barrel's empty. Where is Stefanos?"

"Dead, lad. The Germans shot him."

"Dead?!"

"Aye. In a field far from here. It was terrible."

Joining the other men, O'Malley labored to dismantle the camp. He helped Fotis pack up the radio and ammunition, then borrowed an axe and hacked up the barrel where Stefanos had taken shelter, chopping away at it until it was reduced to splinters.

Setting the axe aside, he paused to catch his breath. Grigoris must have spread the word, he thought, looking down at the broken staves, the mess of wood chips and splinters at his feet. The *antartes* hadn't said a word about what he was doing. They just stood around and watched him.

Behind barbed wire, the Germans watched him, too, pacing back and forth in their little corral. O'Malley swung the axe high in the air and brought it smashing down on the last of the staves. They were right to be afraid, he thought, gripping the handle of the axe tighter. Given half a chance, he'd smash their skulls in with the thing. Pound them into the ground and kill them, same as their friends had done Stefanos.

Merciless, it'd be, a deed like that, but understandable, given the circumstances. After all, they'd started the war, hadn't they?

Shouldering the axe, he walked away. *To hell with them.*

* * *

ELEKTRA JERKED HER head away when O'Malley slipped the bit in her mouth. "Easy now. Easy."

Throwing the saddle on her back, he secured it, then picked up the pile of bedrolls and lashed it to her as well. Hoisting himself up, he rode back and forth, testing the load for balance, not wanting the weight of it to unseat him, pull the two of them off the mountain.

Remembering how much Stefanos had loved the horse, his eyes filled with tears. He brushed them away, thankful for the darkness.

He hadn't wanted to make the journey, but Leonidas had insisted.

"You can't go back to Kalavryta, not now. Germans catch you anywhere near the village, they'll burn the place. Von Le Suire's looking for an excuse."

As always, he'd taken care to address O'Malley as an equal, kept his tone respectful and polite. "Stay with us a little longer, my friend."

Reluctantly, O'Malley had agreed. He was glad of that now; it was better to be on the move. Better than losing oneself to ghosts. He'd find his way back to Kalavryta after they rid themselves of the prisoners. When there weren't so many German soldiers prowling the hills. He'd help Danae and her family. Maybe they could spend Christmas together.

Alexis and another man were leading the prisoners out of the camp. As before, the German, 'Homeros,' was translating for the rest. He'd sensed the *antartes'* change of mood and was all business. "Why are we here? Where are you taking us?"

"We're closing the camp. Moving you out."

Alexis jerked the rope, forcing the prisoners to follow like dogs on a leash. "Keep moving," he shouted.

Roumelis was the last to leave. He was leading a pair of donkeys with tin pans and heavy sacks of grain strapped to them. The weight of the load was tearing into their backs, leaving raw patches in the animals' fur.

O'Malley had always liked donkeys. Unlike in Greece, they were valued in Ireland; an aunt of his had cried bitter tears when hers died. She'd been married to a brutish man who'd cuffed her in public and treated her badly. "Poor friend," she'd said, cradling the head of the dead beast. "Poor brother donkey. We were slaves together."

His pa cherished animals and always insisted that O'Malley be gentle to them. "Make no mistake; they are the same as you, only cloaked in fur and hooves and poor at talk. Always share what you have with them and treat them kindly."

Getting down from his horse, O'Malley loosened the straps on the donkeys and did what he could for them. Wishing he had some liniment, he used the bandages he'd brought from Ireland and pasted them over the open sores. He tore his bedroll in half and laid it on their backs as a saddle blanket.

After O'Malley finished, the cook dug out a bottle of *raki* and handed it to him.

"May the giving hand never falter," O'Malley said, taking a swig and handing the jug back. "You're a right man, Roumelis, don't I know it. Daylight's own fellow." The *raki* burned on the way down, set his insides on fire.

The cook glanced back at the camp. "Feels strange to be leaving."

"You know this place we're going?"

"Sure. Mazeika. It's up in the hills."

"Far from Kalavryta?"

"Two kilometers, no more. A stone's throw."

The trail was steep, almost straight up. Unwilling to risk Elektra, O'Malley got down from the saddle and led her with the reins. The others were ahead of him, over one hundred men making their way up the mountain. In spite of the ropes, the POWs were in a jovial mood and sang as they marched—Nazi songs, judging by from the sound. As the night wore on, they too fell silent.

The moon was now directly overhead, the shadows of the trees like etchings against the pale rock. Far below, O'Malley could see the river and the legendary waterfall that was its source. Like a stream of liquid mercury, it was, cascading down from the shattered crest of the mountain. A mist was rising from the surface of the water. It seemed a thing alive under the moon, floating up from a secret place in the earth.

The Greeks rode back and forth on their horses, herding their captives like cattle. The fog was soon everywhere and it gradually overtook them. Worried, Fotis suggested they light lanterns against it, but Leonidas forbade it, saying the Germans might see them. "If we stay together, it'll be all right."

As before, he took the lead, spurring his steed forward. The others quickly followed, disappearing one by one into the mist. The fog eventually vanished, driven off by the rising wind, revealing the deep rift of the gorge again. O'Malley dropped back, preferring to be the last in line. Elektra was barely visible in the darkness, her labored breathing the only evidence of her presence. He crossed a small pond a few minutes later formed by run-off from the snow. The still water reflected the moon overhead, the ice along its banks like shards of broken glass.

Leonidas drove them hard, pausing only to do reconnaissance before pushing on.

They continued to climb. O'Malley recalled the area from a briefing in Cairo: Kalanistra, it was one of the highest points in the region. The wind was fierce and it whipped his clothes. A few clouds were rising from behind the mountain. Ragged lines of gray, they were ghostly in the moonlight.

He wondered how Leonidas had found his way. There were no paths, no landmarks to judge distances by. Only the sky and a wilderness of stars. He could see the Milky Way, the neat symmetry of it, the North Star beckoning just below it, a few others that he recognized.

A light seemed to be moving across the sky. *A boat*, he thought, *in the Gulf of Corinth, the sea at one with the night sky*. Too large for fishing, it was probably a German vessel patrolling the coast. The Wehrmacht had a large force in the city of Patras; it was their main area of supply. An infinite number of mountains stood between the *antartes* and the town, or so it seemed. Here and there he saw other lights. Villages, he thought, high up on the hills.

The *antartes* had dismounted and were leading the prisoners toward the edge of the precipice. The slope was heavily forested, thick with cypress and fir. "You should pull back," O'Malley called, coming forward to meet them. "The rocks aren't steady."

Alexis was in the lead this time. The prisoners were still roped together, leaning against each another and struggling not to lose their balance. Alexis jerked the rope. Two other men were helping him, O'Malley saw. He didn't know their names, but had seen them around the camp.

He tried a second time to get their attention, more urgent now. "You're too close. Pull back!"

Alexis gave the rope a savage yank. The force knocked several of the prisoners down.

Then O'Malley knew.

Alexis first demanded the prisoners surrender whatever gear they'd been carrying, their greatcoats and their boots; then he ordered them at gunpoint to line up again. He and five other men dragged them over to the edge of the cliff, forcing them forward until the Germans began grappling, fighting to hang onto the rocks and secure a foothold, anything to keep from falling. Frightened, they began to resist, screaming and begging for mercy.

The one called 'Homeros' was the most vocal, yelling in Greek for Alexis to stop. "*Afto den einai sosto!*" This isn't right. He dropped to his knees and held up his bound hands. "*Stamatiste! Stamatiste!*" Stop. Stop.

Alexis motioned for him to get up. The prisoners grew more and more restless, the ones in front backing into the men behind them, clawing and pushing at them as they tried to get away from the cliff. They were all yelling now, and a few had soiled themselves.

Alexis raised his gun and shot the first POW in line. The man tumbled off the cliff, dragging the others down with him. The Germans screamed as they went over the side and reached out with their hands, their anguished cries echoing and reverberating in the darkness. The Greeks rushed forward and pitched the ones who hadn't already fallen off the mountain. O'Malley could hear the sharp thump of their bodies as they hit the rocks, the wrenching animal sounds of the unlucky few who'd been impaled on the trees. Alexis and the others fired off a few rounds to finish off the wounded, then shouldered their guns and retrieved their horses.

In less than ten minutes, it was over.

The silence that followed was far worse than the screams had been. It felt like an indictment to O'Malley. As if God Himself had turned His face away.

Fotis was standing off to one side, tears running down his face. "I told them not to. I told them no good would come of it."

Haralambos and Leonidas were with Fotis, all of them well back from Alexis and the other two men. It was too dark to see their faces.

"Why'd you do it?" O'Malley screamed. "For the love of God, why'd you kill them?"

It was Haralambos who answered, "The order came from ELAS headquarters to move out. That was the message Leonidas received. There was no way we could take the POWs with us. We don't have enough men to guard them, enough food to feed them."

"So you decided to kill them?!"

"None of us was willing at first. Finally Alexis volunteered. We didn't want to kill them near Kalavryta. That's why we came this way. We thought if we did it here, the Germans would be less likely to discover the bodies."

He looked out at the night. "We are soldiers fighting for our country," he said. "We had our orders."

* * *

CROSSING OVER THE spur of the mountain, the *antartes* started down. The men were subdued; no one spoke for a long time. The majority took care to stay well away from Alexis and the men who'd assisted him.

"Won't help you," O'Malley muttered, seeing what they were about. "The sin is ours. The blood is on all of us."

They were in a narrow valley, moving steadily west. It was overgrown with trees, a wild and inhospitable place. Centaurs had once lived here, one of the men said. O'Malley looked up at the shadowy walls. *Aye*, it was easy to imagine them here. All manner of pagan beasts.

The men behind him were discussing a region to the south, a place called Mani. It remained Free Greece, they were saying, one of the few areas the Germans hadn't conquered.

"They have a harbor in Mani, boats?" O'Malley asked. He was thinking seriously about leaving the unit tonight and never returning. He'd fetch Danae and go, her father and aunt too, if he had to.

"Yes," one of the men said. "Many of the villages can only be approached by boat. It's a Godforsaken place. Like the gorge, one of the entrances to hell in ancient times. The dead were escorted across an underground lake or river that ran through the heart of it."

Recalling the coins the women had placed in Stefanos' coffin, O'Malley asked if they'd paid the ferryman in the old days.

"Sure. The family would place coins on the eyes of the dead to ensure their safe passage to the underworld. Without the coins, Charon would refuse to take them and their soul would wander the world of the living forever." He pulled something out of his pocket. "You go to Mani, you'll need this." He handed a coin to O'Malley. "Use it to pay for your passage to hell."

A dark story. Still, O'Malley thought he'd keep Mani in mind when he left.

"They say the largest tree in Mani is a cabbage," another man volunteered.

Getting down from their horses, the group rested for a few minutes, the men teasing each other as they stood around. Those from the bigger villages calling the rest *vlachoi*. Peasants. Keeping at it until the others called them out.

Although the sparring appeared good-natured, there was an edge to it, a roughness. O'Malley's cousins had needled him in much the same way, belittling him as a 'bogger' and making a show of inspecting his boots for manure whenever they saw him, for no other reason, save that unlike them he'd grown up on a farm. It was the same here.

He'd noticed other divisions within the group as well. By and large, the men from Messenia in the south were less enthusiastic about ELAS and its teachings than the ones from the north, a few even going so far as to speak out openly against it. That attitude would cost them if civil war broke out. Haralambos and his friends, they'd see to that.

The Greeks appeared eager to fight, desperate for anything that would distract them from the events of the night.

Near daybreak, Leonidas led them through a small hamlet. Using the mountains as cover, they'd circled around Kalavryta during the night, O'Malley now saw, and were approaching it from the west.

18

A HEAD LAY A ruined watchtower. As they rode closer, O'Malley saw a small hut, constructed out of mud bricks built into the base, a length of burlap across the entrance.

Pushing the cloth aside, an elderly woman came out to greet them. Her long white hair hung loose on her shoulders, as wild and curly as lamb's wool, and she had a cane clutched in her hands. She wrapped a dirty shawl around her and asked what they wanted.

"Refuge," Leonidas said, making it clear it was not a request, but a demand.

She nodded, went back inside and returned with a metal ring full of keys. The small door led into the tower. It was made of wood and looked to be original to the structure—a heavy slab of walnut with rusting iron hinges. The woman put the key in the lock and turned it, undid the chain that wound through the handle, and pushed the door open. A pair of teenage boys had come out of the hut and stood watching her.

One by one the *antartes* entered the tower, bending almost double to protect their heads. Leonidas patted the lintel with his hand as he passed. "To prevent someone from coming in with a drawn sword," he told O'Malley.

Trust the Greeks. Keeping their portals low to protect themselves. Savages to a man.

In the cellar of the tower were three adjoining rooms, accessed by a stone staircase. Empty now, they were swathed in cobwebs and knee-deep in filth, some of it human, judging by the smell. A flock of chickens were secreted there, pecking at the cobbled floor, the smell of their waste so strong it made O'Malley's eyes water.

He climbed back up the stairs. Let the *antartes* bed down in that prison. He for one would sleep outdoors.

Haralambos, of course, saw it differently. "You've done well for yourself, little mother," he told the woman. "Living in a castle, keeping chickens when others have none. How'd you come to be so lucky? The Germans lend you a hand?"

"I inherited it," the woman said. " 'A castle,' my father told me. I'll be a princess, I thought. A queen." She waved a gnarled hand at the tower. "And now look at me. What am I queen of? Chicken shit and rocks."

"Count yourself lucky. Many have far less than you."

"What do I care what others have?"

She demanded payment for the use of the space, said she'd have to clean up after them, deserved a few drachmas for her trouble. The Germans had taken all the livestock and grain, even the firewood she had stored. Did the *antartes* perhaps have some food they could give her? A few eggs, perhaps? Some bread?

She backed off when they refused, sulked a little. "How do you expect me to get by?" she asked.

"What do we care?" Haralambos said, giving her words back to her.

She laughed, nodded. But she was too old to teach the lessons of communism to—the 'one for all and all for one,' too old for the era she found herself in. "I prayed and prayed." She stared off into space, watching something only she could see. "Wore myself out praying. Prayed for the Turks to die."

The men exchanged glances.

The two teenage boys were her grandsons and looked after things for her, she said, protected her from the Germans. She introduced herself as Kyria Demetra and said that she'd lived in Mazeika all her life.

The oldest grandson, the boy named Kimon, told them there'd been a shooting two weeks prior. He and his brother had been herding goats with their cousin, Theodoros, and blundered into a German patrol. They'd tried to escape into the woods with the animals. The Germans had shouted something at them, but they hadn't understood and kept running. Their cousin had been shot in the back, killed in the woods not far from here.

Though the boy did his best to appear manly and describe the killing without giving way to tears, it was hard for him. Cursing the Germans, he vowed to avenge his cousin's death. "I'll slit their throats. Murder them while they sleep." He sounded very young to O'Malley. His voice hadn't changed yet.

He was dressed in better clothes than his brother, a man's jacket that had been cut down to fit him and heavy wool trousers. He had thick features and a pronounced underbite, his lower jaw jutting out like a boar's.

Kimon said he and his brother wanted to join ELAS, fight the Germans same as the *antartes* had done in the gorge. He knew everything about the battle, or so it seemed. The number of Germans killed and how the four wounded men had been taken to the hospital in Kalavryta. He even knew the name of their commanding officer, Reiss.

As gently as he could, Leonidas declined his offer. "Someone has to defend Mazeika. Protect your grandmother and the people here."

Kimon insisted, saying he and his brother were good with guns. Not afraid to die.

The old woman murmured her approval. *Heard it all before*, O'Malley thought, watching her. *Been hearing it every day since the shooting. None of this comes as anything new to her.*

In Greece these days it was as inevitable as the coming of winter—the haste of the young to die.

Stomping his foot, Kimon refused to be put off. "Listen to me," he squalled. "Listen to me."

O'Malley decided he didn't like Kimon much. All petulance and bluster, he reminded him of Alexis. He hoped Leonidas would tell him no. A boy like that, he'd only bring them trouble.

* * *

Behind the tower stood a few buildings, a village of sorts. The old woman pointed to the church at the center. "Aghios Haralambos," she said.

At the entrance to the church was a metal box with a slot for coins. Pointing to the box, she motioned for the men to put money in, scowled at them when they didn't. The frescoes on the walls were primitive and blackened with age, the bodies of the saints so elongated and wracked with pain, they were grotesque. Judging by the name painted on the icon to the left of the altar, the church was indeed dedicated to Saint Haralambos just as the old woman had said. She knew what she was talking about. She wasn't that far gone.

O'Malley studied the icon. The saint's face was dour and full of condemnation, his high Byzantine forehead furrowed with rage. *Another one who finds us wanting. Just like his namesake.*

He wondered why Leonidas had brought them here. He didn't feel safe in this place, exposed as they were on the hill.

A military strategist of sorts, the old woman offered any number of suggestions as to how they could defend themselves and hold the tower in the event of a German attack. "You can do like the ancients did in *Aiges*—repel an invasion by tying torches to the horns of their goats, misleading their enemy into thinking reinforcements had arrived."

She was far more intelligent than she let on, O'Malley thought. Haralambos had been right not to trust her. This one bore watching.

* * *

SEARCHING FOR SOMETHING to eat, the *antartes* spread out and explored the area. "Oh, shit," O'Malley muttered when he saw Fotis pull a frost-blackened plant out of the ground. "*Horta.*"

Roumelis scooped up two of the woman's chickens and cut their throats with a knife, laughing when she protested. "We're hungry, little mother, and you have food. What can we do?"

"Thieves!" she bawled, hitting him with her fists. "Thieves!"

She tried to herd the rest of the chickens into her hut, but it was an impossible task. Still shouting, she pushed the burlap flap aside and disappeared inside. Her grandsons trailed after her, cursing the *antartes*.

Roumelis quickly built a fire and set about roasting the chickens. He threw a handful of potatoes into a pot of boiling water along with the *horta* and whatever else Fotis and the others had scavenged. After he finished cooking, he divided up the food and gave everyone a share. Although he was very careful, there was barely enough to go around, a few mouthfuls maybe.

O'Malley took his plate and sat in the corner. Chewing slowly, he tried to make the sensation of eating last as long as he could, to hold the taste of the chicken in his mouth. He hadn't eaten in forty-eight hours and would gladly have eaten mice if he'd had to, bugs. The songbirds in the trees.

He sang a song from Ireland:

> Oh, the praties they grow small
> Over here, over here.
> Oh, the praties they grow small
> When we dig them in the fall
> And we eat them coats and all
> Full of fear, full of fear.

Leonidas, sitting beside O'Malley, asked what a 'pratie' was.

"A potato. It's a song from the famine."

After they finished eating, the *antartes* spread their blankets out on the floor of the tower and prepared to sleep. Drawing on his cloak, O'Malley got up and walked outside.

Roumelis came out and joined him a few minutes later. "We must celebrate the moon," he said, pointing up at the sky. "Drink to its well-being."

O'Malley reached for the bottle the cook was carrying. "Smoke in me gob and a drink in me hand. What more could a man ask for?"

* * *

THE COOK PAUSED for a moment before speaking again. "Worst thing I ever saw was in a village to the west of here. The local police were working with the Germans and they killed a man I knew in ELAS, cut off his head and left it out in the square as a warning to the others. I still see that man's head sometimes, the awful pallor of his face. I swear it grows every time I think about it, grows and grows."

He and O'Malley were sitting on the ground with their backs to the wall. They'd both had a lot to drink, emptied a full bottle of *raki* between them.

"Awful," O'Malley said with feeling. He'd seen similar things. A woman's body burned beyond recognition, only the charred outline of her breasts indicating what she once had been. The Australian in the road after the tanks had run over him, barely recognizable as a man. He'd never spoken of these things. There was no way to. They were living things, the horrors. Growing like Roumelis' severed head, growing and festering inside him.

"What makes it worse was he was killed by his own people, by Greeks."

O'Malley took a swallow. They were getting drunk because of the POWs, though neither of them said it. O'Malley could still hear their anguished cries, thought he'd probably go on hearing them the rest of his life.

He held up the bottle. It wasn't Murphy's Stout, the mother's milk of Cork, but it had done the trick, provided him with the oblivion he was seeking. He prodded the embers in the fire with his boot. The wood crackled as it caught, a shower of sparks spraying up into the night.

"War makes you something you weren't before. The lucky few, it makes better. The rest of us, it ruins."

Roumelis nodded. "There was a butcher I knew. Big, red-faced man. Bad-tempered, everyone in the village was afraid of him. One night the Germans caught him in his shop after curfew. I'll never forget the way he just stood there wringing his hands. 'In or out,' he asked as meek as a lamb. 'In or out.' Imagine that. Asking the Germans where you should go so they can kill you, whether you should stay in your shop or come out in the street. I'll never forget it. I could feel his fear. Taste it. Only people he knew how to beat up on were women."

"Germans shoot him?"

"Yes. The wife, too, when she tried to stop them. Left them both bleeding in the doorway."

O'Malley could feel the wine turning on him and darkening his mood. In a hoarse voice he described the death of Stefanos, the awful moment in the field when he'd realized the boy was gone. "Lad was like a brother to me."

"*Slipitiria*," Roumelis said in a low voice. I feel sorry with you.

O'Malley recognized the expression, had heard it countless times at the child's funeral. The mourners had consoled the family with it. Deeply touched, he nodded. *Aye*, it had been like that with him and Stefanos. They had been that. Family.

* * *

O'MALLEY SAT UP, uncertain as to what had woken him. Taking his gun, he walked back through the tower, but saw nothing. He shook Roumelis awake. "I'm going down to the bottom of the hill. Tell Leonidas."

Secreting himself amid the olive trees, he kept his eyes on the tower, planning to keep watch until morning. A dog was barking up by the houses. It had heard something, too. Knew there was an intruder about.

He fell asleep and awoke at dawn, dappled sunlight warming his face. He lay there for a moment, listening to the early morning call of the birds. Barn swallows, they were, like a cloud of arrowheads whirling about

A group of women in black were filling their jugs from a nearby spigot. One of them pointed at him and spoke to the rest, protesting his presence apparently. They all took flight a moment later, jabbering in Greek. O'Malley watched them go. *Crows*, he thought to himself. Mazeika was a village of crows.

It looked to be a poor place, 'mean' as they said in Ireland. The houses were built deep into the hill, the entrances as dark as mineshafts. Swallows were living under the eaves and their mud-splattered nests added to the forlorn quality of the place, its overwhelming sense of decay.

O'Malley picked up a clump of dirt and crumbled it between his fingers. Farming would be difficult here, soil this poor, like tilling sand. *Not crows. Chickens. Aye, chickens, scratching in the dust.*

A little girl was watching him from a doorway, her baby brother playing at her feet. She giggled when he waved to her. Barefoot, she was dressed in a torn dress, her dark hair cropped short like a boy's. Her eyes tilted up a little at the corners; and her smile, when it came, was joyful and innocent. She'd be a beauty one day.

She whispered something to her brother and pushed him back inside. Her tone, a mixture of exasperation and love, reminded him of Danae's, the way she talked to Stefanos. *Aye*, she'd been a girl like that once, Danae, a girl laughter came easy to.

Hungry, he returned to the tower to see what was for breakfast. He doubted anyone in the town would feed him. The old women hadn't liked the look of him—that was for sure. He wondered what it was about him that put them off. He'd come with the *antartes*. Surely they realized he wasn't the enemy.

Or maybe he was, come to that.

They'd been starving, those women—way their clothes hung off them, the cadaverous look of their faces. They'd heard about the chickens and thought he was the same. Just one more thief come to rob them. No wonder they'd fled.

Roumelis gave him a crust of bread and a cup of bitter coffee. "Horses need tending to," he said.

"I'll see to it."

Leading the animals down the hill, O'Malley pastured them in a stony field. It was a sunny day and he could see Kalavryta clearly in the distance. Not far, he judged—an hour's walk at the most. The town looked vulnerable from where he stood. If the Germans ever succeeded in breaking through, it would go badly for the village, surrounded as it was by mountains.

Like being in the palm of a hand if the Germans came. A hand about to make a fist.

* * *

HE STOLE A chicken from the old lady in the hut and carried it, hidden beneath his cloak, to Kalavryta late one night, intending to present it to Danae—the first of many gifts he planned to bestow upon her. The chicken had objected to the *journey* and soiled itself, making O'Malley's entrance less majestic than he'd wished.

"How will I explain it to my father?" Danae asked, eyeing the chicken nervously.

"Tell him it wandered in out of the blue, begging to be eaten."

"He'll know it was you."

"What if he does? It'll cook up fine, even if I was the one brought it. It's meat, isn't it? Better than the poor scoff you've been eating."

In the end, they turned the chicken loose in the field, thinking Danae's father would discover it and congratulate himself on his good fortune. O'Malley's role would remain a secret.

Later the two of them wandered over to the rabbit hutch. The animals had caught their scent and O'Malley could hear them moving around inside, thumping excitedly against the wooden floor.

Dressed completely in black, Danae was barely visible in the darkness. Her voice was husky when she spoke of Stefanos, recalling how much her brother had loved the rabbits. "He called the one with the droopy ear, Foufou, and that one there, the white one, he named Bobo."

She and her aunt had gathered up the boy's things that morning, she told them, and put them away in the closet. "I brought you these," she said. "They were in his pocket." She handed O'Malley the carved wooden animals.

19

~~~

THE SENTRY SHOUTED out a warning. Father Chronis was walking toward them, leading a mule with a man laid out across the back of it. A great shout went up in the camp a moment later. "Fotis, it's your brother! Costas is here."

Grabbing the reins of the mule, they escorted the priest into the tower. Father Chronis' eyes were teary and his cheeks were chafed with cold.

"We'll build a fire for you."

"No, no," the priest protested. "See to Costas first."

Fotis' brother was trembling violently, so weak he could hardly stand. Fotis demanded the old woman surrender her mattress and he helped his brother down, cradling him in his arms like a child. He swaddled him in blankets then gathered up wood and built a fire next to him.

"Slaughter one of your chickens and make him some soup," Fotis ordered the woman. "I'll pay you for it."

O'Malley was surprised when she consented. Since the arrival of the *antartes* in Mazeika, food had become increasingly scarce in the village, whatever supplies there'd been slowly dwindling into nothing.

Perhaps it had been better to throw the POWs off the mountain, he now thought. No one in the camp had eaten anything but *trahana* for the last twenty-four hours and it was unlikely they'd eat more than that today. Perhaps it was better to fly out into the darkness and come crashing down on the rocks. Better than this slow ebbing away, the life leaking out of you. Scrabbling in the dirt as his ancestors had done, searching for nonexistent potatoes.

The priest sat down next to the fire and rubbed his hands. "After I told His Eminence, the bishop, that Ebersberger refused to meet with you, he went to the German headquarters himself. He told von Le Suire the situation had become intolerable and that it would serve no purpose to delay the exchange and take a chance on more men dying."

The priest was relieved. Drunk with relief.

"It took some convincing, but von Le Suire eventually agreed and released Costas into His Eminence's custody as a gesture of good will. I would have brought him here sooner, but he was too weak to walk. I had to find a mule for him to ride and mules are hard to come by these days."

"What does von Le Suire expect in return?" asked Leonidas.

"The prisoners you're holding."

The *antartes* looked at one another. O'Malley watched them, curious as to how far they'd go, whether they'd lie to a priest.

"We no longer have the prisoners, Father."

"What are you talking about? Where are they?"

"They're dead."

"Dead?" The priest cried, his face full of anguish. "But how can that be?"

"It just is, Father."

"All of them?" He was trembling.

"Yes."

"But this is madness. Von le Suire will retaliate. He'll burn Kalavryta."

* * *

FOTIS' BROTHER SLEPT for the rest of the day. He was a small man with thinning hair, skin so pale O'Malley could see the veins pulsing in his wasted neck. Gradually, a spot of color returned to his cheeks. However, he remained very weak, barely able to swallow the soup the old woman concocted.

His story was a simple one. He'd been caught in a raid and dragged off to Gestapo headquarters. There the SS agents had formed a circle around him. Drawing closer and closer, they'd baited him a bit, hitting him with batons and laughing at his terror, mocking him when he wet himself. They kept him housed in a cellar and tortured him until they tired of the game. Eventually they left him alone, apparently thinking he'd die before morning. He'd regained consciousness in the darkness and that's where he'd stayed until yesterday, living off potato peels and garbage.

Worst thing about his incarceration had been the hunger, he said, the way the Germans had starved him into submission, throwing rotten vegetables and spoiled meat into his cell once a week, offal their cooks had no use for.

"I knew some German words from school and that was what saved me. '*Danke,*' I'd say to them, bowing like they were kings. '*Bitte.*' I took care always how I addressed them. Always spoke respectfully and gave them higher ranks than they deserved. '*Herr Hauptsturmführer der Waffen-SS,*' I'd say. '*Herr

Oberscharführer der Waffen-SS.' They fed me potato peels and soup that was mostly water. The guards used to torment me about the soup. Said it was piss, their piss, in my cup."

"*Drakoi*," Fotis whispered. Monsters.

Haralambos took notes as the man talked, asked him whether he remembered the names of the Gestapo agents who'd held him, said there'd be a time of reckoning, a day when his suffering would be avenged.

The *antartes* stayed up late that night, discussing what they should do.

"I say we go to their headquarters and engage them there," Spyros said. "Von Le Suire is expecting us to bring the prisoners. He'll give us free passage. We should take advantage of it."

"Good way to get killed," Leonidas countered.

"We can split up, enter the village at night." He was an older man with a grizzled face, deep-set, angry eyes.

"What do you stand to gain from all this?" Haralambos asked him.

"Nothing," he said, startled by the question.

"You sure no money changed hands? The Germans aren't paying you to deliver us to them?"

Leaping to his feet, Spyros made a great show of being insulted. "I am Greek. Greek, same as you. I'd never sell you out, never. I'd sooner die than see you perish at German hands."

He laid particular stress on the last two words, as if saying them aloud dirtied his mouth, as if he were swallowing glass.

"You betray us, we'll kill you," Haralambos told him. "No matter where you go or what you do, we'll find you and kill you."

* * *

Roumelis continued to raid the old woman's pantry, serving the men eggs for breakfast and, on occasion, roast chicken for dinner. They supplemented their diet with *horta* and olives, cans of macerated fruit they'd found in an abandoned cellar. It was never enough and O'Malley often went to bed hungry.

News from the front was good. Messengers reported ELAS and EDES guerrillas were pushing the Germans back all over Greece. It was only a matter of time now, everyone thought. A month or two and they'd be gone.

O'Malley alone remained on guard. One of his masters in Cairo had told him, 'The English always won the most important battle … the last.' In his experience, the same was true of Germans after a fashion. They never retreated without leaving a river of blood in their wake.

You're a cynical bastard, he told himself. Still he wondered what would happen, where the river of blood would come from and what form it would take.

What Father Chronis had told von Le Suire about the missing men remained unknown. A second ELAS unit had surrounded German headquarters and was shelling it, inflicting heavy casualties. According to reports, von Le Suire was preparing to withdraw before Christmas, a few weeks away. Evidently, the fate of the seventy-seven German POWs no longer concerned him.

* * *

O'Malley continued to visit Danae at night. Sometimes he saw her watching for him in the window as he crossed the field, her face visible through the glass. She always seemed to know when he would arrive and wasted little time coming out to meet him.

She remained subdued, muted almost.

He'd hoist her up on the back of Elektra and they'd canter as before. For the most part, she hung well back and kept her arms at her sides, didn't cling to him as she'd done in the past.

The horse liked their midnight rambles and would jerk her head, dancing almost as she crossed the river. They spent many hours in the field on the other side—level land without trees. The middle of November, winter was fast approaching and there was frost on the ground, the area a monochromatic wasteland of dead grass and night. The river too had become lifeless, a thin sheet of ice covering its surface. Only Elektra seemed alive to the darkness.

One evening Danae leaned closer, brushing up against O'Malley. "Faster," she urged.

He dutifully drove his heels into the horse's flanks and spurred her forward across the frozen land. It was very cold and he could feel Danae shivering behind him. He longed to stop and pull her into her arms, but decided against it. Grief still held her fast and he must respect it.

They'd have another season, the two of them, when the war was over and this was behind them.

In the meantime, he'd stand by at the ready with his flagship of a horse.

"Things are coming to a head at the camp," he said. He told her about the POWs and how their deaths had divided the men, made it a bitter place. "If the Germans find their bodies, it'll go bad for Kalavryta."

"It doesn't matter," Danae said. "What do we have to live for?"

O'Malley told himself it was her sadness talking, that she didn't mean it, that he must count for something. Still, her words grieved him.

What he wouldn't give to hear her laugh again.

* * *

It snowed later that week, a feathery dusting that started in the mountains and swept down across the plains. O'Malley was out in the pasture with the horses when it began, and he stood there watching it. Settling first on the branches of the pine trees, it gradually overtook the land before him, the forested hills and distant villages, blanketing the raw red clay and softening the jagged edges of the rocks. He leaned his head back and caught a flake on his tongue, enjoying the feel of the snow on his face, the cold touch of it on his eyelids and brows. It made him feel hopeful. In Ireland, white was the color of innocence, purity itself, and so it seemed today.

Leonidas laughed when he saw what he was doing, called him the Greek equivalent of a caffler, a fool.

"Away with ya!" O'Malley made a snowball and threw it at him, caught him hard on the side of his head.

Leonidas quickly retaliated. Seeing them, the other men quickly joined in, gathering up fistfuls of snow and heaving them at each other. Having had little practice, they weren't very good at it, and the snow kept slipping through their fingers or falling in clumps before reaching its target. There was snow in their eyebrows and hair, chunks of it frozen to their beards. Haralambos could barely see, so thick it was on his glasses.

Without gloves, their fingers quickly got stiff, and they abandoned the fight. Although it continued to snow intermittently the rest of the day, it never amounted to much, most of it gone before nightfall, melting away.

It was O'Malley who spotted the plane, circling Kalavryta, it was, as if looking for a place to land. He cursed the British, remembering the airfield they'd ordered him to build, the use it would be put to now. Though the buzzing of the plane lasted well into the night, it never set down.

O'Malley stayed up long after the others, watching the valley with his rifle in hand. A siren had gone off in his head when he'd seen the plane, was sounding still.

* * *

HE HEARD SOMEONE walking outside, voices whispering in the darkness. Getting to his feet, he checked the tower, but saw nothing amiss and returned to bed. They were marching west soon to join other ELAS units, and he didn't want to be tired.

There was frost on the ground when he awoke the next day. In spite of the cold, the old woman was sitting on a stool outside her hut, talking to herself, something about her grandson, what she'd ordered him to do. "I told him if he was a man, he wouldn't let it pass."

She'd brought a length of knitting with her and was untangling the yarn as she spoke. "'Now's a good time,' I said. 'They won't be expecting it.'"

She continued talking as before, confusing the Germans with the Turks, using the terms interchangeably. An enemy was an enemy. *Xenoi*. Foreign. It didn't matter where they were from or what language they spoke. They didn't belong here.

She tended to natter on and O'Malley was only half listening.

Smiling, she reached into her bag and handed him a dimpled apple from a summer long past, patted him on the knee. She didn't ask to be reimbursed for it or mention the theft of her chickens. She's forgotten, O'Malley thought, studying her wrinkled face and milky eyes. *Aye*, age has wiped the slate clean. He didn't know whether to laugh or cry.

He was drawn to her in spite of himself. Never still, she was either sweeping out her house or knitting as she was today, seeing to her endless litany of chores. Like the hag in the Irish legend, the mythical crone who presided over the Fort of Shadows in Skye, who built a castle in a single night, chanting and singing as she labored in the dark.

The old woman would often reminisce, sharing memories of her youth with him. The last few days it had been her wedding she spoke of. The beauty of the crowns she and her husband had worn in the church that day, so delicate they were like haloes.

Today, however, it was only her grandson she talked of.

" 'You must kill them,' I told Kimon." Picking up her needles, she began to knit again. " 'Theodoros has relatives there. They'll help you get rid of the bodies.' "

Not sure he'd heard right, O'Malley bent his head closer. "What's that you're saying, little mother? Who's Kimon supposed to be killing?"

She looked up at him, surprised he hadn't understood. "The wounded Germans. The men in the hospital in Kalavryta."

* * *

Leonidas frowned. "You're sure you understood? Your Greek …." He rocked his hand back and forth. The local gesture for a little this, a little that. In other words, not so good.

"Aye, I understood her all right."

O'Malley had let loose a torrent of abuse on the old woman after he understood. "Brought the wrath of God down upon us, so you did, flicking that forked tongue of yours." The old woman had chuckled. She'd thought he was playing.

He was still so angry he felt like flames were consuming him; he was giving off heat.

Leonidas got to his feet, O'Malley's rage beginning to stir his as well. "I'll go after him," he said. "Kimon's on foot. Maybe I can head him off."

"I'll come."

The Greek put a hand out to steady him. "No. You'll kill him."

"Aye, I will. Come to that."

Leonidas quickly saddled his horse and took off at a gallop. He was whipping his steed mercilessly, spurring it on as he raced down the hill.

The old woman was still sitting outside her hut, knitting placidly. "You needn't bother," she called after him. "Kimon will have finished by now."

* * *

Darkness was falling when Leonidas returned. He was riding slowly, letting the horse find its way on its own. He had a cloth bag with him, stuffed with soiled sheeting.

"The doctor was beside himself when I got there," he said, lighting a cigarette. "He said he tried to stop them, but Kimon had a knife and forced his way in. The doctor refused to tell him which room the prisoners were in, but the nurses were scared and they showed him."

O'Malley noticed the Greek's hands were flecked with blood. "The burned men, they're dead, aren't they?"

Leonidas nodded. "I didn't get there in time."

He rubbed his eyes. "Kimon killed three of the Germans in the ward. The fourth had been shot in the lungs and was having trouble breathing. To keep an eye on him at night, the doctor had moved him out of the hospital and into his house. He is still alive."

He offered this up in a hopeful voice. As if all were not lost.

"I demanded to see the ward. Though the mattresses had been stripped, there was blood everywhere. 'Get rid of this,' I told the nurses. 'Burn all the evidence there were German patients here.' The women hurriedly fetched mops and began to clean up the room, their hands trembling as they wrung out the bloody water. He slit their throats. It was a mess."

He imitated a woman's voice. " 'They were asleep,' the nurses told me. 'They didn't know. They didn't know.' "

As if it made any difference.

"What'd he do with the bodies?" O'Malley asked.

"There were two men with him and they helped him take them away. They told the nurses not to worry, that they were going to throw them down a well. The women were all crying by then."

"A well? That's the first place the Germans will look."

"I know."

"Maybe they won't find them."

Throwing his cigarette down, Leonidas ground it out under his heel. "Trust me, they'll find them."

He had retrieved the bloody sheets from the hospital and told the men to burn them immediately. Roumelis made a fire in a metal barrel and stuffed them in, poking them down into it with a stick. The mattresses they buried in a pit outside the town. Everyone who'd witnessed the attack had been warned to keep silent, that their silence was a matter of life and death for the village.

As a precautionary measure, Leonidas set up a twenty-four hour watch on Kalavryta. The *antartes* needed no urging and quickly spread out on the hills above the town.

That evening the bells of the church in Kalavryta began to ring. They continued to ring on into the night. Father Chronis must have heard, O'Malley thought, and was sounding the alarm.

* * *

LEADING DONKEYS LADEN with household goods, people began leaving Kalavryta the next morning, passing through Mazeika on their way south. The village was in a state of panic, they reported. No one knew what to do, whether to stay or go. It wasn't just the murder of the three wounded prisoners in the hospital they were worried about; it was the seventy-seven other soldiers who'd gone missing in the area. They blamed the *antartes* for their troubles, the long journey they now faced.

A few of the refugees had horse-drawn wagons, but most were on foot. O'Malley had drawn guard duty, assigned to the butte above the road. He spent the day watching the exodus, the slipshod caravan of people and animals filing out of Kalavryta. Every now and then a car would seek to get past the horde, its owner honking and shouting at people to get out of his way.

The refugees had packed in haste, stowing leaking tins of olive oil on top of their bed linens and clothes. For the most part, it was a motley collection, the things they'd chosen to take—icons and painted crockery, rolled up rugs—little that would be of use to them on the trip ahead. Every now and then a toy would show itself, a child's bicycle, its wheels spinning aimlessly, or a china doll. The villagers led cows, too, if they had them, and goats and sheep. A couple of people had chickens in ramshackle cages strapped to the backs of their donkeys, and the hens' squawking added to the sense of chaos.

The people's trudging had an air of finality about it. They kept looking back as if trying to fix the village in their mind. Many of the women were sobbing.

"We're heading to Sparta where we have relatives," one woman told O'Malley. "Hopefully there'll be food when we get there." She had a little boy with her, clutching at her skirts.

"What about Danae Papadakis and her father?"

"As far as I know, they're still in Kalavryta."

"*Peino, mama.*" Her son tugged at her arm. I'm hungry.

"*Siopi.*" Hush.

The child continued to cry. Embarrassed, his mother bade O'Malley good night and walked on with her son. O'Malley could hear the boy weeping as they made their way over the hill. "*Peino*," he kept saying, the words echoing over the darkened landscape long after he and his mother had disappeared from view.

The *antartes* continued to search for Kimon, seeking to learn where he and his brother had thrown the corpses. Leonidas had instructed the men to destroy any evidence they found. Disinter the bodies and burn them. Do whatever was necessary to obscure the fact that the wounded men in the hospital had been murdered.

The old woman had also disappeared.

O'Malley seethed whenever he thought of her. Not the hag in Skye, that one. No, what she'd been was far darker, the angel of death.

If von Le Suire discovered the bodies of the wounded men, he'd remember those seventy-seven others, the ones long dead on the mountain. That many, he'd be forced to take action.

* * *

"I'LL BE CAREFUL. I'll ride like the wind and get Danae. You won't even know I'm gone."

O'Malley and Leonidas had again drawn guard duty and were up on a bluff, watching for German patrols. A pair of hawks hovered above them, riding the currents of air. The birds made O'Malley anxious, and he watched them out of the corner of his eye, circling above him. At least they weren't vultures, he told himself. Not yet anyway.

Snow covered the lower flanks of Mount Helmos. If he and Danae were to leave, they needed to go now, before more snow came and blocked the pass through the mountain.

He had thought this was as good a time as any to tell Leonidas he was going and was surprised at the vehemence of his friend's response.

"Are you crazy? You can't leave, not now!" Leonidas shouted.

Setting the binoculars down, O'Malley turned and faced his friend. "Say what you will. I need to get her out of Kalavryta. Get her to safety."

"Safety? Take a look around you, my friend." Leonidas pointed to Kalavryta, the mountains that surrounded it. "There's no safety here. You're a soldier in a military unit that has neither ammunition nor food. Outgunned and outmanned by the enemy. When the Germans attack, we have exactly enough bullets to hold them off for a day, maybe two. No more."

"I'll take her away then. To Mani."

"Mani's a long way off. People see you, they'll think you're a German soldier and she's your whore. Greeks in the countryside think the devil has red hair, 'Red like the flames of hell,' they say, and they throw stones at them. The way you look, you won't last a week. You saw what happened to her brother. You want her to get killed, too? To get shot dead in a field somewhere?"

"No. I'd sooner die than see her harmed."

"Then leave her where she is, safe in her father's house."

"How long you talking?"

"Until the end of the war."

"Go on outta here."

"I'm serious. The Germans are on the run. Even if they do try and attack Kalavryta, they'll never make it through the mountains. ELAS has men guarding every pass. They'll never get by them."

"Do they have bullets, these ELAS men of yours?"

"More than we do. Enough to hold them back."

O'Malley looked away. He didn't share his friend's optimism. Again, he thought of Kalavryta and the fist. Wondered if his friend had forgotten the Germans had planes.

20

After the initial exodus, the number of people leaving Kalavryta slowly dwindled. Perhaps it was the cold keeping them home, O'Malley thought sourly, beating his arms against himself.

It had been three days since the attack at the hospital, far longer since they'd thrown the POWs off the mountain. Although he and the others still kept watch on the village, there was less urgency now when they took up their positions. Von Le Suire hadn't found the bodies. There was no reason to think he ever would.

Not exactly peace in our time. A truce, more like it. O'Malley prayed it would hold and that he'd be able to spend Christmas with Danae. Just that morning, he'd questioned Leonidas about the custom in Greece, whether her father would take it amiss if he bought her a ring. The Greek just laughed and shook his head.

"*Ehei trelathei apo tin agapi tou,*" he said. Crazy from love.

For the time being, O'Malley had abandoned his plan to spirit her away. Leonidas was right. She was better off staying where she was. He'd do her up proper when the war was over, marry her and take her away in a shiny new car. A convertible maybe, with a horn he'd blow like the trumpet of Gabriel.

They'd spend their honeymoon in Ireland. First to Cork, of course, to see his folks, then on to Glengarriff, where they'd swim in the phosphorescent water, the fiery sea. His ma had always wanted a daughter. Danae's presence would be like a gift to her.

Three times he'd snuck into town to see her, waiting until well past midnight and taking his rifle with him. He'd left Elektra behind and walked there, hidden in a ditch at the bottom of the hill and ventured on. Crossing the field at a run the night before, he'd nearly slammed into a donkey. Scared him half to death, it had, and set his heart pounding.

The donkey had barely stirred. Shying away, it had only flicked its ears and given a swipe of its tail. The grass had been stiff beneath him and he'd lain there for a few moments before taking off again, pausing in the shadow of a village doorway before making his way to her house. He always hesitated once he got there. Then, gathering up his courage, he'd throw a handful of gravel at her window.

She opened the shutters and peered out. Her hair was loose, reaching almost her waist. Breathtaking, it was, the heavy length of it stirring in the air like ravens taking flight.

"*Angle?*"

"Aye. I came to see how you're faring."

She snuck out of the house a few minutes later. She hadn't bothered to change, just thrown a shawl over her nightdress. He'd brought a blanket and they sat out in the field. The clouds had lifted and the sky was bright with stars.

They spent the night there, talking softly.

At one point O'Malley pointed to the sky. "Once, on St. Stephen's Day, I made a mask out of a brown paper bag. Seven, I was at the time, and eager to parade in the street with the older boys, all bedecked as they were in a straw costume and ribbons. The bag was ripped in places, and when I put it over my head, I saw these tiny pinpricks of light. Being a smart lad, I concluded stars must be much the same: holes in the broken parts of the sky where the light of heaven shone through. My pa laughed when I told him, said I'd never be a scientist. My ma, however, was greatly pleased."

" 'You're right, son,' she'd said. 'God's glory is all around. Waiting for us up there in the sky, waiting to bathe us in holy light.' "

For some reason, O'Malley felt like crying. "She's a good woman, my ma."

He'd expected Danae to laugh at him, but she just touched his face with a kind of wonder. Murmured his given name.

"We sang that day in Cork, laughed and sang and celebrated Christmas."

> The wren, the wren, the king of all birds,
> St. Stephen's his Day was caught in the furze;
> And though he is little, his family's great,
> So arise, good lady, and give us a treat.
> Sing holly, sing ivy.

He sang softly to her for a moment and stopped. The words seemed foolish in this place, a mockery even. He'd not be the same boy his ma knew when he got back to Ireland. The one who'd made masks and paraded with the other lads in the street. Who thought heaven was all around, just waiting to be seen. No, he was gone forever. Lost to the war like so much else.

He thought again of Stefanos, lying in the field with his eyes open. Those wounded, unseeing eyes, a dead echo of sky.

At some point he'd taken the *flokati* off and draped it around Danae's shoulders, but she'd pushed it away, insisting they share. Although she was very near, lying in the crook of his arm, he hadn't reached for her. He'd been content to just lie there with her, to watch over her, if only for a time.

"You got food?" he asked. "Enough to eat?"

"Yes. My father is bringing us a goat and we'll butcher it when he comes, so we will have meat."

She was making her pa a gray vest with cables, she said, knitting it under her Aunt Toula's tutelage. "If I have any wool left over, I'll make you one, too." She picked at the *flokati* with her fingers, made a gesture of distaste.

"Now don't go maligning my cape. Served me well, it has."

"Baa," she said softly. "Baa."

A shooting star pierced the darkness. "Make a wish," O'Malley said.

Danae shook her head.

"Come on."

"All right." Throwing her head back, she mumbled something. It sounded too long to be a wish, more like a prayer.

"What'd you wish for?"

"I wished the star hadn't fallen, that it was back where it belonged up in the sky, that everything was the same as before."

Although she hadn't said her brother's name, O'Malley knew she meant Stefanos.

* * *

AFTER LEAVING DANAE, O'Malley had retreated to the bluff with his gun, watching over the plains of Kalavryta. Leonidas always referred to guard duty as 'shepherding the wind,' but O'Malley saw it differently. Standing there on the rock, he felt like he was the captain of a ship, a guardian of sorts, steering the village through a stormy sea. Messengers reported there'd been German troop movement in and out of Patras, but so far he'd seen nothing.

Von Le Suire was withdrawing, had to be. By Christmas, it might well be over. After the initial panic, life in the camp had slowly returned to normal, the main worry now no longer the murdered POWs, but food. All the chickens had been eaten and the *antartes* were living on olives and puckered figs gleaned from the fields. Although the woods were full of quail, Leonidas had forbidden the men from shooting them, saying they needed to conserve their ammunition and the sound might alert the Germans in the area to their presence. O'Malley, for one, was ready to disobey that order—kill the first quail crossed his path. Bite off its head and eat it, feathers and all.

There'd been talk of marching into Kalavryta and bartering for provisions. Again, Leonidas had dissuaded them, saying they'd lose their advantage if the Germans attacked, that it would be better if they kept to the high ground. Judging by the talk he'd overheard, the *antartes* were ready to mutiny. O'Malley doubted his friend could hold them back much longer.

A middle-aged man was climbing up the path toward him. Unlike the other refugees, he carried no suitcase, led no donkey or mule.

"I came to warn you," he said. "The Germans found the bodies."

"When?"

"A few hours ago. They brought grappling hooks and fished them out of the well, laid them on the ground. You could see the wounds in their throats, what Kimon had done to them. Von Le Suire was there, walking back and forth and shouting orders."

"Where was the well?"

Let it be far, he prayed. *Far, far away from this place.*

"To the north of here. About a fifteen minute walk from Kalavryta."

Two days later, the same man returned. "They found more men," he said. "High up in the mountains. All broken apart and dressed in German uniforms. More than seventy of them. My cousin's a shepherd. He watched the soldiers carry them down."

O'Malley felt like he'd been hit by a wave, washed out to sea. "How they'd know they were there?"

"I don't know. Maybe a pilot spotted them. Von Le Suire had a group of Greeks with him and he ordered them to put the dead in coffins. They had been on the mountain a long time and animals had been at them, my cousin said, so it took the Greeks a long time. After they finished, the Germans lined them up and shot them."

"Do you think that was the end of it?"

"No." The man's voice cracked. "They won't stop until they kill us all."

The man said the mayor planned to meet with the German officers when they arrived. Explain that the people of Kalavryta had nothing to do with any of it. It had been the *antartes* who'd thrown the soldiers off the mountain, kids from another village who'd knifed the POWs in the hospital.

"He's forming a committee to welcome the Germans. A fucking committee."

O'Malley looked back at Kalavryta, his face full of longing.

"Ach, Danae," he said in a strangled voice.

* * *

She was standing outside, hanging wet sheets on a line with her aunt, a basket of wet clothes between them. Both women were wearing black dresses and kerchiefs, *tsokara*, cheap leather clogs, on their feet. The grass was damp and their ankles were splattered with mud.

"The Germans are on their way," O'Malley shouted. "You've got to get out of here."

Toula Papadakis waved him off. "Bah, they've been saying that for weeks now."

She gathered up a sheet and threw it across the line, wrestling with it against the wind. The sheet swelled with air, beating against the rope that held it like a sail. Danae's aunt had let herself go since the death of Stefanos, O'Malley noticed, abandoned her lipstick and dyed hair, an inch of white now showing at the roots. A rank odor clung to her and there were lines of filth in the folds of her neck.

"Put your laundry away, woman," he yelled. "Did you not hear? Von Le Suire is coming. He'll take down this place and slaughter the lot of you. In Crete, Germans destroyed a village named Kandanos. Massacred everyone there. Women and children, it didn't matter. Salted the earth and poisoned the wells. I was there. I saw. It'll be worse here in Kalavryta. Far worse."

"Danae's father is bringing the goats down from the mountains. He won't be back until Thursday."

Two days from now.

Bending down, she began going through the wet clothes as if searching for something she couldn't find, her hands shaking.

Danae gently took the basket from her. "Come on, *Theia*. We'll pack the suitcase and leave as soon as Baba returns from the mountains. We'll go to your cousin's house in Coroni."

O'Malley helped the women get the suitcase down from the attic and stood over them, watching them pack. The aunt quickly folded up her dresses, then went to the closet and retrieved some of Stefanos' things, which she placed in the suitcase on top of the rest. His little bag, a couple of sweaters. As if the child would be traveling with them.

As if he wasn't gone.

Danae she left to fend for herself.

After they finished, O'Malley carried the suitcase to the door and set it down. Before he left, he warned them again to get away as soon as possible; with the Germans on the move, they were in terrible danger.

Sprinting across the field, he started back toward the camp. He needed to find Leonidas and warn him, figure out some way to save the village. Judging by what the man had told him, the Greeks didn't have much time.

Danae came running after him. "*Angle*! Wait!"

Out of breath, she handed him a piece of paper. "It's my cousin's address in Coroni."

Grinning from ear to ear, O'Malley fingered the paper. A commitment of sorts, this was, there was no denying it. "Ah, Danae, Danae. My summer's day, my bit of light. Does this mean you'll have me then?"

As always, she soon put an end to his malarkey. "It is only an address. A way to find me."

"Good Lord, but you're a stubborn one. Is it my red hair that's putting you off? My feckless Irish ways?" The note made him bold. She was his and he knew it.

"I am afraid for you," Danae said, touching his sleeve. "I wish you could come with us."

"Can't. Got to fight the Germans."

"I know."

"You got no cause to worry though, not on my account. The Irish, we're invincible. 'Tis the freckles protect us. Keep the bullets from penetrating."

Bad luck to be talking this way, but he didn't care.

He didn't want to remember her crying. He'd enough of that back in Ireland, his ma clutching at him and sobbing. Women's tears weakened a man and he needed to be strong now.

"When will you come?" Her eyes were wet.

"As soon as the Germans turn loose of this place. I'll ride my big horse and come fetch you like in a fairy tale, bear you away and make you my wife. It'll be grand, so it will. You'll see. I'll wear my *flokati* and you'll wear your ma's wedding dress and all the people we love will be there, pelting us with rice and shouting 'halleluiah.' "

Pulling her close, he crooned the words of an Irish wedding jig in her ear.

> Come haste to the wedding ye friends and ye neighbors,
> The lovers their bliss can no longer delay.
> Forget all your sorrows your cares and your labors,
> And let every heart beat with rapture today.
> Come, come one and all, attend to my call.

"After we're done marrying, we'll spend our days by the sea, throw off our clothes and take to the water like fishes, swimming and frolicking and nibbling each other, scandalize the neighborhood with our nakedness. At night we'll lie out on the beach and count the stars, catch the ones that tumble. A few we'll save to adorn you with, to dress up your raven hair. The rest we'll put back. "

"You are such a fool." She was crying openly now.

"We'll have sons aplenty. Big, strapping fellows with hair the color of fire and tempers to match. Irishmen, they'll be, same as their pa. We'll have a couple of daughters, too, to even things out. Dark-haired girls with faces like the Madonna's. Beautiful faces."

He touched her cheek with his hand, did his best to wipe her tears away. "Your face, Danae. Your holy face."

21

"I aim to marry her," O'Malley declared again.

Leonidas gave him a long look. He'd been giving him that look for some time now. As if all the idiots in the world were in a great race, and he, Brendan O'Malley, was about to win the gold medal.

"I know no other way," he insisted.

"Germans coming and you talk of love. Ach, Romeo. What am I going to do with you?" Spurring his mount, he drove it into the herd of horses, whistling to the strays and moving them back into the fold.

Determined to keep the horses out of von Le Suire's hands, he and O'Malley had rounded up the herd and driven it up into the mountains, intending to pasture them in an abandoned corral near the airfield.

Unable to contain himself, O'Malley had spoken of nothing, save Danae, on the long ride there, the vow he'd made to marry her. She'd expressed her love, too, he'd said, albeit a tad more reluctantly than he would have liked. Perhaps that was the nature of Greek women. They were understated and quiet in their romantic passions. Still giddy, he'd gone on a bit, he had to admit, recalling every word of the conversation, offering them up to Leonidas like precious relics, a fistful of gold doubloons.

The Greek had just shaken his head. "Ancient Greeks say 'marriage is an evil most men welcome.' You'd do well to heed them."

"Irish say 'only cure for love is marriage.'"

"There, you see? Be sensible and give up this nonsense. Go to Cyprus."

The sun was going down by the time they finally reached the corral, light slowly ebbing from the sky. Ahead, O'Malley could see the long line of horses, their shadows dark against the hill.

Finding a tin basin, he filled it with water from a nearby stream and set it down on the ground next to them. He pulled up armfuls of frozen weeds and laid them out as well. Like the men in the camp, the horses too would soon be hungry. Elektra danced around him, nickering softly, her breath steamy in the night air.

"Sorry, my lady. Got naught but brambles for your supper."

Leonidas continued to chaff O'Malley, mocking him about his domestic arrangements, his misplaced devotion to Danae.

"*Ah, Irlande*," he cried in a falsetto voice, sashaying around like a woman. "*S'agapo. Filise me.*" Oh, Irishman, I love you. Kiss me. "Ah, Romeo, Romeo!"

O'Malley started to say Romeo had come to a bad end, but then he stopped. Maybe he knew, Leonidas. Maybe that was the point.

* * *

"It might go the way it did in Vysokiotis," Haralambos said. "Germans rounded up all the men and held them at gunpoint for a few hours before letting them go again. They burned a few houses, but they didn't kill anybody."

"Maybe." Leonidas didn't sound convinced.

After O'Malley had reported von Le Suire's discovery of the bodies, the Greeks had immediately set to work strengthening their position, digging foxholes at the base of the walls and securing the mortars.

The *antartes* had decided as a group not to enter Kalavryta under any circumstances. They might get trapped there when the Germans came and put the residents of the village even more at risk.

"It'll be like Vysokiotis," Haralambos kept insisting. "We stay out of it, and no one will get hurt."

"Not this time," Leonidas said. "They are going to level that village."

He'd spoken calmly. Only a slight tremor in his hands as he lit a cigarette betrayed his tension.

A messenger had brought word that morning that Wehrmacht units were being summoned from Aigion and Tripoli in the central Peloponnese, hundreds, maybe even a thousand men to be deployed from the military bases there. Units were also being dispatched to Kalavryta from Corinth and Pyrgos.

North, south, east, and west. O'Malley wondered how long it would take for the Germans to reach the village. The mountains would slow them down, but not by much. Two days, maybe three. By the end of the week, they'd be in the thick of it.

Stukas had been flying low over the area for the last twenty-four hours. O'Malley held his breath every time one appeared, waiting for the pilot to strafe the village, but so far they'd held their fire. Conducting reconnaissance was his guess. Von Le Suire was getting ready.

The *antartes* had undertaken their defense of the town with a sense of fatalism. They had no hope of repelling the Germans and they knew it. They didn't speak much and what talk there was concerned the fate of their wives and children, should they be killed.

"You, there," Alexis had called to O'Malley at one point. "See to the mortar."

O'Malley had ignored him and within minutes they'd gotten into it.

Grabbing the front of the other man's jacket, O'Malley had shoved him hard. "Don't you be telling me what to do, you hear? I'll beat your face in." The anger felt good, made him feel alive for the first time in days. "You're the cause of this, you are. You're the reason they're coming. If you'd only left those poor men alone …."

Alexis spat on the ground. "British." He made the word a curse.

"Be careful," the other men cautioned O'Malley after Alexis stomped off. "You're poking a stick at a snake."

"I know," O'Malley said, his rage now spent. "I know I am."

* * *

THE FOLLOWING DAY, December 8th, a messenger from ELAS headquarters brought word that the Germans were advancing, marching out of Patras and heading east.

The killing started almost immediately. The Germans burned Kerpini first, a village northwest of Kalavryta, and shot all the men there, some forty or fifty of them. They killed eighteen more in Zachlorou, a hamlet high up in the mountains, and threw the bodies into the river. Family members pulled the dead men out of the water and dug graves for them in the sand. The temperature was near freezing and the ground was too hard to bury them in the local cemetery.

Marching on, the Germans torched three more small villages—Souvardo, Vrachni, and Rogi—before taking possession of the monastery, Mega Spileon, in the gorge.

Initially, the monks had treated them as guests, serving them lunch and offering them rooms to rest in. After they'd eaten and slept, the soldiers collected the monks and marched them to Kissoti, the highest point of land in the gorge, where they killed them and pushed their bodies off a cliff. One of the monks was severely crippled and being looked after by a ten-year-old boy. When the boy saw what was happening, he tried to intervene, and the soldiers shot him, too. After they finished, they left the bodies where they fell and burned the monastery.

The similarity between the killing of the POWS and the murder of the monks was not lost on the *antartes*. Fotis and two other men cornered Alexis after they heard what had happened and accused him of murder.

"It's war," Alexis said, backing away with his hands up, his bravado gone. "They were the enemy."

"What did you accomplish by killing them? Did you retake Athens? Did you drive the Germans into the sea?"

"They would have died anyway. We had nothing to feed them."

"At least Kalavryta would have been spared. At least the people there would have lived."

The *antartes* had been watching the monastery burn all afternoon, the surging mass of black smoke rising from the gorge. O'Malley silently prayed for the soul of the monk in the *kalymafki*, the old man who'd asked Leonidas what he should do if the Germans came, the one who'd so feared this day.

In spite of his veil and prayerful existence, he'd seen the world after all, that monk. Seen it as he stood on the edge of the cliff waiting to die, seen it in all its gory magnificence. His precious God had not intervened, had not in fact saved him. O'Malley wondered what the monk had thought about during his last moments on earth. If like Jesus, he'd sought forgiveness for his tormentors—if his belief had been strong enough and he had welcomed the coming of paradise.

Somehow he doubted it. The monk wasn't Jesus. He was a man same as him, and men feared death. It was one of mankind's most defining characteristics. Christianity had been built on it, the idea of heaven and hell—a kind of answer.

The wind was up and it made an inhuman sound as it tore through the cracks in the tower.

Sounds like the wailing of a banshee, O'Malley thought, remembering his mother's tales, how banshees wore cloaks of cobwebs and could change their shape, appearing sometimes as washerwomen and cleaning blood off the armor of those about to die. But always they howled.

* * *

THE FIRST GERMAN motorcycle appeared at dawn on December 9th. It was immediately followed by others, an ever-widening stream, hundreds of them converging on Kalavryta.

The sound was deafening in the early morning stillness, the stench of diesel fuel heavy in the air.

O'Malley and Leonidas were lying on top of the butte, watching the advance through binoculars. They were very close to Kalavryta, less than a quarter of a mile by O'Malley's estimate. He could see the motorcycles clearly.

After a messenger from ELAS had reported the Germans were closing in, the two of them had gotten into position. Their plan was not to attack, but to count the soldiers and determine what weapons they carried. The rest of the *antartes* were higher still. They had been ordered by Leonidas and Haralambos not to fire on the soldiers. Their mission was only to watch and keep track of the number, to alert ELAS headquarters once they knew.

A long line of trucks soon followed. O'Malley counted each truck as it passed and did a rough calculation. Twenty men per truck. At the very least, well over three thousand men. Half the trucks were towing heavy artillery as well, self-propelled mortars and rocket launchers—ten-centimeter siege howitzers on metal platforms.

He grew more and more distraught. Only other time he'd seen an onslaught like this had been the day the Germans invaded Athens. These soldiers seemed to have the same sense of purpose. He could see them peering out of the backs of the trucks and looking around curiously. All were dressed in battle gear and carrying assault rifles—outfitted for war. Some of the guns had small searchlights on them. *Vampirs*, he realized with dread. Even at night, there'd be no getting away.

St. Patrick had transformed himself and his followers into a herd of deer to flee their tormentors. Would that he had this gift and could do the same, clothe the village in fur and hooves and spirit it away.

The parade of vehicles continued the rest of the day. The motorcycles separated from the trucks when they reached the village, the former entering the town directly, the latter forming a tight circle around it.

Immediately after the trucks stopped, soldiers jumped down and set up roadblocks, barring all access.

At noon four more vehicles arrived in quick succession, huge, cumbersome trucks with anti-aircraft guns in tow. The drivers sped up as they neared the village, waving and egging each other on. As if this was Le Mans and they were racing, jockeying to be the first across the finish line. Soldiers were visible through the windshields, their faces young and intent. Like the others, they wore helmets and were carrying StG 44s.

" 'Tis only a village. What do they need guns like that for?"

Leonidas' eyes were bloodshot. "To blow holes in the buildings."

"So they'll be taking it apart then, same as they did in Crete?"

He nodded. "Right down to the ground."

Watching the trucks maneuver, O'Malley prayed Danae had already left, that she and her family had escaped what was surely coming.

"*Ahortagos*," Leonidas said. "That's what they are. Cannibals, cannibals in search of prey. Hitler said, 'When swine are housed with women and children, you must put the house to the torch.' "

"We're in for it, you're saying," O'Malley said.

Leonidas shook his head. "No," he pointed to the village, "they are."

* * *

O'Malley fiddled with his binoculars, working to bring Kalavryta into focus. He could see a German soldier standing on top of a truck with a bullhorn, shouting something, a second standing off to the side, probably translating the words into Greek. So far the residents were staying in their houses. *Poor fools.* He wondered if they'd locked their doors.

The village was like a field mouse he'd once seen in the claws of a cat. The little creature had stood idly by as the cat batted it back and forth, let it go only to recapture it again, stoically enduring the torment that preceded its death. It hadn't tried to flee, hadn't fought to save itself in any way. A chemical was released in its brain that numbed it, his pa had said. Made death bearable.

Standing there, watching Kalavryta, O'Malley desperately wanted to believe there was a human equivalent.

Danae must have left, he told himself. It had been four days since he'd seen her and told her to go. She and her people had to have reached Coroni by now. He'd wanted to visit her house to make sure, but Leonidas had begged him not to, saying his presence would bring the wrath of God down on the village, should the Germans discover him there.

"The wrath of God is already on its way, unless I'm mistaken," O'Malley argued. "What difference does it make?" But in the end he'd obeyed. Danae was safe in her cousin's house by the sea, the little waves—the *kymata*, as the Greek called them—washing up on the shore at her feet and keeping her company. He smiled, thinking of it. She was well out of it; that was the main thing.

A large black touring car arrived a short time later. A convertible, it had red flags with swastikas that snapped in the breeze as it made its way forward. Two men were riding in the back, one in a military uniform, the other in the black garb of the SS.

"The one to the left is Ebersberger," Leonidas told him, watching the car through his binoculars. "The man on the right is Walter Blume. SS, he's well known to us: rounds up civilians during *bloccos* and interrogates them. The driver's name is Doehnert. He speaks Greek, which is probably why they brought him. They'll need him to translate once things get started."

Raising his binoculars again, O'Malley followed the car's progress through Kalavryta. Ebersberger was waving a plump hand at the village, smiling at the people in the street as if on parade.

Blume's face was harder, marred by deep cuts on the right side of his mouth and across the bridge of his nose. Not as disfiguring as shrapnel wounds, they probably came from dueling. Such things were a sign of prestige in Germany.

O'Malley didn't like his sharp, neutral gaze, the way he was inspecting the handful of villagers who'd dared show themselves. An IRA renegade had once passed through his parents' farm, and he'd never forgotten that man's appraising glance. Blume's expression was exactly the same, as if he were measuring people for coffins.

* * *

THE *ANTARTES* REMAINED holed up in the tower, the assumption being they'd be safer there, have the advantage of high ground should the Germans attack. None of the men had any illusions about what was about to happen. They'd been at war long enough to recognize a German reprisal operation when they saw one and a reprisal operation was what this was. All they dared hope for was that the Germans would confine their killing to the men and leave the women and children alone.

They'd been overwhelmed by the number of men von Le Suire had dispatched to drive them out and the weaponry they wielded. The situation was hopeless and they knew it. After much debate, Leonidas and Haralambos ordered the men not to engage the enemy in defense of Kalavryta. "To attack a force of this size would be foolhardy and suicidal," Haralambos told the assembled *antartes*. Such action would only further the destruction, the firestorm about to engulf the town.

Fotis begged them to reconsider, arguing they should try and defend Kalavryta no matter what the cost. They should be like Spartans in Thermopylae, he kept saying. "With only three hundred men, they held off an entire Persian army."

"The Persians didn't have siege howitzers," Haralambos said.

Fotis refused to give up, his eyes bleary with tears. "We brought this on the village. We are responsible."

"So what if we are? We can't do anything. Not against those guns. The best we can do is bear witness. Care for the survivors after the Germans leave."

"*Diloi*!" Fotis shouted. Cowards.

He abandoned the unit immediately after, taking his brother, Andreas, and about thirty other men with him. He spat on the ground as he left, cursing the *antartes* and the cause they served.

"*Prodotes*!" Traitors.

Roumelis pulled Leonidas aside after Fotis left. "My mother lives in Kalavryta. She's all alone and crippled with arthritis. She'll need help if the Germans march them to Patras. I need to be with her."

"Go," Leonidas said. He was pale after the exchange with Fotis. "Go."

Haralambos had been right from a military point of view, O'Malley thought. Wrong from every other one. At least half of the men came from Kalavryta. In effect, he was asking them to abandon their families.

O'Malley walked part way to Kalavryta with the cook. All was quiet, only the long line of trucks around the perimeter evidence of the German presence. Thin wisps of smoke rose from the chimneys, and he could see lights in many of the windows. *People must be having supper now. Putting their children to bed.* A light rain was falling and it dampened the bark on the trees. Somewhere off in the distance an owl gave voice to the approaching darkness.

A bottle in hand, Roumelis lumbered alongside him. He'd offered it to O'Malley, but he'd declined, saying he was on guard duty that night and had to have his wits about him.

"How are you going to get into Kalavryta?" he asked the cook. "Ebersberger sealed the place off."

As always, Roumelis made light of the situation. "On tiptoe." Drawing himself up, he spun around like a ballerina, his great gut wobbling from side to side.

He continued to prance around, raising first one foot and then the other, taking care to keep his toes pointed. He had it down, the bowlegged gait of male dancers and the poses they struck. It was funny watching him barrel around in his tattered pants, wall-eyed, so he was.

O'Malley had a lump in his throat. "You stay alive, you hear?"

The cook didn't answer. He took off a moment later, leaping high in the air as he ran.

Performing still.

* * *

LATER THAT SAME night O'Malley dragged the radio up to the top of the tower and tried to raise the British officer he'd spoken to in the past. After identifying himself as 'Barabbas,' he hurriedly explained the situation: "It's a matter of life and death. The village of Kalavryta is completely surrounded. The unit I'm with doesn't have enough men and ammunition to mount an attack and we need air and ground support, ammunition most of all. You can use the airfield I built, make the drop as soon as you're able."

He worked to tamp down the Irish in his voice, thinking he'd stood a better chance if the man thought he was English.

Enunciating carefully, he gave him the map references for the airfield. "It's secure, high up in the mountains and well away from the German advance. Your planes should have no trouble getting in and out."

The officer on the other end repeated the coordinates back to him and signed off. O'Malley waited by the radio all the next day but heard nothing. Growing more and more agitated, he radioed again that night.

"The British Command in Cairo vetoed the drop," his contact reported. "Due to hostile action against its British field agents by ELAS forces in Greece, the Command will no longer supply them with ammunition." He recited this in a clipped monotone as if he were reading from a piece of paper.

"How do you expect us to stave off destruction if we've no bullets?"

"If you are indeed as poorly armed as you say, Barabbas, I suggest you and your comrades retreat."

"What about Kalavryta?"

"You've been ordered to leave the region."

O'Malley gave up trying to sound like an Englishman. "*Pog mo thoin*," he bellowed.

"Means 'kiss my arse' in Gaelic. And so you can, you miserable gobshit, so you bloody well can."

"I see. You're Irish." The man's voice was thick with condescension.

"Shut up and listen. Germans killed nearly one hundred fifty people here yesterday and burned four villages. Half the people they killed were monks, men of God. They're on a rampage. They'll stop at nothing."

"I will relay your concern to Cairo," the man said stiffly.

"Tell your commanding officer he'll have blood on his hands if he doesn't help."

"I'll make a note."

And with that, he was gone.

"You can't be doing this! You can't! You can't!" O'Malley tore off his headset and slammed it down.

Leonidas picked up the headset and rubbed it against his sleeve. "Even if your friends in Cairo dropped a thousand guns, it wouldn't matter. Not now. It's too late."

"We can't just stand by. We can't let this happen."

"We can and will." Leonidas' voice broke. "May God forgive us."

22

Leonidas sent the oldest man left in the unit, a white-haired farmer named Menelaos, to Kalavryta to find out what was happening. He was convinced the man's age and stooped posture would protect him and allow him to move more freely about the town.

Menelaos took his time getting ready, rubbing dirt on his face and into his hair, perfecting the shuffling gait and empty-eyed stare of an elderly man, half gone in the head. He dressed himself in old-fashioned garb—voluminous, ballooning pants dating from the last century and tall leather boots, a fringed band around his head.

"I'm a farmer, been out in the field."

"That's right. And now you're on your way home."

The wind was freezing and the *antartes* hunkered down in the tower after the old man left. They didn't dare light a fire, lest they alert the Germans of their presence on the hill. It was very misty, fog boiling up from the river and overtaking the land.

Menelaos returned a few hours later. "Germans imposed a four p.m. curfew and are going from house to house, kicking in doors. 'It was like an earthquake,' my daughter said. 'The soldiers were all shouting, their eyes full of murder.' They had a *maskoforos* with them, pointing out where the *antartes* live. I was hiding in my cousin's house, but the window was open and I could hear him talking. They must have brought him in from outside. He isn't anybody I know. They haven't killed anybody yet, been too busy stripping the place. They looted the cathedral, took everything that wasn't nailed down and pissed on the floor. Then they ordered the town treasurer to open up the bank so they could clear it out, too. After they finished, they made him hand over his watch and his wedding ring."

"What else?" Leonidas asked.

The old man rubbed a hand across his grizzled chin. "Ebersberger keeps telling people, 'You have nothing to fear. We won't harm you.' "

"What about Blume?"

"He's interrogated a few people. I saw him standing outside, smoking a cigarette. Looked like he'd been hard at work. Jacket was bloody."

"You think it'll end there?"

"No." The old man's voice was full of gravel. "I think they're just getting started."

* * *

"I ARRANGED FOR my daughter's son, Nikos, to keep an eye out," Menelaos said. "He's a clever boy. He'll be able to get in and out of Kalavryta without being spotted."

He himself had been stopped by the Germans on his second trip to the village and was afraid to go back. The officer who'd questioned him had been reluctant to let him go. Only the intervention of an elderly woman who claimed he was her senile husband, given to wandering the streets, had saved him.

The other men had teased him when they heard the story, saying he'd best be careful after the war was over—that the old woman would come for him, force him to make good and marry her.

Menelaos had laughed until he had tears in his eyes. "She can't have me," he'd cried, thumping his chest. "I will defend my honor."

* * *

THERE'D BEEN A lull after the initial burst of German activity, a three day hiatus. Military trucks were seen leaving town, piled high with furniture.

"That's how they measure their success," Leonidas said. "Not by the territory they seize, but by the tonnage they steal."

"Good at killing, too," O'Malley said, fiddling with his gun. He'd spent the last forty-eight hours cleaning and re-cleaning it, slipping the cartridge in and taking it out again. Pure foolishness, a tic almost. Still, the repetitive motion comforted him, made him feel as if he were still a soldier, not standing idly by watching the Germans devour a village. If it hadn't been for Danae, he'd have proposed he and the others make a kamikaze run at Kalavryta. Go out with guns a-blazing. But he wanted to stay alive now. More than anything, he wanted to stay alive and get to Coroni.

"How many you think they'll kill?"

"In 1941, Keitel declared the Wehrmacht would kill ten Greeks for every dead German. Later he raised the number to fifty. Ebersberger is a man who obeys the rules. That means more than a thousand will die before he quits."

Sliding the bullets out in his gun, O'Malley bounced them up and down in his hand. "Count the dead, do they, same as accountants?" The thought amused him. Some ledger that would be.

"Yes," Leonidas said. "Germans keep track of everything. They are nothing if not thorough."

The old man, Menelaos, had decided he wanted to be with his family in Kalavryta and had left with two others the previous night, further reducing the number of *antartes*. Those who were left in the tower had done nothing but clean their weapons over the last few days, and the lack of activity was beginning to wear on them.

Haralambos spent his time reading and rereading his Communist tracts, while Leonidas spent hours up on the butte with his binoculars trained on Kalavryta, watching and waiting for the Germans to make their move. A young farmer named Babis had taken over Roumelis' job, boiling *horta* over charcoal in the depths of the tower. They'd long since exhausted whatever food there'd been in Mazeika, scouring the fields until there was nothing left save nettles, dandelions and a few frostbitten onions. At the beginning of the siege, O'Malley had feared dying from a German bullet, but now it was the specter of starvation that haunted him.

Restless and unhappy, the men began to fight among themselves, arguing over the death of the POWs, who was responsible for the slaughter.

"Why'd you kill them?" a man yelled at Alexis.

"Because they were Germans," Alexis shot back.

"You stupid cunt."

"I did what I had to," Alexis said, trying to brazen it out. "I did what was necessary. We were ordered to move out, remember? It's on Velouchiotis, whatever happens. Take it up with him."

"Velouchiotis didn't give the order. It was Dimitris Michos."

"No, it wasn't. Michos is from Peloponnese. He'd never risk Kalavryta."

"Well, someone did."

And so it went.

O'Malley spent most of his time with Leonidas, watching Kalavryta from the butte. "When do you think they'll get to it?"

"I don't know. Tomorrow, the day after."

Judging by the circles under his eyes, his friend hadn't slept in days.

O'Malley pitied him. Knowing what was coming, it had to be like watching his family die a second time.

* * *

O'Malley had just bedded down for the night when Leonidas came stumbling into the tower. "A flare just went up. An arc of green light over the village."

A few minutes later the bells of the church began to toll.

"It's started."

It was two a.m., December 12th.

23

THE DENSE FOG seemed to magnify the sounds, the pealing of the church bells, and clamoring of soldiers, the sense of loss they all felt.

Nikos, Menelaos' nephew, arrived a short time later. He'd run the whole way, he said, desperate to give them the news.

"The Germans told everyone to go to the school with blankets and enough food for one day. They're going to move us away from the front, they said. That's why we need food, for the trip. My mother was worried, afraid we wouldn't have enough to eat if the journey was long."

The *antartes* exchanged glances. "Did they say you were being resettled?" Leonidas asked.

"Yes, how'd you know?" the boy answered. "Resettled in a better place."

The *antartes* who had returned to the village, Fotis and the others, had left their hiding places and were joining their wives and children in the school, the child reported. "A German soldier told a neighbor not to go. He said the soldiers were going to kill us, but the neighbor's a drunk and no one believed him."

It was all a game to the child. "My mother said he was a fool and not to listen."

He kept fidgeting as he told his story, unaware of the seriousness of what he was relaying. "My uncle told me to hide in the house and get word to you as soon as I could—not to come back, no matter what. Soldiers were going up and down the street, making sure no one was left. A woman two doors down had a new baby and her husband had stayed behind to help her. He didn't want to leave, but they dragged him off, too. I was scared, but I did what my uncle said. I hid in the chimney and waited, snuck out again when it was quiet.

It was still dark, so no one saw me. The Germans were all standing around in front of the schoolhouse. I looked for my mother, but I didn't see her."

"Is everyone still at the school?" Leonidas asked.

"Yes. The whole town. No one ran away. The mayor asked what was going happen, if they were going to kill them. '*Nein, nein,*' the Germans said."

"Did the mayor believe them?"

"Sure, everyone did. When they first came, they made us stand in the square and listen to a man with a bullhorn. 'I swear nothing will happen to you,' he said. 'I give you my word as a German officer.' Another soldier translated what he said into Greek; that's how I know. The first man said it over and over. He *promised*."

"He gave you his word as a German officer?" Haralambos was taking down everything the boy said.

Nikos nodded. "There's bunch of soldiers in Kepi's cornfield. I saw them when I was coming here. They're setting up machine guns."

O'Malley looked where the boy was pointing.

Almost at our feet, he thought. *We're going to have a ringside seat.*

* * *

AT FIRST O'MALLEY thought it was the rising sun bathing the clouds with fire. Then he realized it was Kalavryta. The Germans were burning Kalavryta.

The soldiers had torched the fields first, apparently counting on the rising wind to fan the flames. Sounding the alarm, a donkey in a nearby pasture began to bray, its agonized cries adding to the horror. The fire quickly grew in intensity, fueled by the olive trees and the brush, the acres of dry grass.

O'Malley watched the shifting smoke through his binoculars, trying to chart the fire's progress, the movement of the flames as they roared toward the village. It exploded like a bomb when it reached Kalavryta a few seconds later. The Germans must have poured petrol everywhere, soaked the place.

Within minutes, the houses began to collapse, and the air grew rank with swirling debris. Flames poured forth from the cataclysm, columns of sparks shooting hundreds of feet in the air.

The Germans had retreated to the far side of the village and stood watching it burn, their faces lit by flames. It was a well coordinated effort, Stukas passing overhead as if on cue, their engines whining as they dive-bombed the town. A few minutes later, the anti-aircraft guns started up. The Germans' aim was unerring, and entire blocks began to fall as if made of sand. Even though he and Leonidas were a good quarter of a mile away, they could feel the force of each blast, the ground shaking beneath them. Somewhere the donkey continued to bray—weaker, its cry faint now. O'Malley felt like he was watching the end of the world.

At 10:30 a.m., a whistle sounded, the little cog train announcing its departure from the station. O'Malley watched it go, stunned by the incongruity of what he was seeing, but then these were Germans they were dealing with and that's what Germans did. They kept to a schedule. Be it for trains or fire bombing a village, they were systematic till the end.

The whistle continued to blow, as forlorn a sound as he had ever heard. The train was pulling a long line of cars this time, more than half of them loaded with animals—sheep and goats mostly—the rest with domestic goods and farm equipment. Taking everything they could, the Germans. O'Malley wondered where the train was going. If there were special Wehrmacht units whose task it was to unload the possessions of the dead.

An hour later, a group of Germans soldiers left the village, marching a long line of Greek men in front of them. They were herding them at gun point into the cornfield the boy Nikos had spoken of, not far from the cemetery where Stefanos lay buried. Many of the Greeks were carrying blankets and parcels of food.

O'Malley closed his eyes. It was as if they were on their way to a picnic.

He could see all the men clearly through his binoculars, the color of the blankets the Greeks had over their arms and the Jaeger insignias on the hats of the soldiers, the dull sheen of their guns.

He heard shouting, watched a soldier prod a man with his gun.

Sloping steadily downward, the cornfield formed a natural amphitheater overlooking the town. The Germans had chosen the site well, O'Malley thought, watching the Greeks file in. It was perfect for their purposes. Many of the assembled were young—boys no older than ten or eleven years old. The faces of the older people in the field were taut with anguish. They were talking to one another, pointing to Kalavryta and gesturing in distress. As Ebersberger had intended, the sight of the Greeks' burning homes was to be their last on earth.

Eight soldiers with machine guns were kneeling on a rise to the rear of the Greeks, spaced evenly apart. Unlike the villagers, who'd been roused from their beds, they were dressed in fresh uniforms, the metal on their harnesses gleaming in the sunlight. Doehnert and Ebersberger were there, too, overseeing the preparations.

The guns the soldiers were manning were MG 42s or 'Spandaus,' as the British called them. O'Malley had come up against them before and thought the German name, 'bonesaw,' was more apt. The machine gun was like a mighty scythe, taking down all before it.

Judging by Ebersberger's gestures, he was explaining what he wanted done to the men. One of the soldiers pointed at the boys in the field and said something, apparently questioning the children's fate. Furious, Ebersberger shouted at him and made a slicing motion with his hand. The soldier gave a curt nod and resumed his position. The rest of the men appeared unaffected by the order they'd been given and went about their work, adjusting the ammunition belts and sighting the guns. A job, this was. A job like any other.

Ebersberger then approached the Greeks.

A man Leonidas identified as a high school teacher got to his feet and came forward.

Ebersberger continued to speak, a benevolent expression on his face. O'Malley was pretty sure he knew what the German was saying: the Greeks of Kalavryta had no reason to be fear. He and his soldiers meant them no harm. All would be well.

Ebersberger put his hand over his chest when he finished, nodded gravely to the crowd.

Like the scorpion in the story

Leaving the butte, O'Malley inched closer, his gun in his hand. He crawled forward until he was almost directly behind the machine gunners, looking directly down onto the field. Leonidas followed him a moment later.

"Careful with the binoculars," he warned. "They'll see the reflection and know we're up here."

The high school teacher was standing in front of Ebersberger, evidently translating the German's words into Greek.

As soon as he finished, the villagers started yelling and catcalling. Raising their arms as if giving the Nazi salute, they turned the gesture into the *mountza*, the Greek gesture of contempt.

Even now, making jokes, O'Malley thought. Those pungent jokes that so defined them as a people.

Turning on his heel, Ebersberger left the cornfield, taking care to keep well away from the line of fire. Seeing him go, the Greeks began to prepare themselves. A few embraced; others reached for the hands of their sons.

Roumelis was standing in the middle of the group. In a loud voice, he began to sing.

"What's he doing?" O'Malley asked.

Tears were streaming down Leonidas face. "He's singing the national anthem of Greece."

As soon as Roumelis finished the song, he started up again, bellowing out the words at the top of his lungs. Waving his arms like a symphony conductor, he urged the men around him to join in. Fotis was there, O'Malley saw, as was the old man, Menelaos. Father Chronis and the boy from the camp, Grigoris. He recognized others, too, but didn't remember their names.

He could see them all clearly, almost hear the words of their song. The cook pulled a little Greek flag out of his pocket and waved it over his head as he shouted out the words. One of the young boys took the flag from him and held it aloft, then passed it on to another, each touching it in turn as if it were a religious relic, a holy thing.

Tears stung O'Malley's eyes. He reached for his rifle, thinking he'd shoot Ebersberger first, then Doehnert. Give the Greeks a few more seconds of life.

He fired off a round, but he was shaking so badly, the shots went wild. Before he could get another round off, Ebersberger shot a green flare in the air. Doehnert raised his right arm when the flare went up and dropped it when Ebersberger fired off the second flare, red this time. It spun as it came down, a thin ringlet of smoke in its wake, and flooded the cornfield with incandescent light.

Roumelis cried, "*Zito i Hellas! Zito i Hellas!*" Long live Greece.

The other Greeks quickly picked up the chant. "*Zito i Hellas! Zito i Hellas!*" They were still yelling when the soldiers cut them down.

24

O'MALLEY LOST TRACK of how many rounds the Germans fired into the crowd. After they finished, the soldiers left their machine guns and walked through the pile of bodies with their pistols drawn. Hit in the legs, Menelaos tried to crawl away, dragging himself backward on his elbows.

A soldier imitated the Greek's crab-like movements, pursing his lips and miming Menelaos' terrified expression.

He put his pistol to the old man's head and pulled the trigger. The report of the gun seemed to make time stop. After he shot him, the soldier grabbed Menelaos by the hair and shook his head back and forth, and then, satisfied he was dead, dropped him back to the ground.

In their search for survivors, the soldiers were very thorough. They kicked the corpses aside as they worked their way across the cornfield. A haze of gun smoke hung in the air, the smell of cordite lingering long after the massacre.

Not much to a man once the life has been taken from him, O'Malley thought as he watched. "A generation of leaves, so is it of men," Homer wrote in *The Iliad*. And so it was now.

Occasionally, a voice would arise from the pile, a muted whimpering. The sound never lasted more than a few seconds and was inevitably followed by a blast of gunfire. The Germans were taking no chances.

It was close to noon when they finished.

* * *

KALAVRYTA CONTINUED TO burn, sheets of flames rising from the town long into the night.

The next morning, the German soldiers formed up and left. Without a second glance, they boarded their trucks and took off at high speed down the road, Ebersberger's black touring car departing immediately after. The trucks towing the anti-aircraft guns were the last to leave. Rumbling loudly, they were too wide for the road and had a hard time of it, the caissons swinging wildly from side to side.

Belonged to an earlier age, a convoy like that, O'Malley told himself. A time long distant, when men hunted with spears and burned the entrails of animals. Cut out the hearts of their enemies.

He examined the faces of the German soldiers through his binoculars. They had little of the energy or sense of purpose that had marked their arrival, and no one in the trucks was looking around today. No, the men in the trucks kept their eyes resolutely averted.

'Where were you in the war, Papa?' their children would ask their grandchildren.

'I was in Greece,' those men would be forced to say, 'in a place called Kalavryta.'

Having been at war for a long time, he had no illusions about himself or the men he'd served with. He'd killed and would kill again. He'd heeded the same call to glory as those men in the trucks, nursed the same wanton desire to carry a gun and fight. He didn't know the reason. Something vainglorious and wanting in the human heart, maybe. A genetic weakness passed down from one generation to the next.

His ma had no use for guns or the men who carried them—be they IRA or their English counterparts, the RIC—and she had never allowed them in her house. The memory of the look she'd given him when he told her he was off to war still scalded him. "I'll not cry over you, Brendan O'Malley, idiot that you are, bringing your mother such grief," she'd said. "Learned nothing here, have you? Now you'll go off and learn nothing elsewhere. Think you'd have seen where it gets you. But no, not you. You'll not rest till you've got blood on your hands. Think being a soldier justifies it, that you'll be able to wash it off once you get home, but you won't. No, it'll mark you, stay on you forever."

His ma was right. War left an indelible mark, dirtied all it touched, stained a man's soul forever.

No matter how long the men in the trucks lived, that stain would remain. A scourge, they'd been and would come to know it, a pestilence like no other.

Would that a wave would rise up as it had in Exodus and engulf them. Would that God would make his displeasure known and destroy them as it had Pharaoh's army.

* * *

"*Eimaste Ellines,*" Leonidas cried. "*Osoi iste zontani fonaxete mas!*" We're Greek. If you're alive, speak.

The *antartes* were in the cornfield, searching for survivors of the massacre. Leonidas staggered as he worked his way through the dead, his hands streaked with dried blood. He rolled over one body after another and inspected them.

"*Eimaste Ellines,*" he cried again.

O'Malley doubted they'd find any survivors. All those bullets fired at close range. No one could live through a barrage like that, least of all children.

Haralambos was counting the bodies and logging them in with a pen. He'd been sick twice and his uniform was flecked of vomit. Leonidas had ordered the boy, Nikos, to stay in the tower, not wanting him to see the body of his uncle, the mess the bullet had made of his head. As for Alexis, he hadn't made the journey down to the killing field.

They slowly untangled the corpses and began laying them out in rows. Judging by their clothes, the dead had been poor men, their pants worn thin in places, and only a few had on proper leather shoes. What was it Yeats had said? "An aged man is but a paltry thing, a tattered coat upon a stick." The food they'd brought with them—their last supper as it were—was equally humble. Onions mostly, random crusts of bread.

O'Malley held one of the onions in his hand. Hard to believe the Germans had stripped the land of all save this. The murdering had begun long before, begun with famine and its attendant diseases. Today's shooting was only the culmination. The older men had tried to shield the boys with their bodies, he saw, reached out to cover them as they died. The faces of the boys were soft in death, babyish. He couldn't bring himself to touch them.

Haralambos was determined to enter every name in his notebook, along with the date and manner of death. Initially, this proved impossible; many of the dead had sustained terrible wounds and were so soaked in blood as to be virtually unrecognizable.

Taking off his coat, Leonidas began to wipe the blood off the dead men's faces, calling out their names while the school teacher wrote them down. He began to weep when he came upon the body of Grigoris, his poor feet still covered with bandages. The priest was there. Fotis, too, and his brother, Andreas. Other men O'Malley recognized from the unit. Roumelis was lying near the bottom of the heap, a deep wound in his chest.

O'Malley bent down and gently closed the cook's eyes with his hand. He felt numb, as if he too were riddled with bullets.

The Germans had shot 1,252 people, Haralambos said, almost the entire male population of Kalavryta.

Piled ten deep in places, the dead were everywhere. The grass was drenched, slick with blood. Haralambos must have miscounted, O'Malley thought, looking around him. A million people must be lying here—the population, not of a single village, but of the earth itself.

Twelve people had survived the attack. Three said they'd fallen to the ground a split second before the Germans fired. The remaining nine had been buried under the dead, so bloody the soldiers had taken them for corpses and let them be. It was all too random for O'Malley. Snake eyes, a man lived. Snake eyes, he died.

The young boys had all been killed, torn up in the blasts of gunfire, and one man had been shot twice—once in the stomach and once in cheek.

Working feverishly, he and Leonidas covered the survivors with blankets and did what they could for them. In spite of their efforts, nine of the wounded men died within hours.

O'Malley paused to wipe his brow, his hands encrusted with dried blood. "Who's that there?" he asked Leonidas, nodding to a body a few feet away.

The Greek didn't answer, just went on with his work.

A small man was lying sprawled on the ground. He was dressed in a knitted gray vest, pristine in its newness.

"Can't be." Kneeling down, O'Malley turned the man's head toward him.

The dead man's lips were drawn back, exposing his teeth, a single gold incisor. *Aye*, it was Danae's father all right. Danae's father, lying dead in that field.

O'Malley buried his fist in his mouth. "No! No!"

* * *

THE DONKEY THEY'D heard braying was lying on its side in a burned field, its open eyes scalded and white. Chained to a gutted tree, it had been unable to get away.

The Germans had burned every square inch of Kalavryta. The smoking debris was four feet high in places. Borne by the wind, charred bits of wood spun in the air, so sharp they bloodied O'Malley's face. For the most part, only objects of metal or stone had survived—door knobs and faucets, dented tin pans. He came upon a cast iron stove in the ruins of one house, looming like a primordial beast in a sea of ash. The local hotel had been leveled by mortars, as had the church.

In the village square, only a single tree was left standing. Even this proved to be a mirage; the tree was not a living thing, only a column of ash that collapsed instantly when he touched it and left a sooty mark across the palm of his hand.

More than three quarters of the houses had been destroyed outright, the rest so damaged as to be completely uninhabitable. Holes large enough to crawl through riddled the walls still standing, bullets having gouged out pox-like patterns in the stone. Like a stage set, a wrought-iron balcony hung off a wall with a carved façade and banged in the wind, the building it had once been a part of almost completely demolished. O'Malley found odd things as he searched for survivors—a Singer sewing machine and a set of keys, a woman's locket with a broken chain. All the windows in the town had been blown out, every door.

Ashes, ashes, we all fall down.

A vortex of gritty air swirled around him. Somewhere, a dog barked feebly. Like the donkey, it had been trapped in the wreckage and was dying. O'Malley wanted to scream but didn't dare, afraid once he started, he'd never stop.

He kept thinking he'd turn a corner and everything would be as he remembered it. The air would be clean, flowers and grass living things.

He felt something crunch underfoot and looked down. Beneath his feet, the street was littered with cut-off chicken heads. The birds' eyes were melted and runny, throbbing with flies.

O'Malley swallowed hard. "Christ Almighty."

Evidently, the Germans had raided a chicken coop, killed the birds where they found them and thrown the heads out into the street. Afterward, the fire had passed over them and seared them where they lay.

A strange silence hung over the village, the only sound the buzzing of the flies.

25

The women could barely stand and held on to one another for support, their skin greasy with smoke. Their faces bore cuts from falling glass, and O'Malley could smell smoke on their clothes. There must have been close to eight hundred of them, standing in front of the wreckage of the schoolhouse. Crowded together, they silently watched Haralambos and the rest of the *antartes* approach, their eyes full of accusation and grief.

"Now you come!" a woman yelled, picking up a rock and throwing it. "Where were you when they were killing us?"

"Cowards!" another woman cried. "You left us to die!"

"You should have protected us! You were soldiers. You had guns."

Feverishly, they surged forward and pelted the men with rocks, fistfuls of dirt, anything they could find. "Murderers! Murderers!"

The *antartes* endured the assault, wiping the spit off their faces and trying not to flinch when a rock found its target. The women continued to claw at them, screaming abuse, until gradually their rage was spent.

Holding up a hand, Haralambos made a placating gesture. "We need to document what happened."

After conferring with the others, a tall woman eventually stepped forward. Dry-eyed, she described how the Germans had summoned them to the schoolhouse in the night and separated them from their husbands and sons.

"My boy was only twelve and they took him. I kissed him goodbye and told him I'd see him in a few minutes. I couldn't stop crying. I knew what it meant."

The soldiers had then locked them up in the schoolhouse. "It has been a prison under the Germans, and there were bars on the windows, so we couldn't see out. We could feel the heat of the fire and we were afraid we would burn to death. Everyone was screaming.

"We kept pounding on the doors, begging them to let us out, but they ignored us. In minutes, the inferno was upon us, the smoke so thick we couldn't breathe. Fire was everywhere, in the air, on our clothes, everywhere. Then the roof burst into flames. My daughter's dress caught on fire and I put it out with my hands.

"Again and again, we cried for the Germans to let us go. I felt like I was suffocating and began to push against the door. The others helped me. We pushed and pushed, shoving and hitting each other as we fought to escape. A couple of old women fell and were trampled underfoot.

"I stepped on the face of a person who was dead. I tried not to, but everyone was crowding me and I couldn't go any other way.

"Under the pressure of our bodies, the door of the schoolhouse was forced open. I don't know how, whether the Germans unlocked it or the lock broke. All I know is one minute we were inside and the next minute we were running down the street."

* * *

THE WOMEN BEGAN to keen when they saw the bodies in the cornfield. Leonidas and the other men had worked hard to clean the blood off the faces of the dead, but it had been a hopeless task. There'd been too many and too many shots fired. A cold mist was rising and it leeched into the hollow and collected around them.

One woman's seventeen-year-old was still alive, clutching his stomach and whimpering next to the bodies of his two brothers. O'Malley didn't know how the *antartes* had missed him. Perhaps the boy had been unconscious when Haralambos and the others had gone through the cornfield.

"*Mana,*" the boy cried. "*Mana!*" Mother.

The rest of the women were not so lucky and fell on the bodies of their dead, screaming and crying. Unlike the old crones who'd sung at Stefanos' funeral, the keening of these women was animal, torn from viscera, their living flesh. He'd never heard anything like it. It was as if the tortured figure in Munch's painting, *The Scream*, had been given a voice.

One woman took off her scarf and wiped the blood off her son's face, moaning for the *antartes* to kill her, too, that her life was over. Eventually, the older women organized themselves and began to sing dirges.

> My child, alone I raised you.
> My comfort, with my own hands I raised you.

You were beautiful and pure like an angel.
Don't go away, my child. Come back ….

Unable to stand it, O'Malley left the field. But the sound of the grieving women followed him, seemed to reverberate in his skull and fill it with spiders.

They stayed in the cornfield all that night and the next, keeping the dead company as was the custom. The *antartes* offered to build a fire for them, but they chased them away.

"Leave us! You killed them!"

Furies and harpies and gibbering fools, they stayed up until dawn, talking to the dead. Sometimes they grieved, their voices heavy with sorrow; other times they shouted out in anger, distraught at being abandoned by their murdered husbands and sons, forced to face the long years ahead alone. At dawn, they rose as a group and set about digging the graves. They had no shovels and had to rely on tree branches and bits of crockery, broken tiles from the rooftops of the ruined houses. A light snow had fallen, and it was very cold.

Again, the *antartes* volunteered to help. "We're soldiers. Let us do this for you. Let us dig the graves."

The same tall woman as before stepped forward. "Soldiers shoot soldiers," she said. "They don't put women and children in harm's way." She gestured at the wreckage of Kalavryta. "In the path of death. You and those men with you?" She spat on the ground. "You're nothing."

* * *

DANAE HAD BEEN in the schoolhouse, a woman told O'Malley. Her aunt had stumbled during the rush to escape and been one of those trampled underfoot. Danae had tried to help her up and that was the last time anyone had seen her.

The inside of the schoolhouse was nearly waist-deep in debris. Part of the roof had fallen in and the charred beams shifted unsteadily as O'Malley climbed up over them. Flecked with ash, the air was so murky, he could barely see.

Toula Papadakis lay half-buried behind the entrance. Three other dead women lay next to her, the lower parts of their bodies burned beyond all recognition.

Half mad with grief, O'Malley shifted the wreckage aside with his hands. "Danae! Danae! Where are you, girl?"

Although he dug for more than five hours, he found no trace of her.

He carried the dead women up to the cemetery and buried them. Even with a shovel, it was back-breaking work. After he finished, he retrieved the body of Danae's father from the cornfield, dug another hole, and laid him to rest next to his son.

He did what he could to mark the graves, piling up stones and scratching out the date on a charred piece of wood. He recited the Act of Contrition and Lord's Prayer; scraps of Latin he remembered from Ireland. Psalms and phrases he'd been forced to memorize in school.

"For we must die and are as water spilt on the ground which cannot be gathered up again."

The clock in the blasted bell tower of the church had stopped at 2:34, the hour of the massacre.

* * *

IN THE DAYS that followed, the women continued to live in the cornfield, laboring on the graves during the day and sleeping beside them at night.

"The residents of Mazeika offered to take them in, but they refused," Leonidas said. "They don't want to leave the dead, not even for a minute. The graves are too shallow and stray dogs will come and dig the bodies up and drag them out." He said the women had asked for a gun to fend off the dogs and he'd given them one.

O'Malley feared sleep now and took to sitting at the edge of the field, keeping watch over the women in the darkness. Occasionally, he'd hear a gunshot and a dog would start to howl. The women weren't very good shots, and sometimes it took the animal until morning to die, the sounds of its struggle haunting the darkness.

He'd walked through the cornfield late the previous night, searching for one of the wounded animals, determined to put it out of its misery. It had been an unearthly scene. Hundreds of women and children lying on the ground fast asleep, the earth around them pockmarked with graves. The dog had been there, too, its eyes gleaming in the half-light, blood leaking out of its side.

The next morning he'd given the women a lantern and a second gun and offered to kill the dogs for them if they wanted. They'd gladly accepted. A foreigner, he was but a witness to their tragedy, a bystander. He'd had no hand in it.

They approved of his search for Danae and his loyalty to her memory. One of them tore a strip off her black dress and gave it to him to wear as an armband, a symbol of grief.

He'd only cried once. It had been snowing and he'd walked up to the corral to check on Elektra, ridden her a bit. Slipping down from the saddle, he'd stood there a long time, watching the sky and weeping. At one point, he'd buried his head in the horse's mane. Disturbed by the sounds he was making, she'd stepped away, disappointed in him, or so it seemed. Crying over a single girl in this world of grief.

* * *

O'Malley spent his days with the women, his nights sleeping in the train station. The old depot was one of the few buildings left standing after the fire, and it gave him a feeling of momentary peace to be there, to see the yellowing train schedule on the wall, the advertisement for a local circus. Evidence of human life, he thought. A museum exhibit almost. But his dreams were dark, haunted by death and faces eaten away by fire. He awoke screaming and soaked in sweat.

He remained convinced that Danae was still alive. She'd not have died at German hands. Not her, not Danae. Perhaps she'd fled to another village and would return, suitcase in hand. The longer he stayed in the station, the more convinced he became. *Aye*, it was only a matter of time until she appeared. The train would arrive and Danae would be on it. It'd happen, sure. He'd have to keep an eye out.

The women in Kalavryta stopped what they were doing and watched him, their faces full of pity. "*Trelos*," they said, shaking their heads. Crazy.

"Only a fool would stay in Kalavryta," they told him. "You should leave."

Concerned, an elderly woman and her granddaughter joined him there one evening. Settling herself on the bench beside him, she rolled down her stockings, complaining that they were tight and hurt her legs.

"I am old," she said by way of explanation. "Comfort is everything."

Her granddaughter tugged at her arm. "Who is he?" she whispered, nodding to O'Malley.

"A soldier."

"Why isn't he fighting?"

"He's lost, child."

And so he was, O'Malley thought. *No point in denying it. Lost in every way known to man.*

Both of the Greeks were dressed in black. He wondered how many people they mourned, the extent of their loss.

"Was anyone you know killed in the war?" the old woman asked after they'd exchanged the customary pleasantries.

He nodded. "My fiancée's gone missing."

"Ah," she said as if this explained everything. "What was her name? Your fiancée?"

"Danae."

She cocked her head, bird-like. "Greek?"

"Yes." He hesitated a moment. "Greek, so she was, the soul of her."

"From here?"

"Aye. Kalavryta. Danae Papadakis."

The old woman closed her eyes. "Is that who you're waiting for?"

O'Malley's eyes filled with tears. Again, he nodded.

As gently as she could, she explained that Danae would not be finding her way back to him. "She's not coming. Not on this train or any other." She was very patient, the old woman, never saying the word 'dead' out loud.

Instead, she concentrated on the train itself. "The Germans use it to ferry timber from the village of Zachlorou to Diakofto," she said. "Now they're letting the Red Cross use it. There are never any passengers on it. Never."

She went on to declare that part of the line had been destroyed by a second group of *antartes* and she and the others were worried the men in ELAS would blow up the rest, further isolating the village.

The Red Cross could still drop food parcels, but bad weather might prevent the planes from flying and there'd be hunger. Many people were fleeing the area, an option O'Malley might want to consider. "You should leave Kalavryta. Go back to the war."

"Never. Not until I find her."

"Not all the women got out alive, you know. A building might have collapsed on her."

"She was a wily one, was Danae. It'd not have happened that way."

* * *

THE LINE OF destruction stretched to the mountains and beyond. Deep grooves marred the fields to the east, a legacy of the heavy German trucks, and trees were charred for close to half a mile. O'Malley wondered how long the evidence of the Germans' coming would remain—how many years—and if Kalavryta would ever be free of it.

The old woman at the train station had hugged him when he started to cry. Held him and rocked him. She'd taken off her cross and hung it around his neck, told him it would protect him when he went into battle. "I can't fight them. I'm too old. You have to do it for me."

"*Einai pethamenoi*," she'd said gently. "*Eisai zontanos. Otan teleiosei o polemos, tha pas stin patrida sou.*" She is dead. You're alive. After the war is over, go back to your country. Go home.

He'd kept the carved animals Danae had given him and he took them out of his pocket and held them in the palm of his hand, fingering the marks his knife had made. Like Danae and the train, they brought him a measure of comfort, served as a kind of talisman. Foolish, he knew, yet he couldn't seem to help himself.

As a child, he'd done the same with a rabbit's ear, thinking if he held it in his hand and wished hard enough, his dog would come back to life, start barking and rejoin the living.

His pa had told him things didn't work that way, no matter what people said. "That thing you're holding. Didn't do much for the rabbit, now did it?"

Still O'Malley had clung to it.

He was retracing the route he'd taken the day Stefanos was killed. Sodden with grief, he didn't feel like meeting up with the *antartes* yet, and he wanted to sear every second of the boy's murder in his memory before rejoining them. Arm himself with it, as it were.

The pile of leaves was still there, and he could see evidence of blood where the child had fallen. The snow had softened it, but he could see the outline of the body in the matted grass.

* * *

Von Le Suire's shadow did not recede until O'Malley was halfway through the gorge. The area around Kalavryta had been completely destroyed; the trunks of the dying pine trees were red orange, their needles curdled, the cones on the ground beneath them as black as grenades. Farther on, the character of the landscape began to ease. Sometimes a tree bore the scars of the fire on one side, but not on the other, a line dividing the living from the dead. The contrast between the two overwhelmed O'Malley and started him weeping again. He saw a single pomegranate tree in the distance, red fruit weighing down its branches. There might be others. He'd have to tell Leonidas, send some men to claim them.

The Germans had bombed the tower not long after the massacre, forcing the *antartes* to seek shelter elsewhere. Choking from the smoke, they'd sought refuge in Mazeika, but the residents had driven them away, loudly proclaiming their presence would draw the Germans and more people would die.

Cowed by their fury, the *antartes* had retreated. A few had wanted to join the forces of Aris Velouchiotis to the west, but the rest had argued against it, saying von Le Suire had marched in that direction and there'd be close to three thousand Germans between them and Velouchiotis.

It had been Leonidas who'd made the final decision. "Von Le Suire thinks he destroyed us, if not in Kalavryta, then when he bombed the tower. We'll be safe in our old camp in the gorge. He's finished here."

Twenty *antartes* were crowded around the campfire when O'Malley arrived. As usual, Haralambos was going on about something while the rest listened, a barstool warrior if ever there was one. Rolling out his bedroll, O'Malley lay down and tried to sleep, the darkness mirroring his own.

26

It snowed intermittently, heavy drifts blocking the pass through the mountains and sealing the village off. The women in the cornfield still labored to bury their dead, but they were growing sick now, coughing up blood-flecked phlegm into handkerchiefs, so weak they could barely stand.

O'Malley tended to their wounds, reassuring them that he was a doctor in Ireland and they could trust him to help them. Finding no sterile dressings for their burns, he used sheets and old clothes, sterilized his tools over the flame of a candle. Every morning he checked for fever and listened to the lungs of the sickest ones with his stethoscope. It had been catch-as-catch-can, but he'd done the best he could. The women called him '*yiatro*,' doctor, or '*Kyrie Angle*,' the Greek equivalent of Mr. English.

The sound of their pneumonia-driven coughing grieved him, and he radioed the British agent, begging him to send food. "Medicine, too, if you've got it. Most of the women are sick. They're in desperate straits. You got to help them."

He'd started out aggressively, describing the massacre in great detail, hoping to shame the Englishman into taking action.

"Children, you say?" the man had asked.

"That's right. Germans shoot every male over the age of sixteen and a lot of boys who were younger, then endeavored to burn the women alive. Diabolical, they were. Diabolical entirely. Before they burned the village, they stole all the food—sheep, eggs, flour, you name it. Forced people to show them where the food was and shot 'em afterwards."

There was a long silence. Finally, the man said he'd work with the Red Cross and perhaps step up the delivery of supplies. "Securing a plane might take some time. I understand there's a railroad line that connects Kalavryta to the town of Diakofto. Shipping the food in by rail might work better."

"Be foolhardy. Germans still control the northern part of the line. ELAS is talking about dynamiting it."

"Counsel against it, Barabbas. As long as there's a train, the Red Cross can get food to you. Winter's closing in and you're in the mountains. Landing a Dakota under those conditions may well prove impossible."

O'Malley fought to keep his voice down. It'd do the women in the cornfield no good if he gave out on this caffler.

"We're living on grass. Grass, you hear? Got no potable water either. Most of the wells are contaminated. Another week and we'll all be dead."

The man went on as if he hadn't heard, "We cannot risk sending a plane in bad weather. Visibility is limited. It's too dangerous."

"I repeat: we will die."

The two of them stayed in radio contact, O'Malley eventually wearing the man down and convincing him to arrange the drop.

He didn't want the plane to land anywhere near Kalavryta—no reason to bring the wrath of God down on the village a second time—and insisted the pilot use the airfield he'd constructed high above the gorge.

"Tonight. I'll set out flares and wait for you."

* * *

THE JOURNEY TO the airfield took O'Malley and Leonidas by the burned-out husk of the monastery. Although nearly two weeks had passed since the Germans lay siege, the rocks where the monks had died still stunk of cordite and death. Vultures were circling overhead, occasionally floating down like black kites cut loose from a string and landing next to a lifeless form on the ground. The birds turned and watched them, their gazes neutral, indifferent to their passing.

O'Malley turned away, not wanting to see what the bird was feeding on, the scraps of black cloth that seemed to be everywhere. He couldn't stop thinking about the monks flying off into space, their robes fluttering about them like failed parachutes, crying out to God as death rose up to meet them.

The airfield was as he remembered it, a faint sheen of snow covering the runway. After tethering their horses, the two of them dug holes in the icy ground with their hands and set out flares. They had very few and decided to hold off lighting them until they heard the plane approach.

Eager to be off, Elektra pawed at the ground with her hooves. Warmer than the cold night air, she was a hazy vision in the darkness, steam rising from her flanks and pouring from her nostrils. The whites of her eyes glowed faintly in the darkness and made her appear otherworldly, mythical even. A horse a goddess might have ridden.

"Pulling the devil by the tail, are you?"

Horses were the grandest creatures on earth, O'Malley thought. Hadn't Jonathan Swift himself said so? At a gallop, freer than all, save the birds.

In the old days, the English had forbidden the Irish from owning decent horses. Nags, the Irish had been forced to ride, mules broken by the plow and not long for the knackers. Perhaps that was why the sight of Elektra stirred him so. It was the Irish in him, the ancient yearning of his people to possess such a creature, to race through the countryside and take a fence at a gallop.

Cupping his hands, he lit a cigarette and handed the pack to Leonidas.

They spoke of the coming drop, carefully skirting around the massacre, the horrors they'd witnessed.

"She's alive, Danae is," O'Malley said after a time. "Irish say you can sense such things, that a person knows when a soul's departed. I'd feel it, I would, Leonidas, if she were dead. A little ripple of sorrow passing through the universe."

Leonidas started to say something, but stopped.

A moment later, the moon appeared. Breaking through the clouds, it bathed the plateau in light. Elektra had stopped her rambling and was staring up at the sky.

"Will you look at that? She's Pegasus, she is. Mark my words, she'll be leaving us for the stars one day. Leaving this sad earth behind."

* * *

THE DAKOTA CAME in from the east. Breaching the mountain, it dropped straight down until it was almost on top of them, its huge propellers stirring eddies of snow on the ground. It touched down a moment later, rocking back and forth as it lumbered across the field.

The men on the plane waved, threw out the boxes and took off again, eager to be gone from the mountains before the clouds closed in again. O'Malley and Leonidas retrieved the boxes, strapped them to their mounts and led them back down the path to Kalavryta.

"*Fagito*," Leonidas shouted when they reached the village. Food.

The women quickly emerged from their huts and formed a circle around the horses, waiting for the food and begging the men to hurry. Their hunger was so all consuming, they'd have braved a bullet to eat.

"No need to ration yourself," O'Malley told them as he tossed the boxes down. "There's more where that came from."

He radioed the British agent again later that day and arranged for him to drop some toys and bags of candy for the children as well. Unused army jackets and bedrolls for the women. Whatever they could spare.

"Headquarters was appalled by your report, Barabbas," the man said. "I'm not sure we could have saved Kalavryta, but you were right, we should have at least tried. You can count on me, count on all of us here. We'll help you in any way we can."

Leonidas contacted Aris Velouchiotis on his own and asked him not to dynamite the train, then radioed the Red Cross and requested that their representative negotiate with the Germans and get permission to use the train to deliver supplies on a one-time basis to the village. Two days later the Red Cross representative radioed back to say he'd succeeded and a train full of food would be forthcoming.

O'Malley rejoiced when he heard the news. With any luck, the women would have enough food to make it through the winter.

The supplies arrived as promised, an entire boxcar full of food. The women gathered when they heard it coming and waited patiently while O'Malley unloaded the boxes. He had volunteered for the task, telling Leonidas he didn't need to send extra men; he'd see that the parcels got delivered.

Leonidas was off by himself when O'Malley returned to the camp that night. Setting the gun he'd been cleaning aside, he signaled for him to come and sit beside him. "Red Cross train come?"

"Yup. Had the devil's own time unloading it."

"The village is going to be swimming in food. The agent radioed. They scheduled another drop at the airfield."

"When?"

"Tomorrow night."

"They say what they're sending?"

"Toys for the children. Everything you asked for."

* * *

THE SUN WAS setting when O'Malley and Leonidas arrived at the airfield, a bright line of red across the horizon. O'Malley panicked at first when he saw it, the fiery play of light across the sky, thinking it must be the Germans, that they'd torched another village. But then he realized it was only the end of day.

Sadly, he wondered if the time would ever come when a sunset would be just that, not a reminder of firefights and death. If he'd ever leave be able to forget the war.

They tethered their mounts to a tree and sat down to wait. Around ten, O'Malley heard a plane approach and hastened to ignite the flares. The air was very damp, and the lit flares were soon haloed with humidity.

The Dakota touched down a moment later. But the whine of the propellers frightened Elektra and she reared up, tearing herself loose from the tree

"Stop!" O'Malley yelled, charging after her.

Leonidas ran to help and together they rushed to grab her reins and pull her to safety.

Unaware of what was happening, the plane continued to roll forward, circling around before coming to stop on the far side of the field. The men on the Dakota quickly threw out the boxes, which thudded when they hit the icy ground and split open, the wood shattering on impact.

Hearing the sound, Elektra grew more and more frightened. She rose up on her hind legs and whinnied, the whites of her eyes showing, then galloped away. She ran and ran, trailing the loose reins, but she couldn't see her way clear in the dark and stumbled into the broken boxes. Neighing frantically, she tried to get up, but fell back down again, her leg shattered, the bone white and exposed.

"No!" O'Malley screamed. "No!"

Distraught, the crew of the plane threw down a bedroll to staunch the bleeding, but the wound were grievous and O'Malley knew she was lost. The horse's eyes were open, beseeching. She nuzzled his hand as the life ebbed out of her.

Like all of us, he thought, *she's afraid to die.*

Leonidas offered to shoot her, but O'Malley refused.

"No, she's mine. I'll see to it."

Closing his eyes, he raised the gun to her head, pressed it against the bone and pulled the trigger.

He insisted on burying her there in a field. Along with the parcels of food, the crew had thrown out tools—shovels and pickaxes—which he and Leonidas used to move the frozen earth. Leonidas had proposed butchering the animal and taking the meat back to the camp, but O'Malley wouldn't hear of it. It took until morning and their hands were raw by the time they finished. The horse was too heavy to lift and they had to drag her over with ropes and lever her into the hole.

O'Malley began to scream then. He went on screaming for a long time, picking up icy clumps of dirt and throwing them into the grave.

Leonidas watched him, but didn't interfere. He seemed to understand that it wasn't just the horse, it was all of them O'Malley was grieving for.

* * *

SAYING HE'D RETURN to retrieve the food parcels, Leonidas left the airfield and went back to the camp alone. It had begun to snow again, a layer of white slowly covering the newly dug grave. O'Malley couldn't stop crying, blubbering and wiping his nose on his sleeve.

"A horse, for pity's sake."

As long as he lived, he'd not forget the sight of her down on her knees, her eyes full of terror as the blood poured forth and drowned her.

Another innocent lost.

Leonidas returned a few hours later with some other men, who quickly loaded up the parcels and rode off again. O'Malley said he'd be along later, that he had something to attend to. Seeing how distraught he was, the Greek didn't argue and left him there, standing alone on the snowy airstrip.

"Don't linger," Leonidas warned, wheeling around on his horse. "More snow is coming. You'll freeze to death."

27

Reaching for his drop pack, O'Malley stowed his bedroll inside. The women would have meat, he'd see to that, and afterward he'd heed Leonidas' advice and get the hell away. Roasted goat would be better than the poor scoff the Red Cross was handing out—the tins of sardines and powdered eggs—and if the women wanted to keep a few of the goats for milk, so much the better. It would be a blessing, it would. His last hurrah.

He shouldered his pack and set off at first light, relieved to see the back of the camp. The *antartes'* mood had darkened since the massacre in Kalavryta. Unable to move out because of the snow, they'd begun to turn on each other, the more bloody-minded bullying the rest and pushing them around. It didn't take much to set them off, and there'd been fist fights over cigarettes and space around the campfire, about whose allegiance to ELAS was suspect and whose family had profited the most from the war.

Increasingly paranoid, Haralambos spoke continually of collaborators and black marketeers, what 'the people's justice' would do to them once the Germans withdrew. The British were omnipresent, according to him, Churchill actively working to undermine the efforts of ELAS and occupy Greece once the Germans withdrew. His agents were everywhere.

"Just a few people playing games," Leonidas had told O'Malley when they'd discussed it.

O'Malley wasn't so sure. Haralambos had been on him again about his loyalty in a way that frightened him, making it clear that he no longer considered him a comrade-in-arms, but an agent of the British government and as such, his mortal enemy.

He'd caught the school teacher watching him the previous night with a scowl on his face.

"What are you looking at?" O'Malley had asked, keeping his tone light.

"You."

"What is it about me that has caught your eye this fair evening?"

"I'm wondering why you are here." Pushing his glasses up, the school teacher had studied him through narrowed eyes. "What your true purpose is."

"Fighting Hitler, same as you."

Haralambos turned away without answering.

"I'm my own man," O'Malley shouted after him, "I'll not take the King's shilling and betray you. Grass on a fellow soldier."

The rest of the men fell silent. They'd all been listening to the exchange.

"You there, you gawking at me?" Collaring the man closest to him, O'Malley pushed him away. "You've got no cause to be staring. I've been here since 1941. Been shot and nearly died defending your friggin' homeland."

He thought at the time that would be the end of it, but he remained uneasy.

No one in the camp ever spoke of Kalavryta, the focus of discussion instead being on the British landing in Salonika and what it meant and how Athens was now under martial law. Many of the *antartes* continued to assist the women in the village, chopping wood for them and repairing their houses, but if they did so, it was as individuals, not as a group. The collective will was elsewhere.

Leonidas had withdrawn completely and no longer played much of a role. He rarely spoke to anyone, save O'Malley and then only when the two of them were alone.

"Remember that war I told you about?" he told him late one evening. They were hard at work, seeing to the horses, bringing them water and scattering hay on the ground for them to eat. "The one you have no place in? Well, it's starting. You need to leave."

O'Malley set his bucket down. "For the love of God, Leonidas, where would you have me go?"

"I can get you as far as Mani, and from there you can take a boat to Cyprus."

"But the Germans haven't surrendered. The war's not done."

"For you it is. Even if you wanted to go on fighting, you're no good to them the way you are. You scream in your sleep and they've seen you crying." He touched his arm as he said this, his voice gentle. "I've heard them talking. They say you're *loxos*." He fluttered his fingers at the side of his head, the Greek gesture for mentally ill.

O'Malley could hear the horses ahead of him, their hooves on the ground as they moved about. Settling in for the night, they were milling around in the shadows of the trees.

"*Loxos?*" he repeated softly. "Aye, maybe I am. Maybe I bloody well am." He'd never felt more alone.

"The British and ELAS will soon be at each other's throats." Leonidas' face was hard to see in the darkness. "Which side will you choose?"

"Yours, of course. The Greek one."

"They don't trust you. You'll only get yourself killed."

The stars were out—so close O'Malley could almost touch them, bat them about with his hand—the mountains, angular shadows against the sky. Such beauty to be had here and yet so much pain. Even after all this time, he couldn't decide which quality best defined Greece.

He blew on his hands and knocked his feet together in an effort to get warm. He could see his breath, feel the dampness collecting in his bones. He wanted to bed down close to the fire like the other men, but was afraid to now.

"I'll go, since you say I must. But there's one thing I want to do before I jump ship. Danae's father kept a herd of goats in the foothills here. I aim to find them and drive them down to Kalavryta."

"Goats, eh?" Looking back at the camp, Leonidas kept his voice down. "You know where he kept them?"

"Got a fair idea." They'd not be far from where he found the ewe, O'Malley thought, dilly-dallying on those same rocks. It'd go all right. He'd keep an eye out for the Germans, hide if he heard anything.

Leonidas seemed to read his thoughts. "With that hair of yours, it'll be the Greeks you need to watch out for, not the Germans. The villagers who think you're the devil."

A stranger in a strange land. So he was and ever would be. Leonidas had no need to remind him.

O'Malley gestured to the men asleep around the campfire. "Don't you go telling them, you hear? They'll eat those goats alive, I swear they will, and me along with them."

Like being hit in the face with a wasp's nest it would be, if the *antartes* found about the goats. They'd swarm all over him and claim possession. Never mind feeding the women. Never mind anything, save their ravenous hunger.

They were maggots, all right. "You hear me, Leonidas? It's on me, this thing. On me and me alone."

Herding goats was about all he was good for, come to that. Kalavryta had undone him, undone him entirely. There was no denying it. The shooting and hellish landscape after the fire.

And Danae. *Oh God, Danae, Danae.*

He closed his eyes, fought to get a grip on himself.

With any luck, fetching the goats would set him to rights. He'd round them up and drive them to the village. Shoot off his revolver and whoop like a cowboy. The women would rejoice and all would be well again.

It would be good, that. Him, Brendan O'Malley, bloody Father Christmas.

* * *

LEONIDAS HAD WRITTEN out a list of names and starred their locations on a map. "Some are ELAS supporters," he said, "others are my relatives. You'll be safe with them. They'll feed and house you, tell you when it's safe to move out. Take my horse," he urged. "You'll cover more ground."

O'Malley shook his head. He was done with horses. Elektra was the last one he would ever ride. He was polite about it, said he preferred to walk, that it would be good for him, clear his head.

Leonidas let the lie stand. He'd caught up with O'Malley not long after he set off, had come charging up over the rocks, shouting his name. The little mare he was riding was trembling all over, her coat damp with sweat.

Pitying the animal, O'Malley pulled a blanket out of his pack and rubbed her down a little with it. He didn't welcome the task.

"Take it easy on her," he warned Leonidas. "Way she's heaving, she'll take sick, you're not careful."

After he finished, he stowed the blanket back in his pack. "Well, I'm off then."

"Brendan …."

"No need to linger." Shouldering the pack, O'Malley started down the path. "I can see my way out."

And with that he was gone. He could feel the Greek's eyes on him, but he didn't look back.

* * *

UNWILLING TO PASS by the monastery again, the reeking cliffs, O'Malley headed up into the hills. He planned to circle around and approach the cave from above. The area was unfamiliar to him and he got his compass out. At some point, he heard water running and searched for the stream, thinking he might know it and that the landmark would anchor him.

After the claustrophobic life in the camp, it felt good to be out in the open. He'd sleep rough and accept food from Leonidas' contacts only if he had to. They'd not know what to make of him, the natives, and though polite, would surely keep their distance. Wouldn't be the red hair kept them at bay, not this time, no. It would be the sad state of him, his bloodstained *flokati* and God-awful stench, the rank odor of fire and death he carried with him. *Aye*, he was a ruin, all right. Same as Kalavryta. A ruin entirely.

Perhaps if he gave himself a good scrub, it would go better.

He found the stream, stripped his clothes off and waded in, set about scrubbing his skin with twigs. Dipping his head underwater, he came up, roaring like a savage. "Jaysus, almighty cold, so that is."

Grabbing his *flokati*, he dragged it over and wetted it, rubbing the fur with his fingers to get the blood out. It was a hopeless task, the icy water running red down his arms and chilling him anew. All he succeeded in doing was spreading the stain. Shivering, he got dressed again and walked along the streambed.

A covey of quail exploded from the underbrush a second later, rattling the sky as they rose. The sound startled him and set his heart racing. Afraid something had set them off, he flattened himself against the ground and stayed there. But all was quiet, save for the raucous clamor of the birds.

"Must have been me spooked them."

He thought he'd kill a few and roast them for supper, but he was too slow and the quail had disappeared. They were surprisingly graceless in flight, their wings small and seemingly misplaced, the feathered tufts on their heads jiggling like flimsy crowns. Hares were also in evidence, the dirt underfoot soft from their tunneling. After Kalavryta, the land seemed impossibly lush, awash with abundance.

The birds continued to caw, and O'Malley wished he had been more careful. Stupid, that. Give him away, it could.

He headed up into the rocks, keeping a look out as he climbed. The wind was merciless, so cold it made his eyes run.

"Got its back up, it has."

He paused to catch his breath. He was standing in a strand of olives trees, shaggy and overgrown. Unpicked olives dangled from the branches, thick bunches of them, so evenly spaced they might have been hung by a human hand.

A man planted them for his sons and grandsons, Leonidas had said. It takes a generation for them to bear fruit. Old patriarchs, the trees before him were majestic. Mute testimony to a man's belief that he and his kind would endure.

O'Malley wondered what had happened to the people who owned them—if they had perished in the war, leaving the grove abandoned.

As the shadows lengthened and night came on, the sky grew more and more radiant, the moon emerging from a bank of marbled clouds. 'Twas like a vast mussel shell, the sky, he thought, awash with silvery light.

Ahead was a hamlet of sorts, a smattering of houses on the spur of the mountain. A teenage boy was herding sheep through the tall grass, the animals' wool coats bright in the fading light. A woman called from a doorway, telling the boy to hurry; it was getting dark.

O'Malley hid in the trees and watched them. He could smell meat cooking, onions. The simple domesticity of the scene stirred him, the thought of a family, untouched by the war, sharing a meal.

He wondered if the woman was aware of what had happened in Kalavryta, what she and her son had been spared. He, for one, would never tell her. Let her stay as she was, watching her son drive the sheep home for the night

Coming out from behind the trees, he stood where the woman could see him. "I'm a British soldier. I mean you no harm. I got separated from my unit."

The woman stayed well back. *Believes I'm a German*, he decided, seeing the expression on her face, the fear in it.

"I've been fighting with Velouchiotis."

The woman recognized the name and nodded. "ELAS," she said.

She volunteered that she herself was from Athens and had fled here after the Germans came. It was bad in the city, she said. People were dying in the streets.

"They shot twenty men in my neighborhood," she told him in Greek. "Usually they roll up the clothes of the men they kill and throw them on their families' doorsteps like newspapers. But the last time, they stripped the bodies, put the clothes in a room and made the women go through it. A neighbor of mine found her son's jacket. After that, I left."

Her hair was cut short, marceled in tight waves, her brows so thin they might have been drawn with a pencil. *A city girl*, he thought. *Knows more about shellacking her hair than bringing in a harvest.*

"Where do you come from?" she asked.

"Ireland," he said.

She continued to question him. Who else had he served with, where in Greece had he been? *What brought you here?* she seemed to be saying. *Why are you troubling me tonight?*

He wished she'd leave off. Talk didn't come easy to him anymore. He seemed to have lost the knack.

Reluctantly, he described his parents and the farm he'd grown up on, trying to give her a sense of himself. Told her a story that had always brought laughter at home.

"Had a dog, name of 'Connor,' was supposed to see to a herd of sheep we had. But he was a blackguard, old Connor was, and mauled a pair of Jehovah's Witnesses who came calling, seeking to convert us. Bit 'em and bit 'em. Aw, the puss on them when Connor did that. You should have seen it. ' 'Tis to be expected,' my pa said. 'Connor's an Irish dog and they were Englishmen, so they were.' "

The woman didn't get the joke. After she went back inside, O'Malley stood there for a time, staring out at the darkness. It wasn't just being foreign, he told himself. No, he could deal with that. It was what he'd seen in Kalavryta that was distancing him from human life. His grieving heart, a wall around him.

* * *

THE STORM BROKE near midnight. O'Malley kept moving, afraid he'd freeze to death if he paused to rest. He thought about returning to the hamlet where the woman was, but decided against it. She didn't want him there. Her seeming curiosity, the questions she'd asked, had only been a way of making sure he was who he said he was, not an enemy soldier in disguise. There was no shelter to be had in her house, not for him, no warmth.

Pulling the goatskin over his head, he plunged forward through the sleeting rain.

As the night wore on, it grew colder and colder, the rain slowly changing over to snow.

Still damp from the washing, his goatskin slowly froze as the temperature dropped, moisture clinging to it and weighing it down until he felt encased in ice. O'Malley grew more and more frightened. If he didn't find refuge soon, he would die out here. He heard water roaring in the distance and stumbled toward it, thinking it must be the waterfall at the head of the gorge. The cave was somewhere above it. He'd find it and wait out the storm inside.

Flushed with rain, the river was a raging torrent, leaping and flashing as it poured over the rocks like a monstrous school of salmon. Climbing on all fours, he started up the cliff toward the cave, pausing now and then to wipe the snow from his eyes. He'd lost all feeling in his fingers, and his hair and beard were beaded with ice.

He thought of Stefanos and Danae as he battled his way forward through the storm, remembering the hours they'd spent in the cave. He could still hear the child's manic laughter and see Danae's face in the gloaming. Gone now, the both of them.

He paused when he reached the entrance.

Just a place now, he told himself. *A place like any other.*

28

O'Malley thought at first it was his *flokati*, the snow magnifying the rankness of the thing, but then he noticed the droppings on the floor. So the goats were here, just as he'd anticipated. The brush he'd gathered with Stefanos lay undisturbed, stacked up neatly by the entrance. He used it to start a fire. He found the jug of water, poured some into a pan from his kit, and set it out to boil, thinking to make himself some tea. His fingers stung as the feeling returned to them and water trickled down his neck from the melting snow in his hair. He shook off his cape and laid it out next to the fire. Within minutes, it was steaming like a geyser, the ends of the fur slowly curling as they dried.

He removed his rifle and laid it down, thinking he'd have little need of it here. Germans would never venture up to the cave. It was too hard to get to, for one thing, and once here, they'd be trapped. It was no good for their purposes. He prodded the fire with his boot. He could hear the wind howling outside, the storm raging still.

He wondered how the goats were faring in the blizzard. In medical school, he'd seen a cat that had frozen to death, its body arched in death, its mouth frozen in a silent scream. He'd leave the goats where they fell, if that had been their fate. Let the vultures take them. Unrolling his bedroll, he made ready to sleep, threw a last log on the fire.

The log slowly caught and the fire grew in strength, the shadows of the flames leaping and dancing on the walls of the cave. The movement unnerved him. Haunted, this place was. Haunted and always would be.

* * *

He awoke when the fire went out, the cold wrapping itself around him. Below, the rocks were covered with snow, a vast blanket of whiteness disturbed only by fallen branches and the hieroglyphics of birds. He could see the river in the distance, gleaming where the snow bled into the water.

He relit the fire and drank his tea, ate a pack of biscuits from the Red Cross. When he finished, he pulled his cape around him and exited the cave. Outside all was quiet, the snow muting even the cry of the birds.

The goats had weathered the storm well. Spread out along the base of the cliff, they had sought out crevices and fissures in the rock and stood huddled there, keeping their heads buried in the fur of their chests. A few watched him approach, their eyes leaden.

As he drew nearer, they started to shy away, the huge unmilked udders of the ewes swaying from side to side as they sprinted up the rocks.

"Where you bound, you bloody scuts?"

It was a peculiar dance, they did, galloping off, only to turn back and stare at him. There was no challenge in the look they gave him, no intelligence whatsoever. They changed their tactics a moment later and charged him, intent on pushing him off the cliff.

Swinging a stick, O'Malley hit as many as he could. "Back, you trotters! Back, you puddles of dog piss! I'll kill you, I will!"

But the goats kept coming. In an instant they were upon him, a tidal way of goats. Falling on the old billy in the lead, he grabbed the animal's horns and twisted hard, brought him down the way a cowboy does a steer. The other goats stopped dead in their tracks. Like Germans, they only knew one game, apparently, and it was follow the leader.

The old goat got to his feet and shook himself off. He charged again, but weakly this time, the horns never connecting, the pawing of the ground a bit of male bravado, the animal's way of having the last word.

* * *

Whenever the billy goat lagged, O'Malley nudged him in the anus with the stick. He'd discovered the technique by accident and been astounded at how well it worked. As long he kept the goat in his sights and prodded him in the rear with a stick, he could control the herd and keep it moving. He didn't understand it, but there it was.

Adept only at scaling rocks and soiling the earth, goats didn't amount to much that he could see. What energy they possessed was focused mainly on eating. Their appetite was prodigious, and their teeth were surprisingly human. Reminiscent of the dentures his granny had kept in a glass, they were square and yellowish, and the goats displayed them often. He'd have thought they were grinning at him if he hadn't known better.

What was it the Irish said of goats? 'More beards than brains.' O'Malley chuckled. If he'd been Noah, he never would have let them aboard.

The goats were relentless as they trotted through the empty fields of Kalavryta, yanking up everything in their path and gulping it down. Their gluttony reminded O'Malley of the Germans, the way the soldiers had overrun the village and taken everything

Aye. They belonged on the streets of Berlin, all right.

* * *

THE HAWKS STILL occupied the rocky highlands, their high-pitched screams echoing across the wintry hills. Frightened by the sound, the goats drew together, climbing atop one another, instinctively seeking safety in numbers.

Would that he and the *antartes* had done the same, O'Malley thought, watching them. Rallied 'round one another when a predator threatened instead of abandoning the lesser among us, the way we did the people of Kalavryta.

He could see heat rising from the makeshift chimneys in the distance, a faint shimmer against the gray sky. A few women were toiling outside, waif-like in their black clothes. There were far fewer than he remembered, and they stopped what they were doing and watched him, shielding their eyes from the sun.

O'Malley gave a half-hearted whoop when he reached the square, mimicking a cowboy at the end of the trail, but his heart wasn't in it. The town was no longer a living place; it was a butcher's yard, an abattoir. All was blackened and stank of fire. The very stones that bound it together seemed awash with loss.

Yesterday's storm wasn't cleansing as sometimes occurred in Ireland—raindrops sparkling on blades of grass, the sky aching in its purity. Here it had only wetted the ash and coated the ruins with scum.

He distributed the goats as fairly as he could, giving them out to the women with children first, then the others. He counseled the women not to kill them outright, but to save them for milk. They would slaughter three of the animals later, he told them, and deliver the meat to those who were elderly, wounded, or sick. The rest would be shared, cheese to be made and given out.

Waving their aprons like bullfighters, the women shooed the goats toward their hovels, a horde of unkempt, giggling children tagging along behind. As ever, the goats went where they wanted, scampering to the top of the festering piles of rubbish and peering down, feinting and bucking and bleating all the while. Nearly as sure-footed, the children went climbing up after them, roped them and dragged them down. The roundup went on for some time, everyone enjoying themselves.

It was the first time O'Malley had heard the women laugh since the massacre and the sound cheered him. A Christmas of sorts, this.

They didn't thank him. Just took the goats and left.

"A word of gratitude never broke anyone's teeth," he muttered under his breath, watching them go. He was nothing to them, he knew. Perhaps not a proper member of ELAS, he was a soldier nonetheless. And soldiers they'd had their fill of.

He'd roped two goats himself, planning to take them to Danae's house and leave them there in case she returned. He couldn't bear the thought of her going hungry.

* * *

He led the two goats down the road and deposited them in the field behind Danae's house, erecting a barrier of tree branches to hold them there. Goats took it into their heads to leave, they'd leave. Nothing he could do about it. They were a force of nature, goats, locusts with hooves. He gathered up leaves and threw them in after them, dragged over a fallen poplar tree, thinking it'd keep them for a time. They could eat snow if they got thirsty. They'd be all right.

He studied the land around him, the looming mountains to the east and west. He could see the firebreak in the distance, the place where blackened forest gave way to green. It made a line around Kalavryta and probably would have reached here, had it not been for the stream.

Caught up in his memories, he walked toward it, remembering the hours he'd spent on its banks with Danae and Stefanos. He was startled to see that the rabbit hutch had survived.

"Poor Bobo and Foufou. Who will look after them now?"

If the rabbits were still alive, they might stand a chance in the wild. He tramped through the underbrush, determined to turn them loose.

The ground in front of the hutch was mossy and damp, the reeds ticking with moisture. The glade where it was buried was pooled with shadows, burnt pine needles and ash collecting along the surface of the water, washed downstream from Kalavryta.

He heard a faint, rustling sound. Not rabbits, something else.

Cautiously, he inched toward it.

His breath caught in his throat. "What the devil! Who's there?"

He feared trickery, witchcraft even. Could be another girl, he told himself, his grief playing tricks on him. Still he let himself hope.

Raising herself up on her elbows, the girl turned and looked at him.

Aye, it was her all right.

Danae.

***

At first, he could only stare at her. She'd been badly hurt, a cut on her head edged with fresh blood. The part of her arms that he could see were mottled with burn marks, tiny blisters seeping pus. The smell she gave off was cloying and unhealthy. Her eyes were terrified, her body poised for flight, every muscle tense and on guard. Pity filled him as he watched her struggle, fight not to run away. She was dressed in a man's coat, same as she'd been the first time he laid eyes on her. Khaki, it was this time—the fabric, like her skin, burned all over.

"Lord God, girl, what happened to you?"

Her eyes filled with tears and she shook her head.

As gently as he could, he helped her down from the hutch. She'd lost weight, probably weighed less than eighty pounds, but her eyes were as he remembered. Amber. *Aye*, amber when held up to the light, amber all shot through with gold.

She was too weak to stand and collapsed against him.

"Danae. Oh, my sweet girl, Danae." O'Malley grabbed her fingers and felt them, touched her skin, her hair, marveling when he felt her breath on his hand, unable to believe she was real.

He couldn't keep the tremor from his voice. "'Tis a wonder, this. A wonder entirely."

Fetching his backpack, he laid out his medical instruments and quickly set about dressing her wounds. Although a four-inch clump of hair was missing, he was relieved to see the gash on her head wasn't deep. Only a scalp wound, it might have bled copiously, as such injuries were prone to do, but would heal in time. He dipped a cloth in alcohol, cleaned the area and bound it with a cloth, then bandaged up her arms. The flesh here had been seared in places and was scabbing over now, burgeoning scar tissue evident on both of her hands. She'd probably suffer a slight crippling in the future as the skin tightened, but it'd be a minor thing, and there was no evidence of infection or gangrene. Something eased in his heart. Danae would not die of her injuries.

A neighbor woman had been looking after her, she said, bringing food and water to the hutch. "The rabbits kept me warm."

"Sailed close to the wind, you did, I'll not deny it. But you'll be all right. Your wounds will heal in time."

"I don't want them to." Her voice grew stronger. "I want everyone who sees me to know …."

He touched her cheek. "To know what, Danae?"

"What they did to us."

***

BEARING A BOWL of soup, the neighbor turned up not long after. Like the rest of the women in the village, she was dressed entirely in black, her hair covered by a soiled kerchief. She was very old, her skin crosshatched with lines like the neck of a tortoise. Tortoise-like, too, was her pace.

O'Malley wondered what her age was, how far she'd come this day to bring food.

Just another old crone haunting these mountains.

Talkative, she described how she'd been fetching water in the river when she'd heard someone groan. "Then I saw the hutch."

A cagy old peasant, she shifted her eyes and took a step closer, not wanting Danae to hear. "Papadakis is dead, I thought, the boy, too, from what I heard. Who's going to know if I take a rabbit for my supper? Then I saw her lying there. At first I thought she was dead. She was burned, poor thing. *Panagia mou*, how she was burned. Half her hair was gone."

She'd fought with her sister and brother-in-law, who'd taken her land and left her with nothing. Consequently, she'd withdrawn from village life and lived out here, just over the hill, kept her own counsel.

She seemed a cantankerous old biddy, full of rancor and spite, a type familiar to him from Ireland, who kept track of their grievances, grew them in a dim kind of garden like poisonous toadstools.

That's why none of the others had known about Danae. The old hag hadn't told them.

Together she and O'Malley half walked, half carried Danae to the train station, the old crone yammering the whole time. Given the damage to the town, it was the only place O'Malley could think of to go. It'd do until he could rebuild her house. It had a little ceramic stove he could feed wood in for heat, a bench along the back wall where she could sleep. Other women, too, as the need arose. *Aye*, it'd be fine, the depot. He'd turn it into a clinic, a hospital of sorts.

Before they left, he opened the cage to set the rabbits free. A majority of them were dead, the few that remained, so sickly, they could barely hop. They backed away when he undid the latch, working their noses, their whiskers, unwilling to leave the hutch. Reaching a hand in, he pulled them out, one by one, by the scruff of the neck and set them down on the ground. "You get along now, you hear? Don't stay out here in the open. Hawks will get you. Eat you, sure."

He pitied the starving creatures, doubted they were long for this world.

The neighbor told O'Malley she knew a short cut to the train station and led them across a field that smelled of horses and up a shallow rise. She had a rolling sailor's gait and used a staff to support herself, digging it into the ground and pulling herself forward. Her clothes had been recently dyed, and the fresh black that had pooled on the fabric gave off a faint chemical smell. She didn't speak of what had befallen her family, and O'Malley didn't ask. He was growing used to this world without men, populated only by grieving women.

Exhausted, Danae fell asleep almost immediately after reaching the station. But her rest was uneasy and she thrashed around, mumbling to herself and crying out.

The old woman told O'Malley Danae had been like that since the day she'd found her. Sometimes she was all right and talked like a normal person, other times not. From the beginning she'd had trouble sleeping and would mutter and whimper all night.

"*Baba!*" she cried, imitating her. "*Baba!*" Father.

"She vomit?" O'Malley asked, thinking Danae might have a concussion. "Her eyes lose focus?"

"*Oxi*," the old woman said, shaking her head. "*Einai poli lypimeni.*" She has sorrow.

Later that night, she gave him a pail and asked him to fetch water from the river, saying she wanted to make a broth for Danae, a concoction of grasses and herbs to help her regain her strength.

The moon was directly overhead when O'Malley emerged from the station, the land before him as bright as day. Pine saplings no bigger than a fist were everywhere, fighting for purchase in the ashy soil. A forest of them, bluish in the moonlight. Miraculously, the fire had released the seeds and blown them here. The scent of them made him think of Christmas and he wondered what day it was, if the holiday had come and gone. *Aye*, must have.

He took the saplings' presence as a sign. Whatever injuries Danae had suffered, physical or otherwise, one day she'd recover just as the forest had.

Before him, the river glowed like metal, moonlight making a path across it, ripples of light ebbing and flowing with the currant, a roadway almost. Normally, O'Malley would have feared the exposure, but now he took it as a blessing and welcomed it. If the world died, died as it had in Kalavryta, he would aid in its rebirth. It was enough that the moon was there, lighting his way this night.

29

O'MALLEY HUNG A sign outside the depot that said '*nosokomeio*'—hospital in Greek—to keep villagers from thinking he and Danae were up to no good inside. Not that the girl would be up to anything for a long time, not in the state she was in.

He felt a little drunk, out of breath and jittery. "Grand, us being here," he told her as he prepared supper that night. "Grand, so it is."

At first, the two of them had been formal with each other, asking politely where each had been when the Germans arrived and what they'd done. The way folks in Ireland did when a bridge washed out and they had to go around, had a spot of bother.

Danae was too weak to sit up and he held her in arms. To celebrate, he'd wanted to prepare a feast for her, roast one of the goats and give it to her whole, but given her fragile state, he thought it would be unwise and had settled on the old lady's broth instead.

She had a hard time swallowing.

"Take your time." He tipped the spoon in her mouth. "There you go."

Between mouthfuls, Danae told him about the old woman. "I would have died if Kyria Anna hadn't found me."

"That her name, Anna?"

"Yes. Anna Plakotaris." She studied him. "She said she heard there was a foreign soldier waiting at the train station for me. She said all the women in Kalavryta were talking about it." Danae smiled awkwardly. Unsure of him now.

"It was me, if that's what you're asking. Lost my wits for a time after you went missing." He gave her another spoonful of soup. "Why didn't your Anna speak up? Say that she'd found you?"

"She was afraid. She didn't know who you were or what you wanted."

He scrapped the spoon across the bottom of the pan. "Eat up, my girl. Everything's going to be all right. Your hair will grow back and you'll be yourself again." He couldn't stop smiling, buoyed up by her presence.

"No, it won't."

"What's that you're saying? Of course it will."

"I'll never be myself again. She's gone, *Angle,* the girl you loved. She got burned up in the fire." Danae spoke without emotion, as always, simply stating the facts.

"Nonsense. Aren't we sitting here together, you and me, same as we ever were? Me wanting to have my way with you, to run my hands all over you, and you having none of it."

He worked to keep his voice light.

"In full bloom, so we are."

* * *

DANAE CLOSED HER eyes. "Sometimes at night I see my father. The dead are more real for me than the living."

Earlier that day, O'Malley had been heading off to fetch firewood when she'd asked to come along. He'd hesitated for a moment, afraid the journey would prove too much for her, but then agreed, thinking the fresh air might do her good. She kept up well at first, but then lost her balance and would have fallen if he hadn't grabbed her. He helped her to sit down on the ground and covered her up with his *flokati*. The clouds were gone, the sun so bright on her head that he could see her wounded scalp, count each matted strand.

Noticing the stain on the *flokati*, she gave him a questioning look.

"Horse splintered her leg," he said. "Bled out in my arms."

"Elektra?"

"Aye, Elektra." He was embarrassed by the thickness in his throat. "Great, thundering savage, she was. Rope couldn't hold her. 'Twas all my fault, her dying like that, my fault entirely. I should have tied her down better, but I hadn't the heart. I liked the wildness in her, the spirit. It was like riding the wind, being on the back of her. Glorious."

A wave of color overtook him and he blushed furiously. "You think I've gone and lost my mind, grieving over a horse in this kingdom of night."

She shook her head.

"What then?" There was something in her face.

"We are the same, *Angle,* only for you the hurt does not show. You have no wounds people see." She hesitated, struggling to find the right words. "But still you hurt. You've seen too much death. You can't get away from it. Day or night, you're always in the war."

O'Malley felt tears start in his eyes. "I hear it in my head, I do. Can't seem to turn it off. The whining of the bombs and the earth quivering when they hit, buildings caving in and women screaming. See the faces of the men I fought with, hear 'em crying out as they die. Truth be told, I never was much of a soldier, Danae. Couldn't bear it, couldn't bear the sounds of battle, the purpose of it—men dying at my hand."

She reached up and touched his face. Her bandage was leaking and she left a faint skim of blood on his cheek.

"And still you cry for a horse."

* * *

DANAE PICKED UP a walnut and rolled it around. "My aunt and I were out gathering walnuts the day the Germans came. My father had returned from the mountains and we were rushing around, trying to get ready to leave for Coroni. Aunt Toula didn't think we had enough to eat and she wanted some walnuts to take with us."

She looked off for a moment, her face full of sadness. "Remember Stefanos, how afraid he was, how his teeth would chatter? I was like that when I heard the trucks. Still, I thought we'd have time. I never thought they'd get to us.

"A local woman was bringing water up from the river. I remember the way she paused, the look on her face. Even though they were still far off, we could all hear them. The woman's clothes were damp, glistening with drops of water from the river. I know it's silly, but I thought they were crying—her clothes, I mean."

Raising her arm, Danae threw the walnut into the river. The movement caused her fingers to bleed a little, but she didn't seem to notice.

"And then, suddenly, there were soldiers everywhere. How they gleamed, those soldiers with their buckles and their guns—like freshly pressed coins, I remember thinking. That afternoon, they started taking things out of people's houses, but my family didn't have much and they quickly moved on. It took them two days to empty all the houses. After they finished, they loaded everything up on the train and I thought that would be the end of it. Maybe they'd hang a few hostages, but then we'd be free of them. But then, when it was still dark outside, they woke us with bullhorns and told us to go to the schoolhouse."

A true winter's day, all was quiet save the wind, knocking the branches of the trees together. No living thing but us, O'Malley thought. *Aye*, it was a suitable landscape for what he was hearing.

"The soldiers were polite at first. They told us to bring food and blankets;

we were going to be resettled. One of them said something to my father and waved for us to go back to the house. I think now he was trying to warn us, but my father didn't understand German and we kept walking. Kalavryta was on fire by then. I stopped and watched it burn for a moment, then ran to catch up with the others."

The haunted look in her eyes grew more intense.

"They separated us when we got to the schoolhouse. 'All males over fourteen,' the soldiers said, but they took a lot of boys I knew who were younger. Two old men from my neighborhood were clinging to each other like they were drowning and all around me people were crying—even the men—crying like girls. They took my father away with the rest. He embraced me and told me to be brave. They marched them off and shut the rest of us up in the schoolhouse. Then the guns went off and the women all around me started screaming. They went on screaming for a long time. I put my hands over my ears. I didn't want to hear."

Holding a wake, she is, O'Malley judged. *A wake with neither whiskey nor laughter, with only me in attendance.*

"I was standing next to a window, looking out, when the shots came. It was very strange. Inside, the women were screaming, and outside, everything was the same—the mountains and the fields, just as they had always been, places my father would never go again."

Migrating birds had appeared in the valley the previous day, hundreds of them, rising and falling in fragmenting clouds of wings and chatter. They'd settled in the trees by the stream and O'Malley watched them for few minutes, not knowing what to say to Danae or how to begin to console her.

"I was about a quarter of a mile away," he finally said. "Watched the whole thing through binoculars. Germans herded them into a cornfield and killed them. Went fast, Danae. Soldiers were efficient; they didn't linger at the task."

There was more he longed to share with her, but he held his tongue. What good would it do to hear how the men had sung as they died, showed the flag as the Germans shot them down.

"Went fast," he repeated.

Danae continued on as if she hadn't heard. "One of the women pushed past the soldiers and started running. They caught her, dragged her up the steps and threw her in again. Another woman was holding a baby, and the soldiers knocked the baby out of her hands. The baby cried for a moment when it hit the floor, but then it went quiet, and I didn't hear it again. A soldier who'd been guarding us picked up the baby and handed it back to the mother, made a gesture as if to say he were sorry. It had been the others who had done it, not him. Then he shut the door again.

"The fire was very close by then. I lost sight of my aunt. I looked around and tried to find her, not wanting to be alone." Her voice was hoarse. "But everything was burning and my aunt was lost. Everyone started pushing against the door and somehow we got out. My aunt fell down and they trampled her. I tried to get her up, but a burning piece of wood fell on me and set my hair on fire. Anyway, it didn't matter. My aunt was dead. Outside, it was chaos. You never heard such sounds.

"I was afraid the soldiers would come back, and I looked around for a place to hide. The hutch where my father kept the rabbits would be big enough, I told myself. No one would think to look for me there.

"When I got there, I opened the door and crawled inside. It was a flimsy thing, good only for rabbits, rough wood and wire only. I caught my dress and jerked it free. There was a big rip where the nail had snagged it. I was upset at first, afraid of what my aunt would say, but then I remembered she was dead.

"There were eight or nine rabbits in the hutch. They didn't like me being there and they fussed for a moment, thumping their hind legs and making noises in their throats, but after a while they settled down again. I turned so that I was against the back wall of the hutch and had the rabbits in front of me, hiding myself behind them. The hutch was filthy, full of rotten vegetables and droppings. It smelled bad and made my eyes water. I could feel the noses of the rabbits, wiggling, and their whiskers working against my skin. They felt warm against me—like a blanket almost—and I felt safe lying there with them.

"It wasn't bad. I just lay there, feeling the hardness of the wood, the warmth of the rabbits. Fighting not to feel anything else. Not to cry. My head was bleeding and my hands hurt, but that was all. Then I heard someone making choking noises and I thought for a moment it must be the baby in the schoolhouse, the one who'd fallen on the floor. It was a helpless sound, a bleating almost. Then I realized it was me. I was the one making the sounds. In the distance, I could hear women screaming. After the soldiers finished at the schoolhouse, they turned on the animals, bringing out oxen and mules and shooting them, too—animals that were too big for the trucks.

"I saw a group of soldiers joking in the field behind our house. It was easy to see through the wire and they were nearby. One of the men was holding up something he'd stolen, and the others were teasing him about it. It was the chalice from my church.

"The fire soon reached me and it was very smoky in the hutch and I couldn't breathe. I was afraid the Germans would hear me coughing and I grabbed one of the rabbits and buried my face in its fur." A tear rolled down her face. "I clutched it so hard I broke its back.

"After the soldiers left, Kyria Anna found me and gave me some food. She wanted to take me back to the shed where's she was staying—they burned her out, too—but I didn't want to go. She told me I was lucky, that the Germans had killed over a thousand people that day and burned all the houses. She kept saying how lucky I was.

"I didn't feel lucky. I stayed in the hutch. It was very cold, but I didn't care. I thought about my aunt and my father, the baby I'd seen die. I tried to remember them, to hold on to everything I knew about them. Every word they'd said. How they'd looked. My father most of all. I didn't cry.

"After the food she brought me gave out, I lived on things I found. Berries and leaves. It was all right. I didn't care about eating."

30

Nightmares continued to plague Danae, and she often woke O'Malley with her cries. 'Battle fatigue,' the medics in Egypt had called it, a misnomer if ever there was one. 'Fatigue' played no part in what was wrong with those who suffered from it. 'Battle shock,' more likely. Like touching a live electrical wire, being in war was. It left no part of a person untouched, the sights and sounds of battle blistering their insides, a kind of emotional gangrene.

Some people never recovered, and he feared Danae might be one of them. Like the Dada artists, who used paint to work off the horrors they'd witnessed in the trenches during World War I, who drew men with gas masks instead of heads all their lives, amputated arms and hands with no fingers, limbs that were weapons.

Danae would do the same now, if you gave her a pencil.

She'd jerk around for hours at night, talking to herself and crying out for her father.

Hearing her, O'Malley was reminded of the terrible lines from Richard II, when they'd brought word to the queen that her grandsons were dead. "Oh, let me die, that I may look on death no more."

It filled him with despair. In her weakened condition, Danae needed to rest. It was imperative. She wouldn't make it otherwise.

Unable to stand her crying anymore, he'd woken her up the previous night and tried to comfort her. But the minute he turned her loose, she got into his medical bag and seized one of his scalpels.

"Spartans cut their hair before going into battle!" she yelled, grabbing a fistful of her hair and sawing it off, then another. "I'm a Spartan and I'm going into battle! I'm going to kill all the Germans!"

"That's crazy talk," O'Malley said. "Put the scalpel down."

He thought she was going to commit suicide and tried to wrench the scalpel away, but she fought him for it, screaming and clawing his face.

It took him until dawn to subdue her. Forcing her down to the floor, he wrapped her up tightly in a blanket, swaddling her like a baby. "Hush now," he kept saying, stroking her ruined hair. "Hush now."

O'Malley had learned the technique in a hospital ward, the ward where they kept schizophrenics, people irretrievably lost.

* * *

TWO DAYS LATER, O'Malley followed the river back to the place where he'd seen the quail and shot eight of them. Threading them onto a stout branch, he rigged up a spit and roasted them, When the birds were cooked, he cut strips of meat off and fed them to Danae, who devoured them eagerly.

He glanced over at her and smiled. "Good, huh?"

She was gnawing contentedly on a bone. Putting the bone down, she smiled back at him. A fleeting thing it was, that smile. Sunlight on water.

He retrieved the two goats from the field where he'd left them and turned them over to the old woman, who made feta out of the milk, pouring it in a vat and sprinkling salt on it, leaving it by the fire to ripen.

Well pleased, the old woman did a little dance when the chore was done, clapping her hands together and whirling around unsteadily. Reaching for O'Malley's hand, she endeavored to dance *kalamatiano* with him, humming off-key a song from the region. He'd gone along with it, blushing furiously.

Still, he was glad of it, remembering the way she'd eyed him that first day by the hutch, when he asked her to help him carry Danae to the station, as if he was the devil incarnate, the red-haired devil Leonidas had warned him about.

Seeing his devotion to the girl, Kyria Anna had softened toward him over time and often kept him company now at the station in the evening while Danae slept. She'd laughed aloud when he said he intended to marry her after the war, rebuild her father's farm and settle there. Her cousin, Stelios, was a priest, and she said that for a small fee she'd summon him to Kalavryta when the time came and prepare a wedding feast for them.

"Have you asked her yet?" She squinted at him.

"No, not yet."

"Better to wait. Girl's no good now."

A kind of chaperone, the old woman only came in the evenings after the sun went down. She was like his ma in that, didn't think people could sin during the day.

She didn't like it when he spoke English and would wave her hand in front of her face as if the foreign sounds were a cloud of gnats. But in the closed confines of the station, the language difference gave Danae and him a measure of privacy, and he often resorted to it when the old woman was around. Not that Danae ever said much. No, he was the one who did most of the talking.

For the most part, Danae acted as if he wasn't there, the silence between them lengthening and filling him with sadness. Sometimes they'd talk, but never for long. Like spent dandelions was their time together, the fragile chaff he used to blow as a child.

Even inside the depot, Danae kept a blanket wrapped around her, scruffy thing that it was. She'd insisted the old woman dye it for her, loudly declaring that from this time forward she would only wear black, that she'd be in mourning forever. She had only one dress left, the one she'd been wearing the day of the fire, and a single pair of shoes.

Seeing how thin the soles were, O'Malley made a pair of slippers for her out of the skins of the dead rabbits he found in the hutch, laces to hold them on from strips of their hide. Although he took great care, they looked like something a Neanderthal might have worn, clumsy and heavy. However, Danae was greatly pleased. Rejoicing in the warmth they provided she took to padding around the station in them.

Watching her shuffle, O'Malley wondered why ghosts were always portrayed as white when black would have suited them better. For a ghost Danae surely was in that dyed blanket of hers.

A strange kind of backward ghost, who though she walked among the living, was haunted by the dead.

* * *

At night, after she'd fallen asleep, he often lay awake and watch her. A smattering of burn marks covered her forehead and cheeks. Microscopic things, they didn't mar her savage beauty, only served to enhance it—the way tears sometimes magnified a person's eyes, intensify the color.

Remembering the words of Yeats, he sometimes recited them over her as a benediction, as a prayer:

> How many loved your moments of glad grace
> And loved your beauty with love false or true
> But one man loved the pilgrim soul in you
> And loved the sorrows of your changing face.

31

As soon as the soil was soft enough, O'Malley planted a vegetable garden behind her house, a row of cabbages so symmetrical he could have drawn a line through them—turnips and radishes. He'd found the plants a mile from Kalavryta in an abandoned garden, dug them up and replanted them. The ground was wet and mud clung to his shoes, pulling him down as he walked back through the rain-soaked field. An apt symbol, that mud, the red-stained earth he would never be free of.

Danae grimaced when she saw the cabbages, made a face.

"What's wrong with you?" he asked. "Cabbage is a respectable vegetable. It's what my people eat."

"And look at you. Rusty hair and skin like flour."

He grinned at her. "You're saying I'm not handsome, so you are."

"I'm saying I won't eat cabbage."

It was the first time he'd heard her laugh since he'd found her. Coming back to him, so she was.

The next day he searched through Kalavryta for other things he could give her, but found nothing. The place had been stripped clean. As in everything else, the Germans had been thorough.

* * *

The Red Cross continued to supply Kalavryta, although deliveries were more sporadic now. The pass through the mountains had opened, and people were abandoning the village in ever increasing numbers. The need for supplies was less urgent as the population declined, and the Germans were in the process of reclaiming the railroad for military purposes.

The last Red Cross supply train was due to arrive the first week in March. A group of *antartes* rode in on horseback to help unload it, Leonidas among them.

O'Malley was glad to see his old friend, who'd found him working in the garden behind the house. Like Danae, Leonidas didn't think much of O'Malley's agricultural endeavors—the tidy rows of vegetables—and teased him about them. "Left the war to grow turnips. British should shoot you."

"Probably will if they catch me. So far, no one's come looking."

The Greek had dark circles under his eyes, fatigue clinging to him like dust. The unit was no longer camped in the gorge, he told O'Malley, and had relocated far to the west. He and the other men had ridden all night to get here.

"Haralambos is the same—the voice of the proletariat. He and Velouchiotis are busy planning the next stage of the war. Everyone's optimistic. Russians entered Poland. It won't be long before they reach Berlin."

"Coming to an end then, is it? What about after? There really going to be a civil war in Greece?"

"It's already started. ELAS is negotiating to stop the fighting, but even if both sides agree, the peace won't hold. The minute the Germans leave, we'll be at each other's throats again."

Leonidas paused to light a cigarette and shook the match out. "I can still get you to Cyprus, you want to go."

"No. I'm here for the duration."

"Thought you might be." He eyed him for a minute. "The women in the village said you'd found her."

"Aye. A miracle, it was. She was here in Kalavryta the whole time, hiding down by the river in a rabbit hutch."

"Hurt?"

O'Malley nodded. "Got burned in the fire. Hands mostly. Can't make a fist to this day and may never be able to. Worse is what it's done to her spirit. Broken her, it has. Concussion can cause all manner of strangeness. Could be that's what's wrong with her."

"And you aim to heal her?"

"Do what I can for her, yes."

"And after?"

"Marry her. Stay with her always."

O'Malley walked back with Leonidas to where he'd tethered his horse. Snow white, the horse was, a magnificent creature well over sixteen hands high, skittish and high stepping. Austrian, from the look of her, a descendant of one of those Viennese stallions people were always going on about.

"Where the hell did you get her?" asked O'Malley, drinking in the sight of the beast.

"Belonged to von Le Suire," Leonidas said with a smile. "I captured her during a raid on German headquarters."

"Spit in von Le Suire's eye, did you? Fair play to you."

"It was a hardship at first, the language difference, but we're doing better now. I'll steal a panzer next, drive it straight to Berlin. You're welcome to join me. Men respect you. There's a place for you among the comrades."

Both men laughed.

"No, I'm done with all that," O'Malley said. "It's your fiddle now."

He paused, holding on to the reins of the horse. "There is one thing though."

"Anything, my friend."

"Will you explain to Haralambos what I'm about? Tell him to leave me alone? I don't want to get shot as a spy."

"Sure. I'll take care of it. I'll tell him, 'O'Malley's so love sick, even Churchill has no use for him.' *H agapi ton exei trelanei.* 'He's lost his mind to love,' I'll say. 'A fool on a crusade, hell-bent on matrimony, the idiot.'"

"I am that, Leonidas. A fool entirely."

"It'll be hard, this life you're planning," Leonidas said, his voice growing serious. "Even if you do find a priest—a living, breathing priest the Germans spared—he won't marry you. Not with a name like Brendan O'Malley. Along with your homeland, you'll have to give up your faith and your name."

"You having me off?"

Leonidas shrugged. "Name has to be Greek. That's just the way it is."

"A saint's name?"

"No. Only a Greek one."

"I'll call myself Achilles," O'Malley declared, recalling the legendary warrior in *The Iliad* who'd tied the body of his dead enemy to the back of his chariot and dragged it around Troy.

Would that I could do the same. Would that I had a chariot and von Le Suire by the heels, him and Ebersberger both.

Wouldn't I just.

* * *

RETRIEVING ONE OF the Red Cross parcels from Leonidas, O'Malley carried it back to the depot, thinking he'd stack the tins next to the bench, the cocoa and biscuits, other luxuries. He'd arrange them so they'd be the first thing she saw in the morning.

He'd bought her a rose-colored scarf in the market that had sprung up in Kalavryta, commerce apparently indispensable to human life, an enduring feature like cockroaches and lice, appearing wherever people gathered.

The scarf was a pretty thing, with little metal coins that jingled on the ends. The vendor had smiled broadly when she saw O'Malley eyeing it, had wrapped herself up in it and shimmied like an Arab woman, her ponderous breasts swaying beneath her loose robe. Salome and the dance of the seven veils.

Gold, the thing should have been—the price he'd paid for it.

Danae refused to put it on. "Why'd you buy me this?" she asked angrily. "You should have saved your money."

He begged her to try it on just once, even went so far as to drape it over her shoulders. "Please, Danae. You'll not be wearing black forever."

She pulled the scarf off and flung it down on the floor. "Why are you doing this? I'm in mourning, can't you see? All I see are graves. This is who I am, *Angle*. All I am now."

She choked back a sob. "I lost everything."

"Not everything," he said, picking the scarf up and stuffing it in his pocket. "Not entirely."

* * *

O'Malley removed the last of the bandages from her hands later that week. "Now lift up your arms and flex them. Keep on flexing them, like a strong man in the circus. Come on, come on. Now your fingers. Curl them." Holding his arms up, he demonstrated what he wanted her to do. "There you go. You're doing it. Good girl!"

He continued to coax her, tickling her under the arms when she lagged. "Now curl them under. That's it. Smashin'. You can play the piano, you choose to. Do anything you please. Just like before."

After she finished the exercises, he led her outside toward the river. The cold had eased, and it was a beautiful day. New grass had appeared, blanketing the red earth and camouflaging the fire-ravaged fields. The clouds had become fleeting things, shadows passing swiftly over the greening plain. O'Malley had been surprised to see fresh shoots emerging from the charred trunks of the olive trees, the world giving way to spring even here.

The banks of the river were wet with snowmelt, and wildflowers carpeted the soggy ground. There were tiny, star-shaped daisies—*margaritas*, Danae called them—irises and anemones, the color of water. Poppies were in evidence, too. So red they seared the eye, they'd overrun all of Kalavryta as the weather warmed, blooming between the cracks in the walls and on top of the heaps of ash. They gave the ruined town a jaunty air—festive, yet off somehow—Christmas tinsel hung by a drunk.

O'Malley couldn't get over the sight of them. They filled him with joy, hope even, and he gathered up a handful and gave them to Danae.

"You should never pick poppies," she said, letting them drop to the ground. "They don't last."

"They'll last," O'Malley said, losing his temper. "As will every good thing, Danae. Winter's come and gone. Take a look around you."

She walked ahead of him for a few minutes. Then, as if she'd come to a decision, she turned back and picked up the flowers. She stuck one in the buttonhole of her dress and placed another behind her ear. Her hair had grown out a little, the curls soft on her head like a child's.

She gave the rest to O'Malley, who put them between his teeth and sang her a song.

For want of a better game, they played hide and seek for a time, unwilling to go back inside. O'Malley ducked down and secreted himself behind the leafy trees by the river. Danae knew the hiding place and came chasing after him. Her cheeks grew redder and redder as she sprinted across the grass, the skirt of her dress fluttering in the wind. A haze hung over the water and it filled the glade with diffuse, milky light.

When she reached him, he jumped out and grabbed her around the waist, spinning her around and around. She was so thin, he needed only one arm. Pulling her closer, he recited the most famous passage from The Song of Songs:

> Rise up, my love, my fair one, and come away.
> For, lo, the winter is past, the rain is over and gone;
> The flowers appear on the earth;
> The time of the singing of birds is come,
> And the voice of the turtle is heard in our land.

"I thought the Germans shot you," she said, clinging to him for a moment after he put her down again. "I thought I'd lost you, too."

It was the first time she'd addressed him directly, acknowledged she cared for him and that his passing would grieve her.

O'Malley was careful when next he spoke. "And yet here I am, standing before you. Same as I always was. You kept me alive, so you did, Danae, only you. I'd have died, save for the thought that you might still be alive."

He moved to take her hands, but she jerked them away, hid them in the folds of the jacket.

He gently pulled them free and kissed them.

"No, no. They're ugly," She flexed her fingers, grimacing. "I can do nothing with them."

"Of course you can."

"What?"

"You can hold me."

She started to cry then, soundlessly at first, then louder.

Pulling her close, O'Malley stroked her hair and drank in the smell of her. "There's nothing ugly about you, Danae. You're perfect in every way. They tipped the sun and its light spilled down upon you, so it did, and caught in your raven hair. You are an angel brought to earth, Danae. You're the lyre the heavens play."

He could feel her pulse beating in his hands.

"Ach, *Angle*. What's going to happen to us?" she asked.

He stopped for a moment, struck by the way she was looking at him—a seal breaking the surface of the water to breathe.

"I'll tell you what's going to happen," he said. "We're going to get married after the war is over. I'll summon my folks from Ireland. My pa and me, we'll rebuild your house and make it better than before. Raise sheep, same as we did at home. Goats, too, if you insist. They'll take you to heart, my folks, and you won't be alone anymore. You'll have a family again. We'll sit around the fire in the evening, swapping stories, cook ourselves a meal. The simple thing, done right.

"We'll see the winter through and watch the spring come in. And next year we'll do the same and the year after and the year after that. And when the weather warms, the two of us, we'll take to the fields when no one is looking and gambol about, rolling around and kicking up our heels, come home with grass in our hair and smelling of clover. Nothing will stop us, Danae. You and me? We'll be like wild horses running free. You hear? Wild horses running free …."

He bent down and grabbed a fistful of dirt, closed her fingers around it. "Love is like the earth, Danae. You'll see. It endures."

LETA SERAFIM IS also the author of the Greek Islands Mystery series: *The Devil Takes Half* and *When the Devil's Idle*. She has visited over twenty-five islands in Greece and continues to divide her time between Boston and Greece.

You can find her online at www.letaserafim.com.

CPSIA information can be obtained
at www.ICGtesting.com
Printed in the USA
FSHW010806160219
55718FS